WEREWOLF

THE FIRST CHRONICLE OF MICHAEL CAVENDISH

BY

PHILIP A BURNHAM

Published 2005 by arima publishing

www. arimapublishing. com

ISBN 1-84549-049-5

© Philip A. Burnham 2005

Printed and bound in the United Kingdom

Typeset in Garamond 10/16

arima publishing
ASK House, Northgate Avenue
Bury St Edmunds, Suffolk IP32 6BB
t: (+44) 01284 700321

www. arimapublishing. com

About the author

Philip Burnham is 63 and lives in Derbyshire. He is married for the second time and had to take early retirement due to ill health. He has been writing for most of his life and has had short stories, in dialect, published in a writers group anthology many years ago. It was his wife who encouraged him to try and get his work published now. He has also had lots of encouragement from some of his friends. In addition to writing he also enjoys reading and watching films.

To my wife Ann without whom Michael would have never got finished.

To Val who read Michael and used a red pen liberally.

To Trevor who put Michael on one disk.

And to Mum and Dad who introduced me to the wonderful world of books.

Contents

The Valley-Part 1

Katji screamed in her sleep, the man beside her was instantly awake, his hand closing over the butt of the pistol he had near him at all times. Automatically he cocked it, listening for any sound that could bring trouble to the girl that lay at his side. Tibor lay quietly listening, he heard nothing save the soft moan of the wind in the trees. Nothing disturbed the darkness of the long winter nights. Katji screamed again, Tibor shuddered at the sound of it. Night after night the child had dreamed her dreadful dreams. Only when the long hours of winter's darkness had given way to the pale light of day had the girl found some respite from her nightmares. Katji had awakened cold and sweaty, every fibre and nerve end of her young body screaming for relief. Tibor could not be sure if it was the fear of what she knew or if it was something more sinister. He saw the thin film of sweat on her top lip. He gently touched her face, it was hot. He eased himself from beside her, once clear of the bed he made sure that the sheets still covered the girl. Moving as quietly as he could, Tibor crossed the room. It was hot inside the cabin, a hot stifling stickiness caused by the stove in the corner and the sealed windows. It could not be helped, he had to keep it this way, the child had to be kept warm. He lifted the lid of the stove, the heat was intense on his face, red, yellow and blue flames raced over the wood in their rapacious dance. He let the lid fall back, plunging the room back into semi-darkness.

Tibor stared at his child bride, she was resting peacefully for the moment. They had warned him, explained she would experience these times. The power of the Wych was being called on, and he, he would perhaps be called on to protect her. He allowed a grim smile to cross his lips, too late to complain now. He had known all this when he had taken her to be his wife. "No, no" He hadn't taken her for his wife, he had obeyed the law of the old religion, and he had been born to be a Guardian. His marriage to a Wych was taken for granted, the choice was never in question.

Tibor had been chosen at his birth to be a Guardian, the hand of the Fallen One had touched him, created him. He had sworn the oath and had drunk from the cup held in the hands of the Fallen One.

Tibor Vajek Khan, born into the family of the travelling people. He had stood, a tall gangling sixteen year old. He had stood before the cowled figure and had trembled at the touch of the ice-cold hands. He had knelt, fear burning into his mind and soul as the cup had been pressed to his lips. He had fixed his eyes upon the Fallen One, listening as the cold impassioned voice droned on, passing on the law that would rule his very existence. He was to become an exile from his family and friends. He would find a place far from where he now stood, he would build himself a shelter. He would make sure that it was safe, away from the eyes of those not connected with the old religion and there he would wait for the Wych who would become his bride.

"Go now Tibor, go and prepare all that has been asked of you. One day, it may be soon, it may be years from now, I will send you your bride." The Fallen One had reached out and held the youth by his shoulder. He pulled Tibor towards him. "Remember all that I have said to you, burn it into your mind and soul. One last warning to you Tibor Vajek Khan" The Fallen One had gripped his shoulders until he, Tibor, had cried out in pain. "Never take the Wych woman, never touch her or know her as a man knows a woman, until the time of the calling of her powers has come and gone."

Tibor was lifted high, his feet clear of the ground. The Fallen One threw him from him. Tibor struck the ground, the breath knocked from him. He lay unable to move. This would be the only time Tibor would know naked fear.

"Death, if you touch the Wych bride, Death." The Fallen One had turned and walked away. Tibor had staggered to his feet. He stood alone in the clearing, his family and friends had gone, and his exile had begun.

Tibor shook his head, trying to clear away the memories. He turned to gaze at his sleeping child bride. He felt the weight of the pistol in his hand. He held it before his eyes, the cold metal promised peace. He could end it all, the pain that Katji was going through, the anguish of a man twenty years older than the woman he loved. "Such a beautiful child."

Tibor walked slowly over to the bed, "Why did they pick you?" He sat and watched as she slept, a small figure in the big bed. He almost touched her smooth face, he felt a longing start deep within him. He wanted to hold her to him, to hold her close, to feel her body against his. To feel her soft breath on his face, to love her, man to woman. The effort to restrain himself, from touching her caused sweat to gather on his face.

Once more he stared at the gun he still held, knuckles white from the pressure his hands exerted. He let the pistol fall onto the bed and buried his face in his hands.

He prayed that he and Katji were the last of their kind, with the death of either Katji or himself the race ended. Unless she was called on, they could never consummate their marriage. If they should break the law he would certainly die. The penalty paid by the Wych would be even greater, she would spend an eternity in the depths of Hell.

The giant smiled, he could not hurt her nor could he hurt himself. He rose stiffly to his feet. He would stand there, as he had done in times past. He would stand there all night, not moving, silent, protecting her. For had he not promised to protect her even unto death. His eyes rested on the pistol, let it lay, death would come in its own time. That was the one certain fact in their lives, eventually death would knock on the door of their existence.

Tibor's lips moved in silent prayer. He whispered his prayer to any Gods that cared to hear him. "Let us be the last of our kind, if it pleases you to grant us a child. Take from it the tarnished curse of our race. Give us peace, give us rest, give us freedom, if only briefly, to find happiness."

Katji moaned aloud, her small frame tossed and turned in the bed. What was she seeing in her troubled sleep? What was it that disturbed her so? What terrible or wonderful things controlled her nights? Leaving her pale and shaking in the mornings. The Wych's powers had surfaced six nights ago. The strength and extent of them had disturbed the man. After all the warnings he had been given nothing, nothing had prepared him for the sight of a Wych under the influences of the power.

The hairs on Tibor's neck stiffened, he actually felt the cold chill of fear crawl down his spine. Katji screamed, they reverberated around the cabin. She sat bolt upright, eyes wide open, her eyeballs strained against their sockets. A terror gripped Tibor. Katji was shaking, her mouth open. The scream was stuck in her throat, Tibor could see clearly the strain on her face. Her head was bobbing back and forth, she was trying to force out the scream. Tibor held her tight, felt the strength of her as she fought the nightmare. Katji was shaking, the intense trembling of her body shaking his own. Tibor clasped his hands around her. The hard powerful muscles bulged. He started to sweat. It ran down his face and arms in rivulets, at the concentrated effort required to hold the girl on the bed. Katji's possession was intense, it almost lifted them clear of the bed. Tibor sobbed aloud, he could not hold her much longer, even his giant strength had its limits.

The girl gasped like a fish out of water, struggling for breath. She threw back her head, a low croaking sob escaped her . She moaned from between clenched teeth. The sound tore at Tibor's heart. Then a sound from the very depths of her soul broke free. She gagged, spittle burst free and sprayed the giants face. Tibor blinked trying to clear his eyes. He dare not release her. Saliva dribbled from the corner of Katji's mouth. An unnatural fear gripped Tibor as the thin dribble became thick and slimy. He shuddered yet again as the stuff dripped onto his arm. The touch of it sickened him, its hot fetid smell causing him to gag. Tibor pressed lips tight, against the threatening bile that churned within him.

Katji struggled in his arms, her tiny frame straining with an almost uncontrollable strength. The agony she was enduring was written in her face. Tibor tried to ease his aching muscles. He flexed his shoulders, he was reaching the point of no return. At the final moment when even his giant's strength was beginning to fail, Katji screamed.

A sound that released all the devils pent up inside of her. It tore at Tibor, ripping into his heart and numbing his brain as it went on and on. The girl stiffened in Tibor's arms, her body rigid. The sound of her voice jolted the giant. Without realising it, Tibor let go of her. Katji fell back on the bed, she reached up and grabbed his arm. Nails dug into his flesh, blood seeped from between her fingers. "Moon child". She whispered, "A Moon child comes." Katji clenched her teeth, eyes closed, the lids betraying the rapid movements beneath them.

Tibor prised her fingers loose, felt the pain as slivers of flesh were torn from his arm.

Katji, her face hot and sweaty, lay on the bed. "Moon child." Tibor heard the soft spoken words, his mouth was suddenly dry. "He comes". The girl's head began to shake. "He is in pain, hurt, he comes for shelter."

Tibor reached and gently wiped her face, brushing the wet tendrils of hair from her eyes. "The law." Katji spat out the offending words. "He has broken the law and killed." Her hands fluttered like a trapped bird, Tibor closed his massive fingers over hers. "Vengeance, he killed in anger." Her fingers twisted and turned between his, "Not in defence of the pack, not to protect."

With a force which caught him by surprise, Katji pulled her hands free. She moaned aloud, reached for the man. Tibor held her in his arms. One of her fingers touched his face, he looked at her. Katji smiled up at him. Tibor felt the anguish and pain of that smile burning at his heart. "His own kind, he has murdered one of his own, in anger." Her head fell back, her eyes rolled, "He comes soon, soon." Her sense gone, she fell into a deep trance.

"Katji, when?" he cried, "When, stay with me Katji, you must tell me. When will he come? I have a right to know." The girl's eyes opened, she stared at him blankly. Tibor saw no sign of recognition in her vacant stare.

"Moon child" she whispered, Once more Tibor felt the spine tingling thrill of terror, mouth dry, tongue fast against the roof. He forced himself to secrete moisture. It had finally happened. After all the years of waiting and praying that he would never be called, it had begun. The coming of the stranger was the reason he had been born. The reason women like Katji were born to give shelter to the children of the Fallen One.

For countless decades, the Guardian and his Wych wife had been the last line of defence. The final safe bastion on the path of the werewolf. Tibor fell to his knees and prayed to all the gods of the old religion to aid them in their protection of the Moon child.

The pain in his arm reminded him of where he was and what he had to do. A tiny part of his brain asked, as he rubbed his arm, would he forever carry the scars of Katji's nails. He looked at the pistol, knowing that it would be of little use against the Moon child. He still reached for the cold comforting feel of the gun.

The wolfman was exhausted, curled in a ball, he lay as far back in the concealing shadows as he could. Here in the comparative safety of rocks and bush he would spend the night. He needed to regain the strength his flight for freedom had robbed him of. He was in a half altered state, more human than animal. His throbbing brain told him he had a much better chance of survival as totally beast.

He needed to think, to rest, perhaps even to sleep, if only for a brief hour. Somewhere behind him, how far he did not know, hunted the pack. He had made himself an outcast, a thing to be driven away, shunned by all those who carried the same curse. He had broken the law of the pack, he had killed one of his own kind through anger and hate.

He had forced Julius into a fight, and had taken a terrible pleasure in destroying him. But he had not escaped the battle free. Julius had hurt him badly. An open wound ran from armpit to thigh. Unless he found help he would die, at worse he could be a virtual cripple for months, if not years. In this condition he would be an easy prey for the vengeful pack. Michael lifted his nose and sniffed the wind, snow, he could smell snow.

He must go on, he needed better shelter than he had now. Hands pressed hard against the ground, he pushed himself erect. He stood and listened, hardly daring to breath in case he missed the slightest sound. No sound, nothing save the sighing of the wind in the branches of the trees.

Go, he had to go on, run, the first wet flake of snow fell on him as he began to run. He was following a path to safety, he had only heard about. A story, legend, spoken of and handed down from pack to pack. The legend of the Wych and the Guardian was his only salvation. Michael fought the change as he ran, he could feel bones popping , trying to alter his shape. Sinews stretched in a vain attempt to accommodate the change. He fought it off, how many more times would he be successful in this battle.

The light flurry of snow changed, it became thicker. Fat heavier flakes carpeting the ground he ran across. The snow came thick and fast. Snow on snow, thickening, deepening into a blizzard. He did not feel the bitter wind that drove the snow against his body. His only thought was that the pack could not follow his tracks in the snow. Seconds after his passing, his footprints vanished under the white blanket.

Michael pulled up, chest heaving, gasping for breath, legs trembling. He crawled under the bush, here the ground was dry. Here he could rest for a short time. Michael had experienced many snowstorms in his long life, but to his tortured mind there was a difference about this one. He had prayed for help and the elements had come to his aid. He had never believed the tales of the dark gods or existence of the Fallen One. He had always challenged their power, was this their way of showing him they did exist? Was it possible they were laughing at this puny creatures effort and were only playing with him before they brought him down?

The wolf inside of him growled, the man reached round and touched the wound. The blood had clotted, forming a hard crust. Still it pained him to touch it. Yet it was slick to the feel. The bitter icy wind had frozen the wound closed with his sweat. Snarling and growling he pushed his way out of the bushes. His half altered state allowed him to think rationally. It also increased his stamina. But it left him prey to his human frailties, he had been falling asleep.

Snow hurled itself at his naked frame, battering him. Change, his mind screamed at him, change, accept it. Let the nature of the beast take over, become wolf. Change! Be free of your human side, as the grey one you will survive. He howled his defiance at the swirling snow, how far had he come? How far did he have to go? Eyes blazed a feral yellow, he pushed himself on. The whole of his left side burnt with the fire of pain such as he had never known before. Body slick with sweat and snow, each faltering step an effort he staggered on. The wolfman was reaching a pinnacle that not even his great strength would carry him over it. Michael missed his footing, his momentum carried him over the edge of the slope. He shot forwards, his body sliding over the frozen snow. He could see the tree before him, there was nothing he could do to avoid it. He struck the tree with his left side and rebounded into a second. A cry, half human, half animal was ripped from him. The pain exploded through him, the fire that was his wounded side, intensified. Rage and anger numbed his brain at the battering his body was taking. There was little the wolfman could do to save himself as he rolled over and over.

The wolfman was not aware he had come to a halt. He did not feel the impact of the tree on his battered body. He was only aware that he lay in deep snow, he could feel the ice beneath him and the cloying snow around him. A strange wearisome warmth descended on him, the pain was gone.

Michael was completely numb. Sleep, his battered and bruised body cried, rest, don't fight it, sleep. Michael closed his eyes, head resting on a pillow of snow. Slowly, and without the usual pain the change came over him. He was becoming wholly human, though he did not realise it, he was also giving in, soon, Michael would be dead.

THE WANDERER- Part 1

The horse was running at full stretch, hooves pounding on the hard packed dirt of the road. The man lay as close as he could to the horses back. His face pressed against its sweat streaked neck. The man risked a look behind him. In the gathering gloom of the evening, they were still visible to the naked eye. He put his spurs to the beast's flanks, urging it on. If he lost the race, his reward would be a hanging. The big black responded, from somewhere inside that powerful frame it found strength. Horse and man had covered miles and hours from the moment they had been forced to flee the field of battle.

It should have been so easy, one among thousands running from the troops of Cromwell. But, he had chosen the wrong group to run with. It was only when a troop of Cromwell's men had taken after them had he realised he rode with the young Prince.

How long ago and how many miles ago since he had lost contact with them he did not know. At this particular moment in time, he did not care if he could not outrun the Roundhead cavalry, he would pay the price. A royalist cavalier, the first born of a Noble, Michael Cavendish, the son of Lord Chetwynn would be a coveted prize.

He heard the crack of the pistol, grunted as the ball burnt along his ribs. His horse was beginning to tire, if this was not the case, they could not have hit him with their shots. They fired again, the horse reared, screamed with pain, a deep bloody furrow across its flanks. The rider pulled hard at the reins, digging the metal bit into the horses soft mouth. This time they had not missed, a ball struck him high   on the shoulder, a second struck his back. The cavalier fought to stay in the saddle and control his horse at the same time. His left arm hung, blood poured down his fingers, dropped to the ground, trampled under hooves of the pursuing riders. He placed the reins between his teeth and pulled the pistol free of its holster. Michael turned in the saddle and fired, more by luck than skill his ball found a mark. The Roundhead was knocked from his saddle, he bounced once and lay still. Thrusting back the spent pistol, he reached over for the second gun.

He had no time to pull it free, a ball from one of the Roundhead's troopers struck his horse. The horse tossed its head, the reins were pulled free, the horse veered sharply and headed into the trees. Michael grabbed the horses mane and hung on for his life. Running free, reins trailing the horse ran deeper and deeper into the forest. He heard its wind coming in deep wretched breaths. He felt its body between his legs, chest heaving with the effort of running legs trembling. Its strides became shorter, its breathing harsher. The black stumbled, recovered, a few strides on it stumbled again.

Despite the branches of trees, through which they were fleeing, threatening to pull him from his horse. He risked turning to look back, the hat was torn from his head, a branch whipped his face. There was no one behind them, he was safe for the moment. Beneath him the horse gave a violent shudder, a scream was torn from its throat. The black horse went down, Michael catapulted over its head, he struck the ground. Once, twice he bounced, and came to rest. The horse ploughed a bloody furrow across the soft soil between the trees. Flesh was ripped from its face and chest. Bones snapped under the impact, the horse was dead long before its broken and battered body came to a halt.

Michael stood, fell, stood again, while all around him the trees whirled. He put out his hand, like a drunken man seeking support. He went down yet again. Struggling, fighting his way out of the blackness that threatened to engulf him. The bile rose in his throat, what food he had been able to grab in the last few hours, erupted from his mouth. He stayed on his hands and knees, emptying the contents of his stomach. "God" he thought, "What a way to die."

He felt sick, how long he lay there he had no recollection. Only when his sense returned did he realise the situation he was in.

Michael was lost in the forest, he had no way or understanding of which way he should go. He had no food, he was without his horse, and he had no weapons with which to defend himself. As distasteful a job as it could be he checked the pistols on the saddle, broken beyond repair. His blade had snapped on impact with the ground, only a few inches remained below its hilt. He had turned from the accusing eyes of the dead horse, sick to the heart at what he had been responsible for.

His wounds were minor, only the over heating of his body had caused them to bleed freely. He held the broken sword before him and stared at the dead horse. There was food, the blade was good enough to carve meat from the carcass of the horse. "Do it," his brain told him, "At least you will eat."

Michael threw the blade from him, he had asked too much already of the animal. He would survive, of that he was sure, somehow he would get out of this forest, reach the coast and find his way to France.

"But" he told himself before he tried to reach the coast and find a ship. He needed to be out of the woods, he desperately needed a change of clothes, which way?

He pulled one of the buttons free from his jacket, plain on one side, the engraving of a wolfs head on the reverse. "Plain left and my friendly animal, right" He flipped the button upwards, watched it twist and turn in the air before it landed wolfs head up. "Right it is then," he bent and picked up the button, turning he ground his boot into the dirt. "Without shield or spear?" He lifted his head and looked up at the night sky. "So, Mars my God of war, is this my first step on the road to a different destiny?"

Words prophetic, for there would come a time when Michael Cavendish would gladly have died in that forest in the land of his birth.

Weeks later, dirty, bedraggled, wild eyed and stinking, he stumbled onto the camp. The old gypsy and his wife stared in disbelief at the ragged creature the young Lord had become. Hardly able to walk, just about managing to croak out his need for food and water. The old man took hold of him and carried him towards the steps of the caravan.

"A royalist" he said, the old woman sniffed and carried on with her tasks.

"He'll bring us nothing but trouble husband."

"He's only a boy, and he needs our help. Come on woman give a hand." Together they helped Michael into the caravan. The man, Carlo, undressed him, saw his stinking raw furrows caused by the pistol balls.

"They will heal themselves, he looks a strong boy, food and rest is all he needs." The old woman thought better of her reply, her husband had already decided to help. She paused at the top of the steps, the old fool never knew when to say no. "Damn the silly old fool." What would he say when Cromwell's men found them. It wasn't easy being a gypsy in any land, the first to be accused when any stealing took place. The first to be dragged before the judges if some idiot farmer accused them of bewitching their livestock. Apart from the Jews they were always the ones to be moved on. Still mumbling to herself, she gathered Michael's cast off's and threw them onto the fire.

While the forces of Cromwell and the Roundheads gained control of

England, Michael gained strength. On the day Parliament took the head of a King, Michael stood with Carlo in a small market town, thirty miles from the coast. Michael had just finished bargaining for two chickens when Carlo took his arm. Before he had time to ask what was the matter, Carlo had turned into an alley. "Roundheads, dozens of them."

"What do they want?"

"What they always want, royalist sympathisers." He held the young man by his shoulders. "Listen, and when I finish, walk away as if all is well."

"What is it?" he asked, "Carlo, you look frightened."

"True lad, today is the start of an evil time for the likes of us." Carlo took a deep breath, "The news that Cromwell's men bring is bad, today, Cromwell has murdered a King." Michael shook his head.

"Not even Cromwell dare that, no true born Englishman would let it happen."

"The deeds done, the crime committed, come boy, we must run. Once the news is abroad, these towns people will look for someone to blame."

In a daze Michael followed the old man. No, it was not possible, not even Oliver Cromwell dare to have a King beheaded. Even though he had fought on the side of the royalists he had understood the reasons of Cromwell and his followers. Freedom to worship, and the basic freedom of all Englishmen, the right to work and play in their own way. The right to own their own land, their God given right of never having to crawl to any man, King or otherwise. Yet to kill a King for all of this, was wrong. Cromwell had won, did he not yet realise that, his Ironsides had destroyed the armies of the King.

Lena, the old woman wasted no time in putting the horses into their harness. Equipment was bundled inside the caravan. The ground where they had camped was wiped clean. Soil scattered over the spot where a fire had burnt. A last look, careful in case they had missed anything. Michael helped her up the steps, ran round and joined Carlo on the seat. Carlo, flicked the whip and the pair of horses moved off. He let the whip strike the animals rumps urging them on, the pair broke into a trot.

"We must be clear of this region by nightfall." Michael said nothing, he had lived with the gypsies long enough to observe the treatment they received at the hands of his countrymen.

He had, had it all, rank, privilege, wealth. He had never known want, now he understood how those on the lowest rung of life's ladder felt. Carlo and Lena were born outcasts because of their race. He was forced to hide from his own people because he had dared to fight on the wrong side. "We have friends on the coast." Carlo broke into Michael's thoughts. "With luck it may be possible for them to smuggle all of us to France or Belgium."

"You keep many secrets friend" said Michael, his mind racing ahead, he already saw himself on a boat on the open seas.

"It is always better to use drops of knowledge my young friend than to squander it all in one drink." Carlo let the whip just flick the rump of the horses, "We have four hours of darkness left to us, soon we must find a place to hide. We travel only by dark, and we eat and drink only cold fare. If possible, we avoid contact with any others." Carlo turned to Michael, "It may be boy that we are forced to defend ourselves, both myself and Lena are able to use guns, when we stop I will show you something, easy lad, don't be so eager to know." Carlo grinned and knocked on the caravan. A panel opened and Lena looked out, "Look under my bunk, you will find a package, take it out please." Lena snorted at him and continued to stand there, staring at the road as it twisted and turned through the forest.

"I smell the sea husband." She drew in a deep breath, "Tomorrow night we should be looking on it."

"True woman, and with the help of the Gods we shall soon be sailing it."

"Out of this damnable land, back to where we belong."

"We have enemies there too, strange that a man cannot be free from prejudice in his own home." Carlo slowed down the horses, looking from left to right, "Look for somewhere to hide us Michael." It was nearly dawn before Carlo found the place he was looking for. Carefully he pulled the caravan deep into the bushes. Leaving Lena to see to the horses, he took Michael with him and returned to the road.

"Here" he said, handing Michael the beezum. "Sweep over our tracks while I hide our passing through here." Not until Carlo was satisfied did they leave the road and return to the caravan.

"Now we sleep, we talk later, go Michael, get your rest, I'll call you in a few hours." Carlo sat with his back against the steps, from where they hid he could see the road clearly. No one passed along the road, and not until the sun had reached its appointed place in the sky, did he move.

"Husband" Lena's voice stopped him and he turned to her. "Let him sleep, he is young and the young need more rest than the old, come, sit and talk."

Carlo sat down beside her, slowly he put his arm around her. The old woman smiled at him, Carlo lent forward and pressed a kiss against her lips. "My sleep is troubled husband and I have dreamed again of death. "

"You, we, are old, remember it is many years since we had to call on the second sight."

"Too long" sighed Lena, "We have travelled too far, too many different lands, we should have stayed in our own lands."

"And I" said Carlo. "Would be dead, we knew the risks and we took them, our time together has been long my wife, my love."

"Keep your foolish talk and thoughts to yourself old man, I do not talk of what we did, I cannot see what will be, I only tell you that I dream the same dreams that once I saw a black cowled death hovering around us, I see bodies laying dead upon the ground, yet husband, I do not see their faces and I know it is not from among us that death will claim his prize."

"Then it matters little what you dream."

"Husband, do you not understand, death sits on the shoulders of the boy. And you will place death in his hand this night."

"The sword," Carlo shook his head, "There is no magic in the blade, it has lain for thirty years beneath my bed."

"I don't know, I don't know, I only know that something or someone is calling to me." Carlo saw fear in his wife's eyes. "The power inside of me is awakened and I know here" Lena pressed her hand over her heart, "Before the moon sets a third night, I will be called on to use those powers."

Her old head rested on his shoulders, Carlo pulled her tighter to him. Not after all these years, no it couldn't be possible. Not since she had turned twenty had his woman ever needed to call upon the powers. And then she had only used them in their defence. "Carlo I will have to use them even though I don't want to."

"Then why use them at all?"

"If I don't husband, the boy will die."

"Then I won't give him the sword and we will bypass Tarfleet."

Lena sadly shook her head, she knew they must go to the coastal village of Tarfleet, it was their only hope of escape. It was one of the few places in England where they had true friends.

"No, what must happen will happen, and what I and you must do" she held his hand tightly, caressing and kneading it between hers, "We will do."

They sat silently, holding each other close, each with their own memories of the days that had been, and never would be again. Lena sighed deeply and held onto her husband. Soon their lives would be over and what they had been to each other would be carried into the grave with them. She had enjoyed a life time of love from her Carlo and he had willingly taken the love she had returned. Memories crowded her tired mind, happy days and sad ones, each giving and taking a little part of them.

Michael held the sword high, moonlight glinted along the blade. From the hilt to its tip, the blade was an inch wide. The end of the blade was severed off at an angle. Each edge of the blade was razor sharp. From pommel to tip, the blade was thirty six inches long.

"It's beautiful" said Michael, holding his hand flat against the cold steel. Slowly he twisted it and watched the light of the moon play along its cutting edges, "So beautiful".

"You hold death in your hands boy" Carlo took the blade from the young mans hand. "It was created from a piece of heaven that fell to earth. Then a craftsman of wondrous skills fashioned death. It took him two years to create this weapon, heating and reheating the metal constantly folding it layer by layer until he was satisfied with it. It took him another year to fashion the scabbard, so sharp was the blade it had to be carried in a sheath of steel."

"How do you know all this?" he asked "How did you come by it?"

"For over a thousand years my family have carried that sword. Generations of my fathers have used it in battle. I have used it only once in anger." Carlo held up his hand, "I will not speak of it. Ask nothing of my history, I give it to you because you are going to need to defend not only yourself, but my wife and I. Take it boy, my Lena sees the stamp of death upon you. She has been shown the future and feels the old power surging through her veins."

"I owe you my life Sir and I will gladly defend you both this you know."

"This we know Michael, and what we say is of little use to either of us. Talk is cheap and I fear that my Lena has seen something that even she is afraid of, come boy, the hours pass too quickly and time is important to us all."

"You speak volumes, yet tell him nothing" said the old woman to her husband when once again they were on their way to the coast. "What do I say to him?" Asked Carlo, "Shall I tell him that you have visions. That sometimes the future opens up to you? I think not, for you have been shown a glimpse of his future, not ours."

"Worry not my husband, we will survive, you, I, Michael, we will all live to remember what must happen."

Tom Martin held the dagger out to show his drunken comrades. "Took it from a bastard Jew in York." Tom belched and put out his hand for his ale. "Had to burn his feet to get his money." One of the Roundhead troopers poured more beer into their jugs.

"When next you see him, thank him for the ale he bought us."

Tom laughed and turned the dagger over and over in his hand. "Glass" he said, "See that, the points made of glass, shatters on impact. Kill a man in a matter of hours, poisoned see, full of poison."

"Poison ain't no way for a man to die Tom." Tom Martin glared at the man, the big Yorkshire man stared back, he wasn't afraid of his corporal. The third man at the table spoke, breaking the tension between the two.

"There ain't any easy way for a man to die, tell us Tom, why are we here?"

"That's easy Jed, some one told our Captain that a lot of royalists escaped to foreign parts from here."

"Do it make any difference who they fought for now?" the Yorkshire man said, "We beat them fair and square."

"And Cromwell cut off the snakes head." Jed made a chopping motion with his hand.

Tom Martin shook his head. "Tain't so boys" he said, "You don't know 'em like I do, you don't carry their marks on your back." He heard one of them whisper "Weren't hard enough." Tom Martin glared around him, he did not have to guess who had made the whispered comment, that smart bastard Calthorpe. Martin said nothing and went on, his favourite subject, persecution by the rich. "They don't think the likes of us have any rights, they treat their animals better than us."

"Cromwell said, 'Put in Jed, hoping to ease the drunken Tom into a merrier subject.' That we were to forgive but we had better not forget." For a while the three men sat silent, the big Yorkshire man watched Martin play with the dagger making stabbing motions with an imaginary foe. He'd never liked Tom Martin, then few men did, he was a braggart and a bully. He could quite believe the man's story about the torture of the Jew and how he got the dagger.

And he never for a moment doubted Martin's story of a flogging at the hands of the gentry, no doubt he'd deserved it. Martin was a foul man, a snake who would use any man, woman or child to get his way. And above all he liked to be the one in charge, that was the reason they were sat here drinking, just because the captain had heard rumours about fleeing Royalist. And if Martin could bag one, well who knows, promotion? Calthorpe doubted that, Martin was too stupid to catch himself falling.

The Yorkshire man, longed to go home, he had not wanted to fight in the first place. He had no bones to pick with the landed gentry or anyone else for that matter. He wondered how his farm was with only his wife and daughter to run it, things must be hard.

Damn it, he'd done his share, a King was dead, a young prince had escaped and them that fought for the royalist had gone home to their families. Desertion, that was the answer, others had done it, and he could too, he wouldn't be missed. Amos sat quietly, it needed thinking about, once done, there would be no turning back or saying sorry. To hell with them all, Cromwell and his plans, and all of them that hung on his coat tails, he'd do it, tonight.

All thoughts of his defection from the Cromwellian ranks were pushed from his mind, the inn door banged open in the strong wind blowing in off the sea. Amos glanced at the trio, an old man and a young one supporting the old woman. They looked cold and travel weary, the two men helped the woman to a seat beside the fire. The old man walked slowly to the bar. "We need food and a hot drink landlord."

"Good food and excellent ale is what I serve sir." The man continued to wipe the bar. "There's beef or lamb, hot or cold and if you don't fancy that my wife has a chicken soup on the boil."

Carlo placed his hand on the bar, spread his fingers and pulled back his thumb until it was at a right angle. "Venison would make a right royal meal."

"Difficult to come by on the coast."

"It's difficult to come by at any time" replied Carlo, The landlord looked at him then down at his hand on the bar. The sign had been given and answered. "I'll take two bowls of your good ladies broth and a serving of beef."

"And who is the meat for sir, if it's for the lady, I'll find a tender cut."

"No, like me, my wife's teeth are old, give the boy the meat."

"Strong meat for a strong young man."

"Aye, young bucks need their strength especially in flight."

Carlo had passed on the second sign, nothing to do now but wait for the landlord to arrange their escape. Carlo looked around the room, at the sight of the Ironsides, Lena's insistence that they wear clothes of the style and cut of country folks was a wise choice. Carlo turned, one of the men didn't seem to be able to take his eyes off them. So close, the last thing they needed now was to be discovered. He watched Michael tending to Lena. Perhaps he should not have given the boy the sword. Carlo knew, should the Ironsides give them trouble , Michael would fight. The old man's lips moved in a silent prayer. "Here boy" he said aloud. "Take your meal from the lady." Carlo took one of the bowls and sat near his wife. "Take your food wife." Lena touched his hand, "All is arranged."

"I still see and feel death," Carlo put the spoon in her hand, and helped her take the first mouthful of the thick chicken broth. "Husband"

"Hush, eat, rest, I have a feeling the days will be longer until we set foot on foreign soil."

Michael looked up, the landlords wife stood before him. "Fingers" she said in a low voice. "You're a bumpkin, and bumpkins don't use a knife and fork." Michael nodded and picked a slice of the meat and tore at it. He stuffed the fresh baked bread with it and began to chew.

The months with the old couple had changed him. He had grown leaner, harder. His skin was tanned by the weather and the beard he had grown, hid most of his features. Michael doubted that his own father would be able to recognise him. That fickle fingered lady known as fate was going to prove him wrong.

Amos knew that there was going to be trouble, he could smell it. Five times in the past few weeks he heard the same words pass between landlord and travellers. He had said nothing to Tom Martin, one escaped royalist was one less to bother about. The big Yorkshire man even knew the names of those involved. He looked at Martin, "To hell with it."

He had decided he was going home. It couldn't be the old couple, he knew from contact with them and others like them, they were gypsies. It had to be the young one, he had noticed what had passed between him and the woman. If he could get Tom Martin and Jed out of the inn, then what happened between the three and the moonrakers would be a thing past in the morning. "Come on Tom, time to go."

"What?" Tom Martin gazed bleary eyed at Amos, "What is it?"

"Time we got to our beds, and Jed looks the worst for drink."

Tom Martin placed his hands on the table and pushed himself up. He reached over and shook Jed. "Wake up, come on stir yourself." His hand on Jed's shoulder, he looked across the room. Michael chose that moment to stand and turn towards him. Both men stood and stared, Tom Martin was the first to react.

"My God," he cried, "It's not possible," The Roundhead was sobering his brain clear as he looked hard at Michael. Then he smiled a cold, happy smile, he flexed his shoulders at the imaginary feel of the whip. "Vengeance is mine sayeth the Lord."

He moved around the table, his hand finding the hilt of his sword. "But not this night my Lord Chetwynn, tonight I pay you and your kind back." The blade was pulled partly free, Michael's insides churned, if he had to fight, then he would. The man had been drinking perhaps he could convince him he was wrong.

"You mistake me for another master, I'm just a traveller, these," said Michael pointing "Are my grand parents." Michael saw the old man's hand go into his jerkin, he saw the butt of the pistol. "I'm sorry if I cause you confusion sir." From the look in the man's eyes, Michael knew that he had been recognised.

Tom Martin shook his head and grinned, the sword was pulled completely free, the time for pretence gone, the man intended to kill him. Michael pulled the strings holding the cloak around him. He placed his hand on the hilt and pulled, the sword hissed, metal against metal as it came free. "So Tom, what's it to be, you never could beat me with a blade."

"Times change, perhaps I've learnt a thing or two about using a sword." Martin turned to his companions, "Watch the old people, while I settle old scores."

Without another word he flung himself at Michael. Steel met steel with a strike. Martin's blade slid along Michael's, clanging against the hilt. Michael twisted his blade, pivoted on one foot and brought the sword across in a slashing motion. Tom Martin just avoided it, the tip of Michael's blade slicing through his leather jerkin. There was no science in the dual, no fancy or practised moves. Cut and slash was the order of the day, each man striving to land a killing or crippling blow. Sweat flowed freely on the two men as they cut and hacked, seeking a weak spot. Michael stepped back, breathing heavily, "It seems you have learnt some small tricks Tom."

"Enough to kill you Chetwynn." He gasped out the words, a thin trickle of spit hung on his lips, his eyes were wild. Michael knew he had to kill him, a wound would not suffice, only death would stop Tom Martin. The treatment received at the hands of Michael's father, real or imaginary had driven Martin over the edge. All the rights and wrongs of Tom Martin's life had accumulated in the face and form of Michael Cavendish and the point of his sword was their rectifier. Michael backed off, moved sideways and slashed at the exposed man's belly.

Steel sliced through leather, wool and flesh as Michael pulled the sword across Martin's midriff. Tom Martin screamed at the burning touch of steel. Placed his hand on his stomach and stared stupidly at the gout's of blood that spurted from him.

His sword dropped to the inn floor, he pressed both hands hard against the cut, trying to staunch the flow of blood, "Bastard".

Tom Martin crashed to the floor, Carlo fired, the ball hit Jed between the eyes, it exited from the man's head, spraying the wall with blood and brains.

Amos, the pistol still held in his hand, stared at the bodies of his recent companions and slowly shook his head. With a slow deliberate movement he let the arm holding the pistol fall to his side.

"It's over" he said, he stared down at the ever widening pool of blood seeping from beneath Tom Martin. "It's time it was all over." He looked across at the two men, Carlo held a second pistol in his left hand. "If I place my gun on this table , will you allow me to walk out of here?"

"And you promise to say nothing?" Michael shook his head, "I find that hard to believe."

"You have my word on it, I just want to go home to my wife and daughter." Lena took hold of Michael's arm. He looked down at her, she nodded.

"He speaks true, take his word for it,"

"I'll stay until you are gone" said Amos, "I can wait a little while longer to go home." Michael sheathed his sword and moved towards him, he held out his hand, "You have my word." Repeated Amos. Lena walked wearily over to the two men, the Yorkshire mans eyes opened wide in terror. Lena turned.

They gaped in disbelief at the figure of Tom Martin stood there before them. One hand holding in his entrails, he swayed. A dead man refusing to die. His face was a sickly yellow, when he opened his mouth, blood seeped from between his teeth. With a strength that was unbelievable, he grabbed the old woman. The dagger was lifted high and brought down with venom. At the last instant before it reached Lena, Michael moved between her and it.

The dagger struck Michael in his left shoulder blade and the glass tip shattered. Shock followed shock as the poison entered Michael's system. He stood unable to move, arms, legs, his body began to shake uncontrollably. His eyes rolled, a white foam coated his lips, his mouth open and closed of its own accord. Tom Martin tried to speak, his mouth opened and blood spewed out and covered Michael. "Dead" he managed to croak before he fell lifeless to the floor.

"A Jews dagger" Lena turned at the Yorkshire man's cry, "It's full of poison." He managed to catch Michael, holding the young man to him. Michael jerked in the man's arms. Amos gritted his teeth as the poison did its work. Michael's bodily functions rebelled against the poison. Both he and the Yorkshire man were soiled by them. Amos lay Michael on the table, having to hold him down as the fits took control of the young man's body.

Lena tore at the fabric of Michael's shirt, ripping it open. Already the wound was beginning to ooze pus and the area around it was an angry red and swelling. Lena touched it and gently pressed, a shard of glass came free. A thin rivulet of evil smelling pus dripped from her finger. "I must cut and cut deep." She turned to her husband, "I need the box, and all it contains." Carlo nodded and turned to go. "Carlo" she said, "All it contains, all."

"Can you save him mother." asked Amos, "I know of your people. Where I come from their skills in healing are legend."

"I need hot water, clean cloths, sharp knives and all the help I can get." She smiled at the man, and gently touched his face, Amos reddened, "I've never been called a legend before, and" she said still touching his face, "It's a long time since I was called Mother." The man's face turned a deeper shade of red. "Go on," she said to him, "Fetch what I ask for."

"Can you make the boy fit enough to travel." asked the landlord, Lena looked up from her probing. "How long do I have" she asked,

"Two days, at the most." The landlord shrugged his shoulders, "We cannot give him more."

"That is plenty of time." Gently she wiped away the pus from around the wound. "If I cannot save him tonight, tomorrow matters little, for the boy will be dead." She threw the soiled cloth in a bowl held by the landlord's wife. "Can you remove the dead from my sight."

Carlo returned as the landlord and Amos carried out the bodies of Tom

Martin and Jed. Carlo put the box on the table and waited for Lena to tell him what to do. Carefully the old woman unwrapped the instruments in the box. Knives of varying thickness were placed in a row, each one tested for its degree of sharpness. Next she laid out five boxes of different colours opening them she sniffed the contents. The last item was of ivory, about six inches long and three round, with a sealed lid. This she did not open, but placed near the very edge of the table.

"Rub this on his lips, it will help him through the pain."

Carlo dipped his finger into the box and then gently smeared the clear pungent grease on Michael's lips. Michael ceased to struggle, his body became limp. Lena grunted and taking one of the boxes, she put her fingers deep into the green waxy contents, this she smeared liberally on Michael's wound. Gently, but firmly working it into the raw hole. "It's time, get me some water and it must be boiling."

Lena looked at the face of the boy on the table, she didn't doubt that she could save him, it was the cost of saving him that worried her.

Lena held the knife in the boiling water for seconds, she then placed the tip in one of her boxes. The thin blade was covered by a purplish film. Lena carefully rested the blade on the would and pressed, the thin blade went deep. A glutinous stream of pus erupted from the cut, Lena turned her head. She breathed deeply, the stench of the mess running down Michael's shoulder causing her to gag, once more she took a deep breath, turned and cut again across the wound. Blood, a thin pinkish colour ran free, the old woman placed her fingers either side of the wound and pressed. A mixture of blood and pus poured out, Lena pressed again, the blood was cleaner. She reached out and picked up the box, twisting off the lid, she let the contents drip onto the open wound. "Hold him still, now the pain begins". Carlo and the landlord held Michael's arms hard against the table. "Take his legs". Amos grabbed them and Lena let more of the clear liquid drip onto the wound. The young man held fast on the table went mad with pain. His mouth opened in a silent scream, his body reacted violently to the invasion of the cleansing fluids Lena had caused to invade his body. "Tighter" she cried, "You must hold him still."

Michael thrashed about on the table, it took the combined strength of the three men to hold him. Sweat poured from every pore of Michael's body, his bodily functions worked themselves. Lena pulled the young mans soiled trousers from him and wiped him clean. She bent over the wound, the clear liquid had turned a vicious red, she touched it. It hung from her finger like glue. Lena reached for her knife, a wafer thin blade touched the wound. Lena pressed down with all the power of her body. Blood bright red spurted up around her fingers, quickly she twisted the blade. The stream of blood became a torrent as she tore out the infected flesh. She emptied the entire contents of the box onto the raw flesh. The wound sizzled and smoked, the smell making the landlord lose most of that days meals. A bubble of burning flesh broke, blood boiled and congealed sealing the knife cuts. "The poison is too deep." The old woman sat down on a stool, her face was white, she looked completely drained. "I don't know if I can save him." She looked pleadingly at Carlo. "It acts too fast to control." Her head dropped, suddenly she looked what she was, an old tired woman. Slowly she lifted her head and stared hard at her husband. "Use it" he mouthed. "I dare not" There was no help in the face of her man.

Carlo released Michael's arm and bent down to his wife. "Use the power wife, if you don't he dies." Carlo could see the struggle going on inside his wife. If she could not control the flow of poison with her medicines, she had only one option left to her.

"It is a poison unbelievably potent, I've never known one so powerful. God forbid that man could create such filth." Lena held onto Carlo's hand, not wanting to let go. She allowed him to draw her to her feet. Carlo folded his arms around her and she buried her head against his chest. "Pray that I do not curse him for the rest of his life."

She took a deep breath and drew herself up on tiptoes, stretched her arms, "I need tongues, fire tongues," Tentatively she reached out and lifted the sealed box. She gripped the top of the box and twisted it. "God forgive me, I have no other choice." From inside the box she removed a metal cylinder, she turned it until the base was pointing towards her. The three men felt a strong desire to hold their breath, for what seemed like an eternity, Lena's gaze was held by the pentacle stamp.

She put the seal down by the fire, finally she gripped the seal with the tongues and put it into the flames. The minutes dragged by with the length of hours, slowly, very slowly the metal began to glow. First it turned red, then it began to glow. Lena left it until the metal was white hot. "Carlo". The man jumped at the sound of his wife's voice, it boomed in the quiet room. "Carlo, take the bottle and pour the whole of it down his throat, he must swallow it all." She turned back to the fire and put the tongues firmly around the seal. "Say when he has taken it all."

"He's taken it all."

"Hold him." The three men watched her move slowly towards them, then the glowing metal grabbed their attention. With a speed that belied her age, Lena placed the white hot metal to the wound. A smell of roasting flesh, Michael bucked, he gave one loud gasp of pain, his tortured body gave way and he fainted. Only when the seal began to darken through loss of heat did the old woman pull it free from Michael's flesh.

"Forever, he will carry the sign and my people will know what had to be done." She held out the seal to the Yorkshire man, "Take it, destroy it, it is of no more use to any one."

"Will he live?" asked Amos, knowing full well what he had witnessed, and if he ever spoke of it a fire waited for him.

Lena took her time in replying to Amos's question for the simplest of reasons, she did not know. All that could be done for the boy had been done. The potions from the boxes had been used, some of them so powerful that Michael's body may reject them. All her training in the arts, all that she had learned at the feet of the priest of the old religion, all this and more she had done. Until only one road lay open to her, to call on the dark god of her religion, the Fallen One, and use the pentacle seal.

"He will live," a sadness tinged her voice, "but at what cost I don't know." Lena's soft spoken words faltered, "By using that which you hold, I have set his feet on a very dangerous path." Amos put his hand on the old woman's shoulder and gently squeezed, Lena in turn reached up and pressed hers on his. "I will not be there to guide him, he will be alone."

"Do you speak of death Mother? You seem to be in good health."

"No, not my death, but once I used the seal I forfeit the right to be near him." The sadness he had heard in her voice was now written plainly on her features. "We have come to a parting of the ways. He will never be entirely alone for he will carry the scar of the pentacle to his grave. There are those among my people who know what the scar means and from these he may ask for help, it will be given freely."

Her voice faltered, Amos saw the tears mist her eyes, there was a tremor in her voice when next she spoke, "The path he travels is twofold, only time, circumstances and fate will decide which one he takes."

Carlo laid his hand on Michael, under his touch the boy lay rigid, hardly breathing, the rising and falling of his chest barely visible to the naked eye. The old man seated himself and lent close to whisper in Michael's ear. "I know you can hear me boy, and I must speak now for the time between us grows short. My Lena has given you life, I ask that you use that life well, for in the giving we must forever part. That is the price we have had to pay, what price is asked of you, only time will tell. Try to remember us boy, sometimes when you are alone, at those times in the dark of night when sleep is a thing that passes you by, remember us." Carlo stood, he felt a hand on his arm, "Lena" he said, the hand tightened.

"Say your goodbyes old man," Her fingers reached past him and gently touched Michael's lips. "Goodbye."

Three people watched the ship until it was out of sight. Carlo held her close to him, not wanting to let her go. "Soon it will be dawn, we must be on our way."

"Which road do you take?" asked Amos, "For I feel it would benefit us all were you to take my way." The Yorkshire man grinned, "Things have passed between we three, and besides my farm is a big place. There is plenty of room around the fire and a man's children need grandparents."

"What is your name man?" asked Carlo, "For you offer us a gift beyond price."

"I am Amos Calthorpe,"

"Then Amos Calthorpe, we accept."

Far out in the Channel the ship was lifted and dropped on the surging waves of the sea. In one of the cabins the man called Michael Cavendish slept.

THE VALLEY - Part 2

Snow fell steadily on the wolfman, he was warm and comfortable, he had no conscious desire to move. Michael's eyes closed he was experiencing a jumble of memories. Faces, voices, figured from a dim and distant past raced in and out of his mind. Wind drove the falling snow, it began to drift around the man. Soon it had covered the wolfman's upper body, the flakes that fell onto his face stuck. He was being covered by a white quilt of death and he was welcoming it.

The voice low and gentle forced its way into his mind. It invaded his brain, insistent, it droned on and on. Never letting go, begging, pleading, threatening, refusing to be ignored. A soft child like voice. "Live, come to me." The wolfman stirred, opened his eyes, and gazed blindly at his white coffin. A movement, a thrust of a hand, the wolfman forced away the clinging snow. "Rise moon child, come to me, come I am waiting for you, live."

The wolfman pressed his hands and knees hard down and pushed himself free. Snow pummelled his face, the wind whipped around him, he felt the coldness of it chilling his body. On his knees he swayed, his confused brain whirled, the voice returned to him. "Again, moon child, one last effort, come to me." It required a titanic effort on the part of the wolfman to be able to stand erect. With all the powers which his dark god had infected his blood, the wolfman regained his sense. Swaying, reaching out for support, he fought against the agony that now tried to take control of his body. A sky filled with a million blinking lights, a landscape white and endless, broken by rocks and trees, merged into one. It whirled before his eyes, the wolfman howled, his world stopped spinning.

Fully human, Michael suffered the ravages of freezing wind and snow on naked flesh. Turning his head, he strained his ears searching for the voice. There, no, only the wind playing among branches. "Moon child". The voice of the child. Michael forced down the pain that burnt body and soul. Again the voice whispered in his ear. "Come to me, follow my voice."

A spiteful wind tore the voice away from him, Michael fell on his knees in the deep snow, arms outstretched, he threw back his head. "Help me." The elements laughed at him. The cold wind danced through the trees driving the bitter cold snow against his unprotected body. "Help me, help me," His voice lifted high, the wind snatched it from his lips.

The Wych girl Katji sat up in the bed, she threw to one side the blankets which covered her. "I hear you Moon child. fight, listen to my voice."

The giant Tibor dropped the mug he was holding, Katji's words rang like gunshots in the confines of the small cabin. He turned, opening his mouth he stared at her. Katji sat bolt upright, eyes closed, Tibor was sickened at the sight of her face. The flesh appeared to be drawn to the point where it must split, rings, deep and black beneath her eyes, teeth clenched. "Listen to me, hear me moon child, I will lead you". Tibor licked dry lips, tried to swallow, fear rooted him to the spot. On feet of lead he crossed the room, he pulled the blanket free, and wrapped her in it. Katji stared at him. "He comes, in pain, confusion, but he comes to me"

Michael fastened onto the soft childlike voice, he moved like a puppet on strings. Each step manipulated by some other force, in this dreamlike state he followed the voice. This way, that way, the puppeteer lead him on. The elements howled their anger and defiance at one who dared to rob them. The sound of her voice, soft and low, full of the promise of life, leading him on. Mechanically he placed one foot in front of the other, fell, gained his feet and staggered on, forward, always forward, the Wych woman pulled him.

Katji called the giant, "Help me Tibor, help me to my feet." She saw the concern in the man's face, a weak smile brightened the ravaged features of her face. "It's alright" she said, her voice a weary sound. "I must get on my feet." She struggled to throw off the constricting blankets. For a big man, Tibor moved fast and with the grace of a dancer. He was by her side in an instant, holding her, he pulled the twining blankets free. She stood, a doll in the arms of the giant. "Soon, very soon, he will be here." Tibor did not speak, he would hold her until she regained some of the strength she needed. He felt her hand on his. Katji looked at him, "A chair," she asked, "Place me on a chair in front of the door." Her fingers tightened on his, Tibor squeezed it, then he lifted her in one arm and carried her to a chair. Katji wrapped her arms around his neck and buried her face in the folds of his shirt. She could feel his heart pounding, she pressed herself harder against him. Even in her present state, body and soul weary, mind numb from the exertions of the power she had, had to use, she felt it. She felt the love that beat in the heart of this gentle giant. She knew she was safe in his arms, she knew that the mighty strength contained in flesh and blood would defend her to the last. That Tibor loved her, worshipped the very ground on which she walked, was no secret to her. From the moment she had first set eyes on him from the moment his massive hand had held hers, she had known.

A silly little memory invaded her mind, broke through the dark circles which held it. A red faced giant, shuffling his feet at the entrance to the cabin. Hands hidden behind his back, the laughter and the stamping of feet in a pretended anger. The remembered tears and the joy on his face when she had buried her face into the bunch of wild flowers he had brought.

A vision entered her thoughts driving them away, a man, tall, wounded nearly to death, staggering, fighting. "He is here". She touched Tibor's hand, "He stands before our door."

Tibor put his hand in his trouser pocket, he felt the comforting touch of the pistol. Placing his hand on the bolt, he drew it back, he pulled at the catch, the door opened. The half frozen naked man fell forward, Tibor caught him before he hit the floor. "Welcome moon child," said Katji.

THE KEEP - Part 1

Michael rested his face against the horses neck, he gently stroked its muzzle. "No battle for you today old friend." The horse nibbled at the gloved hand seeking its usual treat. Michael pressed the apple into its mouth. "Today I run to meet the enemy, and you, no sounds of battle, no charging to the sound of trumpets." He patted the neck and let his hand slowly travel down to the horses chest. "Rest and wait for me to return." He lifted his eyes to the mountain peaks, the first grey streaks of a new dawn were dispelling the darkness.

No mistakes today, Gasper had underestimated the enemy and it had cost them dear. What had looked like an easy target had proved costly, the pass to the Keep had looked to be defended by peasants had surprised them. They hadn't faced pitchforks and rusty guns, they had run full tilt into cannons and a concentrated field of bullets. Somewhere below the mist which never seemed to lift higher than a mans knees, lay the dead. Hundreds of his comrades in arms lay there, when the bugle sounded, he and the others would need their dead as stepping stones to reach the barricade.

Slowly the fingers of dawn slid down the mountains and with them the breeze that would disperse the mist. White tendrils of mist were lifted and blown by the breeze, they carried high into the morning air. There they vanished, blown far away to some other killing ground. All too soon the bodies of yesterdays dead were visible, their corpses already bloated and falling prey to deaths handmaidens.

He looked along the line of his men, half awake, cold and probably hungry. A hand waved at him, Michael waved back, Sven Thorson grinned, twisted his thick yellow beard and spit towards the enemy. Michael had no such ritual, to him a battle was a battle, a fight only a fight. He did not begrudge the Swede his idiosyncrasies and had lost count of the times he had seen it happen. It was the Swedes opening gambit in the game of life and death.

For over fifteen years he fought, laughed, cried and loved in the company of Sven Thorson. He had stood back to back with the man, he had got roaring drunk with him. And he had cradled him like a child, sobbing at the death of his mother.

All thoughts of what had been were driven from Michael's mind as he heard the whine of cannon balls. He felt the ground beneath his feet tremble with their impact. From somewhere behind him he heard them explode, then the cries of injured men. The musket ball plucked at his jerkin, he felt it nick his arm. He heard the cry of "Fire". Gasper shouted the order and twenty cannons answered the defenders. Before the defenders had time to reload, Gasper's trained men fired. Twenty guns in unison, twenty screams of death hurtled towards the opposing lines.

The defences were ripped violently apart as the earth beneath the defenders erupted. Great sods of the battered ground flew high into the air. Mingled with these sods of earth, wood and straw bales, an assortment of the defenders limbs. Almost lazily the headless torso did its grotesque dance in mid-air before falling to the ground. Michael tried to swallow, licking his lips trying to moisten his mouth. As always before a fight it was dry, his tongue, thick and tacky. It would go once the call to charge was given, it would go. With sword in hand charging towards barricades the dryness would go and the adrenaline would course through his veins. He felt the sweat of his hand in the glove, pulled it off and wiped it on his leather jerkin. He rubbed harder, felt the hardness of the sweat stained leather. Michael clenched his fist, flexing his fingers, did his hand so ache to hold a sword. He looked down the line of waiting men, did he look like them. Eyes wild, lips drawn tight against gums, teeth clenched, dogs of war straining at the leash.

Men ready to die for a bag of gold, men ready to die for a paymaster they would never see. They knew these men that not all of them would survive this day. They also knew that those that did survive, the reward would be greater. He smelt fear, terror, even the lust of death was strong among them. The stench of cordite in his nose, smoke stinging his eyes, Michael reached for the hilt of his sword, once the smoke had cleared the sound to charge would be given.

The clear strident call of the bugle, the answering call of three hundred men screaming at the top of their voices. The sound of six hundred feet pounding towards the enemy. The crack of muskets, the shrill whine of their leaden death, the sobs, the cries and screams of downed men. He heard the harsh panting of his laboured breath, loud in his ears.

The heady scent of battle, the smell of gunpowder, sweat and fear, the bitter brassy taste of blood on his lips. Michael threw himself at the defenders on the barricade. Thrust hard with his sword, the blade sank deep, an obscene sucking as it was pulled free. Not the time or the place to use the fancy moves taught by the fencing masters, only time to hack, slash and cut. No time to think, no time to see how his comrades in arms fared. Like others before him, in the thick of battle, Michael was alone. His arm ached, his head throbbed, legs trembled. He slashed at the face before him, it split like an over ripe melon. He stumbled, fell, struck by the dying man he went down. The dead man lay across his back, hands pressed to cold ground, he pushed. Free from the restraining weight he got to his feet, the wooden hayfork hit him hard. Michael grabbed the prongs of the wooden weapon as the man tried to deliver a second blow. He thrust his arm away and thrust, a look of surprise on the mans face as the blade passed through him. The man fell backwards pulling Michael with him, Michael placed his foot on the mans chest and pulled.

The blast of the exploding cannon ball caused him to stagger, the heat scorched his face. A hand grabbed him, "Come on, Englishman". Sven's face was streaked with the grime of battle , rivulets of sweat leaving thin white paths. "This is no time to rest, we've broken their backs". Michael pushed the Swedes hand away. "The final rush Michael and the pass is ours." He watched the Swede rush to join in the final onslaught.

The last minutes of a pointless battle in a place few had ever heard of was a thing of nightmares. The company took revenge for their commanders mistake in underestimating a foe. The spoils of victory was the slaughter of every man, woman or child, even animals were killed in a frenzy of blood lust.

Michael sat on the steps of the church, around him the dead of both sides. His head hung down, he breathed deeply, the cold air of the mountains harsh on his dry throat. He still gripped his bloody sword in his right hand. A strange weariness , a cold aching in his bones, his head still full of the cries of battle. His stomach churned from the stench of blood and the incessant buzzing of the flies.

Flies, always the flies, after every battle the flies, shining blue wings, incandescent blurs feeding on the blood of the dead. It disgusted him to see them crawling into open wounds, buzzing, flitting from corpse to corpse. Growing fatter with each feeding. He flicked at them with his blade disturbing them in their feasting on the congealing blood. They flew angrily around the blade, some even landing on the red coated steel, it distracted them only for moments before alighting on another corpse.

Michael watched them settle on the dead woman's face, running into the open wound. He stared at them, how could a god create such filthy creatures.

Anger rose like bile in him, he kicked out at the corpse, wanting to squash the seething mass. His booted foot connected with the woman's head, the body began to roll over with the force of the kick. The body slithered down the steps, twisted onto its back, the accusing dead eyes stared up at him.

She had been beautiful once, but pain and death had raped that beauty. Michael shuddered , closed his eyes, trying to blot out her grimace of dead accusation. He felt a dead weight in his hand, he still held the sword in a vice like grip. His eyes ran down the length of the blade, blood stained its usual brightness. A picture of the old gypsy Carlo became fixed in his mind. What would the old man think of him now? What of Lena, would she give congratulations on the way he used their gift. He had not thought of the old couple in years, he could not recall their parting. He had awoken a stranger in a strange land, in a world beset by wars. Petty Princes fighting petty Princes in their petty little dispute. Michael became a player in this game by accident, a company of mercenaries had passed through on their way to fight for one of the Princes. The Swede Sven Thorson had been their captain, with nothing save his sword, it had been easy to convince Michael to join them. Over the years Michael had learnt his trade well, he became a most competent killing machine.

Michael snorted, what was the point in trying to recall the lost years. He had fled his own country because of a war and become embroiled in countless little wars. Why this pass was important he did not know or care, the price they had paid had been too exorbitant. There had to be an end to it, Gasper wanted men to take the small Keep and hold it, the thought appealed to Michael. Maybe he could find a little peace, time to heal himself from his tortured thoughts.

Michael's mind cleared, he saw the offending mess on his blade. He tore the dead woman's garments and wiped it away. He twisted the sword in his hand, wiped it once more, then rammed it home in its scabbard. "It's over." He heard somewhere in the distance. "Michael, it's over, we've won." Michael turned, "What?" He asked. Sven saw the strange look in his comrades eyes. "Are you hurt , Michael?" Concerned he grabbed Michael's shoulders, "Are you hurt?"

"Hurt?, no I'm not hurt, I'm sick." Thorson looked at his friend, he could see the pain and anger plain on Michael's face. "Sick?" he said. "Sick of this." said Michael waving his arm towards the scenes of carnage, "Sick to the very depths of my soul with the smell of death, sick of the sounds of battle." Thorson recognised that his friend had sunk deep in the throes of mental and physical fatigue. He would have to choose his next words with care.

"We have been fighting too long, we have seen too much death." He was struggling to find the proper words, a phrase, anything to draw Michael from his despair, "We do what we are paid to do, we are paid to fight and to kill. It is the way we live." Sven's words were not an excuse, he spoke the truth. He could see his words were having no effect on his friend. "Come," he said, "Come, let's drink and talk."

Michael laughed, "Drink." he said, "Will that solve all my problems? I doubt it. Don't you understand?" His voice grew louder, "I don't , can't live like this any more." He tried to smile, he did not want to hurt his friend , they had stood back to back too many times. They had shared too much, Sven would never understand how he felt at this moment. To the Swede things were so simple. He was a soldier, he sold his blade to the highest bidder. "Leave me alone for a while old friend." The Swede shrugged and turned away, Michael watched him go, within the hour Sven would be drunk or wrapped in the arms of a camp follower. The battle, the slaughter of the defenders, the loss of comrades, all would be forgotten. Michael wished that he could be like his friend, able to forget everything in a cup of wine. The woman's face returned to haunt his thoughts, these had not been trained opponents. True they had used cannons, but after the first flush of success, they had not known what to do. Had they been trained Michael doubted that any of the company would have reached the barricades.

Thorson did not go to find drink, he stood a distance away and watched the Englishman. The Swede was worried about him, ever since they had taken the small town a month ago, Michael had changed. He had become reckless, taking foolish chances when there was no need to. The fact that he still lived this day had nothing to do with his skills as a soldier.

The Countess's last line of defence to the pass, it was her last throw of the dice. The defenders were little more than farmers, more at home with plough and pitchfork than with a musket and blade. Sven shrugged yet again, it wouldn't be long before Michael got himself killed.

Thorson stepped back as the horse and rider came to a stop before him. Sven looked up at Gasper, he grinned, so the little Frenchman had come out of hiding. Gasper glared down at the Swede as if he could tell the man's thoughts. That the Swede or his company did not like him did not disturb him, he paid them and they fought. His master the Prince Mica wanted the lands of the Countess, but most of all he wanted the Keep for to own it was to control vast areas of the mountains. And with that control came the use of immense powers and the Prince Mica longed to be a powerful man.

"Come with me Captain." Without waiting for an answer the Frenchman pulled at the reins and turned his horse. Thorson followed slowly, no need to rush, let the Frenchman seethe a little. When the Swede had joined him, Gasper turned and pointed down the pass to the Keep. "The last hurdle." he said.

"It will be hard to take, if the Countess's men are inside, it will cost a lot of lives." Thorson rested his back against the cold rock of the mountain, "Is it worth it?"

"Whoever holds the Keep, holds the pass," Gasper tugged at his beard, "And my Prince wants it".

"And the Countess, does he want her too?" asked Thorson. "It is said she is a rare beauty". Gasper tugged constantly at his beard, twisting and turning the hairs between his fingers. Gasper stared hard at the small Keep, built into the living rocks of the mountains.

Twenty, perhaps thirty feet in height, only a few openings in its walls. These set at such angles as to cover the approach to the Keep all ways. The entrance, from what he could see was a large door, this would be wood, and wood burnt. The portcullis was a different matter, it was iron and iron did not burn. His tired mind turned over the use of cannons, pointless, it would take better cannons than those the Prince had provided. Many men would die if the Keep had defenders, too many had already died, he could not, dare not loose any more. Gasper was not thinking of the men under his control, the way back was dangerous and to be without sufficient protection would be stupid. Gasper was not a brave man, but no one had ever accused him of being a stupid one, not where his own life was concerned.

"I am not privy to my Prince's personnel thoughts." said Gasper. "Only his orders, which I obey, and you would do well to obey."

Sven stared hard at the little Frenchman, who stood tugging his beard.

Thorson allowed the Frenchman's words to mull over in his mind and he also gave some thoughts to the man they were fighting for. The Prince Mica was a weak minded despot, a creature more used to seeing men die for him than fighting himself. Thorson could never remember seeing the Prince near the battle lines, "Obey". he asked of Gasper, "You did say obey?"

"You serve the Prince, therefore you obey." said the Frenchman. The words of the Swede when he answered caused the Frenchman to step back in fear.

"Obey," snarled the Swede, "I don't have to obey anyone and I'll be damned if I'll die for a nothing."

"No man is my master." roared Sven, the muscles on his face tightened, he jabbed at Gasper with his thick fingers, "I fight for him because he pays well, and more importantly, he pays on time." The little Frenchman was seething with righteous anger, how dare this peasant refuse to obey their master.

"And if the Countess offered more, would you fight for her?" Gasper's hand moved to the butt of his pistol, a look at the Swede told him such a move would be extremely dangerous to his continuing health.

"Probably," said Thorson, "But I won't and she has not offered". Sven turned away, stopped, turned back and levelled a rigid finger at the Frenchman. "I hold my life dear Frenchman, and the lives of those who follow me, I will waste no more for you or your Prince." Thorson was white with anger, the little Frenchman had nearly got him, played him like a donkey with a carrot, offering a prize then threats when that failed. Sven shook his head, had Gasper not used the words of "Obey" and "Master" he would have gone to take the Keep. Perhaps Michael was right, perhaps now was the time to call it a day, to allow the sword to rest in its sheath for a while.

"I'll send the Englishman." said Gasper "He'll go and the men who serve under him, if any are alive, will follow." Michael would go, Sven was aware of that, but he wouldn't go and neither would any of his men. Sven finally found his voice, he stared down at Gasper. The Frenchman found himself looking into eyes colder than the Swedes homeland.

Thorson took hold of the horse's reins, ignoring the Frenchman, he swung himself into the saddle. Sven pushed his feet into the stirrups, Gasper made no protest at the loss of his horse. "I'll take my men and go." He made to reach for Gasper who stepped back, "I give you warning Frenchman, if Michael dies, I'll find you, and then you die." Thorson slapped his heels against the horses flank, his eyes searching for Michael among the men who had listened and witnessed his exchange with Gasper. Michael was stood on the edge of the crowd. Sven lifted his hand and motioned to him. Michael saw the look on the Swedes face as he rode to him.

There was worry and a great deal of concern in Thorson's voice as he begged Michael to leave Gasper to his own fate and ride away with him. "Don't do it Michael, please." Sven could tell that his pleading had fallen on deaf ears. If Michael was not aware of it Sven was, they had come to the parting of the ways. And when at last Michael spoke he knew he had lost his friend forever.

"We all have to die sometime, so why not sooner than later?"

"Don't be stupid," Sven shouted, he had to keep trying to get through to his friend. He saw the looks in the face of his men, a sadness on them that told him even they knew he fought a useless fight. Thorson lowered his voice, "Michael don't die for nothing, if you must die, then find a reason of importance."

"I have taken the Prince' gold."

"So have I, but I won't throw away my life or the lives of my men." He reached forward and grabbed hold of Michael's jerkin. Michael closed his hand over Sven's . "I won't let you do it."

A sad smile touched the Englishman's lips. "How will you stop me, old friend, do we fight?"

Sven groaned aloud, he wanted to strike Michael, knock him to the ground, hold him down and pound some sense into his cold English brain. Sven did not because he knew he could not strike his friend.

"I won't fight you Michael, you'll not find death at my hands, find the way to death on your own."

"I have every intention of doing so Sven, I'll find my own road to my own personal hell."

"Then do it," roared the Swede, anger, frustration and the utter pointless waste of it all sickened him. "Do what you want, go to hell any way it pleases you." The gulf between the two widened, "Don't expect me to mourn your stupid death."

Michael hung his head in shame, he knew what he was doing, he was hurting deeply an old friend. "Sven" Michael wanted to reach out over the void that had come between them. His knuckles whitened as he squeezed hard on the pommel of the Swede's saddle. What had happened to him, what cancer was eating away at his soul? He did not have to try and take the Keep, he could ride away. He could and should be able to turn his back on this one battle. One little fight in many, countless battles for little Lord's, how many had he killed? How many deaths for those little Prince's who craved to be big Prince's. He lifted his head and set his eyes on the Keep. Nothing compelled him to fight, it was almost certain death. What was wrong with him? Did deaths maggots hold him? Did he want to die?

"Old friend," Sven's soft words disturbed his thoughts. The old Swede had to try, just once more. "Come with us." Michael looked up, saw the outstretched hand of his friend, he grabbed it. "Come home with us". Thorson saw the slow almost hypnotic shake of Michael's head. "Then we will go without you." One last try to reach Michael. "Come with me, together we will fight for your lands in England."

"England," Michael murmured the word, soft, low, lovingly. Thorson would have pushed the point but Michael stalled him, "Too late, far too late to even consider going home, I must stay." The Swede seethed with an emotion he was finding hard to control, he gripped Michael's hand with a vice like strength.

"Why? We owe no man, what is wrong with you?"

"I have to stay Sven," Michael tried to pull his hand free, Sven held him even tighter, "I don't know why, but I must stay."

"I ask only once more, come home with us, please Michael."

Michael pulled sharply but the Swede's grip was stronger, also being astride his horse helped. Michael was lifted until he stood on tip toes. Eyes locked, the two men stared deep inside each other. "We were brothers once, what has come between us?" Was all he said. How could he tell his friend what he himself could hardly believe. That here he would find what he was seeking, that here was his own personal road to his destiny. That something deep inside of him, a thing that had been buried, but was now resurrected, was forcing him to stay. And if needs be, die. Sven could see that his words had fallen on deaf ears, further arguments were wasted. He released his friends hand, Michael staggered back. "I will ask no more." Thorson reached inside his jerkin and pulled free a small parcel which he handed to Michael. Michael felt the weight of the object inside, he pulled at the wrapping. A plain silver cross some six inches long, its cross piece three, it carried no crucified figure. Strangely it was sharpened to a point. "It is the only thing of value I have, I leave you in Gods protection for I have this feeling we shall never meet again. And this causes me sadness." Sven looked at the Keep, its cold walls, lifted his eyes to the high peaks of the mountains and lowered his eyes to meet Michael's. Thorson shook himself, this was a bad place, an evil place, here he was leaving his friend to the fates. Thorson was not a deeply religious man, he did believe that there had to be a God. Sven Thorson was a highly superstitious man and he firmly believed that here in this dark valley between the mountains something worse than death waited for his friend.

Thorson shivered and crossed himself and for the last time clasped his friends hand. Here in a cold insignificant little place was the friendship of fifteen years ended. The pain and sorrow of its ending was written plainly on the men's faces. "Goodbye Michael Cavendish, may your God be with you." Words stuck in Michael's throat, he could not speak, he dare not unless the emotions he was feeling overcame him. "Sven."

"We were brothers once." Thorson kneed the horse, tugged hard at the reins, raked the horse with his spurs. The beast fought back, rearing and stamping against this unaccustomed treatment. Thorson clung hard to it until he had regained control and without looking back rode away.

Michael stood and watched until the last man had disappeared beyond the rim of the mountains. He pulled the cloak tighter around him and turned his face towards the Keep.

The pathway to the Keep lay in shadows, the setting sun throwing the mountains shadow onto the small band of men. The men, Michael included seemed to sense a presence, something intangible. Whatever it was they felt it had wrapped itself around them the moment they had set foot on the pathway to the Keep. The very rock gave out a coolness more bitter than the harshest winter night. Michael could almost touch the unease that had entered his men, his own body was chilled with it. He knew it was not the cold of the coming night, it was something else. He looked up at the sky between the mountains, the moon, white and cold was visible on the rim of the high peaks. They must move on, once the moon had set it would distort the shapes of the rocks, plunge the pass into a deeper darkness, long before true night gripped the world around them.

Michael shivered, a dread of the supernatural forced its way into his whole being. Did his men feel the same? Had that cold maggot called fear entered their souls? It was not the fear of an enemy, as yet there had been no sign that the Keep was defended. It was not the fear of death, the companion that settle on every soldiers shoulders. What Michael felt, what they all felt, was the fear of the unknown. Here on this mountain pass was a sense of something unspeakably evil. The hairs on the back of Michael's neck bristled. "Turn back." An inner voice called to him. "Turn back, before it is too late." He heard the muttering of his small band, voicing their fears aloud. Trying to drive them from their minds. A cold rivulet of sweat ran down his back. Icy fingers played along his spine. He had the strangest desire to stamp his feet, he pushed cold fingers deeper into his gloves. He was freezing cold. Michael grinned to himself, that was it, there was nothing unseen to fear. There was no supernatural force at work here, only the cold. It was the cold of the changing season, winter would soon be on them. It was the all embracing cold of the rocks that never felt the warmth of the sun.

Michael's blade hissed, steel on steel reverberating in the still air of the confining pass. The entrance to the Keep was before them.

The portcullis was drawn up, the door stood open, an invitation to enter, there was no sign of defenders. Michael pushed the door fully open, ten feet high, by a foot thick. It swung back noiselessly on well oiled hinges. "Jesus, Mary protect us." The whispered prayer loud in his ears, Michael swung round, ready to chastise the speaker. The man, Michael knew was a harden fighter, had from somewhere produced a torch, which he had lit. The man with the torch crossed himself, his eyes riveted to the wall above the door. Damn, now was not the time to start getting nervy. Michael looked up, whatever the man could see was lost in the darkness to his eyes. He grabbed the torch and held it high, flames spluttered and jumped on the oiled rags, tendrils of burning oil fell to the cold rocks as Michael reached as high as his arms would allow.

A wolf's head, its fanged mouth open, sightless eyes carved from the living stone. Baleful, daring them to pass beneath its snarling effigy, and enter. Michael lowered the torch, it threw grotesque shadows across the faces of his men. He moved it closer to his own face, allowing the men to see him clearly. Michael prayed that he did not show the fear he was feeling. He held his sword before them, the flame of the torch reflected along its shining length. "Well?" was all he said as he threw away the torch and entered the Keep.

The entrance hall of the Keep was brightly lit, torches hung in brackets on its walls. Stalls for their horses empty and cleaned. Shelves and hooks for bridles and saddles waiting. If man and animal had used this place recently there was no sign of their occupancy. Michael had been in such places like this many times, but never one so clean. Animal shelters in Keeps always, always carried the scent of its previous occupant. It was as if the place had been specially prepared for them.

"Search." His voice loud, he startled the men, why was he shouting? Was he allowing things to get to him? The easy way they entered the Keep, the wolfs head over the entrance, the place lit, but by who? "Search." he ordered yet again. "Someone must be here." He looked at the steps leading from the hall to the balcony. Here he knew he would find the living quarters. "Otto, take two men and search the ground floor". He tapped one of the men with his sword, "Guard the door, no one leaves, that is if this damned place is occupied, you," The last man stiffened slightly, "Come with me."

The sound of their booted feet on the stone steps echoed in their ears. Michael bent and touched the stone. "Damp." He turned to his men, "Washed and swept my friend." The man sniffed and moved slowly up the wide stone stairs, "Nothing." he muttered, "No sign of man or beast Captain." Michael did not answer him, where were they, there had to be someone here. Who had cleaned the place? Who had lifted the portcullis and left the door open? "You on the door." Michael called out, it did not appear to matter that anyone heard him. Whoever was in residence would be aware of their presence. "Signal Gasper, let him know we have access to the Keep and we met no resistance." Two more steps to the balcony, which ran the width of the Keeps interior, two more steps, which way should he turn. To his right lay darkness, to his left an open door and a well lit room. "Stay here." he said, his voice sounded harsh to his own ears. Michael swallowed, strange, there was no dryness, for the first time in his life, a last moment before he stepped into the unknown, his mouth was not dry.

The door which stood invitingly open was intricately carved. Trees, that he would swear seemed to move in the flickering torches, as if blown by a gentle breeze. A wolf running, its muscles bunched ready to launch itself at its prey. Michael's eyes followed the carving down the door, he blinked, had he actually seen what his eyes told him to believe. Impossible, carvings on a wooden door could not move. The situation he was in, the stillness of the Keep. The uncertain light from the torches had played tricks with his senses and his eyes. Yet it had seemed so real, the carving of the running wolf had actually changed into a man. Michael stared stupidly at the last carved panel, it was the figure of a man. Michael shook his head and looked around him. "Damn this place". Using the point of his sword he pushed open the door.

"I bid you welcome to my home, enter of your own free will, and when you leave. Leave behind a little of your true self within these walls".

THE VALLEY - Part 3

Michael opened his eyes and looked around him, as the mist cleared, he saw table and chairs, pots hanging in a cupboard, a pot bellied stove and a man bent over the stove stirring a pot. He saw the pile of wood to feed the stove and the guns, a rifle within easy reach of the giant and the pistol strapped to his waist. He heard the cry of the wind, foiled in its attempts to find cracks in the cabins construction. Through the blurred glass of the cabins only window, shadows of the blizzard, snow thrown against the glass. Michael was warm, he felt the softness of the beds covers, he moved. Pain raced through him, attacking every nerve end in his battered body. Michael was unable to stifle the groan that escaped his lips. Tibor turned and looked towards the man on the bed. Michael examined the mans face, his eyes etching every line and curve of it to memory. Michael guessed him to be around forty, a weather beaten face, framed by thick black curly hair. Eyes deep dark pits staring at him from under bushy eyebrows. The nose thick, broken at sometime, it kinked in the middle. His lips thin and peevish under the heavy moustache. The wolfman noticed how tall he was, a giant of a man, broad shouldered, heavily muscled, large hands capable of breaking a man in half. Big, heavy, yet when he moved he moved with the grace and speed of a panther. A dangerous man to tackle, a man who knew no fear, and then Tibor smiled.

It transformed his face, the harshness became kindness, the lips no longer petulant. "Welcome moon child," Michael tried to speak, his voice a feeble croak. "Rest easy, you are safe." Large hands with long blunt fingers pushed him gently down. They pulled the blankets back up to his chin. "You have found what you were seeking". The giant smiled and said. "The Wych Woman called to you and you came to her". "Wych" The one word nearly tore out the back of Michael's throat. The giant shook his head. "I am not the one, I am the Wych's guardian, the Wych sleeps." Tibor looked down at Michael's face, cold, pain, illness had ravaged it. The skin stretched tight, making the handsome face a sickly yellow skull. Michael was barely conscious, drifting in and out of waking and black oblivion. "Sleep moon child, soon you shall see her, sleep." The wolfman tried to speak, Tibor pressed his fingers to Michael's lips, his voice when he spoke was soft and low. "Forget what you are, for now you are safe, sleep." Michael drifted back into his hazy world, the soft sound of the giant's voice compelling him to sleep.

Tibor heard the drone of the planes engines, they were flying low down the valley, searching. He rubbed hard at the frosted glass, the crooked cross emblazoned on the plane shining in the winter sun. The fighter dived, pulled up at the second it seemed he would plough into the ground. It rose high, circled and rolled over, then dived again. Tibor did not doubt for one moment the pilot had found what he had been searching for.

Two nights ago he had stood before the cabin and watched the glow of fires and heard the sound of the bombs. In the white light of the moon, black winged shadows had flown over his valley, and he had known where they were going. The Jewish community in the next valley, Tibor had no love for the Jews, but he did feel a sorrow for them.

He had felt a guilty gladness their community was over thirty miles away. They would bomb the valley relentlessly, then the troops would go in. It would not be the regular soldier's it would be the specialists, the black uniformed extermination squad. "Still," he murmured and managed a grim smile, some of the Jews must have escaped the intended massacre, otherwise they would not have been searching his valley. Here, he and Katji were reasonably safe, the cabin well hidden, the forest heavier in this valley. If any stranger did find them, Jew or German, Tibor felt no compunction over killing them. True the cabin could be approached from behind and it was possible for them to be surprised. But only if they found their way across the mountains and the glacier which guarded the entrance into the valley. Tibor's valley was as safe as it could be, only he knew the way in and out.

"Safe." No, that wasn't strictly true, in winter the valley was safe, but when the snows melted. Once before in his travels before the arrival of Katji he had witnessed the destruction of a valley like his. Machines and dynamite had raped the land and the impregnable valley had been penetrated. It could happen here, they would come with their powder and earth movers and he could not stop them, not alone.

The stuttering cough of the guns made him look up. He heard the whine of lead fired down its rifled bore, he saw the flames as the bullets left the barrel. The planes engines screamed, it pulled up sharply, nose pointing up at the heavens. He saw the black object drop from its belly and fall towards the earth. In the clear light of the winter's day, orange flowers blossomed on the valley floor. The anguished sobbing of the valley, rock, soil, snow flew upwards as the earth was torn apart. Trees screamed and cracked, trunks splintered, branches ripped from them.   Centuries old goliath trees falling in slow motion. Anger rooted him to the spot, forcing him to watch the destruction. Anger and frustration at man and their reasons for destroying his beloved forest. "Damn you." he cried aloud, fingers gripping the window sill. "Damn you". Behind him the wolfman groaned aloud, his rest disturbed by the bombings, Tibor turned, the moon child tossed and turned in a fevered sleep, should he waken Katji, no, let her sleep. The Wych girl had spent sleepless nights tending the wolfman forcing strange brews down his throat. Once he had found her on her knees beside the wolfman speaking in the guttural tongue of the old religion.

On the bed something half man, half wolf had snapped and snarled. Cried out in both human and animal voice. A thing with claws where there should have been hands, eyes a hot burning yellow, feral wolf's eyes, a snout where there should have been a nose, teeth, dripping with saliva, bony, sharp, the tearing teeth of the beast. The rapid changes, the thick grey hair disappearing from the mans body leaving smooth flesh. The creaking and snapping of the joints, the popping of sinews stretched to their limits. Katji weaved her magic over the creature, talking soothingly, touching that obscene thing, that they were sworn to protect.

It was the first time Tibor had ever witnessed the changing of a moon child. He had heard of it, been told of it by other guardians. But he knew that despite all of the tales told around the fires of the peoples of the old religion, it was over two hundred years since a guardian and a Wych had actually witnessed the transformation of the Werewolf.

Tibor realised that without Katji the thing on the bed could easily turn on him, it almost compelled the giant to call her from her sleep. Katji was not only his safeguard, she was the moon child's only hope. Tibor gripped the butt of the pistol for comfort, he knew it would not stop the moon child, but Katji needed to rest. The next instant Tibor was thrown forward, the sound and force of the explosion ringing in his ears. The giant struggled to his knees, his senses reeled, Tibor gasped at the power which had struck him. Gathering his strength he managed to stand upright, like a man under the influence of strong wine, his vision blurred and the room whirled before his eyes. He threw out his arm seeking something to hold onto. His fingers found the edge of a shelf. A flour bag, split open, poured its contents over his hand and arm. Tibor shook his hand, as if in a dream he watched the fine white powder fall to the cabin floor, dancing in the beams of hazy sunlight, which sparkled off the glass of the window.

Far away he heard the asthmatic cough of the guns, the whine of the climbing plane. The sound and feel of exploding bombs, the cabin rocked with their impact. Feet planted wide, Tibor walked stiff legged, lurching towards the window. He stared in horror at the sight before him, a large smoking hole which lay less than a hundred feet from the cabin door. Trees burnt, fire climbing rapidly along trunk and branch. Smaller trees and bushes were blasted into burning match wood, Tibor shook his head, forcing his brain to see what his eyes refused to. Between the savaged timber, less than two miles away, he could see the wide expanse of the valley. Distant figures small and black against the landscape, running, scattering, trying to hide from their relentless pursuer. The plane roared low over the tree tops, the pilot aiming its nose at the running figures. Once more the guns rattled out their message of death, small pockets of snow were thrown up. One of the figures stopped running, was thrown forward and lay still on the ground. Under the rhythm of the guns, a second, then a third did a funny little twisting dance. Then there was silence in the valley, the plane flew on, no need to check on the still fallen figures. Tibor knew that had he been closer that the dark stains around the still bodies would be red.

Tibor could not tear his eyes away from the smoking hole. A bomb dropped too soon had nearly achieved what countless others had failed to do over the centuries, kill the Wych woman and her guardian. They had been lucky, had the pilot intended it, he, Katji, perhaps even the moon child would have been blown to eternity. A distant memory, how long ago had it been? Two, perhaps three years ago?, two men with instruments measuring the valley. Somehow they had found their way over the mountains and across the glacier. But they had stayed too long and he had buried them deep and destroyed their instruments and papers. He had never told Katji of them. He had never felt the need. Tibor clasped the big hands that had squeezed the life out of them, this was his valley and Katji was his to protect.

If what the giant believed to be happening in the outside world was true, then his valley was no longer secure. He would have to take his bride away from here, go deeper into the mountains. Tibor would take them to the cave he had found in his wanderings around his domain, there they would be safe, for a while. The invaders would come, not yet. Not until the snows completely melted, but they would come. At the sound of Katji's voice Tibor turned, her hair tousled, eyes still blurred with sleep, the giant looked at her and the decision was made. He would leave this place that had been his only home for more years than he cared to remember. He would take Katji with him, and if need be, he would carry the moon child to safety.

"We have to leave here Katji". There was no easy way to say it, it would be pointless in pretending that it never happened. "We are in danger". The girl shook her head, "No" she mouthed, "We must child." He said, child, he was not talking to a child, she was his wife, she was a woman. "The invaders are in the next valley, look out of the window, see what has happened here today."

Katji moved over to the window, she was still trying to shake off the effects of too deep a sleep. Tibor stood behind her, saw her body stiffen and heard the stifled sob. "Today the old Gods protected us." Tibor went on to tell her what he had seen and the cause of what had so rudely awakened her. "If frightened men fleeing for their lives can cross into the valley, think what the machines of war can do. You know of the way things are in the outside world, we have spoken of it many times. Remember the things we witnessed there remember the treatment handed out to those they considered inferior by those in power. Think, remember how you, even you cringed at the sight of the black uniform and the crooked cross. Remember how you smelt death on them."

Tibor felt her body go limp as she fell against him, he put his arms around her. "For the moment," he said, "We are safe, but when the snows melt and the pass is clear, then they will come."

"But it will be weeks yet before the pass is clear," she said "And we have the moon child to think of". Katji gestured towards the sleeping man, "We can't leave him behind, we dare not". Tibor smiled down at her, when he spoke his voice was soft, but Katji could hear the iron in it. She knew that no matter what she said, Tibor's mind was made up, when the time came they would move.

"I won't leave you, you know I could never do that, and I know that we cannot forsake the moon child. But" he said, "All I say to you is true, the invaders will come."

"You will protect me Tibor?" She smiled that shy child woman smile of hers, knowing, hoping it would break Tibor's resolve. "You are the guardian."

"Katji," Tibor broke Katji's train of thoughts, she was trying him with her wiles. It had worked in the past but he could not allow her to distract him this time. "I can protect you against most things human and animal. But against guns and bombs Katji, not even I," Tibor spread his arms leaving his statement unfinished. He saw her allowing his words to spin around her mind. Realisation of their situation slowly overcoming the years of safety the valley had afforded them. She would be heart broken to leave the valley, here she had known a little peace in her troubled life, "This is my home." She said. "I wanted to stay here forever, just you and I." Tibor looked into her eyes, she had understood that she must leave. "When must we go?" she asked. The giant placed his large hands on her shoulders. He reached out and lifted her chin, gently he touched her face with a finger. Tenderly he brushed away the tear, he watched the tear slide down his calloused blunt finger.

"I know a place little one". His voice full of understanding at the pain she must be feeling. "It is a safe place, and when," He pressed her to him, folding her tiny frame against his giant one. "And when it is all over, as one day it must be, I promise you I will bring you home." Katji looked up at him, love flowed from her for this gentle giant. Did he know? Did he feel anything for her? If he did, would he ever tell her he loved her, perhaps one day.

"I fear that if I leave this place, our home, we shall never return." Tears flowed freely down her face, Tibor held her face in his large hands, "I would give" he began, Katji touched his lips and shook her head. "Will we ever know real happiness you and I, will we carry this terrible burden forever.?"

"We did not ask for it Katji."

"We never had a choice did we, we were born for it". She tried to wrap her arms around him, buried her head against him, face pressed against the coarse material of his shirt. Silently he cursed the old gods and the fallen one for choosing this child. "We were born for it." Katji sobbed while the giant held her close to him. Tibor did not reply, what was the point in debating it yet again. He, like her had been marked from birth. He would remain a guardian until the day he died, Katji now had a chance, all be it, a slim one. There was hope for her. And should things and circumstances favour them both, he too had the chance for happiness with the woman he worshipped. When Katji reached twenty, which he knew was not far away, he would tell her the secret he had carried for the last three years. Tibor held her tighter to him, he would tell her, if he still lived, he would give up his secret. That he had already killed to protect her. Until then he would remain quiet and pray to his gods.

On the bed the wolfman stirred and through half closed eyes examined his surroundings. How long had he lain here? He remembered the world gripped by winter's hand. His animal instincts told him the seasons had changed. The scent of Spring was in the air, carried by the winds, but not just yet, but it was there, the sweet smell of new grass, Michael sniffed a strange scent mingled with the smell of fire, then it came to him, a scent he had smelt during many battles, cordite, the smell of powder? and the lingering stench of death? When he was on his feet he would ask the giant, until then he must be content with listening. He stared at the man holding the woman. Michael listened to them talking . He heard the giants explanation and reasons as to why they had to leave the cabin. So, the giant was a guardian of the old gods, but the girl, it seemed impossible that this frail looking child was the Wych woman he sought . How could she have guided him through those long hours, how could she be the saviour who had dragged him back from the brink of death. Michael forced himself to move, pain enveloped him, but he must move, he had to be on his feet when he greeted the Wych for the first time. She had brought him safely here, and from the look of, it had caused her much pain, she deserved, no demanded his respect.

Katji was the first to realise that Michael stood watching them, she pulled away from Tibor. She saw a tall man, flesh wasted on his bones, hollow eyed, dark rings of illness visible beneath them. A vivid red scar, an inch wide from armpit to thigh. Countless other scars marked his body, most of them ancient. "The moon child". she whispered, Tibor let go of her and moved between her and Michael. The moon child moved towards them on unsteady legs, the effort it caused was plain to see. His face was peppered with sweat. He was breathing hard looking close to collapse.

"I am Michael Cavendish, Werewolf, and I ask, beg, for the protection of the Wych." Katji moved away from Tibor, slowly she walked towards Michael, she laid her hand on his arm, the wolfman still found it hard to believe his life was held in those tiny hands.

"While I live, you are protected moon child, this I promise."

"And" said Tibor "While I live I protect you both." Even in his weakened condition, Michael understood that what the giant meant was that he protected the girl. Michael did not answer, even at the height of six foot one, he had to look up at Tibor who towered over him. The effort of looking up caused his head to spin, he staggered, regained his footing . His mouth was dry , he was struggling to release the words. He needed to say the words to the man, he had to convince him, say it, tell him. "I will not hurt her." He said finally, the effort causing his chest to rise and fall rapidly. Looking directly into the giants eyes he said, "I give you my word." Michael placed his arm across Katji's shoulder, he needed a crutch , his legs had turned to jelly.

"Food" said Katji, "He needs food."

"What kind of food moon child, there was stew on the stove but," he motioned to the mess thrown across the cabin floor by the explosion of the bomb.

"I heard you," said Michael, the strain of speaking taking its toll on him. "I heard you say this place was no longer safe." Katji helped him back to the bed, the wolfman flopped down on it. Michael tried to collect his jumbled thoughts, fought against the dizziness which threatened to engulf him. "Tell me how long do we really have left?" Tibor smiled, so the moon child had listened to them, at least it saved time on further explanations.

"Six to eight weeks, before the new season claims the valley, it all depends on how badly they want to get into the valley." Michael looked at the Wych girl, she looked little more than a child, He knew what he had to ask for and for some strange reason he hoped his next words would not offend her.

"I could eat your stews big man but,"

"My name is Tibor Vajek Khan, I am husband and guardian to Katji the Wych."

"Then Tibor Vajek Khan, you know what I must have," The giant stared hard at the wolfman, true Tibor did know what he needed. At any other time they would have brought the wolfman out of his illness slowly. The wolfman had understood the urgency of the move, Tibor snorted, then all animals realised when they were trapped.

"I need raw meats."

"Yes I know," answered Tibor, "I'll get you some." Michael fell back on the bed, the effort of speaking and moving was too much for his tired body. Katji placed her hand over his, she could feel the heat of his fever. The wolfman lifted his head and looked at her, "You don't have to stay and watch" he said. "It will not be too pleasant to look at." Katji touched the wolfman's shoulder, touched the star shaped scar.

"You too were chosen," she said and smiled down at him. "It's alright, I do understand." At the sight of the plate of raw meat in Tibor's hand, Michael's stomach began to churn. He needed those raw bloody hunks of meat, he needed them that he might live. He needed to put the bleeding cuts into his mouth, they promised him life.

"Make her leave." his tone almost begging, his eyes pleading he asked of Tibor. "Ask her to go she should not be forced to watch this." His mouth was eager to take in the meat, juices filled his throat. Tibor said nothing, but he held out his hand to Katji who reluctantly took it. Both men watched her until she had left the room and closed the door behind her. She would stay outside until he had finished eating, he prayed. Michael picked up one of the hunks of meat, licked his lips in pure animal anticipation. "You don't have to stay." he said, suddenly aware of the giant staring in fascination at him. Tibor shook his head, walked over to a chair and sat down.

The wolfman sniffed the meat almost delicately he put it in his mouth and began to chew. He tasted the salty bitter taste of the blood, felt its life giving fluids seep down his throat. Strong canine teeth chewed the meat into sizable pieces, Michael swallowed. Tibor sat and watched trying hard not to show the disgust he was feeling. Around and around his brain chased the word he longed to speak aloud. "For this we were chosen, is this all my life will mean as a servant to this creature."

Tibor's resolve failed when the wolfman put the plate to his lips and drank the blood. Vomit caught in the giant's throat and he was forced to rush out of the cabin. On hands and knees the giant allowed the sickening mess to sweep out. Gagging, fighting for breath, determined not to bring up the contents that still remained inside him. He looked at Katji, who smiled sadly back at him, Tibor cursed the fate that linked him and the Wych inextricably to the fate of the werewolf.

The cool breeze that played among the trees wafted gently on the giants face. It caught the tears and dried them on his cheeks, it touched his lips and carried away from him the smell of his sickness. Tibor rested his head against the tree trunk, he heard the twittering of birds. Dimly to his troubled mind the sound of something running. He opened his tear filled eyes and looked for a long time. He stood there allowing sight and senses to drink in the familiar sounds and sights of his beloved valley. An overwhelming feeling of dread, fear, terror, call it what you will, entered the giants heart. "No." he sobbed from between clenched teeth, "No." But the feeling remained caught deep inside of him. Like Katji he knew that when they left the valley they would never return.

Tibor walked to the barrel of water beside the cabin door, he plunged his head into its icy contents. Drinking deeply, swilling out his mouth with its numbing wetness. Once more he pushed his head into the barrel until the need to breath forced him to remove it. Again the playful breeze came to him, as if with spite, it drove the icy droplets into his face, chilling his lips. His mind clear, his brain functioning, Tibor stepped up to the cabin and pushed open the door. The Wych sighed, held back the tears as he entered the cabin, Tibor would do what must be done, to help Michael, no matter how distasteful the task, through her tears her love for this giant shone brightly.

Michael held out the cleaned plate, "I told you not to watch." he said . Tibor could see strands of red meat stuck between Michael's teeth. "Do you have more?" he asked. Tibor nodded his head and held out his hand for the plate. The giant man was fighting his revulsion towards the man on the bed. Michael recognised the look. He saw no trace of fear in Tibor's eyes, the man did not fear him, only what he was. "You have no need to fear me guardian, I will not harm you or the Wych woman."

"I have no fear of you moon child, but you bring a harm with you I cannot fight. What will happen because of you I have no way of knowing, but here," he said, resting one hand over his heart, "Here I know, the life we have known is coming to an end."

"I had no other choice." answered the wolfman.

"Neither do we, you are what you are, and we are sworn to protect you. I will get you more food." Tibor turned and left the room, Michael stared hard at the giants back, why was it that those who gave him succour always had to pay a price. Michael looked up, Tibor stood before him, another plate was held out to him.

"In one week I should be able to travel." said Michael, "Now," he said by way of an apology, "I must eat." This time the giant turned his back , he would not, could not watch. Michael ate the meat, relishing the sweetness of it, drinking the blood, licking the plate clean. No more, he couldn't gorge himself, it was the first time for many months he had reverted to raw flesh. He needed his system to digest it, to become once again used to the feel or it. He lay back, how to engage the giant in conversation, he had eavesdropped when they had been unaware of him listening. He needed more, he had to know the reasons the giant would brook no refusals on their need to know.

"Tibor Vajek Khan." The giant turned to him "I would speak with you." Tibor moved over to the bed, Michael forced himself into an upright position.

"Tell me what it is you fear. Tell me what is happening here. Tell me how long I have lain here."

"The last one is easy, you have been with us six weeks and in all that time Katji was the one who tended you. To her you owe your life." Tibor pulled the chair over to him, placed it before the bed and sat down. "Your first question must wait until I have answered the second." The giant wrinkled his nose, the smell of blood on the man prevailed over all others, Michael saw and understood and tried to move out of the giants senses. "Be still moon child, I have smelt blood before."

"Perhaps," said Michael, "When you have told me what I need to know, I can tell you a little about my world." Tibor did not answer, he did not even look at him. In a low voice he began to speak of what he knew and what he suspected was happening in the world beyond the boundaries of the confined world of the valley.

Of the man called Hitler and his meteoric rise to power Michael knew. Of the kind of men who clung to him who defied him of their desire to wipe away all they considered inferiors, he knew. That, because of one mans desires war would take place between the great powers of the world, a world he hardly knew. Of the overwhelming desire of the new order of Germany to conquer all of Europe he did not know. Tibor spoke of a war machine that was supposedly unstoppable, but must somehow be stopped. He spoke in a voice tinged and bitter, of the camps and the extermination squads that ran them. He spoke of mans inhumanity to man, and he spoke without thinking of the nature of the beast.

"I have dreamed a dream moon child, I had dreamed I would like to spend the rest of my natural life here, in this valley."

There was no bitterness in the look Tibor gave Michael, only a sadness at the thoughts of what could have been. "Men have always dreamed." said Michael, "I too have dreamed. I see into your heart Tibor Vajek Khan, I see your love for the Wych woman." Michael forced himself higher on the bed, with an effort that made his head spin he struggled to his feet. "You do not need to answer my first question, I see the answer in you face. Your heart and soul belong to the Wych woman," Michael, each step causing him pain, moved towards the window, Tibor watched him, the wolfman gripped the window sill with both hands and lifted his eyes up to gaze at the sky.

Time had passed all too quickly, night had come to the valley. The wolfman feasted his eyes on a million twinkling lights that peppered the heavens. For what seemed an eternity to Tibor, the wolfman fixed his eyes on the cold orb of the moon.

Deep inside his brain, memories stirred, he was remembering the times he had run on all fours. A time when he had lifted his face to this same moon, in a different place and a different time. Memories crowded from his tired mind. This was neither the time nor the place to be lost in thoughts of what had been. "Have you ever known peace Tibor Vajek Khan?" The question surprised the giant and for a long moment he stared at the wolfman.

"Many years ago, when I was a boy, I knew peace." Tibor looked at the wolfman seeking an answer in his face as to why he had asked the question. "Before" he went on, "Before I was told what I was, and what would be expected of me. Since then I have not known much peace." The giant touched his forehead. "Not even here."

"I cannot remember a time when I did know peace. There are years lost to me. I cannot recall. I know what I am." Michael laughed and turned towards Tibor, "I even know who I was, the youngest son of an English Lord, does that surprise you Tibor Vajek Khan, no, it does me, but." He said sadly, "that was long ago, perhaps my family no longer exists to see the monstrous abortion that I have become!" Michael turned back to the window and returned his gaze to the moon, he closed his eyes, not wanting to see the mockery on the moons face. "It might have been better had I died that night." Then he surprised Tibor by saying, a grin on his lips. "The night will be long, would you care to hear something of my life Tibor?" he said. The giant waited, Michael did not turn around, he continued to gaze hypnotically at the moon. "I feel a desire to talk."

THE KEEP - Part 2

The woman was beautiful, her eyes a large liquid brown, her nose, small, her lips full and sensual. The lips glistened red, slightly parted to reveal small sharp white teeth. Dressed as she was, covered from throat to as far as Michael could see, her body threw out a sexuality that confounded him. Michael had been in the presence of beautiful titled women before, but this woman held him in a vice. Her eyes were sending him messages his brain refused to believe. She was seducing him with her eyes, looking into his secret places. He had come to conquer, to kill if necessary, instead he stood like a love sick suitor. He was slowly succumbing to those eyes, eyes that stripped him of his manhood, probed and dissected him. Eyes that promised things beyond even his fevered imagination.

"The night is cold." Her voice was as low and seductive as her look. "Pray sit and take wine with me." Michael could not believe he was hearing her words. A few scant hours ago he and the others of Gasper's company had slaughtered her people, yet here she was offering him wine from her table. The woman was tall, Michael could not remember her moving, but here she was beside him. Smiling, the Countess took her place at the head of the table, a table that lay ready and waiting for guests. Michael stood there like a fool, open mouthed and staring. He accepted the goblet she offered him, in a trance he raised it to his lips and toasted her. The wine was sweet, yet Michael tasted a bitterness in it that left his tongue numb.

"Your sword." she said, Michael followed her eyes down, he still gripped his blade firmly in his right hand. Michael felt himself go red with embarrassment, and like a chastised school boy caught out in class, he hid the source of his embarrassment in its scabbard. "Better sir," said the Countess and smiled at him. Michael noticed the sharpness of her small teeth and how one, each corner of her mouth rested on her bottom lip. "Pray do as I ask of you sir, sit." Michael seated himself. No, this was not right. He should not be taking wine, he should be. What in God's name should he be doing, the woman had him in a trance.

"You appear perplexed, sir." Michael was unable to answer her, again the Countess smiled that seductive smile of hers. She was toying with him, showing him that despite his strength, despite his weapons, she and only she ruled here. The Countess was still the Keep's mistress, and she knew that to be true.

"I am," she said pointing her goblet towards him. "The Countess Elizabeth Dressler, this is my home, and welcome you are, for all guests are welcome in this lonely place." Her smile slipped and anger replaced seduction in smile and eyes. "Why do you enter my home with a weapon in your hand?"

Michael pushed back the chair and stood before her, "I am Michael Cavendish." He bowed to her, "On the orders of Captain Gasper and the Prince Mica." The countess did not let him finish, instead she laughed, a hard brittle laugh that left Michael speechless.

"A silly little man who craves to be a King." She laughed again, an ugly sound from the lips of one so beautiful. "A despotic coward." The words were almost a snarl, hatred was plain to see in her face, she lifted the goblet and drank deep. The Countess laughed again. Michael was beginning to hate the sound of it. Elizabeth Dressler lent forward, resting her elbow on the table and stared at the Englishman. "Tell me," she said the words given as a command, "Why do you fight for such a little man?" The Countess waited, fully expecting an answer from the man.

Michael felt his spine stiffen, he would never know if it was the bestial look on the Countess's face or the simple fact that he did not like anyone man or woman talking down to him. "He pays me in gold, madam." He bowed low, hoping he was showing some degree of contempt in his manner.

"So you fight for gold." The Countess smiled a crooked smile at him and waved her hand. As if by magic a man appeared from behind a curtained alcove.

Michael snatched at the swords hilt, damn it he was growing too careless. "Stay your hand sir, you have nothing to fear from Julius." The man Julius walked forward, on the tray he carried was a single silver decanter. He bowed towards his lady, gave Michael a brief mocking glance before bowing. He lifted the decanter and offered it to him. Michael could not help but notice the thick coarse hairs that covered the mans fingers. Julius was dark skinned, and had it not been for the petulance he was showing, some would have described him as handsome. The man seemed to have a permanent scowl carved into his features. Michael found it easy to instantly dislike him, he had about him the air of a man who would see and hold a grudge where there was none. It was also plain to see that the dark skinned Julius was the Countess's dog. Michael felt like grinning in the mans face, he could picture Julius sat at the woman's feet waiting to catch the titbits she threw him from the table.

"Julius, tell the others, the captains men and my servants, they have nothing to fear, and we likewise." She looked to Michael for an answer, "Is that not right?" she asked.

"No Countess, it's better I tell my soldiers." He glanced towards Julius, this time he did not smile. "One look at your scowling friend and Otto will split him down the middle," Michael's smile broadened at the sight of Julius stiffening in anger. "You have my word Countess, you and yours are safe from me."

"Thank you Michael Cavendish, it is nice to know one is safe in ones own home." Julius laughed, lips curled, it came out as a snigger, he muttered under his breath, "Julius."His head snapped back at the sound of her voice. "Get out and send Anna to me." Julius bent almost double. "Madam" he said, never taking his eyes off Michael's face.

"Not a man to turn your back on." observed Michael. That slow seductive smile spread across the Countess's mouth. The tip of her tongue ran over the fullness of her lips. Michael's eyes were drawn to the red moist flesh. He felt an urge to take her, to press his lips to hers, to touch and taste those lips. To gaze into eyes that were full of the mysteries of love and life. Michael closed his eyes, when he opened them the spell was broken. For one brief moment he thought he saw the anger of failure flash in the woman's eyes. "I must go and speak to my men. They are somewhat touchy" "Do so sir." she said, the Countess leant back against the arms of the chair. "And then you must tell me what happens now." She draped her arm across the chairs back, the other she placed across her breasts. Michael was about to ask her what she meant when suddenly the Countess held up her hand. "Wait Anna." He saw the curtain in the alcove pulled back, saw the slim hand disappear. Did the woman have some sixth sense, twice she had been aware of her servants being present. "You did not answer my question sir."

"At this moment madam, I'm not sure what your question is." Once again she was treating him like a child asking for answers when he didn't know the question. Damn the woman. Then it dawned on him, he realised the situation they were in demanded an answer. "Yes." was all he could think of to say. The Countess lifted an eyebrow and gave what she hoped was a quizzical look. "Yes." she repeated, Elizabeth Dressler felt good, that the man was dangerous she did not doubt, she could also sense that his appetites were as strong as hers. He would be good, she could use him, for a time anyway, he could be used. It was a long time since she had held a really strong man in her arms. She raked her bottom lip with her sharp teeth, tasted the blood she drew from them. This one would last longer than the others who had been foolish enough to enter her home. She smiled, she could hear Anna's harsh breathing from behind her. So the red bitch also wanted this man, good, she could use him tonight. She needed the man occupied, there were matters only she could attend to.

"Do I become the spoils of war?" she asked of him. "Yours, your commander's, your men's, anybody's."

"On that I cannot comment." Michael pushed away the drink she offered. "But I see no purpose in treating you in such a way. You ask me what is to happen, I believe Gasper will leave men to hold the Keep. If it is of any consolation to you I will ask for the command." The Countess did not answer him, she sat and stared, Michael felt hot and uncomfortable under her rigid gaze.

"I suppose we must wait for this Gasper's orders then." The man nodded. "Are you afraid of me Michael?" The Countess laughed aloud, this time a softer, gentle pleasant sound full of mockery. "Don't ever be afraid of me or for me." She placed a long slim fingered hand over his and squeezed. Michael looked down. A tangle of fine golden hairs grew on them. "Go now." she said. "Do what you have to do, then return to this room."

Michael turned at the door and bowed to her, the Countess lifted her goblet to him. She waited until the door had closed behind him, "Anna". The young woman stepped from behind the curtain. Green eyed, flaming red hair, a wondrous body, only the small scar on her right cheek detracted from her beauty. "The scent of lust is heavy on you Anna, do you crave a man so badly?"

"I desire a fresh one Countess, and he his fresh and looks strong." Replied Anna licking her lips at the prospects of a strong man in her arms. She turned towards the Countess as the other woman uttered a small snarl.

"Tonight I must be away from here." The Countess reached for and held the Anna's hand in a vice like grip. "You know why and I take Julius with me, and you my precious Anna, you must entertain our gallant Captain." She heard Anna's deep throaty laugh, she smelt the scent of her sex, the red bitch was in heat. "See to him when he returns, quarter him well, the rest I leave to you, but Anna. "Elizabeth Dressler pulled the woman towards her and down until she could look directly into her eyes. "He must not be hurt, understand that, do not hurt him."

"It is only his body I want Countess, the rest I leave to you, when the time is right."

"Good, see that you do just that. Go now and prepare a room." The Countess tapped her nails hard against the top of the table and considered her plans. Whatever had to be done had to be finished this night. She would have preferred to take Anna with her, but she had work to do here, the Countess smiled , Anna would not call it work. The red bitch lived only for and to pleasure herself, she would make sure she entertained Michael all of the night.

Her lips curled as she thought of Julius, he was becoming too familiar. He needed to be taught his place in her scheme of things. He would need watching this night, bloodlust could not be allowed to override common sense.

Michael shrugged his shoulders, it was pointless even trying to give Gasper advice. Let the little Frenchman rattle on, once he was clear of the valley, out of the mountains he, Michael Cavendish was in complete charge. "Four men are all I can spare." Gasper bent his head over the map. "These are dangerous times Captain and you know I must reach the Prince with the news of victory." Michael shrugged once more, he would make sure he had supplies for both men and beasts. Despite Gasper's protestations that they did not require horses, Michael had insisted on them. "If we need to get away, speed will be of the essence." For a short while Gasper had baulked at the idea of so much food and animal fodder being taken into the Keep. But in the end, Michael had won, he had given the commander a simple ultimatum. Since he was to stay here for at least a year, certain of his request must be met. Gasper had finally capitulated with an ill grace and dismissed the Englishman from his presence.

Gasper made his plans quickly, he wanted to be on his way before nightfall. Baggage was thrown onto wagons, men ate their cold fare with haste, and when the four men left the company to return to the Keep, no farewells were said. Gasper watched from a distance, he had no intention of entering the Keep or meeting its occupants. For him the war was over and a return to the luxuries of Mica's court beckoned. Let the Englishman stay, and those who had decided to stand with him. If they managed to hold the Keep all well and good, if not, such were the casualties of war. Gasper turned and without a backward look ordered the company to move out.

Michael blinked his eyes against the flurry of fine snow. The skies above the mountain tops were grey and angry. The threat of winter hung over the mountains and the Keep. He pulled the cloak tighter around him soon it would be night. At the entrance to the Keep he turned. The flakes were fatter. If it continued through the night, by morning. "By morning, we could be snowed in." His voice sounded strange to his own ears. "By morning." He said aloud. Michael suddenly realised that the day was not yet over. Impossible, had it taken only these few hours, the meeting with the Countess. His talk with Gasper and his return to the Keep. Had all this happened in a few short hours? "By morning." For the third time he spoke aloud. The pass would be closed and they would be cut off from the outside world.

He banged the door to the Keep shut, closing out the rapidly falling darkness and the weather. Here they had food and warmth and a year wasn't a long time was it?

"My lady retires early tonight Captain." Anna held open the door to a room, "She bids me see you comfortable." Anna brushed against him yet again, allowing her hand to touch his thigh. The woman could not have made it more obvious what she wished from him unless she had spoken the words aloud. Michael allowed her to move against him, this time her hands lingered on his groin. Michael swallowed, surely she could feel the thickening of his manhood under her hand. Anna rubbed her hand against him, then slowly she moved backwards to the large bed. She locked his eyes with hers, the invitation for him to take her plain to see. Slowly she moved her hands to the cords which held the dress to her shoulders and pulled. The dress fell in a whisper of silk around her ankles, Anna stood naked before him, she stepped away from the fold of her discarded dress and lay back on the bed, slowly and provocatively spreading wide her legs. "To the conqueror the spoils." she whispered huskily . With two fingers she opened herself wide to him.

Michael stripped away his clothes, he stood over her. His penis engorged with lust, he lowered himself down onto her. Anna sighed as he thrust himself deep inside of her, she dug her nails against his flesh as the man moved in and out of her. Her sex was wet and slippery with lust, and with each thrust of his manhood she felt the juices flow. She cried out as he fastened his mouth to her nipple and sucked, she felt his hands touching, probing her body, his finger rubbed hard at her opening.

He touched the tiny button of hard flesh and pressed his fingers to it.

Hands manipulated her breast, lips sucked and his tongue licked her nipples. His mouth kissed her neck, her ears, her eyes, and fastened onto her lips. All the while he toyed with her body he pushed his penis harder and deeper and faster in and out of her. Anna sobbed her pleasure aloud, her body writhing in pure lust. Her sexual appetite matching his stroke for stroke until her body was carried over the brink. Anna climaxed with a scream, covering Michael's penis and soaking the bed clothes with her juices. She climaxed yet again as he filled her with his seed. Spent, satisfied, weak with their efforts, they lay wrapped in each others arms. Between their legs the mixture of both of their satisfaction dripped in a combined pool.

How long she had lain asleep Anna did not know, she had awoken to the heady scent of their mingled love juices. Gently she lifted the sleeping man's arm from across her and cautiously she moved away from him. The man had taken her more than once that night, she could still feel his mouth pressed against her. His tongue forcing its way between the lips of her sex. He had licked and sucked her until she nearly begged him to stop. At the instant before she would have flooded his mouth with her juices, he had pulled his mouth away from her. He had opened her legs and gently pushed himself inside of her. Anna had clung to him while he rocked back and forth bringing her and himself to a climax. Her body was covered with his sperm. It clung to her white and sticky, Anna caressed the parts he had ejaculated on lovingly. She knelt over him and lowered herself. After this night he would be the Countess's, Anna bent her face close to his. One last kiss, she had earned one last kiss. Michael picked that moment to turn in his sleep.

Anna's eyes opened wide in terror, her heart missed its beat, panic gripped her as she scrambled off the bed. She stood trembling afraid to make the slightest move. She did not, dare not wake the sleeping man. Bending she picked up her dress, without putting it on she moved with extreme care to the door. Each sound came to her with a clarity brought on by terror. The sound of naked feet on carpeted wood, the rustle of silk against her naked body. Slowly, gently she pressed down the latch. Its well oiled movement sounded like thunder in her ears. Outside the room she pressed her nakedness against the cold stone walls of the Keep. Anna shivered, not from the chill of the stone but from the thing she had seen.

Etched deep into the man's flesh had been the mark of the Fallen One, the five pointed pentacle of a chosen one. Did the Countess know? No it wasn't possible, she, she had been the one who had given herself to him. She tried hard to drive from her mind all thoughts of sexual pleasure she had derived from him. She tried to remember the law, "So long." she sobbed, so long since she had needed to use it. What would happen to her, what could she do, had she actually broken the law? If so, how, would the Countess know, would Julius, no, he would not, the Countess had not yet taught him about it. Anna tried hard to probe her memory, only once, many years ago had she reverted to the law of the dark angel. Remembrance of it still brought anger to her heart and the taste of bile to her throat. Julius should have been destroyed. When the opportunity had arisen, she should have killed him. Anna wrapped her dress around her shoulders, it was too late for regrets, the deed was done. As she ran down the dimly lit stairs she wondered how the Countess would react. She, not Anna should have given herself to the chosen one.

From far away came the cry of the wolf pack hunting . In the bed Michael buried his face deeper into the pillow, not quite aware of what had disturbed him. In her room, Anna sat, the dress still around her shoulders, arms clasped around her knees. She heard the howl of the hunting pack and buried her face against her knees and began to sob.

"Impossible," The Countess Elizabeth Dressler thrust herself out of the bath tub with such force she overturned it. She lay spread eagled where it had tipped her, the hot contents seeped into the rich Turkish carpets. She grabbed at Julius's arm and pulled herself upright. "It's not possible, I would have known." She stood there in her nakedness not caring that the others should see her. It mattered little, Julius had spent more than one night servicing her and over the long lonely times, she and Anna had pleasured each other many times. "Me." she screamed, "It should have been me, not you." She turned on Anna, one hand raised, Anna waited, she was pleased to see fear and panic in the other woman's eyes. The Countess unclenched her fist, Anna smiled at her, knowing full well the Countess would not attack her, "I should have known, I should have felt something." Anna handed her the robe, almost dismissively she draped it over her. "All these years Anna, all those long lonely years we watched and waited. The hundreds and thousands of minutes which ticked by while we waited for the one who carried the Dark Angels kiss. The chosen one." The Countess pulled at the thin robe, anger blazed from her, the material ripped apart, she looked down. Slowly, deliberately she tore the robe into shreds. The red haired Anna stood, watching and waiting while the Countess vent her anger on the robe. Deep inside of her she smiled, so, not even the Countess knew what to do.

"He has to be made one of us." At the sound of Anna's voice the Countess turned. "He belongs to us," She threw out her arm, watching the rags that had been woven from fine silk fall onto the carpet. "I can turn him." said the Countess. "But how to keep him from the secret of what he is and what his coming means to us, to you and I Anna."

"Let me kill him." Anna stifled a cry and the Countess turned with a surprised look on her face at Julius's words. "He would be better off dead, for all our sakes."

"You." said the Countess, contempt on her lips, scorn in her voice, "You would kill the chosen one?" She laughed at him, "I think not my pretty lap dog." She gently tapped his face with her hand. "Don't snarl at me so Julius." She pouted her lips at him. "It spoils your beauty and," she whispered, "That's all you are, a pretty beautiful man." Her lips curled as she went on. "And a lap dog, my lap dog, so keep you place in the kennel or I will let Anna finish what she has begged me to do for centuries." Julius seethed with anger and embarrassment at the words and treatment he was getting at the hands of the Countess.

"One day you will push me too far, even you my lady and her." He turned towards Anna , "The red bitch is jealous because I will not bed her."

"Get out of me sight." Cried the Countess, reaching for something to throw at him, her eyes settled on a hand mirror. The Countess drew back her arm, "Get out, back to your kennel." Julius retreated back, his hand behind him, searching for the door. "And Julius, don't come to my room again, until I send for you."

The Countess breathed deep when the dark skinned Julius had left her and Anna alone in the room. "Tell the others to watch him, I don't think he will try and kill Michael, but with a man like Julius you can never tell."

"Do you think" said Anna, "That all we know of the chosen one is right?" For a moment the two women stood and looked into each others eyes. Elizabeth Dressler touched the woman's hand, held it, slowly turned it until she was stroking the fine red hairs that grew along the length of Anna's fingers. For the briefest of time the bond that had once been between them, was there again. The Countess could see the sadness, the longing in the red haired woman's eyes.

"Even if all the legends are true Anna, even if they are not, you, I, we can never go back to what we were." The Countess reached for a dress from the alcove. She held it before her, twisting left and right before the long mirror, smiling at the sight of the blood red silk against her pale skin. She noted with a great deal of satisfaction that not one single line appeared on her smooth flesh. Elizabeth Dressler had been a beautiful woman when she had been turned all those decades ago. She held her head at an angle with pride and arrogance in every fibre of her wonderful body, she was still a most beautiful woman. "Look at me Anna, no sign of age, not a line or a wrinkle to mar me. I am still twenty five and I am still beautiful." She let the dress fall, she cupped her breast in her hands, "Still firm," she murmured, her fingers traced a path down her body. She rubbed her hips and thighs, allowing her fingers to slide between them. Touching herself, feeling the tingling beginning to build up inside of her, "Still desirable." The tension between her thighs grew too much to bare, she pulled away her hand as from hot coals.

Anna saw the way her nipples had hardened under her touch, the way the Countess had gripped her own hand firmly between her thighs. She had witnessed the misty clouding of the Countess's eyes, the teeth gnawing the lips. The thick white hairs that covered her spine, the movement of supple flesh reverting to hard coarse skin of an animal. Then she snarled and with an effort regained her composure. "Do you think me a beautiful woman Anna?" The Countess did not wait for an answer, "I like what I am, I like to be young and beautiful and healthy. I do not nor will I ever wish to return to what I once was. Now," she said, "Help me dress and I will entertain our gallant Captain." She looked at Anna, a gaze full of triumphant lust, he is mine, said the look in her eyes, he is mine.

Otto watched his captain stare moodily into the dark crevice that split the mountains in two. Michael had been stood on the very edge of the pathway for over an hour, not moving, not speaking, just staring down into the bottomless darkness. Otto flexed his shoulders, did it never get warm here, was the sun so afraid of the darkness it dare not penetrate the pass. He was not the only one to notice the change that had come over the man. The others had complained that he was not in his right senses. There had even been the whisper of desertion, the continuing cold, the short days, the claustrophobic atmosphere of the Keep was making them all a little volatile. Fights had broken out over the serving women, one man had been badly hurt and died four days later of his wounds. Complaints had been voiced over the way their animals were cleaned. The food they were served. The general grumblings of the common soldier were turning into a nightmare for Otto. While the captain paid service to the Countess he strived to hold the command together. How long had it been, less than three months, surely four men who had all they ever desired, food, warmth and female company, should be able to stand the sight of each other.

The females were a mystery to Otto, you never saw them until the night-time. In his wandering around the Keep, the only two women he had run into were the Countess and Anna. The man Julius who took an instant dislike to him which Otto reciprocated, and a pair of what could only be described as peasant workers. The servants to the Countess seemed to please themselves with their comings and goings.

Otto placed his hands on the wall of the Keep and looked down. The captain had gone, no doubt he was finding solace in the bed of the Countess. Who could blame him, she was a rare beauty, and the damn days and nights were cold here. He grinned to himself, perhaps the red haired wench would be available tonight, she could play a tune on a man's fiddle like none he had ever used before. The howling of a wolf brought him out of his reverie, many times over the last months he had heard them. He had even found their prints before the door of the Keep, but no one had set eyes on them. The mournful howl went on and on, it rang down the pass. It seemed to bounce off the mountains themselves. It grated on Otto's nerve ends causing him to clench his fist. The sound entered his brain and sent shivers down his spine, then an unnerving silence which struck an unnatural fear into his heart. The man was no coward, he had proved that countless times, but even he would admit, it was fear that drove him from the walls. Pray God the Captain would sicken of the woman, for surely she was the only thing that held him, them, confined within the walls of the Keep. The German had made up his mind, like it or not he would put forward the men's request and his own. Give up the Keep and let them all return to their homes before it was too late.

The Countess straddled across Michael's loins writhed with lust. She thrust her sex hard against the man beneath her. Michael rubbed his hands hard against her breasts, squeezing the nipples, the Countess pressed forwards and down, pushing him deeper into her. Michael rubbed harder. She responded to his harsh treatment of her breast by rotating her hips against him, her hands pressed down on his shoulders, fingers dug painfully into the flesh, Michael reached up and pulled her down to him, he fastened his mouth on her nipple and sucked. The Countess gasped her pleasure aloud, the harder Michael sucked the harder she thrust herself onto him. Michael moved from breast to breast, sucking, biting, licking. The heady perfume of mingled sweat and sex overcame the other scents in the room. Their bodies, slick with the efforts of their love making, glistened in the lights of the candles. The shadows thrown by the meagre lights could not hide the ugly face of lust stamped across the features of the Countess.

There was no gentleness in their love making, no tender words of endearment passed between them. The Countess wanted sex, nothing more than that, and he had provided her with it every night for the last month. The invitation to share her bed when it came had not been a shy tentative approach, the Countess had simply said, "I need a man, I need to feel a man inside of me." Michael had obliged her, but her sexual demands were becoming too great, there was no enjoyment in their coupling now.

He felt the touch of her lips on his and tried to respond. Her mouth had moved on, teeth, hard and sharp against his shoulder, he felt their pressure on his flesh. He felt the flesh taken between them and the tongue that darted between the nipping teeth to lick his sweaty skin.

He cried out in pain as the teeth penetrated his flesh, he pushed hard against her, his hands sliding on her sweat slicked skin. Nails raked across his chest leaving furrows of burning pain. The pain became almost intolerable, Michael thrust his body up off the bed, his back arched, the Countess sank her teeth deeper. Michael pressed his hands up against her hips and tried to push her off. The Countess prevented this by pushing down at him and grinding her hips, thrusting his member into her. Slowly she began to move, each gyration coating his penis with her wetness. Briefly the thought had crossed his mind to refuse her, but her incessant thrust was bringing him to a peak he had not thought possible.

Somehow, he could not remember how, she lay beneath him, he let his full weight rest on her and he pushed hard into her. Harder, faster he thrust into her, wanting, trying to hurt her, to cause her pain. Then her teeth met in his flesh, he heard the grinding of ivory on bone, then utter agony as the flesh came away from him. Michael cried aloud, pushed with all his strength and broke free of her embrace, straddled across her he looked down. She was unable to disguise the total pleasure she was experiencing. Blood speckled her lips, a tiny shard of skin hung from between her teeth, eyes closed in orgasmic ecstasy. He felt the beginnings of his own orgasm and he knew he could not last much longer. The intensity of his orgasm when it came, surprised him. It seemed to come from the very roots of his loins, it shot from him with an indescribable force, filling the inside of the woman. It poured free, coating him with its sticky hotness and trickled slowly onto his thighs. He lay still on top of the Countess, body, mind numb, but unbelievably his member was still hard inside of her. He hardly felt the touch of her lips on the spot she had bitten him. The Countess's tongue lapped gently over the wound she had caused, and slowly the hurt subsided.

Long after he had fallen asleep across her, The Countess continued to lick at the wound she had finally managed to infect. She lifted the man off of her with ease, for a moment she considered waking him. She wrapped her fingers around his penis, slowly moving them up and down Michael's flaccid shaft. She watched his manhood stiffen under her touch, smiling she bent her head towards his chest. The Countess lapped at him, her tongue relishing the salty tang of his sweat. The man murmured in his sleep, her tongue moved down his chest to the thick pubic hairs. She buried her face against them, smelling him, she moved her face to his thigh, licking gently she traced a wet path towards his penis. The scent of her own juices mingled with his, sent a violent tremor through her body. She opened her mouth and took Michael into it, her head bobbed up and down, the taste of him creating an uncontrollable desire to drink from his throbbing shaft. Moaning she reached between her own thighs and thrust her fingers deep into herself. The wet slickness of her sex, the velvety touch of vaginal lips soaked in the thick cream of Michael's orgasm. She rotated herself against her thrusting fingers, shiver after shiver causing the muscles of her vagina to contract. Her grunts of pleasure muffled by Michael's penis gripped deep into her mouth.

Her body exploded into a nerve tingling climax. She snatched her dripping fingers from her flooded sex. Her teeth raked along Michael's member, she sucked, licked, swallowed the thick creamy fluid he released into her mouth. The Countess threw back her head, no moan of pleasure but the snarl of an animal escaped her lips.

Hair, thick and white burst from her flesh and spread over her body. Her eyes bulged in their sockets, her nose thickened, becoming a snout, fangs replaced teeth, her mouth stretching to accommodate them. Hands became claws, hard talons replacing finger nails, the claws became paws and the creature bent over the sleeping man howled in bestial joy.

The she wolf crawled off the bed, anger seethed within her, too soon, he could not see her like this. She had nearly ruined everything, in this state she could have quite easily killed him.

The Countess stood before the long mirror and stared in horror at the sight reflected back at her. What would her sleeping lover think of her at this moment. She needed to regress. Face still fighting to control its human features, a body covered in thick white hair, the Countess forced her brain and body to act, every thought she had demanded regression. Such was her state of mind, body still sexually charged the change was a long time in coming. Her head hung low, her body trembled with the effort, until she was once again in control of herself. Exhaustion clawed at every fibre of her being, begging her to let it rest. She smelt the mixture of wolf and human upon her, she saw a face ravaged by the demands she had forced upon herself, she saw a body trembling with an unaccustomed fear. She needed the man Michael Cavendish, they all needed him, if they were to survive and he carried the dark angels kiss. He had been infected, he would become one of them, then, only time would tell if he was capable of handling what he was to become.

She wrapped herself in a sheet, Julius would have this man dead, then Julius was a fool. Only when it had been too late had she realised that allowing Anna to create Julius had been a mistake. Only the law stopped her from letting Anna kill him, but then how close had she come herself from writing stop to his life.

The Countess lay down beside Michael, she pulled the sheet over them both, cradled his head against her breasts. She would not have him dead, she dare not, so very nearly she herself had come within an inch of taking his life. He stirred against her, his arm reached out and pulled her against him. His leg found hers and wrapped itself around her. The Countess stroked his hair, fingers tangled themselves in the thick grey locks. Michael Cavendish would be hers, hers alone, she would nurture him in the beginning, she would be the one to teach him.

Strange thoughts raced through her tired mind, misty half remembered memories of the way things had been. Was it possible that after all these long lonely years she was actually falling in love. On this almost unbelievable thought the Countess closed her eyes and slept.

Michael's shoulder burnt, a cold fire which penetrated the bones. He had examined the wound more than once this day. The old star shaped scar red and inflamed, a thin red strip running across where the woman had ripped it free. No amount of water would cool it down, yet, when he touched it with his fingers it did not make him flinch. He found he could actually press down on it without it causing him pain. The pain that he felt, the pain that was burning him was constant. What had possessed her to inflict such a bite on him, had their lovemaking been so ardent.

He stood gazing out across the pass, seeing nothing, his body and mind trying to forget the pain he was feeling. The bitter cold wind whipped at his cloak, tossed his hair across his face, Michael pushed it back. Darkness came quickly to the pass, the mountains refusing to allow the daylight to linger. Night came early, mornings come late, nothing and no one moved along the pathway through the pass. The wind blew its cold fingers along the pass, seeking, probing for the least line of resistance. Above the rim of the mountains the moon was beginning to rise, dark spiteful clouds scuttled towards it wanting to hide its light. The clouds passed over the face of the moon, the moon's light played on the last reluctant fall of snow. Briefly the frozen snow flakes shone like jewels before dark clouds once more plunged the pass into darkness.

Michael rubbed his shoulder, the full ache had turned into a deep burning, the burning into a throbbing agony. His head pounded with the pain, his body felt like the fires of hell were licking at it. The joints of his fingers caused him to cry out. . They were in turn hot and then freezing cold. His eyes filled with tears that trickled down his cheeks, he pressed them tight. Was it his fevered imagination that made believe they were being forced out of their sockets. He ground his teeth together, opened his mouth wide, trying to give them space to grow. He clasped his hands to his jaw, pushing hard against it, squeezing, pressing, anything to make the pain go away. Michael gripped his throbbing head and staggered away from the wall and lurched into the darkness of the Keep. He leant against the cold stone wall, begging, sobbing, screaming for the hurting to stop.

Eyes open, his tortured mind refused to believe what his eyes told him he was seeing. He could see every laid line of the stone masons work. He could see where time had smoothed the stone, where centuries old mortar had begun to crumble. He could see the thin gossamer strands of the spiders web where it sparkled in the feeble light of the moon. Michael, unable to help himself in his agony slid slowly down the wall. He wrapped his arms around his knees and rested his head praying for relief. Slowly the pain subsided to a dull aching, and the tortured man gratefully accepted the whirlpool of darkness which gave him rest.

The guard found him and called for Otto. Michael still sat in the same position against the wall. When they tried to speak to him, his answer was incoherent, a jumble of words impossible to decipher. Otto and the guard carried him to his room, past a smiling Julius. The stench when they attempted to strip him was revolting to sight and senses. The men looked at each other, not wanting or willing to clean away the foul smelling excrement which covered Michael's lower body.

"Get out of my way." The Countess pushed Otto aside easily, she looked at the man on the bed. Elizabeth was pleased she had her back to them, she would not have liked them to see her smiling. It was beginning to work, the man was experiencing the first stage of the turning. "I'll see to him." she said. The Countess motioned to the red haired Anna. "Fetch me hot water and clean linen." Anna bobbed her head and left the room, she was forced to step around Julius. He was staring sulkily at the sight of the Countess tending the man on the bed. Anna looked at him, "The Chosen one." she whispered, Julius snarled at her and turned away. Anger in every stride as he left the room.

The Countess turned to Otto and the two other men still in the room. "Whatever ails your Captain will not be helped by your standing there." Otto stepped forward and gave the Countess his customary bow. "Madam." He began, the Countess held up her hand, "See to your men and I will look after your Captain." Otto's courage failed him under the Countess's stare, he clicked his heels together and turned away. He ushered the other men from the room leaving the Countess alone with Michael.

"I don't like this." said one of the men, "The Captain was in fine health this morning." Otto nodded, he didn't like it either, he had followed Michael for many years, and never had he seen a man laid so low from no apparent cause.

"I do not know how, neither can I explain why the Captain is so afflicted. But" he said looking at the two men, "He has acted strangely for many a day. From this moment on we see to ourselves, cook our own food and if need be fetch in snow to boil for water." He looked from man to man in their turn, they appeared to huddle together. "Tonight." he said, "I will stand guard in the Captains room." Otto sucked his long black moustache, years of living by his wits and weapons had instilled in him a kind of sixth sense. It was a defensive sixth sense that told him he had better be prepared or pay a price.

When they had found the Captain, the fears the men had voiced became real. The sight of Michael curled in a ball whimpering like a new born babe had sent tremors of fear through him. For the first time in years Otto had taken out his crucifix and kissed it. Had he been able to see in the Captain's room at that moment the fears he felt would have been manifold.

The two women were cleaning Michael with their tongues, lapping at the filth that encrusted his body. On hands and knees they bent over his still frame. Each was in a stage of change. Anna more so than the Countess, it was the first time since the night he had taken her, that she had been able to touch him. The Countess crawled up him, letting her body touch his in intimate contact, her lips touched the wound. She opened her mouth, the teeth extended becoming fangs, delicately she pressed the fangs to Michael's wound. She sank them into the wound she herself had inflicted and infected. Her fangs punctured his flesh with ease, blood spurted up around them, once the fangs were removed the tainted blood ran freely down his chest. With a muffled snarl Anna pressed her mouth to the trickle of blood and sucked. Grabbing Anna's head the Countess tore her away from her feeding, she pressed her breast against Anna's mouth. The red haired woman bit hard and deep. Pressing her fingers to the bleeding marks the Countess moved over Michael. Anna held his head still, the Countess pushed her blood soaked flesh against Michael's mouth. The blood dripped slowly into the mans mouth filling it, finally he was forced to swallow it before it choked him.

The Countess gave a deep sigh and surrendered her breast to Michael who sucked at it with the ferocity of a thirsty man. Eyes half closed the Countess saw Anna take Michael in her mouth, she watched the red haired bitch run her tongue around his tip. Anna slid her tongue the full length of Michael's shaft before clamping it hard in her lips. So intent were the two women in the obscene enjoyment of the man's body they failed to see the burning eyes of Julius watching them.

That night the first of the men left on guard the Keep died. Otto found him outside the Keep's doors, snow and the freezing cold had helped rigor mortis to set in. The man was frozen solid, his mouth opened in a cry for help that was never heard, his eyes wide with terror, his throat torn out. Otto's first thought had been to go and tell Michael, he realised that was a pointless exercise , the Captain was deeper into the illness that had taken control of him. Otto had visited the room earlier, the stench had repelled him. Michael had lain rigid, unaware of his presence, his face carried the touch of deaths hand. The Countess sat in a chair by Michael's bed undisturbed by the smell, Otto had been forced to hold a cloth to his nose and mouth. They had not spoken, Otto disliked the Countess as much as she disliked him. It was the presence of the third person that disturbed Otto, the dark skinned bastard Julius. The man was a yellow cur, forever following the Countess , waiting for the chance to wag his tail. Otto backed out of the room, never taking his eyes off of Julius. He had no choice but to leave his Captain in the hands of the Countess and her maid, but he would watch the dark skinned Julius like a hawk watches a rabbit.

"Toss him into the ravine." said Otto, the man looked at him with revulsion, "Throw him over for gods sake."

"He was a comrade."

"He's dead." said the German and pushed the body with his foot. Otto watched the body bounce off the rocks and finally disappear into the darkness of the ravine. Another dead soldier without a marked grave. Did he have a family, wife, children? Otto did not know, he doubted that it mattered very much now anyway, the man was dead.

The second man died sometime during the following night, he too had bore the marks of a frenzied attack. The third man died sometime between sunset and daylight on the fourth night.

It was the silence that had dragged Otto from his sleep, damn, he had not intended to sleep so late. He knew from the way the shadows fell it had to be late afternoon. He should have been roused hours ago, strange, there was nothing, no sounds at all. The horses, Otto leapt from the bed, he couldn't hear the horses. He placed his foot on the top of the stairs, the door to the Keep was wide open. The sword hissed from its sheath, he held it out before him. Nothing moved, he searched the shadows, no sign of anything or anyone. The horses were gone, had the bastard deserted him, anger blazed like a torch inside of the German. If ever he set eyes on the man again, then he saw the man's leg.

What remained of the man had been propped up against the wall. Otto, had he not known the man would have found it difficult to identify him. He had been literally torn to pieces. Otto crossed himself, he dragged what remained of the man to the edge and rolled him over. Somewhere down there in the cold darkness of the ravine perhaps he would find his comrade.

Otto slammed the door shut, he could count only on himself now. His Captain was of no use at all, he would make the decisions. Damn the Keep, let who wanted have it, damn the Prince Mica. He would take Michael, even if he had to carry him. Otto knew places to hide the Prince Mica had never heard of. The Countess may prove a problem, she would most probably rant and rave at him, but a sword point or a pistol brooked no arguments. It was too late to leave tonight, the pass was dangerous in the dark, besides he needed provisions if he was to get them away from here. Otto began to make plans mentally going over everything they would need. Only one obstacle remained, the Countess, time to tell her what was going to happen, time to get it over with.

"In the morning, but that's impossible." Otto knew his words had troubled her, disturbed her, he saw something in her eyes. Concern for the Captain? No, a fear, that was it, fear, she was frightened because he was taking Michael away. The Countess drew breath, she did not have to be told, the man had read it in her face. Stupid, so stupid, she should have controlled herself, still it mattered little what the man thought he knew, guessed. Michael Cavendish would never leave the Keep and this man would be dead, very soon. Pretend her brain told her, pretend to go along with him. Let him think that he and not she held the upper hand, pretend.

"If that is your decision." said the Countess, "I have no choice but to allow it to happen. But" she said, looking at Michael, whose features were still pale and drawn and lay motionless as if incapable of any movement at all, "Your Captain may die, I doubt if he could survive the travel."

"We will still leave"

"Then I will instruct the servants to see to your needs. You will need grain for your animals and food for your men."

"There are no horses my lady, neither do I have any men, it seems they strayed too far away from the Keep." Said Otto. Surely the woman knew of the deaths, she was not deaf or blind, nothing happened within these walls she did not hear of, "And your servants also appear to have vanished."

"They come and go as they please," she answered. "But I assure you they will attend to you when I tell them to." Otto grinned at her for the first time in weeks, she felt some measure of relief, he had made his final decision, they would leave in the morning. He bowed to the Countess and turned to leave the room, he had hated every second he had been in her company. "I will instruct Julius to provide mounts for you." Otto turned back, inclined his head towards her, "They will be ready for you in the morning." You are dismissed said the look she gave him.

"Until the morning Countess."

"Anna." The red haired woman lifted her head and looked at the Countess, she had pretended to wash Michael all through the conversation between the Countess and Otto, "We have very little time left to us, he must be fully turned tonight." She pulled the sheet from Michael's body, she wanted him, the stirring in between her thighs cried out for him.

The Countess pushed these thoughts to the back of her mind, Michael was very close to death, he needed more of her infected blood. She had to give it to him now, time was so short, she had not believed the amount required to turn him. She was weak, in the early hours of this day she herself had nearly died. Only the loud erratic booming of her heart had told her she had allowed the man to drink too much. Her head had whirled and the beating of their hearts had become one, Anna had torn Michael's mouth from her breast. She touched the place gently, it was tender and sensitive to the lightest touch.

"It has to be you Anna, you must give it to him, I cannot." There was a pleading look in the woman's eyes, she pulled open her bodice, and held both breasts towards Anna. They were bruised with his sucking, the fang marks red and inflamed. "Use him." She saw the gleam in Anna's eyes. "He has to remain alive, he must live."

"Otto." said Anna, wanting to use Michael but needing, wanting to know more of the Countess's plans. "He intends they should leave in the morning." The Countess began to laugh a high pitched hysterical laugh, Anna backed away from her all thoughts of the man driven from her. She watched the Countess's face undergo transformation, she herself could not hold a half altered state. Once into the transformation she had to complete, transformation and regression were painful for her , her body suffered the agonies of hell.

"Dead men don't leave." said the Countess from behind the bestial mask which was her face, "We will kill him." Anna felt the blood lust combine with the sexual need she had for Michael. The Countess grabbed Anna's arm, she winched at the pain that the other woman was inflicting on her. "We have need of only this man." The Countess had regressed, she was fully human. "I leave you to enjoy yourself with him."

Anna stood looking down at him, since that first night he had caused strange feelings to surface in her. Night after night she had stifled her frustration in the darkness of her room. The Countess did not love this man, but she did.

The Countess only wanted what it was promised the chosen one alone could give them both. Anna touched the lips of her sex, already they had started to swell, her fingers felt their wetness and the trickle of juices that ran from her.

Anna crawled onto the bed, she positioned herself over Michael, dug her nail deep into her breast and held the bleeding nipple to his mouth.

Otto's sixth sense returned to him, only once before in his life had such a feeling overwhelmed him. That day one thousand German troops, under his command, had been slaughtered. He was uncomfortable , he was sweating for no reason, the cold finger of the grim reaper had settled on his shoulders. Otto had the strangest feeling that this was to be his last day on this earth. The fates had decreed he would die here, miles from home, in this god forsaken hell hole, the Keep. So be it, if he was to die then others would die with him, he prayed that one of them would be Julius. The conviction of his approaching death did not stop him loading his pistols. He would have liked the Captains sword in his hand but he could not find it. He would check the horses, see that all was ready, then he and the Captain would leave this accursed place.

Julius cringed, the Countess struck him with the flat of her hand. The second blow struck his jaw, Julius was knocked back. Before he had time to recover, a third blow smashed against his head, he tried to stand, he failed. He rolled, trying to absorb the blows of her hands, the painful contact of her feet. "Fool." she screamed at him. "Stupid, pathetic idiot." The thin rod she had grabbed came whistling down across him. Julius snarled, defiance on his face, fear in his eyes. Again and again she rained blows on his unprotected body. "If the chosen one dies because of you, law or no law, you die." Blood seeped from a dozen cuts on his face, the back of his shirt stained red.

The Countess bent and took hold of his shirt, she pulled him towards her. Julius tried to avert his face, not wanting her to look into his eyes. He waited, expecting the blow, when it didn't come he turned to look at her. She hit him with all the strength she could muster, his head rocked on his shoulders. She let him fall, Julius curled himself into a ball. "Because of you I must destroy one of the pack. Because you took it into your own hands to kill the two men you almost destroyed the chosen one." It would have been easy just to have killed Otto on his way down to check the animals. Now she had no choice but to murder one of her children, Julius had instructed one of the males to take the

German down to the horses. She looked at Anna and the others of her pack, nowhere did she see a glimmer of sympathy for the beaten Julius.

That Julius should die for disobeying the Countess, this they understood. That the young one who had listened and helped Julius had to die they found hard to accept. "I can do no other, he has broken the law, and this thing," She kicked the whining man who grovelled at her feet, "He lives only because you made him. Anna, take the others and prepare, soon the young one will forget who rules here and go for the kill." The Countess pulled her leg free of Julius's clinging hands. She touched him with the rod, "Do not move from this spot or you may yet die."

Otto fired the pistol, the black wolf was thrown sideways. It bounced once, gained its feet and turned. Behind him the man sent to fetch him screamed, the man fell down the stairs. Hands clawed at the red wolf which had him by the throat. The black wolf launched itself at Otto, he twisted slashing at it with his blade. The steel opened up the wolf's side, white bone showing in the cut. Below him the red wolf tore at the man, he heard the snapping of bones. Slavering jaws closed around the mans head and pulled. The head tore free with an obscene sucking. The red wolf held the head in its jaws, almost before Otto could move, it rushed past him up the stairs.

At the top of the stairs it stopped and let the head go. It bounced past him, spraying his legs with blood. Otto had no idea where they had come from, one moment he was descending the stairs to the stables, the next death had hurled itself from the shadows. Death had come quickly and terribly to the young man and now he was utterly alone. The three wolves stared at him, the black was hurt but not down. The dirty brown coloured wolf had not yet made a move. The red one eyed him with something approaching contempt, this was the one to watch out for.

He pulled the loaded pistol from his belt and gripped the hilt of the sword tighter. He was preparing to sell his life dearly. Then he heard the snarl from behind him. Otto felt his insides turn to water at the sight of the white she wolf. She had watched him, she had witnessed his wounding of the black one. She had heard its howl, she had watched while its red blood stained the stones in the Hall. Otto was having difficulty tearing his eyes away from the she wolf, he blinked, trying to regain his mind. It was to be his only mistake and his last one. Under the mesmerising stare of the white she wolf he failed to pay attention to the others. The red bitch hit him hard, taking his legs from under him, the black wolf howled its anger at a downed enemy. Otto struck out, the brown wolf sank its fangs into his leg, the pistol went off, the ball tore away part of the brown wolf's ear, the fangs sank deeper. The black wolf dived for the throat, the red bitch snapped at him. She had taken him down, he was her kill, as she closed her teeth around his neck the black wolf tore at his stomach. Otto tried to scream out his pain, the constricting jaws of the red bitch stopped him. The jaws closed together, fangs meeting in the soft flesh, Otto felt the blood filling his throat and knew he was drowning in his own blood.

The black wolf deprived of the kill went wild with blood lust, it tore open the man and sank its snout into his intestines and began its blood feast. The red bitch let go of the throat, she bent her head and sniffed at the blood, touched it once with her tongue. She backed off from her kill and joined the brown wolf at the bottom of the stairs. On the balcony the white she wolf looked down at them then turned and padded towards the room where the chosen one lay.

Michael Cavendish opened his eyes, he forced himself into a sitting position. His eyes were hot, they felt as if they were full of grit. He blinked to clear them, tears filled his eyes, his vision was blurred, he rubbed harder. Slowly they began to clear and Michael looked around him. He was in the same bed and room he had occupied since his first night in the Keep. And yet it all felt strange to him, why was he in bed? Why did he ache so? He reached up and rubbed his shoulder. It felt all wrong, the scar seemed raised and his fingers ached with a heaviness and throbbing he could not describe. He put his hand before him. It must be the sleep still in his system, the fingers looked thicker, blunt at the end. He could never remember having hair on his hand, he clasped them together. He felt a pain in his back and neck, he closed his eyes rapidly as the room spun around. Somehow he was on his feet, the stone floor cold to the touch, despite the carpet. He swayed trying to hold himself erect, breathing deeply he stood there until he had some had gained some semblance of balance.

Michael was having difficulty thinking, his mind was crowded with a mirage of jumbled memories. A big blond man, and the sound of a thousand screaming voices, the sound of guns, the clash of steel. The sounds of the battlefield, men and animals voicing their pains. A dark stone building built into the side of the mountains. A beautiful woman, fine white hair framing her face, a red haired woman holding him tight, begging him to live. A dark skinned man scowling at him with burning eyes and the memory of pain, an all consuming pain that tormented every nerve ending in his body. A face covered in hair, teeth long and sharp penetrating his flesh. Something licking at him, a rough tongue moving over his skin. Yellow eyes locked to his, unable to break the spell in which they held him. The eyes of a beast reaching into the darkest recess of his soul.

The heady scent of blood, his mouth dripping with the juices of hunger. Hunger, an incessant gnawing, the taste of meat sweet against his pallet. The feel of hot liquid trickling down his throat. With a suddenness that caused him to vomit out all he had eaten, Michael saw what he held in his bloody fingers. Hunks of bleeding raw meat dangled before his eyes, the bile rose in his throat. Michael swallowed hard, gulping back the half chewed meat which threatened to burst free. His eyes filled with hot bitter tears, part of him tried to reject what he had done. But an over riding desire to continue eating took control of him.

Michael tore the meat apart and stuffed it into his mouth. The animal that ruled his mind and soul needed the meat for fuel. The beast within him overcame his human counterpart and the man attacked the meat in a frenzy. When the beast had gorged itself, when the last drop of blood had been licked from the plate, it allowed the man to rest, the healing part of the turning had begun.

On hands and knees the man crawled back to his bed. His back arched, his spine covered in thick grey hairs. Michael Cavendish wrapped himself in the sheets and fell asleep. The woman stared at him, she had not failed, though he had not known it, the man Otto had more than served his purpose. His flesh had been the final act in the turning of Michael Cavendish. When the turning had completed itself in this man, he would be forever hers.

She had prayed to the dark one for this man, many times she had tried to turn men. Very few had been successful, the turning had been easy, it was the blow to their minds. Some had been driven insane when they realised what they had become, the way they would have to live. Others had died screaming in agony as they attempted to effect the change from man to beast. A few had tried to end their own lives, failure had left them crippled obscenities. These she had destroyed, lest somehow they had broken loose into the outside world.

Success when it came, left her with creatures like Julius. A handsome man to be sure, but weak and spiteful. But she had not created him had she? Anna had made him she had been able to turn him, where she had failed. Julius remained what he had been before Anna had bitten him. But now he possessed the strength to kill without thought. He feared her and to a certain degree he went in fear of Anna, and though she was never able to prove it, she was positive he was responsible for the deaths of most of the male members of her pack. One day she would have to kill him, but for the moment he could wait, soon the man on the bed would be hers.

Not since that night centuries before, the night both she and Anna and been turned, had one who carried the dark angels kiss, had come among them. Here was one who would stand by her side, who would fight for her and if necessary kill Julius for her. The Countess closed her eyes, content with the knowledge that for her and the pack a new world was opening up to them. She felt the quickening in her blood, the need to hunt, to run on all fours, now, now it called to her.

Minutes later the white wolf raced out of the Keep along the path to the forest.

Michael turned in his sleep, unaware of the red haired Anna who lay beside him. Anna held him, cradling his head against her, she pressed her lips close to his ear. "Forgive me Michael." she whispered, "Forgive me, but like the Countess I am selfish , you hold a hope for me I did not believe would ever come." Anna gently kissed the sleeping man, she had waited until the Countess and Julius had left the Keep before coming to his room. That she loved this man she would have to keep hidden from the rest of the pack. If the Countess ever realised it, not even the law would save Anna's life. "You will hear my words Michael, this I know, and when you regain your senses you will remember them. I know as I speak them you will not remember who told you. I love you Michael Cavendish, with all my heart and soul. I love you. I do not try to turn you against the Countess, for I know she has already done that herself, she will try to tell you that you need her, you don't. You bear the sign of one who had been chosen, you need no one. Remember you are not an evil man, you are a warrior, think and act like one, fight for the control of your soul. She will take it if she can, do not let her." Anna put her lips against his and kissed him. "Would that I could remain in your embrace forever my beloved." Tears filled her eyes, they overflowed and ran down her cheeks, wetting the face of the man. "Go Michael, leave this accursed place, even though I spend an eternity without you, I beg you leave this place while you can." Michael's arm encircled her waist and he held her tight to him. She felt him stirring against her thigh. "No," she sobbed, "No, it must not be."

Anna struggled against his grip, she forced herself away from him. "It cannot be again." She reached out and pushed his hair away from his face. "You have the strength to leave, take it, use it," She touched her fingers to her lips and pressed them to his . "One day beloved." she said, "If you cannot leave here, if the change is too strong within you." Anna left the rest unspoken. She could no longer stay with him. One day she would hold him to her like a lover, then she would tell him of the things she knew.

At the door she turned and looked to him. She hoped he would be strong enough to accept the turning. She knew that there was strength in his body and he carried no fear in his heart, only let his mind be strong enough to allow him to live with what he had become.

Michael dreamed as he slept, dreams that caused him to moan aloud. He dreamed of an incredibly old man who beckoned him forward. In his dream hands were placed along the side of his face and his head was tilted so that the old man could look into his eyes. The sleeping man cried out in terror at the visions catapulted into his brain. He saw men and women being torn apart by an army of beasts under the control of the ancient man. He saw the wolf, big and grey running with ease through a forest, he saw it pull down the deer. He heard the tearing sound as the wolf ripped open the deer's side, fangs crunched against bone as the wolf fed, Michael looked into its eyes and saw himself. They were his eyes, his features, blood smeared, they were his teeth that tore at the dead animal.

.

Eyes older than the time of man hypnotized him, he saw a time before recording when man crawled on all fours. He witnessed the ancient man bending over one of these crawling creatures. He saw the yellow fangs sink deep into the creatures throat. His tortured soul and tormented mind watched the transfer of blood from the ancient one and the crawling man. Deep in the damning sleep of the turning, Michael witnessed the changing, he saw what he had become and what he would have to live with until the day he died. Into the sleeping man's memory was imprinted the memory of what would be. The knowledge of the transformation of man into wolf, the old man held his face in long thin fingers. Lips touched his, the scent of sulphur filled his nose, the flesh of the old man's lips burnt his. "You may try to deny me man but there will come a time when you know all." The voice was harsh and grating, insidiously planting the seeds into his fevered mind. , "For all eternity you belong to me."

Michael screamed and shot bolt upright in the bed, his body hot and cold in turn. Shaking with an uncontrollable dread of a nightmare he could not remember. His body was stiff with the efforts of one who had laboured for hours. His eyes were hot and gritty from his enforced sleep. Every joint, every nerve ending tingled or ached, his head throbbed with a nagging pain. He knew who he was, he knew where he was, but for how long he had lain there. Michael sat and listened, every tiny sound magnified a thousand times. As his sight cleared, he saw the threads which held the tapestry together. Colours became a vivid riot of reds and blues, browns, yellows. The lights from the candles danced before his eyes causing his head to spin. Michael flopped back on the bed, waiting, perfectly still until he had control of mind and body.

He must have fallen asleep yet again for when he opened his eyes a dozen candles burnt in their holders, a fire blazed in the large open fire grate. Food heaped on wooden platters on the table. A decanter of wine stood on its silver salver, a glass placed beside it. His clothes, washed and pressed hung over the back of a chair, boots cleaned. A tub of hot steaming, scented water inviting him to cleanse himself. The sight of the water tub made him aware of how dirty he was, sweat stained, blood smeared, he could smell the stink that emanated from his body. The sight of food causing his stomach to rumble and the gastric juices to fill his mouth. Unable to contain them, they dribbled down his chin. Hunger became an insatiable lust and with fingers crusted with dried blood he tore at the hot meats, eating ravenously until he thought he would burst. Michael gulped and swallowed forcing the saliva back down his throat holding hard against the vast amount of food he had consumed.

"At last the invalid rises." Michael turned to face the speaker, Elizabeth Dressler stared at him, the fact that he was stark naked, his body encrusted with filth and blood did not appear to bother her. "You have caused us all grave concern Michael." She moved over to him and put her hand on his bare flesh. Michael had his face towards the table, he did not see the smile as she felt the heat of his blood coursing through his veins. The turning had worked, he was now one of them, he would be part of the pack. "There were times Michael when I truly believed I had lost you." The Countess pressed his head against her breasts. Michael could hear the pounding of her heart, the even thump, thump against his face. He could almost believe that he heard the passing of her blood along her veins, the stretching of sinews when she moved. The tightening of her muscles as he pushed her away from him.

"How long have I been ill? Where is Otto? Send him to me I need him."
The Countess ran her fingers through the tangled mess of his grey hair. "Stop it."
he said, pulling away from her, his locks fastened between her fingers, his head
jerked back, Michael reached up and tore her fingers free. "Otto." he said,
"Where is he?"

"My poor darling." she began, absent-mindedly she stroked his bare flesh
with her hand, her nails tracing patterns along his back. "I don't know how to
begin." "Try." was all he said to her.

"You have been ill for so long, we thought that we would not be able to
save you. Michael look at me." She grabbed his face and turned it towards her.
"Look at my eyes Michael, there you will see the truth. From the first day you fell
ill until now, Anna and I have tended you." Michael wished she would stop
babbling and get to the point. Whatever it was she had to tell him, he had to
know.

"The year has turned and turned again Michael, and your friends are
gone." For a moment he sat there and let it all sink in. Impossible, no man could
lay on a sick bed for two years. And Otto would never leave him alone, never,
Otto was his friend. The bitter memory came back, had he not driven away a
friend before, had he driven away Otto in his illness.

"Look at yourself in the mirror Michael, see for yourself. The flesh is
wasted on your bones, see how the skin is stretched to breaking."

Michael pushed the mirror away from him, he did not wish to see. If two
years had passed as the woman said, then the others would think him dead. "I
will care for you until,"

"Until what?" asked Michael, "Until what my lady?"

"Until you are fit and well, then you can decide what it is you want to do.
I would like it should you decide to stay with me."

Michael did not look at her, she was right, though he needed to regain his
strength, until he had he needed her help. "I have not forgotten you Countess."
The woman smiled at him, "I need you to help me and I need the help of the red
haired woman, this I know. But," He could not reject her not now. It wasn't fair,
he was hers.

"Why Michael, Why?" The woman was pleading with him, begging him
to answer her. Michael knew he could not give her the answer she wanted. How
do you tell a beautiful woman she disgusted you, repels you, makes your flesh
crawl with her every touch.

"Because of you I forgot who I was and why I was left here. In your arms, between your thighs I nearly lost my soul, yet there was no love between us. I gave you what you wanted and I needed nothing more."

The woman snarled at him, her face a mask of hate, her fingers outstretched as she moved towards him. Michael did not move as he sat and waited for her to attack, he could not stop her. In his weakened state, she would be able to cause him considerable hurt. The Countess was barely a fingertip away from him when he spoke. "I will leave when the time comes."

"Never." Her voice high, hysteria only a heart beat away. "Never." she screamed, her mouth twisted, her beauty ugly in her anger at the man sat before her. "You'll never leave here Michael Cavendish. For now, for ever, for the rest of eternity your life is here." The woman was breathing deeply, breast heaving with the effort to hold down the blood lust that threatened to engulf her. "You are mine, you were always mine and I shall keep you mine." Michael recoiled from her anger, there had been times in his life when he had had to face angry women. But never had he felt such venom in their voices as the Countess was spitting at him. "You will learn that you are mine and you will also learn to do what you are told." This time Michael did strike her, though not a powerful blow, it did knock her backwards. It was the surprise of the blow which hurt her, not the strength.

She had decided to hurt him to let him learn the hard way that she had to be obeyed, no matter what. Let him learn what it meant to be a changeling, show him, change before his eyes. The Countess began to summon up the turning, she felt her body tense, the pain in her mouth, the shifting of her teeth. Then she looked into Michael's eyes, she did not see him, she saw eyes older than time staring back at her, she saw an old face. A tiny voice whispered in her ear, "Leave well alone, this man is mine, he bears my kiss." She did not call for the regression, it came of its own accord. This man she had longed for, prayed for over the centuries, it was not possible, he could not be the fallen one. He could not be the dark angel himself, yet she had seen those eyes, she had heard that voice whisper to her. She looked at the emancipated man that stood before her, needing to hold the table for support, no he was not the fallen one, she had been given a warning, a second chance to possess him. He could not be forced to do anything, he had to be nurtured, brought along until he was strong enough to understand what it meant to be taken under the wing of the fallen one.

"You will be mine, rest assured of that Michael Cavendish and you will come to me crawling."

"I am not Julius." said Michael, "I will never beg for you lady." At the mention of Julius the Countess laughed in his face. "You find it funny, I remember your table dog."

"I think we have little else to say to each other at this time." she said. The look she gave him caused him to wonder if he had not overplayed his hand. He had hoped that she was so enamoured of him that he could do with her as he pleased. It appeared he was mistaken, he had pushed just that little bit too far. He had made an enemy of her and if that was so then he had made a mortal enemy of the lap dog Julius. "When you are fully recovered in mind and body we will speak to each other again. Rest yourself Michael for the road you travel is a long one. And that, I ask you to believe." Poor man he would learn, his brain was over taxed like his body, he needed nourishment. Anna would see that he received it. Only once before in her life time had she encountered another man like him, that one too denied his changing, cursed her and all of her kind, but he had relented in the end.

The path of the werewolf was long and dangerous. He had to live among his own kind. None had ever lived among the humans for long, the bloodlust of the full moon drove them to kill. And the werewolf always destroyed those who love him. There had been those that had tried to change, to live a normal life, it was not possible. They did not age with the passage of the years, the sight of those they longed to be with growing old, dying, drove many to become rogues. The rogues did not survive long, the word was passed around and the packs hunted them down. The law of the fallen one decreed that werewolf must not kill werewolf, but times had changed since he had uttered those words. When the world had been young and there had been plenty of places to hide, the law could be obeyed.

The passage of time and the turning of the world changed all things. New deities arose even among the tribes of the dark angel, new gods replaced worn out ones. There were those among the packs that dared to challenge the fallen one himself, and when the dark angel did not appear to strike them down the packs changed. Why worship someone who was powerless to harm them? Some were content to live in hidden seclusion, to remain forever hidden from the sight of man. Others roamed where they would, following the Tarter hordes as they raped and pillaged across the known world. It is said that some fought along side the Vikings and they were known as berserkers.

All these tales were told by the travelling people and slowly over the centuries the legend of the werewolf was born. The church denied their existence, yet slaughtered thousands in their efforts to stamp it out. The werewolf became a thing to be feared, a monster that lived on human flesh. Once bitten by the werewolf the fate of those so attacked was to change into a beast themselves and be ruled by the waxing and waning of the moon. The reality of it all was so different, the turning did require that they be bitten by a werewolf, but only a select few among the changelings had the ability or the knowledge to turn others into werewolves. Once the bite had taken place and blood exchanged, the affected one needed to be watched, the infected wound had to be cleaned and tended. A second bite followed, and more blood exchanged and if the victim did not die the third bite was given. Some did become moon children, others died in excruciating agony unable to make the change. Still others committed suicide rather than live the life of the werewolf. Only by their own hand or by the hand of one instructed in the law of the dark angel could they die. Only a select few knew of the third way to die.

Eternity was theirs for the taking, old age, illness, disease did not affect them once the turning had been completed. But to some the laws of the fallen one were not kept secret and the ways of destruction fell into the hands of the church. Zealots from all religions played their part in the hunting down and the cleansing of the world from the scourge of the moon children. Only a few survived those clever enough to hide their afflictions from the braying mass. Those who used their strange powers to move into the corridors of power.

The man who had turned the Countess and Anna had been such a man. A man like Michael Cavendish, born to the sword, a warrior, a man forged in the heat of battle. Elizabeth Dressler had loved this man, if necessary she would have given her life for his. She had lived only to please him, his every wish her loving command. The few years she had lived with him were a joy she never believed possible. She had known that from time to time when his Prince commanded he would have to leave her, but he always returned. She remembered their last day together, she remembered seeing him astride a black stallion, his body encased inside his black armour. His broad sword held high in salutations to her beauty. He never returned from the battlefield, his headless body had been found among the hundreds Prince Vlad had left behind. The bloody battle to free their homeland from the Turks had resulted in a bitter defeat.

Elizabeth had mourned her lost lover for three decades until the time came she dare mourn no more. Her beauty was still a thing to behold and the whisper of witchcraft and pacts with Satan himself forced her to flee. They did not flee in fear from the populace, common sense told her that she required a more secure hide away.

How long it took them to finally find the Keep she could not remember. Over a period of time she did manage to turn a small number to the path of the werewolf. What little her Lord had taught her was not always successful. The villagers at the entrance to the pass became her slaves, serving her with a passion. If they were aware of what the woman and her entourage were they did not seem to mind. The Countess treated them well, if their crops failed she provided food and they in their turn protected her. They never asked how she found fresh meat to feed their wives and children.

She recalled the day the Englishman had walked into her life. The Countess had liked what she saw and she knew it would not be long before he shared her bed. Circumstances had dictated that she let Anna entertain him that first night and when Anna had come to her trembling with fear, she had learnt that he carried the dark angels kiss. From that day on she had been determined that he would be hers and only hers.

His turning had very nearly cost her her sanity, it had taken the combined blood of both women to infect him. For two years the two women had constantly bled themselves that he might feed and now he rejected her. What had happened to him during the turning, what dreams had he had, what had he seen? Even now when revenge against him was uppermost in her mind, she could not shake off what she believed she had seen. The eyes and the face had been of a man she herself had only ever seen in her dreams. The face, even the voice had been that of the fallen one. The dark angel himself. Elizabeth took control of her emotions and without a backward glance left the man alone, he would need her before she needed him.

Julius stood in the hallway waiting for her, she thought about taking her spleen out on him. Julius would accept her anger, her blows and still he would grovel at her feet. The Countess smiled, Julius allowed his grim visage to break out in an unconcealed joy. The Countess took hold of his hand and placed it over her breast. Julius began to gently squeeze it. She allowed his mouth to cover hers, she did not pull away when he slipped his hand down the front of her bodice, his fingers stroking her nipples. This was the way to control him. Allow him to use her, allow him to let his hands roam over her body. The Countess felt the urge to mate begin between her thighs, she reached down and put her hand on him. Julius was thick and hard to the touch, he wanted her and she needed to feel a man inside of her.

Anna watched and waited for the Countess to take herself and Julius into the bedroom. One of these days the Countess would over estimate the lure of her body and Julius would turn against her. Anna herself ached to go to Michael, she ached to hold him, feel him against her but she knew now it would be a mistake. She had heard their conversation, she had heard him reject the Countess, she had heard the vitriolic words of the Countess. And she had taken note of her face as she left the room, something had frightened her. Perhaps the Countess would tell her, she doubted it, she only knew that from now on Michael would have to tread very carefully. The Countess intended that she and only she would own him body and soul. Anna could not warn him more, she had broken the law even whispering his fate to him. But she like the Countess was unaware of the visitor Michael had had in the long hours of his turning.

Time was now the master of all their fate, on the turning of a coin by fates fingers their futures would come to pass. Time would be Michael's friend and his enemy. Time would heal him, help him grow strong. Would time also help him forget who he was, or would time take a grip of Michael's memories and hold them tight until the hour came when he needed them?

Time did possess Michael, it held him, controlled him, leading him gently along. Such were the powers connected to the kiss of the dark angel he carried on his shoulder that what Michael believed to be a few days were in fact a lifetime to a normal man. The months it took him to regain his strength, to believe in himself, to have the confidence to leave the Keep. The world spun relentlessly around, seasons turned and turned yet again and Michael's hours became days. His days became years and the years changed from decade to decade. Michael was not aware of the vast passage of time that had passed him by, he lived only for the moment he would walk out of the Keep.

Michael pulled on his boots, he could no longer put off his leaving, if he had any regrets it was that he had not spoken or set eyes on the red haired woman Anna. To her he wished to say goodbye, he had no words for the Countess. For the dark skinned Julius, he only hoped the man would stand in his way. Michael honestly believed that Otto and the men had not left him alone in the Keep. At the bidding of the Countess he believed that Julius had in some way killed his men.

He needed his sword, it had to be in this room, where would he have put it, hidden it. Michael threw the covers off the bed, reached under the mattress, nothing. He opened cupboards, pulled out their contents, there was no sign of his sword. His search proved fruitless, the blade was gone. His eyes rested on the heavy poker, it would do, it made a reasonable weapon. Michael reached up to take the candle from its holder, a smile came to his lips. There on the wall a pair of crossed axes, he pushed the end of the poker under the fastening and prised at it. The fastening snapped easily, caught off balance Michael staggered back, he came to a stop against the table. Crossing over to the wall Michael reached up and took hold of the axe's shaft and pulled it free.

He weighed it in his hand, surprisingly it was not heavy. Michael twirled around, it felt good in his hand. The balance was nearly perfect, the blade was old but forged by a craftsman. It was still an effective killing tool. Michael continued to look at the wall, stone, of course stone, the Keep was built entirely of stone, and on stone he could sharpen the blade.

Michael rubbed the axe against the wall, under pressure the years of neglect vanished. Slowly the blade regained its edge, Michael ran his thumb along it, pleased when it scored a thin red cut on his flesh. It would serve him well if he had need of it.

Michael hesitated for one brief moment , he remembered a blonde haired man, a man who had been his friend. He recalled to mind the German Otto and as he lifted the axe in his hand he actually believed he would shortly be joining them. He knew they were dead and that he himself could be dead in a matter of minutes. Michael was so wrong, he would not be dead in a few minutes, the moment he opened the door to leave the Keep. He opened the door to his destiny , unaware of this Michael strode purposely forward to face it head on.

Thousands of candles burnt in the hall and along the balcony. Their bright lights causing him to blink, the dancing flames turned the dark Keep into a place of brightness. Michael moved slowly along the balcony , eyes searching, seeking out any foe real or otherwise. Only the sound of his boots on the wooden floor, the sound changing when he stepped onto the stone stairs leading down to the hall.

Hot wax dripped down the hard wood of the balcony, a thousand drops had formed into pools on the stone floor of the hall. He felt totally alone, nothing moved before or behind him, yet his instincts told him he was not alone. He felt eyes staring at him, he could almost taste the presence of one who wished him dead.

He held his breath and stared down the flight of steps. There before the open door of the Keep lay his sword. A candle burnt at the hilt, one against each end of the cross guard, one at its point. He moved tentatively one step at a time, the axe, balanced, ready for use, towards his sword. The hairs on his neck bristled, a tingling down his spine, once again the feeling of eyes upon him. But there were no shadows in which to hide, the glow of a thousand candle lights made sure of that. Who had left the door open, who had placed his sword before it, who had provided all of the candles? He could not be alone, how did he ever believe he was in the first place.

"Good evening Michael Cavendish." Startled Michael turned, he bent one knee and assumed a stance for battle. The Countess stood at the top of the stairs, beside her the ever present Julius. "We have been waiting for you Michael." The puzzled look on his face was not lost on the Countess. "My children and I," she smiled at him and opened wide her arms, Michael shifted the axe in his hand expecting an attack any second. "Turn Michael, turn and meet your brothers and sisters." Julius laughed aloud at her words, Michael returned the hatred in the man's stare, "Turn Michael they have waited patiently for you."

Slowly Michael turned, he had to see what lay before him at the bottom of the stairs, curiosity and fact. It was better to know the number of your foe. He gave the dark Julius one last look before turning, Michael did not like him behind him. Five of them stood at the bottom of the stairs, two men and two women he had never seen before and the red haired Anna. Michael looked at her as if realising that the others did not matter. From a far away void he seemed to hear her voice whispering to him "Too late Michael, it's too late to leave. You should have gone sooner, I can help you no more." There was pity in her eyes and a sadness at his plight, Michael wondered if he would have to kill her to escape. His hand felt slippery on the handle of the axe, wipe it quickly, no time once he engaged them. At a gesture from Anna they moved from the stairs and formed a semi-circle around his sword.

"Why don't you try and take it?" Julius 's words came out in a hiss full of spite and venom. He had not missed the look on Michael's face, he had noticed how the man had calculated his chances in reaching his blade. "Go on, take it." Julius's dark face flushed with anger and pleasure, he wanted Michael to try, he was willing him to be foolish enough to attempt it. "Go on," Julius screamed at him, "Take it."

Michael grinned, he had played these kind of games before. No amount of goading would make him take unnecessary chances, not where his life was the prize. The odds were not in his favour, that was true, but none of the five appeared to be carrying weapons. Michael looked up at the Countess, he saw an eager anticipation of what must happen in her eyes, she wanted to see blood spilt. He turned towards Julius, the dark skinned man had moved a little closer towards him. "How many do you want dead?" He spoke directly to Julius. When Julius did not reply Michael pointed the axe at him, the dark man flinched and stepped back. "Well, are you the first to try me?" asked Michael "Or do you still hide behind a woman's skirt?" Julius snarled and moved forward.

The Countess stepped in front of him, Julius tried to push past her. Michael cried out in surprise at her next move, she grabbed Julius, lifted him from his feet effortlessly and threw him the full length of the balcony. "Stay." she cried, "No more of these silly little games." Julius, stunned, lay curled against the wall, fear had replaced anger on his face. "We do not intend to kill you Michael, we are here to greet you, our brother." Michael heard her words but did not understand them, what in gods name was she talking about, "Brothers."

Anna's words broke into his train of thoughts, "You are one of us Michael Cavendish, you belong among us."

"What are you talking about, brother, among us?"

"He does not understand you Anna." said the Countess. Michael did not know which way to turn, he wanted to keep his eyes on those before him. He wanted to look at the Countess. "Show him my children." she cried out at the top of her voice. "Don't look upon me Michael, turn and behold your family."

The Countess threw wide her arms, "Show him what he is."

Michael felt his legs turn to jelly, fear, horror, disgust crawled along his spine. He stared open mouthed at the sight that met his eyes. The five were in different stages of change, the men had nearly completed their turning. Little of what was human remained in them, with one last muscle stretching effort, wolves stood where there had been men. Two of the women completed their turning, sat back on their haunches and stared at him. Anna was the last to revert into wolf, she screamed, half human, half animal, with the pain of her turning.

Michael clenched his teeth, he dare not let the terror he was feeling escape. He felt as if he must go insane at any second at the thing that had taken place before his eyes. "Time for you to join us Michael." He turned, the Countess stood at the very top of the stairs, she stood motionless. Her dress in folds around her feet. Her body was covered in fine white hairs, her eyes yellow and bulging, a snout pushing its way free. Her mouth stretching and widening to accommodate the fangs that protruded over her lips. "Now Michael Cavendish." The words having to be forced from her, fighting to speak before the turning controlled her completely. "Join us now."

"No." Michael shouted, his voice filling the confined space of the hall. "No." This time he screamed, blood pounded in his brain, he felt it flow hotly through his veins, muscles creaked and bunched. Michael was a man fighting to retain his sanity. He bit hard on his lips, tasted the blood. "No." he screamed yet again, his throat ached with the effort of shouting, "Never."

"Kill him." The dark skinned man screamed, Julius lent over the balcony, he was in part turning, but holding it. "Kill him." His eyes blazed with madness, as he allowed the change to take him over. Michael heard the answering howls of the wolves, he heard the scraping of claws on stone, he turned to meet their charge. He met the lunging wolf with a downward sweep of the axe, the wolf howled, hot blood spurted from it and splashed across his face. The axe severed the front legs of the wolf, it thudded beside him, turned its head, fangs snapped at his legs. Michael brought the axe down across its neck, the blade severed through flesh and bone to clang on the stone of the Keep. The head flew free of the wolf's body, sending the pack into a frenzy as it landed among them. A second wolf, one of the bitches, moved cautiously towards him, twirling the axe, Michael waited for it to attack. Man and beast eyed each other, each knowing that whatever happened one of them was going to die. The she wolf leapt at him, Michael twisted, the she wolf flew past him leaving her back unprotected, he buried the axe deep into her spine. He threw himself forward and rolled over, his body striking the red bitch, Michael came to his feet holding his sword. The red bitch backed off, Anna's eyes telling him she would not fight. Michael spun quickly as the other she wolf attacked and struck blindly at the screaming beast, the blade struck true. The she wolf died like her male companion, headless.

Michael was brought to a halt by the door of the Keep. He reached behind him, one hand touching the solid wood, the doors had been locked during his battle with the pack, there was nowhere else to go. He was trapped, here he would have to stand his ground.

"Do not kill him." The Countess had regressed back into human form.

Slowly, as if in a dream, she came down the stairs towards him. The remaining wolves retreated to a safe distance from the flicking blade held in the man's hand. The Countess stopped and looked down at the head of the male, kneeling she ran her fingers through its coarse hair. At the sight of the decapitated bitch, anger turned her beauty into a mask of hatred. Two of her pack dead, two of her children murdered, pointless, stupid deaths. "Because of you," she cried, Michael prepared himself for another attack. The Countess was not screaming at him, she was pointing up at Julius, "Because of you two of my children have died." Julius gripped the balcony with both hands, he had failed to kill the man. Unless he could find a reason for his actions the vengeance of the Countess would be a terrible retribution. She had turned against him for this man, she had banned him from her bed because of this Michael. Did she not know, did she not realise that Michael would never be hers? Anna did, the red haired bitch knew and understood the man. Could she not see this man would never love her the way he Julius did?

Had he not proved it to her a thousand times over the years. The man carried the dark angels kiss, he was not like him, she would never rule him. Had he not already refused her, even though it was her blood that had infected him, had made him what he was. Was she so blindly in love with this Michael Cavendish that she could not see clearly?

"He will never accept us or what he is."

"You will pay for this Julius." He tried to meet her eyes and failed, only when it was too late would she remember this night. The Countess turned all thoughts of Julius away from her mind. The three wolves lifted themselves and padded over to her. The Countess reached down and twisted her hand in the rough hair of the male wolf's neck. Michael stood with his back pressed hard against the door, the Countess looked at him. He was prepared to sell his life dearly, she smiled, "It is no use Michael, you can not fight it."

"I can die trying lady." She saw his fingers tighten around the hilt. She saw his face suffused with blood, the straining flesh along his jaw line. Michael blinked, was that sympathy he saw in her eyes, the smile on the Countess's lips widened.

"You belong among us." Michael shook his head, "Never." he mouthed, "Never." "Look at you hands Michael Cavendish." Obeying her words Michael looked down at his hands. Thick grey hairs sprouted between his fingers, talons instead of fingernails, he let go of his sword. Before his eyes his hands changed into claws, he opened his mouth to cry out, pain raced along his jaw, he felt his teeth move, widen, lengthen, Michael managed to scream. "No," just once before the turning took control of him. He fell to his knees screaming, he heard cloth and leather rip apart as his back arched. The pain was almost intolerable as his spine arched, bent and changed shape to accommodate the animal he was becoming. His mind refused to believe what it was seeing, fingers, hands, changed to become the forelegs of a wolf. His lower half felt as though a red hot poker had been driven deep into his anus.

The thing Michael was becoming opened its mouth to cry out, to beg for mercy, relief from this agony. Flesh ripped and split, the wolf's snout pushed its way forward, the man's screams changed into the howls of a beast in torment. Michael's human flesh became like water moulding itself around the shape of the wolf. The man inside the beast fought it, anger lent power to his will, part of him regressed. A pain so intense that it burnt into the very roots of his mind overcame all other feelings. A strangled cry escaped from the creature more human than animal. The Countess and Anna watched as the man fought the turning. The Countess watched with an undisguised pleasure, Julius with a hatred so overwhelming that it brought a bitter taste to his mouth. Anna with a heart and mind full of pity and love towards the creature Michael Cavendish had become and was to eternally be, werewolf.

THE VALLEY - Part 4

Tibor had been right, the invaders did come to the valley, and they came sooner than he expected. They arrived before the snows had melted, men on foot carrying tents and equipment. It must have been hard for them to cross the glacier with their loads, but somehow they had managed it. They found a sheltered place and erected their tents away from the cold winds that still blew down the valley.

Unaware that they were being watched the men went about their tasks. Long thin rods were forced deep into the soil, withdrawn and each sample examined and labelled. Small explosive charges were laid and fired, samples from this were also examined carefully. When this part of the operation was completed, the soil and rock samples were boxed ready for transportation.

Then for two days they did nothing, Tibor concealed , watched and waited. He watched them cook, wash, drink and lounge about, the things a group of friends did when camping out. On the third day two of the men, packing a tent and provisions, headed up the valley, they were leaving the valley with their hard won samples, towards the pass. Tibor would have loved to follow them but he wasn't able to be in two places at once. Had the moon child been fitter he could have left him to watch those in the valley while he followed the other two.

Tibor eased his cramped muscles, even wrapped as he was in furs the cold still managed to penetrate. Soon he must return to the others, they had to be made aware of what was taking place in the valley. The man who appeared to be the leader of the group come out of the tent holding a box in his arms. He set it down on a table and began to unscrew the front of it. Once this had been done the man pulled an aerial free. Tibor cursed aloud, a radio, they were in contact with the outside world. He twisted and turned the dials until with a shout, loud enough for the concealed Tibor to hear. The man informed his companions he had made contact.

The giant eased his way backwards from under the cliff overhang, he knew they could not possibly see him, but Tibor did not intend taking any kind of action that would expose him. Tibor was convinced that they had come to stay , why else would they be testing the rocks and soil. These men were the forerunners, once the snows had completely melted others would come. There would be no going back to the cabin, the risk was too great, until they could leave the valley, they would have to remain hidden in the cave.

"You make the noise of a bear mating." Tibor bit his lip to stifle the cry. The moon child had surprised him by stepping out of the shadows. "She is safe." Tibor tried to see Michael's face but the lengthening evening shadows made it impossible.

"Why are you out here? You should be resting."

"I'll rest now you have returned." said Michael. He moved beside Tibor as they walked up the slight incline to the entrance of the cave. Tibor strode ahead of him eager to look upon the face of Katji. Michael let him go. He would have liked to speak to the giant, ask him what he had witnessed in the valley over the last three days. Soon he would speak to him, for now let him go to the woman he loved. Michael remembered the journey from the cabin to the cave, without Tibor's help he would not have made it. He had overestimated his powers of recuperation, the time he had was not long enough. Katji had said there was no urgency to move as the pass was still frozen. The look on the giants face had told him differently and Michael had insisted he was strong enough to make the journey.

Carrying as much food as they could, Tibor had led them up the tortuous mountain path to the cave. The path would have been considered difficult even in daylight to an experienced mountaineer. By night, with only the light of the moon to guide them, it was a nightmare trip. Somewhere halfway up the path, Michael's strength had given out and he had been forced to rest. Tibor had continued up with Katji and then returned for him. Michael had found himself hoisted over the giant's shoulder and carried the rest of the way. Whilst Katji had tended his wound, which had started to bleed again, Tibor had announced his intentions of returning to the cabin.

While he, who supposedly possessed the strength of ten normal men, lay sick and angry at his weakened condition. The giant Tibor had made trip after trip back to the cabin. Katji's beloved books, her clothes, even a table and chairs and on his last trip, pots and pans in which to cook. While he lay fretting at the wound which caused him to be treated like a new born child, Tibor's great strength and resolution enabled him to provide comfort and safety for the three of them. Not for the first time, since he had so rudely arrived in the company of the giant did he wonder how he would stack up against Tibor. He hoped it would never come to that, and there was no reason it should. But Michael knew that should he wish to subdue this giant of a man, he would have to revert to the beast inside of him.

Even now when he was fully fit, it was Tibor who made the dangerous journey to spy on the invaders. It was the giant who risked his life that they might know what was happening in the valley. He would go with Tibor next time, Tibor had not asked him to accompany him but never the less Michael would go. Curiosity compelled him to go, he wanted to look upon these men who had earned the loathing of the giant. Michael pushed aside the heavy skins Tibor had hung across the mouth of the cave. He could see the glow of the fire way back and by the side of it lay the Wych Katji.

Michael looked at the young girl, no young woman, there was a gentle beauty about her and for one so young, wisdom. It was Katji who had taught him many things about the world he would have to live in. She had taught him to read the books she loved, she had spent hours learning him to write. Writing fascinated him to see the black scrawls on white paper turn into words, words turn into sentences. Katji the Wych woman had no fear of him, and Michael prayed that she never would have. Only once since they had moved into the cave had he nearly reverted to wolf. It had been the night Tibor had cleaned his festering wound. Katji had held him, cradling him like a new born baby, crooning to him, rocking him gently against her breast. The changing had regressed and Michael had rested in peace, all the time the Wych woman had sung to him. An old song of the travellers, seeped in their belief of the dark gods of the old religion.

It had surprised Michael to find that he loved this young woman. True he loved her like Tibor loved her, but not with the same intensity. Tibor loved her with a passion that ruled his life, like Michael he would die for her, but Tibor's love was pure and from his heart. Michael would never love like that again, he had loved and lost the one woman, he would never love like that again. With her Michael had never ever been tempted to use the turning, her love had held him in check. For her he had broken the law and turned himself into an outcast. Bitter memories, too bitter to recall or hold, he knew what he was.

Let them call him Moon child, let them believe in the dark angel and their old religion, he was what he was and only death could free him.

He, Michael Cavendish was a werewolf, an abomination on the face of the earth. An abortion that should have been destroyed decades ago. At night when the others slept he would stand at the mouth of the cave, he would imagine he could hear the baying of the pack. The heady thrill of running through the forest, the blood pounding excitement of the hunt. The stalking of those humans foolish enough to try and hunt them down.

What he was he would remain until his dying day, once long ago he had prayed for death. He had courted death like a lovelorn swain, in the midst of battles. Then a stray pistol ball, the blade of an enemy, a cannon ball, all could have ended his life so easily. Michael would have welcomed that with open arms. Now none of these could kill him, hurt him, cripple him, but not kill him. Only one who knew the secret ways could end his torment or one who would end their life through love for him. By the hand of one who loved him, Michael could die

Michael shook his head, foolish thoughts, foolish dreams, better to forget them. Concentrate on the here and now. In the morning he would talk to Tibor. Michael retreated into the cave, he placed more wood on the fire, curled himself down beside it and slept.

The distant sound of blasting woke Michael, a second then a third explosion , so close that they sounded like just one. "They are blasting beyond the valley, deep in the pass." Tibor let the skin curtain fall back into place. The sound of further explosions coming ever closer as the days wore on. Michael could see that Tibor was agitated. He knew had it not been for Katji that the giant would have crossed the valley to see what was happening.

"Do you wish me to go down to the valley?" asked Michael, Tibor shook his head, "I will give you my word that,"

"No." said the giant, he looked at Michael "No." Tibor sat hunched over poking the embers of the fire. Seemingly at a loss as to what to do. When next he spoke there was a choke in his voice, "No, there is no need, I know what is happening."

The giant pushed himself up, reached for the thick coat he wore. Katji took hold of the sleeve. "Not today." she begged, Tibor smiled at her, his large hand touched her face, gently he removed her hand from the sleeve and slipped the coat on. "I will only look." he said. Michael saw the fear in the young woman's eyes, she knew that he would risk his life if he had to.

"Tibor." The giant turned at the sound of his name on Michael's lips. "I will go with you." Tibor started to say no, the look on the moon child's face said that he would not take no for an answer.

"You will do as I say moon child." said Tibor "You will not try,"

"I will obey your every word Tibor on one condition," A puzzled look crossed the giant's face, he turned imploringly to Katji who grinned at his discomfort. "You do not need to ask," said Michael, "I will tell you."

Katji sidled up to the giant and took hold of his hand. She rested her head against him, Tibor felt the pressure of her fingers on his flesh. Listen to him she was telling him, not by word but by deed. Tibor drew in a deep breath and waited, let the moon child speak. If he did not like it he could always refuse to take him with him. "Call me Michael, it slips off the tongue easily."

"And that is your condition?"

"It is the only one, and it would please me to hear you speak my name,"

"So be it". Tibor hesitated, "Michael." He said the name, it felt strange on his tongue. It sounded like some new word he had just learnt. "Michael." he said again, the giant nodded his head, Katji felt those large hands squeeze her shoulders, she was satisfied. Now each had spoken the others name aloud, perhaps with a sprinkling of luck these two could become , Katji had thought of the word friends, but perhaps friends was too strong a word to use at the moment. Hopefully a trust would spring up between them and from it, who knows, friendship could come. Tibor looked down at her, go, said the look she gave him, go, I will be safe. "Come then Michael," said Tibor "And I will show you what needs to be done."

From the comparative safety of the cave Katji watched until the two men vanished into the depths of the forest. Katji returned inside the cave, she coaxed the fire, and set about preparing herself a meal. The men would probably not return that night, once settled they would want to find out as much as they could. She hummed to herself as she worked , soon it would be her twentieth birthday and Tibor would have to tell her his secret. Katji relished the idea of making the big ox suffer, watching him shuffle from foot to foot, trying to find the words to explain it to her. Ten more days and he would tell, if he had thought she had forgotten then he was sadly mistaken. "Right you giant lump," she said, poking savagely at the offending log which refused to catch light, "You will tell me."

The two men lay side by side, silent, not moving. Michael his eyes on the men around the tents, Tibor gazing up the valley. A tiny speck in the distance, circling round and round, closer it came until the drone of a light aircraft could be heard. The small plane banked and got caught in the cross winds, the pilot gunned the engine, the plane responded to the pilots handling. Once, twice he passed down the valley before bringing the plane in to land. The plane taxied towards the waiting men, the pilot switched off the engine and climbed out. Tibor muttered, he could see the agitated conversation between the pilot and the leader of the group. He would have given almost anything to be able to hear what they were saying. The leader pointed in three directions, towards where Michael and Tibor lay concealed. The pilot shook his head, the other man pointed in the direction of the pass, at this the pilot and man began to talk. At the leaders third suggestion the pilot waved his arms and shook his head violently.

"What are they doing?" asked Michael, he turned to Tibor whose eyes were riveted on the two men. When the two men went into the tent, the giant looked at Michael.

"I'm not sure," he said, "I think I know what's going on, but to be sure for certain we must watch a little longer."

"Then I will sleep." said Michael, "When it is dark wake me, I will watch through the night." Tibor did not answer, the moon child was right, he would be able to see better than he in the dark. Nothing happened for the rest of the day, and the watch Michael kept through the night was incident free.

Early the next morning the pilot started his plane and took off, he flew towards the area where the two men lay. He turned the plane and flew back low towards the others. At his fourth attempt he managed to land the plane. Instruments were brought out of the tent, measurements taken and logged. Once again the plane lifted up from the valley, try as he might the pilot was unable to land the plane back safely from this direction.

The ritual of measuring and logging of statistics was carried out before the plane was taken up for a third time. The little plane was pointed in the direction of the pass, Tibor watched it as it climbed above the mountains. The plane turned and headed back into the valley, there was no mistakes this time, the pilot allowing for the wind made a perfect landing. Four times in the next six hours the plane took off, flew towards the pass then returned to land. After each landing the measurements were calculated and logged, one of the men drove a white painted stake into the earth. The leader of the group appeared to be in an exuberant mood as he clapped the pilot on the back and shook his hand. Tibor was now convinced he knew exactly what they were up to.

Deep in the heart of the pass the explosions continued at irregular intervals. At one point the blasting stopped for many hours after one of the explosions had caused a small avalanche. Even from where they lay, the two men could see the thick cloud of dust rise high into the air. Tibor buried his face in the thick grass, Michael thought he heard a sob escape him. The giant lifted his head and turned to Michael, Michael saw a look of pain in the giants eyes.

"I know now what they are doing, and god help us for we are trapped."

"Speak to me." said Michael, "Tell me exactly what is happening." Tibor hesitated for a moment before speaking. How did he explain all this to a man who had just touched the world he now found himself in. Of course Michael knew of planes, trains, electricity and many of the wonders of the twentieth century, but if what he suspected was true. That the reason these men had invaded this isolated valley was to build, then the unreliable news from the outside world had suddenly become reliable and deadly. Germany was once again preparing to wage war, and like the last time, it would be continent against continent.

"The blasting you hear, they are bringing down the mountains so that they may build a road into this valley. This little charade we have watched with the plane, if they can land a light aeroplane here, then what's to stop them bringing in their war planes. Quite simply they are going to build an airstrip."

Michael did not speak, he knew that Tibor would say more when he had collected his troubled thoughts. He could wait, the giant would tell him all he had to know. "There is a cancer eating into the heart of this country," began the giant, "An evil malignant cancer that will bring this world in which we live to war." Tibor looked at Michael. "You" he said, "Have fought in wars Michael, you have probably stood face to face with your enemy. You have learnt of some of the things which have happened, some of which I know you understand, as for the rest, it will be a bitter lesson to you. Men no longer fight with sword or axe, death can be hurled from thousands of feet away, an enemy may never set his eyes on his foe. Death can be dropped from the skies, not necessarily bombs, but a creeping death that eats at the flesh."

A haunted look came into Tibor's eyes. "There are other things I could tell you, but I don't think I will have to. Down there." Tibor pointed towards the tents, anger in every word he spoke. "Down there you will see it, with your own eyes you will witness man's inhumanity to his fellow man. Do you pray Michael?

What gods do you worship? None? Any?" Tibor's voice was low. "Moon child you have chosen a bad time to return and live among us."

"I did not choose to live in this time," said Michael, "I did not choose to be what I am." A grim smile appeared on his lips and he spoke with a savage bitterness, "I would rather be dead."

"In that I cannot help you, nor would I wish to."

"Why do you hate me so?" asked Michael, he saw the giant start, that they could ever be friends Michael knew was impossible, but there could be trust between them.

"I don't hate you moon child, I was born into a people who were created so that they may protect you and your kind."

"And Katji," asked Michael, Tibor sat up, leant forward and clasped his hands around his knees, resting his chin on his hands.

"When I was first told what I was I was proud, proud that I had been chosen to belong to the guardians. I was young and I was proud, I took pride in the fact that I found this valley. Proud of the fact that I built the cabin with these hands."

Tibor studied the large hands with their blunt fingers, the calloused palms, "There was a pride here." he said, touching his heart. "On the day they brought Katji to this valley to be my wife."

"You love her?" said Michael, Tibor looked at him but did not speak, "You love her don't you?" asked Michael.

"Yes I love her," he said, Tibor rubbed his chin against his hands, "I would willingly die for her."

"Then why don't you tell her what you feel?"

"It is not possible," said the giant, "She is a Wych, and though she is my wife," Tibor laughed a harsh laugh, full of the bitterness he felt, "Man and wife, absurd." he said, "For I dare not touch her, I can not hold her to me in love. I cannot approach her as a husband should his wife." he said, "I love her with every beat of my heart, but to take her to me as a true wife, I dare not do such a thing. I told you I am a proud man and I am, I take pride in my achievements and pride in the woman who is my wife. But believe me Michael, pride is a cold bedfellow."

Tibor's head sank into his knees, he breathed soft and low. Michael did not disturb his thoughts, if he sat here silently, soon the giant would sleep. For the day had been long and even Tibor's great strength could not go on forever.

He would watch through the night, he would only disturb the giant if the need arose.

Michael watched the sleeping giant, did the man have no eyes to see with. Did he have no ears to hear with, he had watched Katji with him, love in her every movement, touch and word, was Tibor stupid as well as being deaf, blind and dumb? When Tibor woke he would speak to him, tell him how he Michael felt about Katji. For now, let the man sleep, for he needed to rest. Michael sat and stared at the giant, his, their destinies were intertwined. But Michael knew that he needed Tibor more than the giant needed him. Michael rolled over and gazed down into the valley, lights had been brought outside and hung on the tents, the scratching sound of a hand cranked phonograph carried to him on the suddenly chill wind. Soon darkness would take over the valley, the oil lamps the only focus of light, Michael eased himself into a more comfortable position. It was time to sleep, if anything happened he was relying on his animal instincts to warn him of danger.

There was a feeling of something almost tangible in the air, there was a tension Michael believed he could actually touch, between Tibor and Katji. All his instincts both animal and human told him that an event was to happen here in this valley. The animal inside the man was uncomfortable in the presence of the other two. The angry words uttered by Katji, the resentful glances she directed towards the giant. The sullen half mumbled replies he gave her when she asked anything of him. Michael knew that the matter would soon come to a head, and he preferred to be elsewhere when it boiled over.

The wolfman took to spending his nights watching the men in the valley, suggesting to Tibor that it would be better for all concerned. He could see in the dark, Tibor could not, and besides Katji would feel better if the giant spent his nights in the cave with her.

Tibor was reluctant at first to accept this idea, he still did not completely trust Michael, but a scowling Katji informed him, it was the way she wanted it. Michael was content to be away from the two, yet each morning when Tibor took over the watch, Michael for reasons he could not put a name to , expected the giant to tell him he had spoken to Katji and explained himself. Tibor barely spoke, he settled himself down and gave his full concentration to the men in the valley.

Michael was about to speak when the sound of an engine struggling to contend with the burden being asked of it came into view. Gears meshed and squealed, the engine roared, slowly, oh so very slowly it crested the ridge. The lorry was massive, its eight wheels forcing it up and over and onto the down run into the valley. The engine free of its overworked burden, slowed down, the driver dropped the gears and allowed the wagon to run free. As the first monster pulled to a halt some yards from the tents, a second wagon pulled itself wearily over the ridge and began its decent, a third followed it and drove alongside the others and parked, the noise from the three monsters was deafening, then silence as the engines were switched off. A man in dirty overalls jumped down from the cab and walked towards the men from the tents. Papers were handed over, the one in overalls shouted and men emerged from the first wagon, there was no setting up of tents, no handshakes. It was obvious the men from the wagons were here simply to work. And work they did, supplies were taken from the other wagons , mostly timber, the moment this was unloaded the three wagons started up and were driven out of the valley.

The two men watched as huts were erected, near to the pegged line which dissected the valley. In less than a day six huts had been built, one of the huts erected some distance from the others had a compound built around it. Then the men from the tents began to take more measurements, thick posts were driven into the ground at exact intervals. Tibor slipped away, leaving Michael to watch, Katji must be warned to stay hidden inside the cave.

Michael heard the giant long before Tibor crawled up to him. "They have stopped." said Michael, "All of them have gone inside, I smell food." Tibor handed over the package he had to Michael. Michael ripped it open and took out the food, he was not hungry but he knew that food was strength. His mouth full of food he chewed, his mind was full of questions, but he would eat first before he asked them.

"I have many things to ask of you Tibor." said Michael, "But I see from your face that what they do in the valley is no secret to you."

"What they do down there you will soon see," answered the giant, "You have lived in times different to me, you have most probably witnessed things my eyes dare not look on. Perhaps what you will see will not sicken you, but for me and hundreds of thousands like me this is the beginning of the end, ask me no more questions." For the first time Michael saw that Tibor carried his gun. "This I will say, we have stayed too long in this valley, from this moment on we are in constant danger."

"Go back to the cave Tibor," said Michael, "I will stay and watch, go to Katji, protect her, not me."

The two men looked at each other, Michael could see that the giant longed to be back at the cave, but his training and his beliefs were struggling with his passions.

"You have protected me and helped me back to life, you and your woman have fulfilled your pledge. I release you and her from it." For a brief moment the old religion in which Tibor believed fought with the idea of Michael's words. Then the wolfman spoke and Tibor heard the words he dare not speak aloud. "You are no longer my guardian Tibor, I give you freedom, go to her, tell her of your love. Take her to be your true wife." The giant did not argue, it was true they had fulfilled their destinies, both he and Katji were free of their burden. Dare he go to her, dare he tell her the secret, would she return his love, would she take him to be her man in more than name only? Tibor knew he had put off this time for far too long, she had the right to know. Despite all she meant to him she had the right to make her own choice. Tibor took Michael's hand in his, there was no need for him to speak, he had decided. "Go." said Michael. The giant nodded and began inching his way backwards, only when he felt he was clear of any eyes did he stand.

Michael watched until Tibor had vanished among the trees. How could the man be so in love yet afraid to speak his heart? The hurtful memory of what could have been came back to Michael. How long had he held his tongue before he had declared his love for a woman. Michael drove the unpleasant thoughts from his mind and turned his face to the happenings in the valley.

Tibor saw Katji standing on the ledge, he saw her face break out in joy as she saw him coming up the path. "Inside quickly." He took hold of her arm and pushed her back into the cave. Katji was hurt and surprised at the actions of Tibor. Tibor realising what he was doing let go of her arm. "I, I" he said angrily at himself for treating her this way, "You must never stand on the ledge in daylight." Katji rubbed her arm where he had gripped it, Tibor gently rolled up the sleeve, already it had started to bruise. "I'm sorry," he said, "but the ledge is too exposed."

Tears filled Katji's eyes, she was confused at his behaviour. Never before had he handled her so roughly. "What's bothering you Tibor?" she asked of him, "Why have you been acting so strangely towards me?" The giant could not look into her eyes, he had acted instinctively, he had felt she was in danger, "Why are you this way?"

"Now is not the time to speak of it." he said, Katji stepped back, her eyes hot with tears and anger.

"When will it be the right time?" she asked, "When it is too late? Do not look away from me, turn and face me Tibor." Katji reached out and took hold of his arm, Tibor stood like a rock while she tried to turn him around. Katji spoke softly, "Look at me." Tibor turned from her, the girl followed him, try as she might he could not avoid her. "Look at me Tibor, please." Tibor looked down at her and Katji saw her answer in his eyes and face. She saw it all, all of his feelings towards her were mirrored in his sad eyes. Katji reached up, standing on tiptoes, she brushed his cheeks with her finger. She touched the wetness beneath his eyes, she held up her finger and watched the giants tears slide down it, Katji choked back her own tears and buried her face against the giant's chest. "You stupid, stupid man." She sobbed out the words, "You silly blind man." Katji wrapped her arms around him, hugging him with all her strength. He felt Katji against him, he heard her sobs, and he knew that if he chose to say nothing she would understand how he felt about her. He had known that this day must come, he had wanted it, begged for it, longed for it with all his heart. Now it was here he did not know what to do, how to begin to tell her how much he loved her.

"You do not have to speak," she said, her words took him by surprise, "I know."

"Come." he said. Taking her hand he led her over to one of the chairs he had so painstakingly carried up from the cabin. Gently he sat her down and then knelt before her so that he might look into her eyes. "I must speak," he said, "You and the moon child have called me stupid." Katji put her fingers to his lips and shook her head. "Oh, I am, I am stupid and foolish, you and I," Tibor knew what he wanted to say, but the words would not come, silently Katji sat there holding his hands. "You and I, we are not like other people, we were born to do certain things. We are chosen at birth to do these things, this we both know. Had we met under different circumstances, had we met in a different place and time, I would not have waited so long before I had the courage to speak." Tibor held her hands before him and touched his lips to her fingers. "From the moment I set eyes on you I loved you Katji. I see in your eyes and in your looks that you don't find it strange that someone like me should fall in love."

Katji wanted to speak but once more Tibor held his fingers to her lips.

"When the old ones came to me here in this valley, I knew what they required of me. The Wych child had come of an age to be married, and I was the one chosen to take her for my wife." Tibor continued to speak, he spoke of how after the blessings of the Fallen one, he had left all he had and built the cabin in the valley. How he had travelled thousands of miles to be at the appointed place at the appointed time to meet the girl who would be his wife. "I looked upon this slip of a girl and my heart melted. I, Tibor the guardian, a man who had lived alone for far too long. I fell hopelessly in love with my Wych bride." Tibor looked directly into her eyes, "I loved you then and I love you now."

Katji leant forward and kissed him, slowly letting the touch of her lips linger on his. "Hush now," she said, "Let me speak." Katji touched his face, traced her finger across his cheek and tugged playfully at his beard. "I too journeyed to meet you," she began, "And I was frightened of meeting you, you were a stranger to me and I was so scared, a child about to be handed over to a man she had never even seen. I saw you for the first time on the day we were to be married. Never in my life had I seen such a man like you, you were a Goliath of a man. Then you turned to look at me and I looked into your eyes. I saw your soul in your eyes, I saw a gentleness in your every move. I saw a love that would carry both of us through the travesty we were about to enter. I too fell in love that day, never have you shown me anything but kindness, gentleness and love." Katji took his hand and held it against her breast. "Feel the beat of my heart, it beats for you and the love I carry there for you."

"Now, I must say more, I know your secret, I have known it most of my life. And I love you all the more, because you foolishly believed by keeping it from me it could not hurt me. Many years ago when first I was told of what I was and what would be expected of me, the women of my tribe explained it all to me. They spoke of the law which forbids the carnal knowledge between Wych and Guardian. They also spoke of my twentieth winter."

"That time has come and gone Tibor, did you think that only the guardians were privileged to carry that burden, and I know while we protect the moon child you must not touch me or I you."

Tibor took her hand from his face, "The moon child sent me to you, he knew what I felt for you and he knew I must speak of it." The giant smiled at her she knew of the secret he carried. "But Katji, my beautiful Katji , he releases us, Michael has released us from our vows."

"You are certain of this?" she asked. Please, by all the old gods, let this be true. "You have his word?" Katji could barely contain herself. If it was true, if the moon child had set them free. The face of her beloved spoke volumes, his every word was true. "We are free to love."

"We are free."

"Then hold me, kiss me, love me Tibor, love me."

With the passing of the days, the camp grew steadily, more wagons arrived bringing cables and generators, and fuel to keep the generators going. Within a matter of hours the cables were laid and connected, now they had lights to work by, night and day the men laboured to complete their jobs. Michael watched as men strung out cable on poles the length of the pegged area, then they erected lights on poles to finish. It had taken only six weeks to erect the huts, lay in the electricity and ensure that by night the camp site was lit brightly.

Nothing happened for the next two days. Michael paid only short visits to the cave. Tibor and Katji were so wrapped up in each other that they hardly noticed the wolfman. When on the morning of the third day the lorry discharged its load, Michael lifted himself from under the overhang and made his way up to the cave.

"Dogs." said Tibor, "Dogs, how many? What kind? What uniforms did their handlers wear?" It became obvious to Tibor that he had to go and look for himself. Michael may know the breed of the dogs but not the type of men handling them. "I'll go down with Michael and check this out." He held Katji to him, kissed her, "We won't be long."

"Longer than you think." said Michael. Tibor turned to him to ask what he meant. "Dogs," said Michael "Dogs use their noses to smell, if I go with you I will have to approach them from down wind."

"Damn." Tibor had forgotten what Michael was, these past, joyous days wrapped in Katji's arms had driven out of his mind their predicament. "I'm sorry," he said, "You stay here and I'll go down alone."

Katji looked at Michael, Michael said nothing. Tibor wanted to know what was happening. Providing he took no chances he would be safe, and Tibor was cautious if nothing else, Michael and Katji watched him go down the path to the place where they watched from. "He will be safe." said Michael, "He is not a fool and besides," he put his arm around Katji, "I think he has too much to lose to make mistakes."

Katji blushed to the roots of her hair, she pushed Michael away and pretended she had work to do. Michael felt a need to say more but could not think of a thing to say, he knew that she was worried, he saw it in her every movement, in the excuses she invented to keep Tibor inside the cave by her side. He saw the look in her eyes when the giant had left the cave to go and spy on the camp site.

"Katji," Michael spoke breaking the silence, "I will go and watch him, no he won't see me I promise." The woman smiled at him, it was all the thanks he needed. Without another word Michael left the cave, he did not have to go far, concealed among the thick bushes he could see Tibor stretched out, his ancient telescope trained on the campsite below.

Michael settle himself in the bushes above Tibor and lay down, up here high above the camp the dogs would not smell his scent. When the giant finally fell asleep Michael watched the camp, he watched the guard patrol the perimeter of the camp their dogs straining and barking at every sound they heard. Tibor had been right they should have left the valley long ago, now it would be difficult, not impossible, but difficult.

The wolfman heard the wind sighing in the trees, the flutter of wings as the owls hunted their prey, for a moment he was content to lay there and listen. When dawn became a thin pencil slim light on the horizon he stirred and slowly he crept forward to where the giant lay asleep.

The sound of lorries, their engines throbbing as they pulled into the valley and crested the ridge, the higher singing as the engine made their way down and into the camp. Michael froze against a tree, Tibor had woken instantly, rolled over and trained the telescope on the camp. Six of them, chugging and belching out their diesel fumes rolled slowly towards the wired compound.

The last lorry pulled to a halt some distance from the other five, the canvas flap was thrown back and armed men jumped down and took their positions forming a semi circle around the other lorries.

The sound of barked orders, men, women even children were being hauled out of the back of the lorries. Under the persuasion of a rifle butt and booted feet they were kicked and pushed inside the compound, a long ragged line of beaten and starved people. A man went down and no amount of beating or screamed threats could make him get up. A black uniformed guard turned the man over, looked long and hard before he fired his gun into the mans head. The body jerked, arms and legs kicking and waving then he was still. The guard called two of the prisoners over and made them carry the dead man inside the compound.

"So." said Michael "The Jews are still a hated race." The giant felt his heart stop and then thump hurriedly in his chest, he had not heard the wolfman creep up on him. Tibor gritted his teeth and swallowed hard, it had been all he could do not to shout out. "They carry the pentacle like me," He said. "are they?" He asked.

"No." Said Tibor "They are not like you, they are forced to wear that sign, it is a corruption of their religion, the star of David." Tibor focused the telescope on the lorries and the guards, he had spent hours watching the lorries bring in their loads. Always before it had been equipment, but this was different, there could only be one reason to bring in a human cargo, slave labour.

Both men looked towards the pass at the sound of revving engines. A lorry climbed slowly up the incline and down into the valley, it was followed by three more. These did not stop before the gates of the compound they were driven straight in. Men and dogs jumped down from two of the lorries before they had stopped and their engines switched off. The guards that did not have a dog on a lease, held machine guns at the ready.

At the first sight of the prisoners Michael heard the sharp intake of breath from Tibor, he saw the giants fingers whiten as he gripped the telescope. Men and women dressed in rags were being forced to stand in line. "Gypsies." He said, "Michael can you see what badge they wear? No, not the prisoners. The guards look at the guards."

"It looks like a silver skull."

Tibor felt his blood run cold. "Gestapo." He said, at the bitter sound of the giant's words Michael's memory stirred, he understood Tibor's fear. For whatever reason these prisoners had been brought to the valley, few, if any would leave alive. "Damn it." said Tibor "I need something better than this old glass, binoculars."

"I see well enough for both of us," said Michael "but if you need binoculars I will get them for you."

"Things like this, they are new to you." Michael did not let Tibor finish.

"No." He said "They are not. Mans inhumanity to his own kind I have seen in a hundred different ways."

Tibor got to his feet "Come," Was all he said and began walking away from the happenings in the valley. The stuttering cough of a machine gun forced them to turn back, the Gypsies were making a break for freedom. A hundred men clambered on the wire surrounding the compound, impervious to its ripping barbs. A guard went down under a dozen of the female prisoners, when they ran on they left behind a heaving bloody mass. The compound gates gave way under the combined weight of the men, who fell into a tangled heap before it. The guards opened fire, dozens died under the first raking salvo of bullets. Men and women twisted in a grotesque dance of death, tossed back and forth by the bullets. Those lucky enough to survive the first stream of leaden death died under the second salvo.

A woman went down under two of the dogs, laughing guards urging the dogs on as they tore out her throat. Then turned on each other to fight over her remains. A man threw himself at the dogs and literally tore one of them apart before a bullet blew out his brains. One man was running free of the carnage behind him, most if not all of his fellow prisoners were being slaughtered. The man was pushing himself, he knew that those that had not died would be shot. The Germans had no use for badly wounded prisoners.

A black uniformed guard lifted his rifle and carefully aimed it at the running man. The man had nearly reached the edge of the forest before the guard fired. The face of the running man which was full of hope as he saw salvation in the trees disintegrated into a bloody mess. The bullet entered the back of his head and exited in a shower of blood, brains and bone, he went rigid for a second then he fell his limbs twitched momentarily then he was still.

"Let us go Michael I do not want see anymore." From where he stood the wolfman could smell the heady scent of blood, he could also smell the scent of animals lost in bloodlust.

"Go to Katji." He said "I will stay and watch until I believe there is no danger to us." He stood and watched as the guards walked around the bodies and fired a shot into the back of the head. He saw the man who stood beside one of the huts, hands on his hips, looking on unconcerned at the mass murder of the innocent.

Michael would stand and watch like this many times over the next few weeks as the prisoners were beaten and kicked, forced to work long body sapping hours. It was the man in charge of the whole operation that fascinated the wolfman. He walked around the work being carried out with his instruments, stop and point, measure again and then retire to his hut. He seemed to care little for the comfort or the well being of his workers, and never interfered when the guards took it upon themselves to beat one of them. The wolfman decided he would go down into the camp and take a closer look at this man.

The object of Michaels interest was one Alfred Strobel, chief engineer on the valley project. Alfred Strobel tapped his teeth with a pencil and looked down at the plans. The airstrip was going well the Jews did their work without complaint, Strobel tapped the pencil hard against the top of the desk. When did Jews ever complain, he could not understand their mentality, why did they work like dogs, men, women even their children. He had seen the food they were given to eat, pig swill, the guard dogs ate better fare, how could a race of people allow themselves to be forced into what amounted to virtual slavery. From their files he knew that among them were teachers, scientists, highly educated men and women, yet they accepted their fate, he would never understand them, never.

Strobel returned to the work schedules he had planned, he needed more workers, damn the Gypsies, damn the fat stupid bureaucratic fat bastards sat on their fat arse's in Berlin. He had lost six men because the Gypsies tried to make a break for freedom, and unbelievably he had also lost two dogs. The damned Gypsies had torn them apart, still dogs were easy to replace, workers that was a different matter.

Strobel looked out of the window, work on the airstrip progressed, not as fast as he would have liked but it did progress. It simply meant that the Jews had to work even harder, he picked up the pen and began to write his report for Berlin. He put it exactly as it was, without more workers he doubted the strip would be finished in time. Strobel pulled the calendar to him , how many days did he have left, by the beginning of September it could be snowing. He flicked it open and looked at the date, the twentieth of April, he began to count the days left to him by the start of September. One hundred and thirty three days left, he made a quick calculation, if Berlin gave him another two hundred workers he could be finished by the end of August. That gave him nearly a month to iron out any little problems.

His report finished Strobel got up from his chair and went to stand before the window. He had to get it right, finish the damn airstrip on time then destroy all evidence of the slave camp. Strobel laughed, he liked the description of the deaths of a thousand Jews, destroy the evidence. What did Berlin expect him to do, get the Jews to dig their own graves, still that wasn't such a bad idea, they wouldn't know what they were digging until it was too late.

Strobel reached into his shirt pocket and brought out the cigarette case his wife had given him for his fiftieth birthday. He carefully selected one of the cigarettes, rolling it between his fingers before putting it in his mouth. He savoured the first deep pull he took of it, holding the smoke in his mouth then slowly allowing it to dribble from his nose.

From where he stood he could see clearly the work already carried out, the actual landing strip clearly marked by pegs. The top soil had been removed to a depth of four feet, rocks, brought from the mountains had been laid in, the hardest part was beginning to take shape. Tons of small rocks had to be pounded and flattened before the final surface could be laid. He desperately needed more labour, how many prisoners had he already lost, Strobel wasn't quite sure of the exact number, ten, twenty, a hundred? Some of them the old men and women, virtually useless anyway, had been unable to move quickly and been crushed beneath the wheels of the lorries. Perhaps dozen's of the children had died, due to the work and malnutrition, but it was the death of that one Jewess that bothered him.

Mantz was investigating it, and he knew that eventually Mantz would find the culprits, damn them, damn the girl. The girl had died being raped by the guards, oh they could deny it but he knew, and he also believed that Mantz knew it was the guards. Strobel wouldn't be at all surprised if Captain Mantz didn't already know who they were, and when Mantz had the truth, all the denial by their comrades that they were in their huts wouldn't save them. Of course the rapist would then be shot, Berlin had decreed it, no fraternizing with an inferior species.

A thought crossed Strobel's mind, he would speak with Mantz in the morning. Don't kill the culprits yet if they craved Jew flesh then let them become Jews. Let them live, eat and sleep and work along side the Jews, Strobel liked the idea. And he muttered to himself it would give the other guards something to think about during the long nights.

Shadows had begun to lengthen, night was coming once more to the valley, giving a few hours respite to prisoners. Beyond the limit of the mountains the moon slowly rose forcing down the sun. Strobel looked up at the sky, it was clear, dotted by a thousand little lights, he turned his head, he had seen something from the corner of his eye.

Strobel blinked and looked again he could have sworn it was one of the dogs. But that was impossible Vogel would never allow his dogs to run free around the camp. No, he was seeing things, the only thing Vogel ever considered was the welfare of his dogs. He rubbed his eyes he was tired, that was it, tired, he had spent too many hours pouring over the plans, sleep, he needed to sleep.

Strobel walked over to the door of his bedroom, flicked on the lights and looked at the sparsely fitted room. It contained only a camp bed and a single chair. Seated on the edge of the bed Strobel tried to imagine Mantz's response to his proposed punishment of the rapist. He let himself fall onto the bed, reached out and pulled the cord, the room plunged into darkness.

Strobel did not see the yellow eyes which watched him, he did not see the breath of the wolfman mist the glass. The wolfman flitted from shadow to shadow, he skirted the prison compound. He stared through the wire at the huts, he could smell and taste death. He could hear the tortured, restless sleep of the prisoners, he heard the soft padding of boots on the ground , the lighter sound of a dogs paws on soil. The wolfman moved quickly, he had vanished into the deeper darkness of the forest before the patrol reached the place where he had stood. The guard grumbled loudly at the dog which strained at its lease, whining, it sniffed the ground and lay down. The scent of the wolfman was strong and fear travelled through every fibre of the dog. Despite the guard hauling on the lead the dog refused to go on, it placed its head on its paws and lay still. The dog stared towards the forest emitting frightening whimpers, the guard in turn looked towards the trees.

Fear became a tangible thing to the guard, he felt a coldness along his spine and a movement in his bowels. When he made his morning report to Sergeant Vogel he would swear by all that was holy to him, a pair of yellow eyes had stared back at him

THE KEEP - PART 3

Michael didn't want to believe the evidence of his own eyes, he stared at the man stood before him. The face was always as he remembered it, the nose long , the lips at this moment in time a mere slash, the strong jaw and the grey eyes. The body of the naked man, tall, powerful shoulders and the hard lean body. "Impossible." He said aloud, the sound of his voice loud in the bedroom of the Keep , which he had occupied from the first day . Michael reached out and his fingers touched their reflection in the full length mirror.

"Impossible." He said again, it was against the laws of nature and the laws of God, for a brief moment a smile crossed his lips and the reflection smiled back at him. God, he hadn't called upon that particular deity for more years than he cared to remember. And what, thought Michael would happen if I did call upon God, would a thunderbolt flash from the heavens and destroy him. He doubted it, if there was some omnipotent being sat up there , it was obvious that he didn't care about those he had supposedly created on this earth. For if he, it , had any kind of compassion it wouldn't allow such creatures like him to exist.

The glass held him prisoner showing him the way he would forever remain. The fingers remained pressed against the glass and the man stared hard at his reflection . How many years had it been , how many suns and moons had risen and fallen since that night in the Keeps hall when he had killed two of the pack and made a mortal enemy of Julius? His brain refused to believe the calculation it made, even taking into account his profession, he should have died a natural death, more than fifty years ago.

A strange jumble of thoughts entered Michaels brain, he thought of the Alchemist, those men who sought immortality. How they must have sat and dreamed as they searched their massive tombs of the past experiments of others like themselves who had sought to cheat death. They had sought immortality , they would have willingly opened their hearts to it, Michael tried to imagine how they must have felt . These men had wasted precious years seeking it, and he had been given what they coveted, and he hated it.

Michael could only see it as a curse not a gift, how long would it go on for? How many years must he suffer , would he always look like this, how could he remain as he was while the world and it's people grew old? "It's not possible." He shouted at his reflection, "nobody, nothing can live forever."

"You can my beloved." The image of the Countess appeared beside his in the glass, he had not heard her enter his room. So intent had he been in looking in fear and with a feeling of revulsion at his mirrored image. The Countess was as beautiful as the day he first met her, not a blemish on the smooth skin. Her full breasted body close to his, his eyes automatically travelled to the thick tangle of blonde hairs between her legs. Michael cursed himself, he wanted to forget about the nights he had sought that place, willingly. The nights of sweaty, lustful sex. The nights when he had lost himself deep inside of her, not caring if it was a feeling of love or just lust which called him to her bed. Looking at her stood beside him Michael realised it had never been anything other than a mutual need to satisfy his sexual needs.

"Hating me won't help you," she said, her hand touched his thigh, gently she moved her fingers along it. A hand found his shoulder and he squirmed as her nails travel their slow erotic way down his back. Slowly she rubbed her hand around his backside, her finger slipped gently into the crack and moved between his legs. "Accept." She murmured, her lips raining gentle kisses on his back, he felt her press her naked body against him, her breasts rubbing his back, "Be grateful for what has been given you." Michael jumped as her fingers curled around him, the Countess moving them up and down. Michael felt himself hardening under her touch, the erotic messages she was giving out coursing through his blood.

"You've damned me to hell's eternity." Michael's lips curled in a snarl, he pushed her hand away from him and turned to her. The Countess reached out, he knocked her hands away. "Look at me, am I alive or am I dead?" Michael giggled, the Countess stared at him in horror. "No I can't be dead can I, I breath, I feel, I hurt , what have you done to me?"

"I have given you life. I have given you my love." Michael laughed a cold distant sound tinged with bitterness. She moved to him, her body touched his and she began to move it against him, he felt the tangle of hairs rub over the tip of his penis. She pressed her face against his chest, her mouth pressed hard against it. Sharp teeth nipped at his skin, her tongue ran its wet path over his flesh.

"No, no," He cried, Michael took hold of her shoulders and began shaking her, the thick blonde hair came loose from its exquisite bouffant and fell around her beautiful face, masking it. He grabbed a handful of it, he wanted to look into those eyes, "Is there a way for me to die?" The Countess didn't answer, she just smiled up at him, anger took hold of Michael and he threw her from him. The Countess staggered across the room, she was thrown with such force that she hit the bed. Caught by surprise she was unable to stop herself from crashing to the floor.

Anger seethed through her, her eyes blazed through the tangle of her hair, on hands and knees she glared at the man. She was experiencing something that was foreign to her, a thing which she thought she would never experience again, fear. She could feel his anger directed at her, a cold violent anger which threatened to erupt into a vicious action against her. The Countess caused her fingers to change into claws, she felt her teeth move in her mouth, she considered attacking him. Elizabeth Dressler forced herself to relax, slowly the change vanished from her. Looking at the man stood before her she knew she would fail, the nature of the beast deep inside of her told her he was too strong for her. She pushed the hair from around her face and smiled at him, there was to much hate inside of him, against her but mainly against himself. No, there were other ways of appeasing the beast within him. "I have given you a precious gift," she said as Michael walked over to her, his eyes gleamed with the feral look of a wolf seeking out its kill.

"You have given me hell on earth you bitch." He saw her mouth forming "No." Whimpering she grabbed his legs and began to kiss them.

"Love me Michael. Love me." Michael felt his stomach churn, the she bitch was begging him to take her. He reached down and twisted his hand in her hair and pulled her up, brutally he forced back her head so that he could look into her eyes. He looked down on the most beautiful creature he would ever see in his cursed life. He wanted to hate, and he did, he wanted to strike at her, destroy her beauty forever, his free hand took hold of her throat and he began to squeeze. Her eyes flew open in shock and pain at the pressure his hand was exerting.

Michael put his face close to hers, she could feel his hot breath on her cheek. "Bitch." He snarled, then his mouth covered hers, his teeth pulling at her bottom lip. "Bitch." He said once more, his hand moving over her breast pulling at her hardening nipple. The Countess responded eagerly when Michael's fingers probed between her thighs, she opened herself to his touch. She moaned in alarm as he took his finger away, she felt his arms go around her then she was being lifted.

Michael carried her over to the bed, the Countess felt herself falling, she looked up at him. Michael stared down at her naked body, slowly the Countess opened her legs, fingers parting the lips showing him a glistening opening. Michael climbed onto the bed and covered her body with his, for a time he denied her, the Countess sobbed and moaned beneath him, pushing herself up at him, begging. Finally Michael entered her and the Countess wrapped her arms and legs around him.

Michael moved, he pushed her arm from around him, the Countess, her body covered in fine white hairs brought on by her frenzied coupling, slept. Michael eased himself off the bed and stood for a moment looking down at her. He saw the yellow fangs protruding over her bottom lip, Michael wondered did he look like her in the throes of sex? He reached for his clothes and began to dress, the tangy scent of sex on his body. He felt he should wash away all trace of the Countess from him, but decided against it and continued dressing. He pushed his feet into the boots feeling the supple leather mould itself to him. His fingers touched the swords hilt, the coldness of the metal penetrating his hand. Taking the sword hilt in one hand the scabbard in the other he slowly pulled it free. Centuries old steel hissed on its steel and leather covering. Michael gazed down at the brightness of death, gently he pushed it back, the hilt snapping tight into its lock. He realised that he didn't need it, why fasten it around him, Michael smiled , simple, it bothered the dark skinned Julius. For reasons best known to himself Julius hated and feared the sword. Michael knew that one day he and Julius would fight, and law or no law one of them would die.

He looked towards the plate of meat, some of it cooked, some of it raw, still dripping with blood. He couldn't remember seeing it before the Countess had come to his room. The red she wolf Anna, it had to be her, she was the only one of the pack, apart from herself, the Countess would allow into his room. Michael tightened the belt buckle and moved towards the door, resting his hand on the swords hilt he pulled open the door.

It came as no surprise to Michael to find Julius stood outside his door, he never strayed far from the Countess. Michael did not acknowledge him, he never did, Michael would not hunt with the dark skinned petulant man, then he would not hunt with others of the pack. Despite all her entreaties Michael refused to hunt with the Countess, he only ever ran with one other, the red she wolf Anna. Julius glared at Michael. Michael rested his back against the door frame and stared back, reluctantly Julius lowered his eyes. Michael smiled at Julius and eased himself upright and walked past him. He could feel the anger being directed at him, for the moment he knew he was safe. Julius was still not sure if he could beat Michael.

Michael turned the corner and stopped, he could hear Julius pounding on the door, snarling in anger when the Countess ignored him. "One day he will try and kill you." At the sound of Anna's voice Michael turned and looked at her. "Sometimes you are a foolish man." Michael reached out and stroked her red hair, Anna tried to pull away from him, Michael held her, he saw the fear in her eyes. She was looking for the Countess, Michael lifted her chin and said, "She sleeps and Julius, I don't fear him, besides the law of the pack won't allow him to kill me."

"He cares little for the law, he kills only for his own satisfaction." She held onto Michael's hand gripping it tightly, not wanting to let him go. "Hunt with me tonight Michael." He looked deep into her eyes, he saw that she was troubled, "I need to speak to you, there are things I think you should be told, before it is too late."

"Then Anna, I will hunt with you, find my spoor it will bring you to a safe place."

He let his fingers rest on her lips, Anna kissed them, "Until tonight." he said and walked away. Anna watched him walk down the long stone staircase and the desire to be with him made her body ache. From the moment the Englishman had walked into the Keep all those long years ago she had loved him. Often he had called her to his bed and she had gone willingly, but always the shadow of the Countess hovered over the bed. Tonight she would turn against the Countess and tell Michael the truth, that no one in the Keep, not even the Countess, not herself, not even the pack had a hold on him. Anna remembered the night she had run from his bed and their lovemaking, the sign of the Fallen One burnt deep in his shoulder. He should have been the Countess's, she should have been the one he made love to first, but it had been her. A mistake made by the Countess but a mistake that could still cost Anna her life.

She had witnessed the love making between Michael and Elizabeth Dressler, it was mostly hard and brutal, but not with her. With her Michael was kind and gentle, he used her body with the finesse of a master. He had carried her to heights of sexual gratification she had not believed possible, and she loved him for it.

How many times over the years had she tried to tell him? "Go, no one can stop you." Fear of Elizabeth Dressler had held her back, but not tonight, deep within her she knew that this night she would speak.

Some miles away Michael stripped off his clothes and carefully hid them, he carefully wrapped his sword in his cloak and hid it some distance from his clothing. He knew that the black lap dog Julius had sometimes followed him, and he did not intend for Julius to find his sword. Soon the moon would rise and he would let the change come over him. The red she wolf would pick up his smell and she would find him.

Eyes hot and angry watched the naked Anna lift her arms up to the full moon before lowering herself to the ground and allowing the change to take her over. The Countess cursed the red she wolf and promised her death, she took hold of the dark skinned Julius and pointed at the running wolf. "Follow her, find out where they meet and when he leaves, kill her." Julius smiled and bowed to her. "At last." he said, "They die." A hand took hold of his face, the Countess pressed it hard against the flesh around his jaw and turned him towards her. Elizabeth Dressler was aware that she was causing the man considerable pain. "The red bitch, yes, her you can kill." Julius looked upon the face of a completely evil woman, he saw in her eyes the anger and hatred she felt from Michael's rejection. "Take off Anna's head and bring it back to me, but don't touch him." Julius moved his jaw, forcing his fangs to appear, anything to lessen the pain she was causing him. "Touch Michael and you die Julius." The Countess pushed away the half man, half wolf. "And believe me when I say to you, your death will not be an easy one, go, follow." The Countess stared at Julius, Michael was right he was not a man, he was a dog, not even a faithful dog, but he served her purpose.

Elizabeth Dressler stared at the same moon that Michael and Anna would be looking at. She stepped back, suddenly her face was as white as her hair, she shook her head and moved back to the window. For the second time in her long life she thought the fallen one had spoken to her again warning her to leave the man alone.

Her voice was loud in the room as she looked up at the face of the moon. "But I don't intend to kill him, only to keep him here with me." Why couldn't Michael love her, where had she gone wrong with him? But he would love her, with Anna gone he would have no choice, she knew his secret, she would be able to hold him here in the Keep. Something nagged at her, a little thing but it was causing her concern, did Anna know? The Countess dismissed it from her mind, no she had never discussed Michael with the red bitch, and anyway, shortly it wouldn't matter, Anna would be dead. She would bathe, perfume her body and wait for Michael and offer him everything yet again.

The grey wolf was bounding over grounds which held so many memories of its past life. The barricade where once he fought for his life was a ruin, over the years grass and weeds had made their home in and on it. The grey wolf ran into the small village, many of the houses collapsed and uninhabited. Those who had fought and died to protect the Countess just distant memories. The wolf did not break its stride when the wind caused an ancient broken door to squeal on its hinges. It merely turned its head and let yellow eyes look at it before it suddenly stopped at the stone steps leading into the church.

The grey wolf lifted its head and sniffed the night air, only the scent of decay lingered in the village. Only the scratching of a church mouse, its tiny claws scrabbling across the stone. The wolfs feral eyes followed its progress across the step, fear causing its tiny heart to thump. Slowly the grey wolf climbed the steps and peered into the darkness of the church. Deep in its brain it was remembering the first time it had been here. It saw the struggling sweaty bodies of men in battle, it saw the wounded fall and the triumphant bring down spear or blade. It heard the cries of the battlefield. Wounded men and beasts, the stench of gunpowder and cloying smell of death. How many times had the grey wolf stopped here? , to many times to remember, and each time the same visions.

In its minds eye it saw the woman Michael had struck down, the grey wolf snarled and leapt back. A vision of a skull, dead eyes accusing him, maggots writhing from between bony teeth, a fleshless finger pointing, a rotting corpse trying to lift itself free. The wolf howled its anger at such memories, it had been so long ago, turning, it jumped from the top step into the soft soil. It clung to the grey wolf's pads causing the wolf to stand and shake it free, it saw a pool of dark rain water, bent and sniffed it. The wolf bent its muzzle to drink, once its tongue lapped at the water before the grey wolf lifted its head and began to run. Within minutes it was miles away from the bitter memories, finding joy in running free.

It ran with all its might, a strong heart pumping blood into its veins. It felt the soft soil of the village land give way to the harder touch of rock as it climbed up and out of the pass. The chilling wind which always seemed to blow down the pass giving way to a gentler , softer warmer breeze of a summers night in a moon drenched landscape. The frightened scent of a rabbit, a deer, the hoot of a hunting owl. The grey wolf refused to break its stride. The female deer protecting her young trembled in fear at the grey wolfs passing. The grey wolf lifted its head and bayed its pleasure of running free to all who cared to listen. Tonight the animals of the forest were safe from the grey wolfs fangs, albeit a fragile safety.

The smell of man and the scent of a fire caused the grey wolf to slow down. From the cover of bushes it stood and watched the old woman bend over the cooking pot suspended over the fire. The grey wolf watched the old man skin the rabbit and cut it into strips, his fingers covered in blood dropped the strips into the cooking pot. The distinctive scent of the horse, the sweet smell of soap and flowers mingled with the scent of humans.

Without taking its eyes from the old man and woman the grey wolf circled the campsite. It stared at the sign of the pentacle painted or burnt into the wood of the caravan. He would not harm these people, a distant memory or a half forgotten story told him they belonged to the old religion and if he was in desperate trouble they would give him shelter. Slowly the grey wolf backed away from the camp and turned to enter the forest. Once more it lifted its head and howled at the moon. It carried to a red she wolf eating from her kill, searching for his trail. It carried to a dark skinned man armed with a doubled headed axe who hunted the red she wolf.

The old gypsy smiled paused in his work of carving up the rabbit. "A moon child." He said to his wife, who had pretended not to hear the cry of the grey wolf. When he repeated himself the old woman nodded and carried on stirring the pot. She had no fear of the moon child for their caravan carried the sign of the old religion. "He runs for the joy of living." Said the old man, he chuckled to himself. At times like this a warm summers night, a soft breeze stirring the leaves causing them to rustle to natures tune. When the moon was full and bright bathing all around him in its incandescent light, he envied the moon children. But as always the envy inside of him did not last long for he knew he had more freedom than the moon child would ever know.

"The fire grows low," Mumbled the old woman seeing the dreamy faraway look in his eyes.

"Hush woman," He said "How can it grow low, here?" He said pointing to a pile of freshly cut wood. He bent and picked some up and placed it on the fire. He chuckled again as she muttered at him, the old man cocked his head listening for the moon child. "Live and run free moon child." In a voice so low his wife thought he was grumbling at her. The old man stared into the darkness of the forest the world around them was changing. Different attitudes to their religion were driving them out of many inhabited areas. People like himself and his wife were no longer welcome in many towns and villages. The keepers of the old religion were being forced to find secure hiding places to practise their beliefs and to protect themselves from the anger of a newer deity. The old man wondered how long it would be before the moon children were deprived of their protectors. The smell of the stew drove all thoughts from his head, he turned to the pot and allowed the smell to fill his senses.

The grey wolf found the place he was seeking, a dark gap in the tangle of thick bushes. Belly down it crawled into the hole and pulled itself down the alley way of tangled roots and bushes. Hard claws dug into the soft soil and the grey wolf pulled itself into its secret place.

A flow of warm water came from the recesses of the rock face, it flowed down the channel it had cut in the rocky ground. It fell into a pool it had formed over the centuries, the sandy soil mixed with pebbles aided it to create the pool into which the grey wolf dropped its muzzle. The foliage in the grey wolf's secret place was green and lush, a blanket of thick moss covered most of the rocks, all this possible because of the warm spring.

The grey wolf laying on the blanket of moss feeling the warmth of the rocks below it, lapped at the water. Knowing before it swallowed it it would leave a tangy bitter taste in his mouth. The grey wolf drank its fill and lay down, waiting , willing the change to come over it.

The grey wolf felt the change begin, in its hind legs, flesh stretched , the agony of bones reshaping themselves, muscle and sinews screamed as human features began to take the place of the wolfs. Pain flamed in the wolfs yellow eyes as its lower half became human. The human brain of Michael knew that next would come the mind numbing agony as human shape replaced that of the wolfs chest and face.

Teeth shifted in its mouth, fangs began to shrink and the mouth contracted. Eyes no longer yellow but a dull grey, full of the pain Michael was experiencing as wolfs pads became fingers. The popping of bones, the creaking and stretching of flesh were as loud as gunshots in the grey wolfs secret place.

Michael rolled over onto his back, hands pressed against his face trying to force the wolfs muzzle into regression. . The blood boiled in his veins, his brain screamed at him to hold on, soon it would be over. Michael felt the excruciating pain as the final part of him changed, hard claws becoming softer brittle fingernails.

Then the grey wolf was gone Michael was wholly human.

The man lay exhausted and sweating on the mossy blanket, an empty vessel drained of all thoughts and emotions. Michael pulled himself over the soft moss and slipped into the warm waters. He lay there for a long time letting the water ease the pain in his bones, his body responded to the gentle heat. He placed himself under the flow of water, it flattened his hair plastering it around his face. It ran down his face. Michael opened his mouth filling it, letting the water ease his pain filled gums.

Slowly the pain in his body began to subside, Michael sat, eyes closed allowing the water to cascade over him. Time was unimportant to the wolf man, he knew that here he was safe. Michael stood up and stayed standing knee deep in the pool until every last drop of its healing fluid had dried on his body.

Michael had found this place by accident and it had been his sanctuary for more years than he cared to remember. In the first days of his changing he had hunted alone not wanting or needing the company of the pack. He had hunted for the sake of it and had killed because of the power it gave him. Michael became a killing machine, the thrill of the chase and the dragging down of his prey was how he coped with the curse placed on him by the Countess.

Chasing a fat deer over the tangled canopy of fallen branches the grey wolf had trod on a rotten part. It had fallen through the canopy which covered the spring, twenty feet it had dropped onto the thick carpet of moss. The stunned wolf, its hind quarters injured it had rolled into the water, it had been a man that crawled out of the pool.

A different man, a man no longer filled with self pity and terror, but a man who had started to think again.

Many times over the last fifty years the grey wolf had crawled into this place. And Michael the man had spent days in solitude doing nothing other than thinking. Trying to find a way out of the depths of despair into which he had sunk. Alone he would lay on his back and look up through the hole in the canopy at the skies. Sometimes the sky he stared at would be a summer blue dotted with fluffy white clouds, sometimes it was a dark storm tossed sky. At nights he would lay cradled on the warm moss and see only stars. Hundreds and thousands of twinkling lights, often without realising it he would reach up as if he could grab a handful of stars.

Michael reached up and touched the throbbing scar on his shoulder, it always throbbed before and after the change. It continued to hurt for hours, Michael stretched himself out on the warm moss covered rocks. He looked around him, this had been his secret place, a place of safety and quiet solitude. Tonight he was allowing another to join him here to share his sanctuary.

The red she wolf searched for the greys trail, twice she had lost it, perhaps she should not have stopped to hunt. Her belly full she moved at a slow pace, nose to the ground seeking the grey wolfs scent. At the gypsies camp she had once more picked up the scent, curiosity had caused her to look at the gypsies, she saw the sign and curiosity satisfied she passed on.

Frustration gripped her, she had lost the trail yet again, she wanted to call out to the grey wolf. The red bitch restrained herself, a feeling deep within her told her it would be dangerous to do so.

She found the scent and the entrance but she did not stop, she carried on a further few miles before turning back. She had felt that she was being followed, but she neither found or saw any signs of her hunter. Animal instinct told her that something or someone was out there, something very dangerous to both herself and the grey wolf.

The she wolf spent a considerable time covering both her scent and the grey wolfs before bellying down and crawling into Michael's secret place. She saw the man laying on the carpet of moss, she padded slowly over to him. Her nose touched his side, the man opened his eyes and looked at her, bellying down she whimpered as she crawled beside him. Her tongue touched his chest, her mouth opened and gently she closed it around Michaels throat. Michael stroked her head, the she wolfs tongue licked at his scarred shoulder, slowly she lowered her head and rested it on his shoulder. His fingers twisted into the rough red hairs and he held her close. Eyes closed he listened to the sounds of agony as the she wolf regressed back into human form.

When next Michael held her to him his fingers touched soft pliable human flesh. He heard the heavy breathing of the woman, smelt her breath, tinged with the scent of blood, he turned and looked at her. He pushed away the thick red hair from around her face, she would sleep for hours, Michael wrapped her in his arms and in seconds both were sleeping soundly.

Julius was raging mad, he had lost the red bitches trail, somehow she had tricked him. Snarling he vented his anger on the nearest tree, large chips of wood flying free under the impact of the axes steel blade. It took a considerable time for him to calm down, he had to find the red wolfs scent. He dare not return to the Keep without the red bitches head. Slowly he began a methodical search of the area, stopping and sniffing each time he thought he caught the red wolfs scent. His eyes blazed with an inner anger, she had had to leave some trace of herself. Julius was in a half altered state, his human half thinking, reasoning, his beasts half using all of its animal instinct.

Suddenly he threw himself at the small bush, he wanted to howl his pleasure to the world. But he held himself in check, a small tuft of red hair, Julius held it to his nose. The smell of the red bitch was stronger than that of the bush. His eyes searched the ground around and under the bush seeking for a telltale sign of which way she had gone. "Damn her." The red she wolf had not only doubled back, she had doubled back on her own tracks, hoping to throw whoever hunted her off her trail.

Julius tore off his clothes, leaving them in a scattered pile, the axe he concealed under the bush. Julius squatted on the ground, reached forward until his hands rested on the ground and willed the transformation to take place. As a wolf he stood a better chance of finding the red bitch and Michael. So methodical had Anna been in concealing her tracks and scent that minutes turned into hours before the black wolf finally found her true trail.

It paused before the entrance, yellow feral eyes glared down the passage of twisted roots. Animal self preservation took over, to go down the passage to Michael's secret place was deliberately inviting death. Coward he may be but Julius was not a fool, he could wait, they wouldn't leave together, the only thought that troubled him was if the red bitch left before Michael.

The black wolf turned and began its journey back to where the instrument of Anna's death was hidden. Once he reached that point Julius changed back, but he remained naked, once he had killed Anna he would need the speed of the wolf to return to the Keep before Michael. Julius held the axe in both of his hands and made an imaginary sweep at where the red bitches head would be. He had waited, how many life times for this, to destroy Anna for good. "Michael." He snarled letting the axe fall, the keen blade biting deep into the soil. "One day." He said "One day."

Their lovemaking was tender, they enjoyed the touch and feel of each others body. Hands, mouths, bodies touching, responding , exploring each other as if it was the first time they had mated. Michael felt her lips on the tender parts of his neck, he thrilled as her tongue ran a wet path over him. His body burnt as Anna's teeth nipped the soft folds of skin below his ears, he matched her thrusting with his own. Not in lust, not in a hot quick mating of wolves in heat, but gently, slowly savouring every precious second of these magical moments. And when they were incapable of responding to each others sexual demands, they wrapped their arms and legs around each other. Like innocents in their own private garden of Eden they lay entwined, satisfied with bodily contact.

When they were not making love they splashed like playful children in the warm waters of the pool. Happy and contented believing themselves to be secure in this place, they used each other, hands, tongues, lips, teeth to bring each of them to dizzying heights of sexual pleasure. And when their bodies rebelled and they were forced to rest they lay in each others arms. If they were aware of it, neither of them mentioned or considered the passing of the days.

The wolf man opened his eyes and looked at the woman laying next to him. Michael took joy in looking at Anna's naked body, where the Countess was heavy and full breasted, Anna was small. Where the Countess was large hipped and voluptuous, Anna was slim. Michael reached out and took one of her breasts between his fingers rolling the nipple, Anna sighed and moved in her sleep. Slowly, insistently he rubbed at the nipples feeling them harden under his touch. He lifted the sleepy woman until she was resting against him. One hand cupped around her breast he began to squeeze it, his free hand reached down and touched the brittle texture of the hairs between her thighs. Michael moved his hand with a deliberate purpose until he was touching the lips of her vagina. Gently he probed the soft wet entrance, feeling the warmth of her. Anna opened her thighs and reaching down pressed his fingers into her. Slowly at first then slightly faster she rotated her hips forcing his fingers to go deeper into her.

Michael pulled back her head and their mouths closed over each other, he returned his hand to her breast, pulling, squeezing. He felt the juices run from her covering his probing fingers, then Anna gave a little cry and released the flood of love juice that had built up inside of her. Anna pulled his hand from between her legs, turned and pushed Michael onto his back. Their lovemaking was quick, both eager to reach a climax.

Michael brushed away the wet hair from around her face, he kissed both her closed eyes, the tip of her nose, her lips tasting the saltiness of her sweat. Anna dug her fingers into his back and held him, the intensity of her grip surprising him. She was holding him against her with a strength he had not believed she possessed.

Anna emerged from the water, its silver droplets running down her body, she looked at the sleeping man. She lifted her head and looked up through the hole in the canopy, could she count the millions of stars in that one small hole. A sadness gripped her, why try and count the impossible, Anna knew that this time was coming to an end. She knelt before Michael, something deep within her told her the time to tell him was now. Anna fought against the thoughts that entered her mind, she did not want to tell him, she didn't want to loose him. But wasn't that why she had asked him to allow her to hunt with him. Hadn't she put off this moment a thousand times before, had she not let the years slip by withholding information which would free Michael from the Countess's grip. Why now? Why now, what was leading her down this path?

"Anna," She turned at the sound of her name on Michaels lips "What is it? What's wrong?" Anna shook her head, the wolf man took her in his arms and held her to him, feeling her tremble, "You are troubled," He said "I feel it." She pressed her face against his chest, "Yes." came her muffled answer.

How could she possibly explain it to him, her mind was a jumbled whirling mess of thoughts. Then a thought entered her mind, a darker deeper thought, and she saw with a clarity as if the thought had been written in black on white paper. She was going to die.

She was going to die, she found the very thought of it ridiculous, she couldn't die could she? The impossible thought raced across her mind, there were only two ways in which a moon child could die, and only she and the Countess knew them. The dreadful thought persisted, she could not shake it free, it was numbing her soul, she was going to die.

Had all this, these last few days been her last chance at living the memories of what could have been. The tenderness, the happiness she had found in Michaels arms. Were they a reward from the fallen one for what she was about to tell him. Or was it some perverse gift from the dark gods before she fell into that darkness from which she would never wake.

Michael felt the violent trembling of Anna's body and held her as close as possible. A strange lightness touched Anna's heart. What had to be would be, the outcome of her dark thoughts became a welcome guest. She would know a sleep like she had not known for centuries, no longer would her dreams be tarnished by the fallen one or his dark gods. At last she would be finally free. She pressed her lips to his chest, Michael lifted her head and kissed her. The touch of his mouth on hers was sweet "I love you." Michael was surprised when Anna pushed him away and sat back on her haunches.

"Sit there Michael and please don't move." Michael smiled at her and did as he was told. Anna ran her fingers through the thick grey hair, across his brow and down his face. Fingers touched, nose, lips, chin. Anna was mentally storing up memories. When she reached the scar on his shoulder she stopped with a painful slowness. She traced the outline of the five pointed star. "I thank you Michael Cavendish for these last few days."

"A very formal," He began, Anna pressed her fingers to his lips "Do not speak." she said. Michael looked into those green eyes, he saw love, a sadness that told him that what she was about to say would cause her great pain.

"I must be allowed to speak. I must tell you things you should know." Anna took his face in her hands and kissed him knowing that it would be for the last time. "When I begin to speak you must not interrupt me, and you must believe what I tell you." The wolf man saw the pleading look which came to her eyes, believe what I say to you. Michael blinked, was he being given a look into her very thoughts, was she allowing him to look into the window of her soul? "You must believe Michael." Anna stared into his eyes "Yes." She said "you will believe for I see it in your eyes." Anna smiled telling him the truth would be far easier than she would have believed. Making him leave her when she had done, that would be the hardest part.

"I will begin now Michael Cavendish and when I am finished you will leave me alone in this place and I beg you not to look back, hush, do not weaken my resolve , not now, and did I not say you were not to speak, just sit there and listen.

What I now tell you is part legend, part truth, you and I are living proof of it, part of superstitious folk lore. I cannot go into exact details for I do not know all of them, I can only tell you what I know and the things that are important to you. Things that will help you come to terms with what and who you are when you leave the Keep."

"The legend of the werewolf has been told and retold wherever men gathered in groups. They did not know if it actually existed but they needed a dark force to pit against whatever gods they believed in. Was just a creature of darkness invented to scare children to keep them inside when darkness fell. The secret of the werewolf should have remained just that, a secret, but the priest of the fallen one disclosed it. They rebelled against the old religion because it gave them a way to control the simple minds of those they ruled."

"The actual beginnings of the werewolf are shrouded in mystery, perhaps it was a discredited priest thrown out of the old religion. Could it have been a man foolish enough to tamper with things he did not know about. I have been told and believe it, that the fallen one created the first werewolf on this earth. Remember Michael he was the right hand of God before he was thrown out of heaven, minutes before he fell he was an angel. Could he have been the first one, I don't know. Do you think the creation of such creatures like us was his revenge, a god who refused to let him continue being his right hand. Whatever way it happened it unleashed a hell on earth."

"Are we some colossal joke Michael Cavendish to pander to the darker side of mans superstitions. Is that what we are Michael, a grotesque joke, to prey on humans , to create others like ourselves, to perpetuate the fallen ones revenge. Am I making sense Michael, do you begin to understand anything I am telling you? I know it's almost impossible to believe, it's nearly impossible to explain the reason as we are what we are and why we were created in the first place."

"Look at me Michael, am I not beautiful, I see by your eyes you think so, have we not always enjoyed each others body. Think of the Countess Michael, is she not also beautiful and you have spent many nights enjoying her body. How old do you think we are Michael, how old are you, you cannot begin to guess can you?"

"In the normal span of things we should have died centuries ago, you should have died Michael, you are long beyond your allotted span. You should be a rotting corpse by now and I see by your eyes you know that to be the truth. Look at me, touch my flesh, does it not feel young and firm, a mere child , not much older than nineteen, twenty perhaps. I was like this when Attila the Hun carved his way across the then known world. Please Michael do not draw back from me, please. I was created at the same time as the woman who calls herself the countess Elizabeth Dressler. We were friends back then, young innocent girls who became enamoured to a man. A man like you Michael, a warrior who carried on his shoulder the kiss of the fallen one. I do not even remember his name, but he turned us , both of us. But he did not impart enough of the knowledge to us before he rode away. He never returned to find us."

"As time and years passed us by we were forced to find places to hide. For a while we stayed young, those around us grew old and died. At first it was a wonderful gift to remain forever young, we had immortality. I have looked like this for over four hundred years."

"I will not bore you with the passage of centuries but the immortality we had found became a double edged sword, this gift of ours. We could not remain in any one place for more than a few years, we could not be discovered for what we were. The loneliness was the hardest part to bear, loneliness Michael, two females locked forever in youthful bodies. But who to share it with, oh we took lovers but not for any length of time, we dare not. We tried in our desperation to create others like ourselves but always we failed, we did not have the knowledge. Then one glorious day we found the way, oh it was by accident, but we succeeded. But with the knowledge we sank into a morass of depravity. Try to imagine what we became Michael, try, for unless you wish to remain forever alone this could become your future. I see in your eyes you don't want to create another like yourself. What will you do then, become like Elizabeth a despicable monster living only for self preservation and pleasure at the expense of others."

"What will you do Michael, stay in the Keep forever, until the end of this wearisome world. I doubt it , for you are restless now, you want to move on, only fear keeps you tied to that damnable place. A fear of the unknown, like the superstitious peasants even you fear the unknown. You in particular have nothing to fear, you are strong, a warrior , you are still able to act and think like a rational human being. That is why Julius hates you and the Countess herself fears you."

"I made Julius you know, I made that hateful creature against my better judgement. He has no soul, he is totally evil, he kills for the sake of killing. I created them all and for the silliest of reasons. I was so lonely I wanted, needed to have company. I needed a man to share my bed with, I needed females to talk to, companionship of my own sex. Such a waste for none are completely right, but I dare not kill them, for the law which rules our lives says we must not kill one of our own. You escaped death by a very fine line Michael for you killed two of the pack before you had completely turned. That is why you still have your cursed life, still I have often wondered if we could have actually killed you. I am tired now I need to rest."

Anna stretched relieving muscles cramped from kneeling so long, mouth dry from talking. Michael watched as she bent and drank her fill from the waters of the pool. He did not speak, he had listened to what she had , had to say. He turned her words over in his mind, if only half of what she had told him was the truth, then the need to know more was paramount. How had they brought about the change, even if he never used it he needed the knowledge. Why did the star shaped scar fascinate her and cause the Countess to fear him, he knew now for certain who these mysterious people were who lived by the old religion and would always help him in times of trouble, Gypsies. Let Anna rest, when she was ready she would tell him more, Michael did not know how much more there was, but when she spoke he would listen.

While the red she wolf slept Michael's thoughts returned to the Keep. He did not think of the Countess but of a dark skinned petulant man who cringed behind her like the dog he was. Even when Julius was around Michael likened him to a rabid dog, dangerous, unpredictable, he would never attack face on if the chance to slink in the shadows and wait while his prey was unprepared . Law or no law Michael made a conscious decision that should Julius try and stop him leaving the Keep, Julius would die. The wolf man never even considered the thought that perhaps he would be the one to die. Still there was time to consider his options, when Anna had finished her story, he only knew that whatever she told him the time had come for him to leave the Keep.

The pale rays of moonlight filtered into his secret place through the hole in the canopy, its beams sparkled on the waters. A small rodent oblivious to the two humans who slept wrapped in each others arms, gathered a few strands of moss. It scampered over the carpet of moss, unaware of a pair of unblinking eyes watching. The owl hopped from foot to foot as the rodent disappeared into a crack in the rocks, it had been deprived of a meal.

Sounds of the forest filtered into the ears of the sleeping man, Michael stirred. His keen sense of hearing picked up the sounds of animals both large and small feeding furtively, forever on the lookout for danger. He heard the sound of leaves being torn from branches by a rising wind. The smell of rain was in the air, soon the soft summer night would be replaced by a summer downpour. Michael knew that the forest would welcome the rain after a prolonged period of dry weather. It was needed to replenish the new growth and to rot the dead leaves of winter.

Here in his secret place Michael knew that the winds would not disturb them. A fine tenuous mist caused by the rising heat of the water and the colder air coming in through the hole, clung to the top of the canopy.

Michael lifted himself onto his elbows when he heard the howl of a hunting wolf. The long mournful cry stirred his blood, the lonely howling trailed off when it received no reply. "Is it the voice of a moon child." Michael started at the sound of Anna's voice, "It seeks a companion to hunt with." Anna rested her head against the wolf mans back, Michael heard the tremor in her voice. When next she spoke, "It can't be Julius can it, you don't think he's hunting for us?"

Michael folded her into his arms holding her tight to him, he pressed his lips to her forehead and said "I doubt it, I don't think that Julius is brave enough to hunt us on his own. It could be another member of the pack." When Anna didn't speak Michael began to talk. "Anna I had the strangest of dreams, I can't remember it all. To be truthful I can only remember what must have been its ending before I woke." Michael paused and wondered how he should continue, there was no easy way of recounting it "I saw a dead wolf and I know, don't ask me how I know, I just do. Anna it was one of the pack." Anna stiffened in his arms, catching a sob in her throat. "And I saw you Anna, but you were a long way away from me, I could not reach you." She felt his arms tighten around her as if he never wanted to let go of her. Michael held her from him and looked down at her. "I have the strangest feeling that when I leave this place you and I will never see each other again."

"I too have this feeling and I know it to be true, give me a little time and I will tell you more of what you need to know."

Anna closed her eyes, so he too had dreamed of the dead wolf, did he suspect that he had witnessed her death. No he didn't understand his dream, he looked puzzled and worried by it. Here in Michael's secret place she knew she was safe, with Michael by her side she had all the protection she needed. It was when Michael left she knew that her death at unknown hands would happen. Anna pushed her fears to the back of her mind, Michael sat waiting for her to speak.

"This." She said touching the pentacle "this makes you different to all of us. It was put there by someone who believed in the old religion. It was put there to save your life by one who loved you." Anna's finger was cool on the pointed scar. "No doubt they prayed that you would never meet one of us, but if you did that the one you met would show you the way to freedom." Anna took her hand away, "It puts you totally apart from werewolves like me. And now I must tell you something that the Countess never would, but also remember Michael there are some things you will have to learn by yourself."

"I have told you that I believe the fallen one created us, and when he saw what was happening to us he felt a little touch of pity for what we had or were becoming. For from him sprang the people of the old religion, it matters little now that many have turned from him to their new gods. They were created to protect his moon children, and from among them he picked special people. These he called the Guardian and the Wych, the Guardian to protect unto death the life of the Wych. The Wych, to help the werewolf to survive in a situation that would bring them close to death. The Wych woman has the power to stop the changing, not forever, but long enough for the werewolf to regain his or her strength."

"When danger threatens you, when you are one inch from certain death, she will call to you. You will hear her and her power will force you to live."

"For unless you are killed by a silver bullet or a weapon forged from silver, oh it's true, silver can kill us. But to be killed by such a weapon it must be wielded by one who loves you and is willing to die beside you."

"There is another way to destroy the werewolf, your head must be severed from your body by whatever means possible to your attacker. The priest of the old religion who turned from the fallen one disclosed this to mankind. They have hunted us almost to extinction over the centuries. There is also a way that is not often spoken of among the packs. Two werewolves can fight to the death, not wholly wolf, not whole man but in a half altered state. In such a contest there can be no winner, for by the laws of the fallen one the rest of the pack have his permission to destroy the winner. If the winner escapes he or she must forever live as an outcast shunned by all moon children and their packs."

"Other than those ways I have described to you Michael Cavendish you are destined to live forever. But remember the Wych woman, call to her and she will answer you. She will give you the strength to go on and no matter how long it takes she will guide you to safety. If not to complete safety at least to a place where you can rest and regain your strength."

"I have little more to say to you, except perhaps the most painful thing you will ever have to bear. You can love and live a dozen lives, you will no doubt give your seed to many women, but she will never give you a child. We can create other monsters like ourselves but we can never, ever produce our own offspring's."

"Now I have said all I intend to say, the rest you must learn for yourself. I want you to go now, I wish to be left alone." Anna stood up and turned her back on him. Michael wanted to say something, anything, but he didn't know what to say to her.

"No matter where I go, no matter what happens to me in the years to come I will always carry with me the memory of you." Anna dare not turn to him, she did not want him to see her tears. Michael stared at her back not wanting to leave her here alone, not really wanting to go away. But he knew in his heart that he had to go, he had no choice. "Thank you for all you have been to me and all you have done, farewell Anna."

She heard the man's body begin to change, she felt every second of the painful transformation of man into beast. Anna turned at the last moment and watched the grey wolf disappear down the tunnel. "Goodbye Michael my love may you find whatever it is you seek."

Julius stirred, he heard the sound of claws dragging a body along the ground. He had no fear of his scent being detected, the rain had washed away his spoor. Holding his breath Julius waited, he saw the grey wolf emerge from the tunnel, stand a moment before it began to run towards the forest away from the direction of the Keep. Julius smiled, if the grey wolfs actions ran true to form it would be at least two more days before it returned to the Keep. Now all he had to do was wait for the red bitch to show herself.

Anna stood and looked around Michael's secret place for the last time. She lay on the mossy carpet and began to remember and as she remembered she willed the change to come over her.

The red she wolf pushed her way out of the tunnel, she did not see the axe descend. Briefly she felt the keen edge touch her neck. The steel blade sliced through the neck severing the she wolfs head from her body. The axe buried itself into the soft ground separating the head from the still twitching body. Julius grinned insanely down at Anna's body, giggling he fell on his knees before it and plunged his hands into the open wound. He held bloody hands before his face savouring the smell and sight of the red liquid. Julius smeared his face and torso with Anna's blood. He opened his mouth and allowed the yellow fangs to force their way into his mouth. Bending his head he sank his fangs into Anna's dead breast and tore away a bleeding chunk of it. Julius swallowed the red meat and threw back his head, at the last moment he remembered where he was and what he had done. He dare not let the grey wolf hear his triumphant cry, Julius lay down beside the body of Anna and let the change take him over.

The black wolf opened its mouth and grabbed the hair of the dead woman's head. Anna's eyes and mouth were open wide in surprise at the suddenness of her death. Picking up the head the black wolf turned its face towards the Keep and began to run.

"Michael, thank god you have returned to me." The Countess rushed towards him and flung her arms around him. Michael pushed her away and looked at the woman who had spent countless nights in his bed. That she was glad to see him he could see in her face, there was a joy there when she looked at him. Michael felt his stomach churn as she touched his face with her hand, he knocked it down.

"You call on a strange deity madam." He said his voice cold and distant "to thank god."

"I would call on any of the gods, be they dark or light as long as you return safely to me." The Countess searched his face looking for some sign that he was at least pleased to be in her company, there was none. "Where have you been all this time?"

"I wanted my own company." Michael made to pass her. The Countess stepped in front of him. Michael moved to the right to step by her, the Countess moved in front of him again, "May I not pass madam?" He asked his voice dangerously low and menacing. Michael matched her stare, the Countess saw the loathing he had for her in his eyes.

"Since my concern for you falls on stony ground," she said and motioned him by with a wave of her hand. "It also appears you do not wish my company," she added. Michael bowed low and benefited her with a mocking smile which seemed to say "You are so right." The wolfman walked past her and began to ascend the stone staircase, from the corner of his eye he caught a movement from behind the drapes. Michael smiled, the Countess's dog Julius, he was never far from her beck and call. At the top of the stairs he turned and looked down at the Countess. "Before I leave in the morning, we shall talk of many things, you and I, and bring this dog with you." Michael moved quickly, pulled aside the drapes and seized Julius by his neck. The dark skinned mans fingers tore at Michael trying to prise them from his throat. Michael squeezed until Julius's eyes rolled in their sockets. The wolfman released him, Julius dropped to the floor. Coughing and spluttering, fighting for breath Julius staggered to his feet. Michael steered him to the top of the stairs and pushed, Julius fought to regain his balance, he failed and bounced down the stone steps to land sickeningly at the Countess's feet. Julius stared up at Michael his eyes blazed with an uncontrollable hatred for the Englishman, Julius wiped his hand across his bleeding mouth and looked at his own blood staining his fingers. "One day." He cried, he forced himself to get up, Michael's assault had caused numerous small wounds on the man's unprotected face and arms but he showed no desire to want to fight.

"Why wait Julius, let's finish it now." Michael gripped the hilt of his sword and waited for the dark man to except his challenge. The Countess took hold of Julius's arm and pulled him behind her. "Protecting your lap dog to the bitter end?" Asked Michael.

"No Michael," she said in a voice surprisingly full of concern. "I'm protecting you."

"From what Countess, him?" Michael laughed and pointed his unsheathed blade at Julius "I think not."

"From the pack, to stop you breaking the law, you still have much to learn Michael."

Michael bit his lip and held back the words he was about to speak, no, don't give anything away, not yet. Let her believe that he still needed her. The morning would be soon enough to tell her that he knew everything he needed to leave her and the Keep behind him forever. Michael snapped the sword back into its scabbard and turned away from the Countess and Julius. The dark man grinned, so the Englishman still believed every word the Countess said. Julius wondered how Michael would react when the Countess showed him the head of the red she wolf. If they were lucky Michael would loose control of himself and if that happened, would the Countess let him kill him. He would have to wait and see, but the waiting could be a sweet thing if the touch of the Countess's hands on his body meant anything.

Michael closed the door behind him and shot the bolts, tonight of all nights he wanted no distractions. He had nearly blurted out all of what Anna had told him, and he would have killed Julius given the chance, and the Countess. Her life depended on what was to happen when next they met, strange, he felt no remorse in the fact that he was most probably going to have to kill her also.

Michael touched the blade, it still retained its keenness despite having been sheathed all these years. Carefully he ran one finger along each edge of it, it felt strange to hold its like again, to be prepared to use it for the purpose it had been forged for to kill. "Old friend." He said holding the blade with both hands. "Tomorrow you drink a red wine if things go badly for me." Michael shoved all thoughts of his next meeting with the Countess aside, he lay the naked blade on his bed and stripped off his clothes. He needed rest, he would sleep for he needed to be alert and prepared for what the Countess would do.

The Countess lay on her back, the dark skinned Julius between her legs. If Michael did not want her, she knew that Julius did. She met his urgent thrusting with her own. She clung to him as he drove his penis hard and deep into her, her teeth chewed at the flesh of his throat and chest. Bloody wounds where she had bitten away the top layer of his skin. If Julius felt it he didn't stop, he pushed harder and harder into the Countess's wet throbbing hole.

Elizabeth Dressler felt herself come, it flooded her vagina and ran free from it, soaking the man and the bed beneath them. Her mind raced as a second climax took hold of her, she closed her eyes and thought of another man who should have been laying on top of her. Julius pushed at her, his body lifting then pressing down hard upon hers. An orgasm of almost uncontrollable sexual lust ripped through the Countess's body, her juices poured out in a hot wet, sticky stream. She screamed her pleasure aloud as Julius spent his seed deep inside of her, she heard the squelching as their sexes met and Julius then withdrew his for another thrust. The heady scent of mingled love juices prevailed over every other scent in the Countess's bedroom, and she cried out Michael's name aloud.

Julius in the throes of sexual orgasm heard her call out the hated name and snarling he pulled himself from inside of her. So powerful was his orgasm that his sperm splattered across the Countess's stomach, he almost threw himself from the bed. The Countess's eyes shot open at the sudden departure of Julius from inside of her. Then the realisation of the name she had cried aloud came to her. Julius stood before the bed, black hairs covered his body, fangs filled his mouth dripping with saliva. The Countess smiled at him, "Come back." Julius shook his head. She opened her legs and gave him a clear view of her wet pink sex. Slowly she moved her hand down between her legs and thrust her fingers inside herself. She held the fingers up for Julius to see, they were coated in a mixture of both their juices, "Come." she said. The Countess put the fingers into her mouth and licked them clean, Julius fought to keep his emotion down. A second time Elizabeth Dressler put her fingers deep into her sex and rotated them around inside herself, she held the sex coated fingers up to Julius. "I need you," She moaned. Fingers between her legs she began to move her body in time with her thrusting. "Come to me Julius, I need you inside of me, I need more, I want more."

"Then call on the Englishman." Julius spit out every word, "See if he will service you."

"To me dog." Her face changed, she was no longer pleading with Julius to return to her bed, she was demanding it. "Do to me what you were created for." Julius shook his head and stepped away from the bed, it had taken almost all of his self control to keep his penis from hardening. "I want your weapon inside of me Julius, I want sex, I need sex, do it."

Julius refused to move, he stood there and stared at the wondrous naked body of the Countess. But he could not return to her, she had called out Michael's name, not his. "So." Said the Countess throwing her legs over the edge of the bed and sitting up. "The lap dog has decided to bark." She stood oblivious to the thick stream of mingled juices which seeped from inside of her and onto her upper thighs. "Do you intend to bite me, did I not kick you enough when you were a puppy?" Julius heard the scorn in her voice, every word she uttered driving a dagger into his soul. "Bark for me then." The Countess, hands on hips spread her legs and thrust her sex at him in a rotating movement. "Bark Julius." she said advancing on him, she reached down and began rubbing herself. "Take it Julius, put your face here, bark into this." Julius could not tear his eyes from her dripping sex, the fingers she had inside of her held him riveted to the spot. He was totally unprepared for what happened next, the Countess changed from an alluring woman offering him her ultimate prize into a snarling spitting beast.

Her hand shot out and Julius screamed in pain, hard horny nails ripped him from shoulder to belly button. Unable to avoid the next blow Julius tried to roll with it, the Countess's nails tore open his face, a large flap of skin hung on his chin. White bone was exposed, his arm erupted in a white hot pain as the Countess struck with both hands. Julius screamed again and again as the Countess more wolf than human attacked him. There was no way Julius was able to defend himself against her frenzied attack.

Breathing heavily, eyes blazing with a feral anger, her face a distorted mask of a killing beast the Countess poised herself, ready to deliver another blow over the badly beaten man. Julius whimpered and whined, his hand raised in a futile gesture as if trying to ward off the next blow. The Countess fell to her knees and straddled the man's body, her clawed fingers reached out and took his throat. She tilted her head and allowed the fangs to fill her mouth and bent to him. Hard, sharp fangs broke the skin of his neck, Julius unable to control himself defecated and the wet stream of urine splashed the woman's leg. It saved Julius's life, the Countess began to regress, Julius's misfortune stopped her from ripping out his throat. Human once more she pushed herself up and away from the soiled man. Elizabeth Dressler looked down at Julius, cold feral eyes examined his bloody and torn body , at the wetness that covered his lower body mixing with the mess he had ejected from his bowels, and she began to laugh.

Julius curled in a ball, hands over his ears trying to shut out the sound of her hysterical laughter and the shame that he was feeling. The pain and damage she had inflicted on him meant nothing, but that she should laugh at him.

The Countess looked at her bloody hands, at the strips of flesh and congealing blood clinging to them. She gave Julius a look of total and utter contempt before leaving the cringing man where he lay.

Michael shot bolt upright, wide awake, eyes open, hand reaching for the hilt of his sword. The snarling of a wolf moving in for the kill, the screams of a badly wounded animal. Then he relaxed realising where he was, he had a good idea where the screams were coming from and who's they were. It seemed the Countess had finally lost all patience with her lap dog. Good, it would save him the job of killing Julius in the morning. He lay down again and allowed the nature of the beast to take over, conserving all of his strength and needing a clearness of mind for the coming hours.

Michael made preparations for his journey, he had dressed in warm clothing for soon the first winds of winter would come howling over the mountains and summer would be just a pleasant memory. He had put on his riding habit, leather breeches, wool shirt, a woollen jerkin with fur trimmed collar and thigh boots, why, he wasn't quiet sure there were no horses for him to ride. In the wide belt he stuck two pistols then he strapped on his sword belt, easing the blade in its scabbard, he knew it would come out quickly if he needed it.

He looked around the room that had been his home for god knows how long, he laughed aloud, home. Prison was a more apt name for it, but he knew no matter what happened to him in the outside world he had no intentions of remaining within the walls of the Keep. Once he had escaped the clutches of the Countess perhaps he would be lucky and find a place where he could live out his cursed life.

Michael reached for the door handle, he was ready now to face the she wolf in its lair. At any other time this thought may well have amused him, not now. Michael had only one particular thought in mind. Nothing and no one would be allowed to stand in his way, and he felt justified in killing both the Countess and Julius if they did. Was there such a thing as a justifiable killing, Michael doubted it, the only thing he could think of for what he would do if needs be, was revenge.

Revenge for what had been done to him, revenge for the lies the Countess had told to keep him prisoner inside the Keep. And if revenge was the reason he used to do all he considered necessary to escape, then so be it. He would carry the burden of his actions forever, a memory of a big Swede entered his mind, what would have Sven said, funny he hadn't thought of his past life for many long days. Sven would be dead and buried close to his home, if he hadn't fallen on some obscure battlefield, so would that little bastard Gasper and the despotic Prince he had served.

The silver cross given to him in friendship lay on the table, Michael picked it up, would the god it represented give him the protection he sorely needed? Would it help him stay alive for the possibility that he might die crossed his mind. He put the cross in his belt pouch, this was no time for memories of what could have been. No time for the possibilities of what could be, it was no time for regrets. No regrets for his past, his present or his future it was a time to act. From out of the dim past the voice of his friend came to him, "Go to hell in your own way". No, it wasn't that that Sven had said, Michael remembered the words exactly, "Find death in your own way." And his answer to his old friend rang with the clarity of bells in his mind. "I have every intention of doing so."

The Countess had put him on this slippery path to Hell, and if Hell was to be where he spent eternity, then others would join him, if need be. Michael shook his head and pounded his fist on the table, he felt the pain as splinters of wood entered his hand. He flexed the hand and pulled out the wood, "Get on with it." His thoughts screamed at him, "Act now."

When the door to his room banged shut behind him Michael knew that one part of his cursed life had been forever closed. No matter what happened to him in the next ticking of life's clock he knew he must find new doors to open to him. But first the Countess and that hell spawned dog of hers Julius.

Michael pushed open the door to the Countess's room and walked in, the

Countess was sat in the large ornate, gold painted chair she always sat in. Michael could almost believe time had reverted itself, the woman, the room, the chair, it had looked like this when he had entered this room for the first time a hundred years ago. The Countess raised the silver goblet and toasted him. "Welcome to my home Michael Cavendish." She raised the goblet and sipped from it, then placed it down on the long table that divided the room. She looked beautiful sat at the head of the table, dressed in a body hugging dress of the purest white silk. Her hair carefully drawn back from her face so that all men could admire the beauty of it. "It appears you are dressed for a journey." The Countess laughed, once he Michael had thought the sound of her laughter wonderful, now he hated the sound of it. Her every word dripped with scorn. "And how pray will you travel on this journey of yours?" she picked up the goblet and as she drank she stared at him over the rim.

"Whatever and whichever way is open to me." The Countess put down her drink and almost fastidiously pushed it away with one finger.

"You know there is only one way you can leave here." So, thought Michael the threats begin, he had expected them anyway, but it didn't matter, Anna had told him all he needed to escape this particular trap of the Countess.

"Then that is the way I take." He said, he waited for her to state openly the threats her voice only hinted at. But she continued to smile, to play the concerned friend, a soft voice only thinking of his welfare.

"How will you survive out there Michael, how will you cope with a world that has left your kind behind?"

"My kind?" He said "Do you mean the man I was, if so then my kind will always be with us. Men who are prepared to live and die by sword or pistol ball. I have been and always will be one small cipher in the world's scheme of things." Michael lent forward and placed his hands on the table. "If you mean by my kind the creature I have become."

"How will you hide what you are?" Her lips curled in a sneer, her eyes held contempt for him. "Where will you hide?" Her voice rose higher with each word, flesh whitening as her fingers gripped the arms of the chair. "Who will teach you what you need to know?"

"Teach." The word erupted from Michael's mouth. "Teach me, you evil bitch." The Countess flinched at his words. "I don't need you, I've never needed you, oh you turned me into what I am. But this thing on my shoulder, I was chosen for this fate long before I met you." The Countess reached out to cover his hand with hers, Michael knocked it away. "I know it all."

"So, the red bitch confided in you, did you enjoy her Michael, was she as good as me between your legs?" The Countess reached across the table and pulled the large silver salver towards her. She smiled at Michael before she spoke. "I would have staked my life on the fact that she would betray me." Her fingers toyed with the handle of the large lid. "How good was she Michael? She will never be as good as me, never." She lifted the lid and Michael felt his stomach turn as he fought to hold down its contents.

The Countess had placed Anna's head on the silver salver and around it she had arranged a selection of vegetables. The eyes and mouth were still wide open in shock. Michael turned to look at the Countess, she sat there holding the lid and smirking up at him. "My my Michael, doesn't she look just good enough to eat." Michael found himself unable to tear his eyes away from the horrific sight. Then he howled his pain and anger out aloud. "You bitch." He screamed.

The Countess looked at him and burst out in a fit of hysterical laughter, that was when Michael went mad. He vaulted the table and hit her full in the face as he landed. Her nose split wide open and cartilage snapped, he hit her a second and a third time. Under the impact of his fist her cheek was ripped open and blood poured down her chin to drop its red petals on the white dress. Michael caught her by the throat and lifted her up, holding her so that her feet just touched the floor. Again and again he rained blows on her unprotected face, hearing bones break, her blood splattered his face.

The Countess was thrown bodily across the room, she hit the stone wall and fell to the floor, unmoving. She turned her ruined face and glared at him, through broken lips she snarled, white hair sprang up out of her flesh. Her mouth widened to accommodate the fangs, fingers curled and became claws.

The white wolf flew at Michael, he moved seconds before she reached him, the sword hissed free. Michael chopped at her, feeling the blade bite into flesh, and the white wolf screamed. It turned in mid air, its left side coated with blood, it landed spread legged and looked at the man.

Michael flashed the blade before its face, the yellow eyes followed the passage of the sword. "Come on Countess." Michael taunted the white wolf. "Kill me if you can." The wolf snapped at him, Michael's sword moved swiftly, it ran along the wolfs muzzle and took out its left eye. Snapping and snarling in pain the white wolf rolled over and over. "Change you bitch." Cried Michael "You have to change, you can't kill me as you are." The white wolf halted its jump and came to a skidding stop. "You have to change you bitch, change."

Slowly the Countess got to her feet, blood ran down her left side, Michael had sliced her open from hip to knee, her face was a battered mess, her beauty ruined for all time. She stared at him through the one eye, the empty socket weeping blood.

"I know the ways Countess, death by the hand of one prepared to die with you. I change and we fight to the death, I won't give you that chance. I give you the same death you gave Anna." Half crouching the Countess waited to attack, but the flicking blade held her at arms length. "I intend taking your head Countess."

"Anna was right Countess, we can live as a wolf, kill as a wolf, but to kill one another we have to look into each others eyes."

The one eye of the Countess glared at him from the ruined beauty, an almost ridiculous thought came to him, he wanted to tell her why he was doing this thing to her. Then that was pointless, she knew why he was going to kill her. What happened next almost caught him by surprise, from her standing position she sprang at him. He managed to shift his head slightly to one side, the claws ripped through the thick wool of his sleeve. He gritted his teeth as they scored along his arm tearing flesh, spinning he put space between him and the Countess. He risked a glance at his arm, only the thickness of the woollen jerkin and his shirt had saved his sword arm permanent damage.

She came at him fast and this time he was not able to dodge her, fingers caught his hair and he was dragged forward towards her fangs. He rammed the hilt of his sword into the already battered face, again and again he struck. Bone and flesh were ripped from her face under his violent assault.

He felt himself falling, they hit the table together landing in a tangled heap on the floor. Teeth sank into his wrist, Michael cried out in pain, Michael brought the sword down as hard as he could , steel met flesh and carved deep into the Countess's leg. Free, Michael, using the table heaved himself out of the Countess's grip, as she tried to lift herself Michael struck out with his foot. It caught the Countess under the heart, she opened her mouth in agony, a gargling grunt came from it.

Finding her feet the Countess stood rigid, she had never experience pain like it. Not only had Michaels boot hit her directly on the heart it had broken major blood vessels. Thick black blood poured out of her mouth, she staggered around the table using it to support herself . Her clawed hands scraped along the wood, Michael gritted his teeth at the sound they made. She was still coming after him, she was a dead woman refusing to die. Blood ran into her one good eye, she wiped it clean, the white fur on her arm turned red.

"Die you bitch, die damn you."

The bloody mask erupted into a strangled laugh, he saw a blood clotted tongue run over shattered lips. She was collecting what strength she had left for one last attack. Michael backed off, his eyes never leaving her face, watching and waiting for her attack. He brought the sword down as she made her move, it hit her across the wrist severing the hand from her arm. The Countess threw back her head and screamed, Michael moved fast, the sword hit the Countess just below the chin, it carved into flesh and carried on through bone.

The head of the Countess hung briefly, held by a single strand of flesh before it crashed to the floor. Her torso stood upright, blood pumping in an arch soaking the wooden floor, then it too fell with a thud.

Michael stood there gulping in deep lungs full of air, sweat poured from his face, blinking his eyes to clear them. The saltiness of the sweat stinging, he licked dry lips and tasted the bitter tang of his own fear. He had always known that he must destroy the Countess if he had any chance of leaving the Keep. He now considered how close to death he himself had come, he looked at the clawed arm and realised only a fraction of wool had saved him from being a cripple.

Gently and without any thoughts or feelings of revulsion he carefully wrapped Anna's head in the torn remains of the Countess's dress. He believed he knew where to find her body and he would go there, Anna of all of them deserved a decent burial.

At the sound of Julius's voice screaming with anguish, the hairs on Michael's body stiffened and his blood ran cold. Julius hardly able to walk, his face strapped to hold in place the flesh the Countess had torn free. His arms and upper body swathed in blood stained bandages, Julius stood in the doorway. His eyes riveted on the head of the Countess, he reached out, his eyes begged , implored her not to be dead. Michael gripped the sword tighter, Julius would not prove too much of a problem in his weakened condition. But the man was a dangerous foe, he always had been, the unpredictably of his nature had been stamped in Michaels brain countless times. Hands held before him Julius attempted to walk over to the corpse, he did not have the strength, he fell to his knees emitting a strange sound, more like a cat mewing than the sound of a wolf crying for its lost love, he crawled over to the head. Holding the head in one hand he reached towards the Countess's body and dragged it to him. Sick to the stomach Michael watched him cradle the headless body, a low whimpering crooning came from him. "You bloody bastard." He snarled the words, difficult to pronounce because of his wounds. Michael reached out and snatched the head from Julius, who howled his frustration at him, callously Michael held it out to him and said.

"If I am, she made me so." He threw the head at him, deliberately out of his reach, Julius scrambled after it. He held it against his face and pressed his lips against the bloody trophy.

"You'll die for this Michael Cavendish." Still pressing the dead face against his own he tried to stand. Michael kicked his legs from beneath him and touched his chest with the blade. "I'll make you pay for this." Julius screamed the words at him, blood seeped from the corner of his mouth with effort it mingled with the blood of the Countess. "I'll find you. One day I will find you." Julius managed to get to his knees. "When you least expect me, I will destroy all that you love, everything, then I will kill you!"

Michael, his body still trembling with anger grabbed the man's hair and pulled him close. "Pray to your god that you never find me, this time I'll let you live. Next time we meet." Michael left the sentence unfinished, he let go of the man's hair and turned his back on him. Michael closed the door to the room, behind him Julius had tipped over the thin line, his brain had broken as he franticly tried to force the Countess's severed head back onto her body.

THE VALLEY - Part 5

The airstrip was nearing completion, but never the less Strobel fretted over the length of time it was taking. Plans made for the end of this year would have to be put back, the snows had come early. By the middle of August the valley was trapped in the grip of arctic conditions, all work had been stopped, poor food and inadequate shelter for the prisoners had taken its toll. He had lost at least seventy percent of his work force, somewhere out there in the man made pass a thousand bodies lay frozen. All his begging entreaties to Berlin had been met with the same reply. It was impossible to move men or machines in the present climate.

So he sat in his warm hut, drank his brandy , smoked his hand made cigarettes and fretted over the plans, and waited for the snows to melt.

Like a schoolboy receiving his first kiss Strobel jumped for joy when the first of the wagons, skidding and sliding on the glutinous mud rolled into the camp. His heart fell at the sight of his 'Fresh Labour.' A pitiful line of shambling, hollow eyed automatons. They worked, the guards saw to that, but progress was painfully slow, the number that died far outweighed the living. Strobel was constantly on the phone to Berlin, and no amount of ranting and raving and veiled threats by the men in Berlin stopped his endless request for more labourers.

By the time the airstrip was completed and the test runs were to begin, Strobel received a visit from the Men in Berlin. The short visit by those grey men caused him more than a few sleepless nights. Strobel was under the misapprehension that the men from Berlin, in their regulations leather trench coats, regulation hats and rimless glasses had come to congratulate him on the work he had carried out. He couldn't have been more wrong, they had come to question him on his punishment of the six soldiers who had raped and killed a Jewess.

Strobel when he discovered who the men were had put them to work with the Jews. They were to receive no special treatment. They lived and ate in the prison huts with the rest of the slave labour. Strobel even got Mantz to circumcise them, to him they became Jews, and they would live and die Jews.

He had fully expected being woken one morning to be told the prisoners had murdered them. It didn't happen, why the Jews had not taken their revenge on these men never ceased to amaze him.

The men in rimless glasses had made it quite plain to Strobel that he had overstepped the line. Only his lineage and usefulness to the Third Reich had stopped him from joining the six men.

Death was the only sentence that would pacify Berlin, they had tarnished the blood of the master race by having sexual intercourse with a Jew. "Death." One of the little grey men had thundered banging the top of Strobel's desk between every word, "Death is the only punishment." Faced by these men who had risen through the ranks of the Nazi party because of their liking for brutality Strobel struggled hard not to wet himself with fear. Behind him Mantz smiled, it would do Strobel good to be touched by the fear of a party that had dedicated itself to eradicating a whole race of undesirables.

Strobel was quick to realise he had no alternative but to obey and comply with the orders of the grey men from Berlin. The six men had been brought before the entire company, who had been forced to parade to see the executions. "Shoot them." Said one of the grey men, Mantz stepped forward flipping open his holster. "Not you," Said the man "Give your gun to Strobel, now you do it Major Strobel." For a moment Strobel had looked at the little man, what he saw caused him to swallow and hold onto his bowels. He could imagine him in some cellar in Berlin tormenting some bound and helpless prisoner.

Strobel took the offered pistol and walked behind the men, ordered them to kneel and quickly fired a shot into the back of their heads.

The grey men from Berlin had nodded their satisfaction, walked over to their car and without another word driven away. Strobel shivered at the thoughts of those little grey men from Berlin in their regulation apparel and made a vow. He would blow out his own brains before he ever let himself fall into their hands.

A knock on the door roused him from his thoughts and before he could call out "Enter," Captain Mantz walked in, shut the door behind him and went straight into his mornings report.

"Fresh tracks have been found again this morning sir and that sergeant of yours, Vogel, he his adamant they are wolf tracks." Strobel saw the smile on Mantz's lips, even from a country boy risen high in the social scale, clearly he didn't hold the same opinion as Vogel as to it being a wolf.

Strobel was inclined to believe his sergeant, the man was rarely wrong where his beloved dogs were concerned. And wolves after all was said and done were only dogs and Vogel certainly knew his dogs. "Sir." Said Mantz "There has never been any report of wolves in this part of the area. And as far as I can ascertain, and believe me sir, I have looked into it, there have never been any sightings of the animal."

Strobel thought for a moment before he answered Mantz. "Despite all your research Captain, on this thing I believe we should go with Vogel." He could see that his words were like a red rag to a bull. That he Strobel should take the word of a low life from Dresden against his. "After all dogs are his speciality, come Mantz, sit down."

Strobel moved over to his desk and sat down behind, his hand offering Mantz the other chair, "A cigarette?" He opened the silver case and held it out to the Captain. "A filthy habit I know, But" he waited for Mantz to light his cigarette before he continued, "Captain I want you to give Vogel the order to set traps," He pulled hard at the cigarette. "I want him to deal with it, you and I, we have more important things to think about." From under the large sheet of blotting paper he pulled an envelope and handed it across to Mantz. "I had to get permission for you to see this." He held the envelope tightly and said, "Read this and then forget what you have read, and Captain, apart from certain parties in Berlin, only you and I will ever know of it here."

Strobel watched the young mans face as he read the thin sheets of paper. No sign of emotion was anywhere to be seen, Mantz read the death sentence of millions as if checking a daily report on the shortage of food. Only towards the end of the papers did he see a flicker of disbelief in the young mans eyes. When he had finished reading Mantz put the papers in order and handed them back to Strobel. "Can you imagine what the British or any of our enemies would do if they got their hands on these?" Strobel replaced the papers under the blotter, when Mantz had gone he would put them back in their proper hiding place. "But those papers and what you are doing here, all are a contingency in case of war." Mantz selected another cigarette and said "We are not at war with Britain."

"Our leader believes we will be soon, and there are those who advise him who believe it could be before the end of the year. Nothing and nobody must be allowed to stop the final phase." Strobel handed Mantz a calendar, a red ring around the fourth of June. "On that day Iron Fist will be delivered here, and from that moment on it will only be a short time before he flies."

"So." Said Mantz in a matter of fact flat voice, "The Jews work harder, of course if we had more prisoners." He shrugged his shoulders, "You have my word that there will be no delays of any kind."

"Excellent Mantz, excellent. Would you care for a brandy?"

"French of course." Said Mantz

"Is there any other captain?" He lifted his glass to Mantz, Mantz touched his to Strobel's, "To Iron Fist."

"You are taking too many chances Moon child," Michael looked at Tibor and then at Katji. There was accusation in Tibor's eyes and words and no help from the Wych woman. "Damn you, you are risking our lives." Tibor spoke quietly, there was no threat in his voice, "Think on man, you're not a fool, we can't afford for them to know that we are here."

"Has love made a coward of you?" He snapped back at the man, all the time knowing that the fault was his, he was taking too many chances. Tibor reddened under the insult and his large hands curled into a fist. Katji placed her hand on the giants arm and tugged at him to sit down.

"He does not deserve that from you," she said "Perhaps a little cowardice on your part would help us to survive." Katji stood up and stood before the seated Giant she placed her small hand on his shoulder. "We are in a very dangerous position Michael," she stooped and looked down at the man she loved and smiled at him. "Tibor and I more than you, if they shoot us we bleed, if they shoot us enough times we die, do you?"

"Once is enough," grumbled the giant Tibor, "If it hits the right spot." There was a dangerous scent in the air inside the cave and Michael knew that he was the cause of it. Katji was right, one bullet could end their lives. He could escape any time he wished, but they had not left him when he was too wounded to travel. The giant and the girl, no she was no longer a girl she was a beautiful young woman, had both risked their lives for him. Both of them had done far more than the old religion demanded of them. It was up to him to heal the rift between them.

Michael got to his feet and started over towards them, Tibor moved and gently pulled Katji behind him. Katji saw the hurt, bewildered look on the moon child's face at Tibor's actions. Had she managed to get over her message, did the moon child understand what he was doing to them?

Michael stood before Tibor and Katji felt a strange pride fill her heart, even the moon child had to look up at her man. The tension between the two men was a tangible thing and Katji believed should she reach out she would be able to touch it. Katji prayed to her dark god, "Please don't let them fight." She knew her choice if they did would always be wrong no matter which one she chose.

"Tibor Vajek Khan, guardian and friend I ask you to forgive me for my choice of words." Katji breathed a sigh of relief as Michael spoke to her love. "I would not deliberately bring hurt to you or yours." Michael turned to the Wych woman. "I owe you both my life." He held out his hand to the giant who stared down at it moodily. Katji reached out and covered it with hers, her free hand tugging at the giants sleeve. Tibor hesitated and looked into Michaels eyes, often when they spoke they looked into each others eyes. There both men knew that if anything was being hidden they would see it.

"Tibor," Said Michael, "You have given me many things , you have told me of the outside world, most of all you have offered me a most precious gift, the gift of friendship." Still Tibor hesitated to take Michael's hand, their fingers were almost touching, Katji willed the two men to take each others hand. "Tibor," Began Michael, "I cannot change what I am, only death can do that for me."

The voice of the wolf man was tinged with bitterness as he continued to speak. "And where will I find death?" There was a loneliness in his last few words, a loneliness that was in every fibre of the wolf man's body and soul. Katji saw it in his eyes, his face, in every little movement of his body, Tibor saw a man condemned, a man cursed to live long after those he befriended or loved had passed on, a walking dead man who was not allowed to die.

"I gave you my friendship Michael not for what you are or what I am, but simply because I thought it the right thing to do." Katji clapped her hands and threw herself between the two men, Tibor clasped Michael's hand and pulled him to him. Katji laughed, tears of joy in her eyes at the sight of the two men hugging each other. The moon child looked lost in the giants embrace, Tibor freed one arm and put it around Katji. "Even the best of friends fall out." He said, they stood there for a long time not moving.

Michael sat with his back against the cave wall, he was watching Katji making their nightly meal. He looked across at Tibor , Michael knew the man would be watching Katji. He never took his eyes off her when she was around, always Tibor looked for any sign of danger to the woman he loved. "I will be more careful in future." Said Michael breaking the silence of the cave, he saw Tibor start at his words. "You have nothing to fear." He said, "Do you honestly believe that I would bring danger to Katji or to you?"

"No Michael." He said "No, I don't think you would, but something bothers me." Michael stretched his legs and looked at the man, "I see love in your eyes for my woman but what kind of love I cannot tell." Michael allowed himself a rare smile, the giant was right he did love the young woman. He could not hide it, it was stamped all over his face. It bothered Tibor that he could not decipher this love Michael had for Katji. A faraway haunted look came into the wolf man's eyes when he looked at Katji and he believed no one was watching him.

"I see hurt mixed with love in your eyes Michael. A hurt that neither Katji or I can mend."

The wolf man took his eyes off the Wych woman and turned to Tibor. "I have told you most of my story," He said "Yet, there is one part of my life I cannot yet bring myself to share, not even with you Tibor." Michael lifted his head and sniffed, he could smell the scent of summer coming to the valley. A scent of rebirth on the light breeze, the sound of new shoots of grass struggling to reach for strength from the sun. The sound of buds bursting and branches moving gently showing off their new coat of leaves. Birds busy searching the branches for materials to make a nest before mating time descended on them. Animals both large and small scurrying though the trees eager to have their own love nest completed in time. And the tinge of snow on the breeze carried down from the mountains.

"Soon Tibor, soon I will tell you all." The wolfman rested his hand over his heart "For I have dreamed a strange dream. For I know here," He said letting his fingers touch his chest and feel the constant thumping of his heart, "That when we leave this place I shall be parted from you and Katji forever."

Michael saw that the giant was thinking of what to reply. "Don't ask me how I know," said Michael "But I do, perhaps this curse I carry with me tells me when it is time to part from those I care for. Perhaps these dreams I have are a warning to me that I am going to bring danger to you."

"I don't want you to go down to the camp tonight Michael." Tibor changed the direction of the conversation, he did not want to hear that danger was being brought to his Katji. And the words of Michael had bothered him more than he cared to admit. "Too many times and someone is bound to see you."

"I have already been seen." Said the wolfman, Tibor jumped to his feet, behind them Katji let the metal spoon fall causing the cave to ring with its sound. "The little man who they call the Rat, the one in charge of the dogs."

"So it is not only your heart that tells you we must leave the valley."

"He won't betray me." Said Michael in a cold, flat matter of fact voice which said, I know I'm right. "He does not fear me, and nothing on this earth will get him to violate my trust in him and his trust in me."

"How can you be so sure?" Asked the giant, his mind whirled as he tried to make sense of Michael's words. Sense that a German soldier who held captive a thousand displaced wretches and gave no thought to their comfort or safety should be trusted with his and Katji's life. "I don't like it Michael," He said "You should have killed him. Did you not think of Katji?"

"We are safe." Said Michael "Believe me Tibor you have nothing to fear from Vogel, for when the time comes to leave this valley, Vogel comes with us."

"I think perhaps Michael," Said the Wych woman "You should tell us of this Vogel and why you put so much trust in him."

"Damn you Michael." broke in Tibor, Katji turned to him, she could see concern written all over his face, not for himself this she knew , but for her. "Why Michael, why did you do it?"

"I didn't, believe me I never intended to make contact with him or any of the men in the valley."

"Then what happened, how did it happen?" Katji had returned to her stirring of the stew in the pot, once again these two foolish men had put a strain upon their friendship. "Tell him Michael." She said "We are entitled to know how it came about, after all it is our lives you have placed in danger."

"There is no danger to either of you," said Michael, Katji slowly shook her head and turned her face to him.

"Then why do I see death's shadow hovering over you Michael?" Michael did not answer her straight away, Tibor held her to him, both of them looked to the wolfman for an answer. "Michael." She said.

"It seems to me," Michael rudely interrupted her and said "Death has always ridden on my shoulders, but yes you're right. I will tell you of Vogel."

The little sergeant, was known to all of the men under his command as the rat, not to his face of course, but behind his back. For the rabble who guarded the camp were the dregs of prisons from all over Germany. And most of them either hated him or feared him, for without his good reports of them they could all find themselves back behind bars, doing hard labour.

Kurt Vogel did indeed look like the rodent they had nick named him for. Bright beady eyes set close to a thin nose in a pinched face, his mouth a mere slash. He was a small wiry man who moved like a rat, his every gesture appeared quick and furtive. In any other time Vogel would have most probably remained what he was, a small time thief , a product born of the meanest streets of Dresden and no doubt if he had not joined one of the gangs of Brownshirts , he would have either been in prison or dead.

He had joined the brownshirts for one simple reason he saw them as a means to escape the meanness of his existence. He always avoided the bloody battles that took place between the brownshirts and the communists and it had come as a great shock to him when he was seconded into the new German army. His superiors thought little of him, cleaver, yes, but at this moment in time they needed muscles. Vogel was in short supply of height and muscle, so they assigned him to help and supposedly protect the old man who ran the Zoo.

It was here that Vogel found his niche in life, for the god who had created him gave him a gift. "Never." the old man had once said to him, "Have I ever seen anyone with your talent for making friends with animals." Vogel appeared to have an affinity with dogs, they seemed to like him, for once he had befriended them there was nothing he could not get them to do.

It was there at the zoo that he was noticed by Strobel, the Majors car had broken down and curiosity and a needing to waste time had driven the Major to look at the small zoo. Vogel had been playing with one of the wolves in its cage, the large animal had rolled over and pawed the air while Vogel stroked its belly. It had then sat contentedly while Vogel combed it.

The Major had left and it was not until the plans for the air strip had been approved and the number of workers required and the number of guards needed did Strobel remember the little man at the zoo.

Strobel had used his influence and pulled a few strings and before he knew it Vogel had been promoted to sergeant and assigned to Strobel's unit, for Strobel had concluded that once the prisoners started to arrive, Vogel and his dogs would be indispensable.

Vogel hated the valley, he hated the soft summer nights and the bitter chill of winter snow, and the crisp mornings full of fresh air. He hated the blind obedience of the Jews, doing what they were told no matter how difficult the order, he hated their foul unwashed smell. He longed to be back in the old mans office at the zoo, drinking thick sweet black coffee, Vogel wondered if the old man was getting his coffee now that he was no longer with him. And did the old man still get those foul smelling obnoxious thin cigars he liked so much. Vogel remembered the overpowering heat of the office, a fire burning in the stove winter and summer. He missed the heady smell of the animals, a mixture of urine and excreta, but no matter what, Vogel knew those days would never return.

Vogel snarled and spit out a loose strand of tobacco, then he dropped the cigarette to the ground and put his boot on it. Time to take a turn around the camp to see if his dogs were being treated right, he hunched his thin shoulders in his army greatcoat. The guards would be on the lookout for him, and it gave the little man a perverse sense of power to think that all those big strapping ex-jailbirds lived in fear of him. Still they all knew that one word from Vogel about mistreatment of his beloved dogs to Strobel and the offenders could find themselves in serious trouble.

Vogel spit again, for where he was stood he could see through the window of Strobel's hut. He could see Strobel and that bastard Mantz, Vogel hated the young man with aristocratic airs and graces, the truth was Vogel feared him. Strobel he could handle, but Mantz, now he was a completely different matter, you just never knew which way he was going to jump under any given circumstances. He guessed they would be drinking the brandy Strobel's wife sent him. Well fuck them, let them think the sun shone out of Hitler's arse. Let them act like they were a cultural oasis in this god forsaken valley, he didn't give a shit.

The sergeant watched them toast each other, he would have given a months pay to know what they were talking about. He wondered how long they would last in his world, the real world , a week , he doubted it , no more than a couple of days. His world wasn't populated with terrified prisoners or middle class toadies who jumped each time a Strobel or a Mantz shouted. "Oh fuck them," he said then forgot all about them.

He bent to examine the traps Strobel had had him set, his finger traced the outline of the wolf's paw. Vogel looked around, when he was certain nobody was looking he carefully rubbed the tracks out with his boot. He would have to talk to the man, he was getting careless, familiarity may breed contempt. Bullets from a machine pistol had contempt for all who got in the way.

Vogel stamped around the trap, anybody looking would think that Vogel was making sure the trap was secure. When he was satisfied that all traces of the wolfman were gone he made his way slowly back to his hut. He wouldn't do a tour of the perimeter tonight, let the guards worry a little it wouldn't hurt them. Once inside the hut he made sure his door was locked before putting on the light, moving about in front of the window, somebody was sure to see him. Vogel took his time, put out the light and waited, he could see most of the camp from here, nobody moved out there without him seeing them. He smoked another cigarette and when he was absolutely positive that the time was right he moved over to the back of his hut and carefully opened the window.

Like his namesake, the rat moved from cover to cover until he was on the fringe of the forest. Not until he was in the deeper shadows of the forest did he feel easier. He slipped his hand into the coats pocket, his fingers curling around the packet of cigarettes. With a sigh he let them slip back, he decided not to smoke, a light no matter how well he shielded it just might be seen by one of the patrolling guards. It wouldn't do to make them jumpy, the talk of a pair of yellow eyes had got them jumpy enough. Vogel wasn't worried about the dogs even if the wind changed they would recognise his scent as a friendly one.

Perhaps the man Michael himself would come tonight, perhaps it would be the wolf. It didn't matter to Vogel he would welcome both of them. From that first wonderful meeting when he had unexpectedly come upon Michael in the middle of his transformation back into human shape Vogel had became the werewolf's slave. The old zoo keeper, in his cups, had drunkenly told Vogel, he had been told that not only were such things possible but the werewolf actually existed. He of course had never seen one himself but he knew people that had, "Gypsies mainly." he said "Believers in the old religion." It became Vogel's ambition to meet one of these people, to talk to them, to have them explain the legend of the werewolf. He scrounged all the written material on the legend he could lay his hands on, he even took to visiting the libraries to find material. In the old man he found a scholar of many dead languages and much to Vogel's surprise the old man offered to teach him. How somebody like the old man had ended up as head keeper in a flea bitten zoo Vogel never found out. Strobel interfered with his education, he had managed to learn a lot and his parting gift from the old man was a book, "Kurt." He said, "Don't ever let anybody else see this book, if they do it could mean both our deaths."

The book was old, its pages yellow and brittle with age, to Vogel it was a bible, a possession to cherish beyond all others. Time after time he read it over and over, and its ancient pages told him that the werewolf was real. He knew it to be true, he believed every word in the book. Then came the night in the forest, when sick of the smell of the prisoners he had decided to take a walk to try and clear his head. It was a night when all he wished for came true, all of his desires were granted. He had come unexpectedly on the big grey wolf and had then stood open mouthed as the wolf regressed. Where moments before had crouched a wolf there now knelt a man. Vogel had moved forward unafraid so that the man could see him, his heart thumped against his rib cage.

The man had looked at him with the yellow eyes of the wolf examining him, then the feral eyes had faded and a pair of cold grey eyes had looked at him instead. With a heart bursting with joy the little man had held out his hands in friendship, the man had understood Vogel's gesture that he meant him no harm.

On that night some three months ago there was born an alliance which would stretch over the coming years. To Vogel, the little man from the mean streets Michael was a god to be worshipped. To Michael, Vogel became friend and benefactor, he no longer had to sneak into the compound to find out what was happening, Vogel told him everything.

From Kurt Vogel, Michael learnt what it would be like for him living in a modern world. Michael learnt things from the little man Tibor could never hope to teach him. He liked the little man and trusted him from the first but he still decided to keep him a secret from Tibor and the Wych woman. Vogel in his turn revered both the man and the wolf and declared himself to be a very lucky man. Not every one on this god forsaken planet was granted the chance of achieving their own personal kismet.

Vogel rested his back against the tree and waited, sometimes he sat here all night and the werewolf didn't turn up. Vogel hoped that tonight Michael would come to visit him for they had much to talk about. He wanted to know why Michael had been paying visits to the camp and leaving his tracks plain enough for even the most stupid of men could not miss them. He couldn't keep on destroying traces of a wolf, somebody was bound to find them before him one morning.

In his hard narrow bunk Strobel tossed and turned, he was sleeping and dreaming. A dream which caused sweat to pop out across his forehead and run down his face. He was stood on the landing strip watching and waiting for a plane. By his side stood the grey men from Berlin, constantly checking their watches and saying in unison, "Berlin does not and will not accept failure Major." Close by stood Mantz, immaculate as ever pointing his gun at Strobel's head.

Strobel shouted out and sat bolt upright on the narrow bunk, sweat stung his eyes, his shirt and under garments sticking to him. He swung his legs over the side of the bunk and sat there his feet touching the cold, bare wooden floor. The major was shaking uncontrollably, he needed a drink. He needed something to take away the foul taste in his mouth and something to steady his nerves. Although he didn't want to believe it the visitors from Berlin had unnerved him more than he liked to admit.

"God," He said aloud "I'll be glad when it's all over." He carried his drink to the window and looked out. He was trying to find a change in the surroundings, anything which would break the monotony. He shivered, it was freezing cold in the hut, god knows why, it shouldn't be, it was summer. He sipped at the brandy and felt its warmth find its way into his stomach, Strobel returned to his desk and pick up a cigarette, it tasted awful . The combination of tobacco and brandy caused him to belch. He looked down at his watch, five thirty, in twenty minutes the first fingers of dawn would be creeping over the rim of the mountain and another day would begin.

A figure moving stealthily across the compound caught his eye, Strobel stepped back, even though he knew he couldn't be seen from outside. "Vogel." He muttered, he watched the little sergeant move with his usual furtive movements. "Good Man." No doubt the sergeant would be checking on the men who had pulled night guard. Strobel drew on the cigarette, its red tip reflected in the window pane. "His dogs," Said Strobel, "Of course his bloody dogs." The major smiled to himself as if he had discovered the key to some great mystery. The man thought more about his dogs than he did about the men under his command. Still he was useful, a man with Vogel's ability to handle those damned vicious brutes. Trained to the standard Vogel expected they were worth dozens of human guards, for a start they ate less. They put a fear into the Jews a thousand threats of death couldn't match. Getting the dogs to savage one of the prisoners was better than a dozen beatings by the guards. Strobel lifted his glass in a silent salute to the little sergeant from Dresden.

He was still stood by the window when the first shrill ring caused him to jump, dropping the brandy glass to the floor, it shattered in unison with the second shrill ring. Strobel stared at the telephone as it continued its incessant ringing. It brought a hard knot of fear into Strobel's throat, he fought to control the trembling in his hand as he reached for it. At the sound of the voice at the other end he came stiffly to attention and felt slightly ridiculous for doing so. Strobel listened , hardly daring to breath, not wanting to miss a single word, Strobel spoke only once at the end of the conversation from Berlin. "Understood." He said and replaced the receiver, a grim smile tugged at the corner of his mouth. The waiting was over Berlin had decided to carry out the trials. The major toyed with the idea of having another drink to celebrate but decided against it.

Time to get dressed, wash away the sweat of fear from his body, this morning he would have a decent breakfast. Invite young Mantz, suddenly he was beginning to feel good, everything appeared to be going to plan and running exactly to time.

THE WANDERER - Part 2

The years passed by far too quickly for Michael as he roamed the mountains and valleys of Northern Europe. From the day he had left the Keep and taken his grisly burden to what had been his secret place and buried the remains of the red she wolf Anna along with his sword and curious cross given to him Sven. Michael had searched for others like himself, for he could not believe that the pack he belonged to was the only one in existence. Once he found some, how long ago had that been, twenty, thirty, a hundred years ago. Michael couldn't remember exactly, but he had watched the pack for days before he finally approached them.

Michael's heart had almost failed him when he walked into their lair, he had hoped that they would be like him. People capable of conversation, capable of understanding the nature of things and the way of the law. His hopes were dashed , after all the years of looking he was greeted by a sight that repelled him. They were a filthy unkempt group. Poor mindless scavengers living in fear for their lives. The stench of their bodies and the disgusting state of the cave they lved in was nauseating. At the sight of a pile of bones in the corner Michael felt the bile rise in his throat, the bones were human, the pack were cannibals.

He tried to communicate with them and failed, that they could stand and walk like men and women was the only segment of humanity left in them. They were incapable of human speech and unable to think rationally. They sniffed him, snapped and snarled at him like the beast they had become.

They had recognised Michael as one of their kind, they neither accepted him or rejected him. The sight of one of the females ripping apart the body of a child so sickened Michael that he walked away from the only ones of his kind that he had ever encountered . Michael had never tasted human flesh, or so he believed, the flesh of Otto had been fed him by the countess, that portion of human flesh had completed his changing. That moment in his life was forgotten, he never again craved it, despite what he was, he believed that somewhere inside of him was a human being, still capable of making the right choice.

He moved on, always seeking, always looking and hoping he would find a place to belong. From the dark mountains of Carpathia he wondered down into the lands of Transavania, but nowhere did he find a place where he was able to rest for long. The villages he walked into viewed him with suspicion, here in the land of the Vampire he stayed only long enough to rest for a few days. Often he would rise at the crack of dawn and vanish before the villagers were up and about their daily routine.

From time to time he was forced to approach the caravans of the travelling people. They never turned him away, providing him with food and shelter and clothes and Michael was grateful for these short periods of respite in his search for his own kind. He was told on many occasions by the travellers he could stay with them, become part of the tribe. Michael had always thanked them and politely refused their offer. True they would look after him, protect him if necessary but he knew deep down they were always glad when he moved on.

Winter turned to Summer then to Spring and Autumn and back again to Winter and still the wolfman searched. The wanting, the needing to belong became a hard maggot gnawing at his soul, and he began to despair of ever finding a place to rest.

Then in the middle of a cold bitter winter he heard the cry of the wolf. He changed into the grey one and found the pack. Like the mindless creatures he had encountered years before they did not want him, he was an outcast. He was forced to fight a hard vicious battle with the pack before he was able to retreat to lick his wounds.

The big grey wolf remained in the cave long after the snows melted and summer came to the mountains and valleys. The grey wolf left the cave only to hunt, avoiding contact with the travellers who passed that way. When it smelt snow on the winds, it dragged its kill closer to the cave knowing that the frost would keep it fresh for many days. The grey wolf would lay in a melancholy stupor at the mouth of his cave watching the passing of the days.

The howling of a hunting pack caused the grey wolf to stir itself, as their baying came closer he dragged himself out of the cave. Emotions stirred deep in the grey wolf as he felt himself and his domain threatened. He would defend his cave and his territory to the death if need be. It was the pack he had tried to join, they had rejected him and turned him into a rogue. Standing at the entrance of his cave he growled his challenge at the hunting pack. It started as a low rumbling in the grey wolfs chest and forced its way between fangs to become a full throated growl.

The pack paused in their hunting and listened to the grey wolfs challenge. The leader of the pack remembered the big grey wolf and the members of the pack it had crippled or killed. The leader of the pack bayed its refusal to fight and the pack moved on. The old wolf looked towards the mountains where the grey ones cry came from, he could see nothing. In future, until the grey wolf left the area or fell victim to a hunter's traps, the pack would find other hunting grounds to roam.

Satisfied that his home was safe the grey wolf backed into its cave and lay down its head resting on its front legs.

So it stayed until the season changed and changed again and the world spun remorselessly around. He lay in his cave until the scent of the forest began to enter its brain calling to it. Moving sluggishly the grey wolf crawled out of the cave and from its vantage point looked down on the lush grass of the mountain slopes. As the wolf moved slowly into the forest the scent of a deer came to it. The grey wolf felt its stomach contract and the juice flow in its mouth and it moved slowly forward for the kill.

While the grey wolf had spent decades in lonely isolation the world turned and turned again. Vast armies had fought across Europe, men from the America's, a land Michael had only ever heard of, came and died in the mud of Ypres and Flanders.

Men no longer fought face to face with sword and spike, they now had machines to do the killing for them. They rained death from the air, they slaughtered each other in their millions, not only by bomb and bullet but with gas. A shell launched three miles away fired by a man, its victim would never see, brought death in an instant. Men died in filthy water filled trenches their lives choked from them by a burning gas. And with their victory these strangers left Europe and returned across the seas to their homes and the years continued to pass. And not content with a war which involved men from all over the world man discovered new ways in which to kill and maim its brothers and sisters.

The young deer ate nervously, taking a mouthful of grass then checking on its safety. Upwind of the deer the grey wolf moved ever closer to its prey. One paw down then stop, still the deer ate, another paw down another foot closer, still the deer ate unaware of the grey death about to strike. The young deer lifted its head and saw the leaping wolf too late, fangs sank into its slender neck. Strong jaws fastened around the deer's neck and bones cracked and broke between powerful teeth. Both hunter and hunted carried by the momentum of the grey wolfs attack were propelled forward.

The grey wolf saw the danger it was in too late, the edge of a ravine yawned before it. Claws scrabbled at the soft soil trying to gain purchase, had the wolf not been locked to the deer it might have been able to stop itself. The weight of its kill carried the grey wolf over the edge, just before they crashed into the top branches of the trees the grey wolf managed to free itself from the deer.

The upper most branches broke easily under the weight of the wolf, using fangs and claws the wolf tried to halt its descent. For one brief instant the wolf saw the ground rushing to meet it, then it thudded into a thick branch which turned it over. The sky and earth cartwheeled before the grey wolfs eyes, then ground and wolf met. The grey wolf bounced once, hitting the ground with a sickening thud, it was thrown forward into the unyielding trunk of a forest giant. Unable to move, ribs broken in the fall, the grey wolf emitted a strangled whine before a blackness , deep and full of pain overcame it.

LILITH – Part 1

She was a tall striking young woman who walked with an unerring accuracy through the dense undergrowth of the forest. Only occasionally when she lost the strange sound that had come to her, did she reach and touch one of the saplings. Lilith heard the sound again, a strange mewing cry of an animal in pain. The cry came louder to her, she must be getting closer to the hurt creature. She cocked her head and listened, again the low mewing, the creature must be desperate. Lilith stood still and waited for the creature to call to her again, the sound came from her left.

Lilith held her arms straight out in front of her, her fingertips touched the rough bark of a tree. Tentatively she felt her way around the tree, her fingers touched the spongy leaves of the ferns. Lilith's head almost rested on her shoulder as she searched for the wounded animal. She pushed aside the long black hair, straining to hear again the cry of pain which had drawn her from the forest pathway. The pitiful mewing stopped, the touch of a hand on her foot caused her to take a sharp intake of breath. She almost believed she could feel the blood racing through her veins with the pounding of her heart. Once more the hand touched her foot urgently imploring her to help.

Lilith knelt slowly and reached out, her hands touched the grass and the woman moved them forward slowly. As if burnt by hot coals Lilith pulled back her hands in alarm at the touch of cold human flesh. Her brain registered the fact that the voice of the forest was silent, Lilith lived by sound and touch. The silence of the forest troubled her, but she pushed these thoughts to the back of her mind as she explored the body with her hands.

Her fingers touched the swelling around the man's chest, the open wound in his side, the touch of bone. Lilith ran her fingers over the man's face, a strong face wasted by illness and starvation. The young woman held her breath while her fingers searched with a deliberate precision. A strangled cry of joy escaped her, there she had found it, a pulse. Lilith bent her head until her ear almost touched the man's lips, the almost indiscernible feel of his breath on her flesh. Lilith would have cried out with joy had she been able to, she pushed her hands against the ground and got to her feet. The man needed help and quickly, with some difficulty she found her way back on the forest path. Once again on familiar ground the young woman moved at a surprising speed.

The sound of an axe thudding into a tree stopped her, she waited and listened, once more the thunk of steel on wood. Stepping from the well worn path Lilith honed in on the sound of the axe. A pair of large rough hands grabbed her. "Lilith child what is it?" The voice of her father brought a grunting sob from her, frantically she began to pull at him. She pointed back the way she had come. "You want me to go with you?" Lilith grunted again and tugged even harder at her father's sleeve. Old Markos held his ground and Lilith was jerked back towards his arms. "Easy child," He said holding her to him. The old man turned and shouted, "Peter, Peter." Old Markos called for his son to join them.

A tall well made young man joined the two, Peter Markos had just celebrated his eighteenth birthday and like all young men he tended to blurt out his questions. "What is it, what's the matter with Lilith, is there trouble?"

"Hush boy." Said his Father and beckoned the boy forward and whispered in his ear, Peter smiled and shook his head. He had gone through this a thousand, no a million times, Lilith would come running and he or his father were expected to follow. Old Markos lifted his daughter's face up from where she had buried it against his chest and looked at her. His eyes filled with hot tears at the sight of those milk white orbs that stared blindly back at him. With one calloused finger he brushed a strand of her hair away from her face. Most probably it was some hurt beast of the forest, a bird, perhaps a fox, but that mattered little to the young woman it was hurt and it needed help. The grunting sob of her voice drove daggers into the old mans heart, but he allowed her to pull him on.

Markos was always amazed at the speed his blind daughter was able to attain through the trees. He almost bumped into her when she suddenly stopped. "Hush Peter." he said as Lilith cocked her head and listened. The woman stiffened in his grip and pointed towards the place she had heard the sound. Markos loosened Lilith's grasp and lifting the axe he moved cautiously forward. At the sight of the injured man old Markos stopped and stared , his eyes told him in seconds, what Lilith's fingers had, had to probe for, the extent of the man's injuries.

Markos bent to examine the man and almost jumped back at the sight of the pentacle on the man's left shoulder. Markos crossed himself and unable to help himself said, "Lycanthrope," he turned to see if his children had heard his cry of werewolf. His son was stood with his arm protectively around Lilith's shoulder a look of concern written on his young face. The young woman stood listening waiting for her father to come back to them.

Markos caught his breath as the mans eyes flicked open, then closed , for one heart stopping moment he had looked into the eyes of a wolf. The old mans fingers curled around the axes handle, one quick sweep and the thing would be dead, or would it, how did anybody kill a werewolf? Why him? Why had he been picked to find this thing? Why his family? Better to leave it here, better to let this abomination die here, let its flesh rot into the soil of the forest. The old man opened his eyes and looked down as the thing cried in pain, he stared at the emaciated body, the broken ribs plain to see. Jagged bone poked through the flesh of its leg. A swollen lump surrounding the projecting bone. Tentatively he reached out and touched the angry red lump, a thick yellow pus burst free. It slithered like a viscous glue down the creatures leg, the stench caused Markos to gag. It filled him with loathing and disgust and he rammed his pus covered finger again and again into the soft soil until it ached. Common sense dictated that he leave the creature here, his daughter would believe him if he said the man had died. No, no she would not, for she had exceptional hearing.

It would be better for all concerned, his wife, his children, it would be for the best, don't taint their lives with that of a moon child. Markos looked once more towards his children, the blind, voiceless beautiful Lilith, Peter who had begun to fill out promising to be a fine, handsome well built man. His wife Mina, Mina what would she say if he left the moon child here to die? Markos wanted to laugh at his predicament, he knew what she would say, they had been born into the old religion. They believed in the fallen one, despite all the terrors that made him tremble with fear , he knew he could not leave the moon child here.

Markos wanted to break down and cry, to curse the dark god that made it impossible for him to refuse help to this creature. The one thing he had prayed for all of his life not to happen to him and his had happened, a werewolf had entered their family circle.

"Peter." He called out, his voice unnaturally loud even to his own ears, "Peter." He called again, a little quieter this time. "Come and help me boy, we must take this," The old man's voice faltered, "We must take this man to our home, he needs help." The man stirred in the old mans arms and emitted the cry of an injured beast.

"The ribs are bound husband," said Mina the old man's wife, she was a large woman but she moved around the bed quickly. Taking one of Michael's arms she lashed it to the headboard. Mina did the same with his other arm, testing the strength of the knots each time. Muttering to herself she took another piece of rope and tied the foot of his good leg to the bottom of the bed. When she was satisfied that the rope would hold the man down she went over to the table and soaked the cloth in the bowl of water. This she carried over to the bed and put it down close to Michael's infected leg. Placing two fingers either side of the swelling she pressed, thick yellow fluid poured out of the lump, Mina paused and taking the cloth wiped away the stinking mess. Once more she pressed and pus erupted from the swelling, she turned her head and breathed deep. Not until the pus was tinged with blood did she pause in her work. Mina wiped the swelling with the cloth and pressed again, she was rewarded with the sight of fresh red blood. When it was a steady flow she smoothed pungent oils all over the loose pocket of flesh around the bone.

"Now," Said Mina "It is your turn." Markos did not move, he was staring stupidly at her bloody hands. "What is it husband?" She asked "Why do you wait?"

"That thing," he said "That thing on my bed, in my home." His voice began to tremble and he had to force himself to say the words that stuck in his throat. "It's a werewolf." Mina looked at her husband, sadly she shook her head. Markos was a good man, a gentle man with love to spare but at this moment he was a very frightened man. Why did he hesitate, he knew what he must do, were they not both devotee's of the old religion, had he not carved the pentacle above their door with his own hands? "I cannot do it Mina, I cannot help this creature." There was pain in his voice when he said, "Let it die."

"How?" Snapped Mina "Do you have the secret?" Her voice rose higher. "Well?" She said "Do you know the secret ways husband?" All the time she was talking Mina was gently rubbing the pungent oils into the Werewolf's wound. "Take the leg and pull." She ordered Markos, still the old man hesitated, he was afraid to even touch the thing on his bed. His flesh still crawled with his previous contact with the werewolf, he looked to Mina for help. Had he not carried the thing from the forest, had not he and Peter brought that abomination into the house and laid it on his bed. "Do it." Mina's voice thundered in his ears causing him to step backwards. "Do it or be cursed for the rest of your life."

Markos could hardly believe what she was saying, had he heard her right, was his wife of thirty years threatening him. "No." Said Mina as if reading his thoughts "No I'm not threatening you husband. I would never do that, but you, we took an oath, remember the pledge to our people." Markos saw the love in her eyes and he understood what she was trying to tell him. No matter what he thought of the man on the bed he could not renege on his pledge to the fallen one for if one whisper reached the ears of the dark god, their lives would be worthless.

It was fear of the fallen one that made Markos move to the bottom of the bed. It was fear for the lives of his wife, his daughter and his son, that made the old man take hold of Michael's leg. Markos pulled, Mina saw the hatred in his eyes and the savagery in the pull.

The man on the bed reared in pain, his mouth opened in a silent scream, bone grated against bone. He twisted and turned in agony and fought against the restraining bonds, Markos pulled again holding the leg as straight as he could. The man's body lifted off the bed, his back arched and his mouth opened to allow the howl of the beast to come out. Michael's breath expelled from him in one long gasp, then he lay still. His body was coated in sweat which ran freely onto the sheets below him soaking them, blood welled up from the hole where the bone had been. Mina worked quickly, strapping the leg with bandages, which quickly stained red. She placed the wooden slats against Michael's leg and wrapped more bandages around it fastening the slats into place.

She was sweating freely by the time she had finished her work on Michael's leg. She pushed away the wet rat tails of her hair which fell across her face. "With luck," She said, "He will keep the leg." Mina sat down heavily on the large chair by the bed, she was close to physical and mental exhaustion. "I will stay here tonight he may need help."

"Better he were dead." said Markos, "It would have been better if Lilith had never found him."

"Go away old man." said Mina angrily, "I'm too tired to argue." She rested her head against the back of the chair and closed her eyes. "We will speak again in the morning." Markos opened his mouth to speak then changed his mind, he turned and walked to the bedroom door. Mina watched him go, there was a hurt mixed with love and a sadness in her heart. What was wrong with him, why had he taken this attitude, why was he frightened of the man on the bed? There was nothing to fear from the moon child, he would not hurt them or their family. Was it because he was frightened for the sake of the children, he didn't have to be, they knew nothing of the old religion. Neither she nor as far as she knew had Markos spoken of their people and his and Mina's connection to the old religion. The children had been born here, they had never known of the travelling life of their parents and they never would. She would talk to Markos in the morning, perhaps in the light of a new day things would look differently to him.

Mina looked at the man on the bed, it seemed impossible that this poor sick man close to death could and would, change into a snarling beast. All her life she had heard the legend of the werewolf, stories handed down by word of mouth, nothing ever written down. She had listened to the tales told to her by her mother and her grandmother how her people had been chosen to protect the moon children. It had been foolish of them to try and deny their destiny, how many years ago had she and Markos come to this place. Too many to consider, but he had built her this house and she had given him two fine children and they had lived a normal life.

Mina sighed, she was not a Wych woman she did not have the power to stop the transformation of man into wolf. Markos was not a Guardian, but they were of the travelling people. It was their sworn duty to help this man, to make him strong enough to continue on his way. In the morning they would talk, she would sit and hold his hand and make him understand, he had to understand. Mina closed her eyes, she would rest for a moment, her breathing changed to a slow regular rhythm and Mina slept.

"Mina." The voice came from down a long tunnel. "Mina." Someone was shaking her, "Mina." The woman stirred and yawned and began to drift back into a warm comfortable place. The hand was insistent, it continued to shake her, Mina slowly opened her eyes, the figure before her was a blur, concentrating her mind she allowed the blurred figure to take form. Markos stood before her, a mug of steaming coffee in his hand. The old man took her hand and put the mug in it.

"Drink." He said, Mina still in a daze lifted the mug to her lips and sipped at it, she tasted the hot unsweetened bitterness of the liquid. He always did make his coffee too strong and he never put sugar in it, just because he didn't use it. Then she realised where she was and what had taken place in this room last night. She tried to get up but Markos held her back. "Drink Mina." He said, "The moon child sleeps, I watched him through the night he did not move."

Mina swallowed another mouthful of the hot drink and pulled her face at the overpowering strength of it.

Pushing away the old man's arm she lifted her bulk out of the chair, she felt her muscles creak with the effort. "Sit down Mina." Markos tried to push her back into the chair. "Sit, I'll fetch you some food." Mina shook her head and taking his arm finally got herself upright.

"No." She said, "I will eat at the table like always, nothing has changed." But before she left the room she checked on the man. His breathing was even and regular and he appeared to be sleeping comfortably, gently she removed the soiled bandages from around the wound and applied more oil to it. She examined carefully the place where the bone had broken through, true it was still inflamed but there was no sign of the poison. For a moment she considered loosening the bonds which held him to the bed when she saw the bruises which covered his wrist. "Better not." She mumbled, if the man had struggled so hard in his sleep he was better off remaining tied to the bed.

Mina yawned, she was still tired, spending the night in a chair was never the best way to have a good night's sleep. She walked to the bedroom door, there was nothing more she could do for the man for the present and the smell of food cooking made her stomach rumble. Mina rested her weight against Markos and smiled, the old fool had spent the night guarding her, though of course he would never admit it. The old man squeezed her shoulders and then went downstairs, she heard the sound of his boots on each wooden step and blushed because she found a silly joy in the sound of it. Sighing Mina made her way down the stairs behind him, once he had been tall and straight, now age was beginning to bend him a little. But he was her man and she loved him for all of his faults, which at times drove her to distraction.

The overpowering smell of bacon cooking and the sound of eggs sizzling in the pan drove these thoughts from Mina's head as she made her way to the table. Sipping from the mug she watched Lilith, it always surprised her the way the girl could move around the kitchen. The girl was always able to cook their meals, some inner sense telling her when it was ready. The old woman's heart was full of pride watching her, Lilith put food on the plates and brought it over to the table. As always Lilith would tut, tut, at her interfering brother in that strange way of hers. Mina watching the two of them wondered what she could say about the man upstairs, obviously she couldn't tell them the truth. Still she thought as she applied herself to her breakfast she would find a way. Whenever she had anything difficult to tell the children she somehow managed to find a way. As she ate something nagged at her, something she should have remembered, what day was it. Mina mentally calculated the days, and suddenly realised it was the third Wednesday of the month. Today Markos went to the village to exchange his goods for food, he would have to be warned. Not that Markos would say anything about the man , but Peter, he was a different matter, from what her husband had told her once in the village Peter made his way to the inn. The boy didn't drink much and she wasn't one to refuse the boy a bit of fun, but the crowd he hung about with. From all reports they were a bad bunch, idle and given to tormenting those less fortunate than themselves.

"Do you take Peter with you today Markos?" She asked over the clatter of pots and pans being washed and Lilith loudly scolding her younger brother. "Do you really need him?" She asked.

"Yes." Said Markos sucking on his empty pipe, the old man never smoked until after the evening meal, but he would constantly suck noisily at his empty pipe. "This time I expect to bring back enough flour and oil and potatoes to last us through the winter."

"Do we not have enough vegetables in the garden?"

"No, well not enough to last us, you're worried about Peter?"

"You know how he talks husband, you must impress on him, he's to say nothing about your cousins visit."

The old man flinched at her description of the man upstairs, his cousin indeed, still Mina was right. He had spent the night keeping watch over the man, he still didn't like the thought of him being under his roof. But once again Mina was right, the boy would have to be told to keep his mouth shut. "He won't say a word about him." He said and got up from the table, he walked over to Lilith and put his hand on her arm, Lilith turned and smiled at him. He wondered if she had heard the conversation between him and his wife, she most probably had, she didn't miss much. It was as if the gods to compensate her for the loss of sight and sound had given her acute hearing. "Do you want a trinket bringing back my pretty one?" He said. Lilith's smile widened at his words. "What shall it be?" He looked at her as she shook her head. "A surprise eh?" He bent and kissed her, Lilith threw her arms around his neck and clung to him. "Then my sweet that is what it will be a surprise." Markos managed to untangle himself from Lilith, kissed Mina and went outside to look for his son.

"Peter." The boy came out of the stable leading the old mare. "Come on son, once again the women of the house send the men to do their shopping." Mina watched the two men harness the old mare to the wagon and saw their agitated conversation, her husband pointing back towards the house and finally giving his son a gentle slap on the shoulder. It seemed that the boy had agreed to keep silent about their visitor, at least for the time being.

Her husband and son were still locked in agitated conversation as they climbed onto the wagon. Markos snapped the reins and the old mare moved off, it would take them hours to reach the village at the speed the old mare could manage to muster. Mina sat on the house veranda watching the wagon until it disappeared around the bend in the road. She eased her bulk up from the seat and walked in to the house, it was time to check on the man again. "Lilith come here to me child." The girl left what she was doing and came to Mina, negotiating the obstacles in her way with ease. "I must go and see how the man is." She said to her daughter. "Will you stay here in the house?" A look of dismay crossed the girls face and she pointed towards the forest. Mina held the girls hand and said, "Alright off you go, but be careful." The old woman realised her statement was more than a little foolish, the girl was always careful. "Oh go on then, but Lilith," She said "Please don't go too far today, I'll need you shortly." Lilith nodded vigorously and kissing her mother made her way to the door.

Mina climbed the stairs slowly, she was still stiff and weary from her lack of proper rest . Mina was getting old she would be seventy next birthday and her vigil at the bedside of the moon child didn't help her poor health. Mina was forced to smile, she hadn't really done much last night, only fall asleep in the chair. She pushed open the door and stopped dead in her tracks. "Fallen one help us." she exclaimed.

Michael had broken free, he lay with his arms by his side, Mina saw the bloody mess he had made of his wrist breaking free. Mina like her husband the day before crossed herself when she looked into the yellow eyes of a wolf. Mina found herself unable to tear her gaze from that of Michael's. Her heart beat erratically and she pushed her fist against her mouth to stop herself from crying out. The wolf's yellow eyes slowly faded to be replaced by a pair of grey pain filled eyes of a man.

Michael made a feeble attempt to lift his arm, his mouth opened and closed, nothing came out, his head fell back onto the pillows. Her heart still thumping Mina moved closer to the bed, the man appeared to have gone back to sleep. She bent and lifted the wolf mans arm, his wrists were rubbed raw. Gently she rubbed the pungent oil into the raw flesh, Michael did not move, he lay like a lump of stone. The old woman wiped the oil from her hands and bent to examine the bandages around his leg. She touched the place where the bone had broken through, there was no smell and no sign of infection at all. Mina grunted to herself and put fresh dressings on the leg, she put her hand on her back and straightened up.

Michael was watching her, how long he had been staring at her she had no way of knowing. The mans eyes made her feel uncomfortable, she had the feeling he was trying to see into her soul. Mina licked her lips and swallowed, her tongue wanted to stick to the roof of her mouth. Michael blinked his eyes and opened his mouth, the corner turning upward slightly. "If that is a smile moon child," Mina said under her breath "It is a very poor example. Would you like some food?" she forced herself to ask him, the man's head nodded. "I'll fetch you some." She said, pleased for a reason to leave the room and those probing grey eyes.

Michael fought hard to remember where he was and how he had got there, his last conscious memory was of plunging over the edge of the ravine. He remembered those seconds as he crashed into the trees, the bone jarring impact with the ground and the deep, deep darkness which engulfed him, the blinding light when he had returned to consciousness. A pair of gentle hands that had touched his body, and the smell of a female bending over him and those strange white eyes. He knew that the woman who had just left the room wasn't the one who had found him, she smelt differently, she smelt older. The one who had found him was younger, a lot younger.

Where was he? Who had brought him to this place? Michael was aware that he was inside a house. He could smell the different scents of cooking and polish and fresh washed laundry. He also picked up the scent of two men, again one was a lot younger than the other. He twitched his nose and the smell of tobacco came to him. A family home, a father, mother and two children, this he was sure of, for like all family units they had a very particular smell. Michael tried to lift his head, the effort was too much for him, he lifted his arms and regretted it, pain lanced through him as he tried to examine his wounds. His arm dropped heavily onto the bed, next he tried to move his body, his left side exploded in a burning agony. He was unable to stop himself crying out in pain, slowly, as he lay still the agonising pain subsided. Not contented the wolf man tried to move his legs, this time the pain was a red blinding mist that blurred his vision. Michael gritted his teeth and tried to close his mind to the pain he was feeling.

The wolf man heard the tread of feet on the wooden stairs, the sound of a latch being lifted, and footsteps approaching the bed. Michael did not open his eyes as his head was lifted and the first spoonful of the thick soup was put into his mouth. The smell entered his nose as he tasted the soup and swallowed, greedily he took every spoonful as it touched his lips, licking the spoon clean. He wanted to ask for more, he needed more, he needed every vital spoonful of the hot thick liquid. Michael wanted to beg the old woman to give him more but found he couldn't speak, his mouth could not form the words he needed.

A blind panic gripped the wolf man as he tried to force his throat to open and let the words out. An inner voice told him to be calm, don't fight it, take your time, you're sick, hurt, take your time. He tried to open his eyes, the lids felt like an iron weight, this time when the darkness descended he welcomed it. Over the next few days he welcomed the sound of the soft footsteps on the stairs, for he knew they would be bringing him food. Soups at first, then meats and bread. But why he was not able to open his eyes and look at the woman who fed him like a baby was a mystery to him. It was no mystery to Mina who had laced his food with a drug that caused the moon child to sleep. If Mina was correct it would not be long before the moon child was fit enough to travel. It had been a wonder to the old woman just how quickly the broken bones and wounded flesh of the moon child had healed. The bones had knitted perfectly, the gaping wound had healed over, fresh skin replacing the old. Mina would at any other time or with any other patient taken credit for his return to good health, but she knew that she had only assisted the healing power of the fallen one's child.

The wolf man opened his eyes, the sound of a woman's voice calling out had awakened him. "Lilith." Michael heard the name of the girl being shouted, "Lilith, where is that girl?" The sound of plates clattering onto wood, metal pans moving on an iron stove. The sound of voices, a man, no two men and a woman all talking at once. His nose twitched at the smell of roasting meat, his mouth filled with his own juices. Michael moved, there was pain but unlike the last time he had tried to move he found he could sit up, it was slightly uncomfortable because his chest was bound tight in bandages. He looked down at his leg, at the wooden slats that were strapped to it. Michael held his breath and moved the leg over the edge of the bed, there was no pain. Gripping the edge of the bed Michael stood up, briefly the room spun before his eyes. Michael took his time, carefully he placed the injured leg onto the smooth wooden floor. There was a little pain but only for a second or so, Michael swayed, fought to control it, then stood perfectly still. Like a child who had found its feet and realised it had the ability to walk the wolf man moved clumsily around the room. When he believed he was in total control of his body Michael moved towards the bedroom door.

"And how's my cousin today?" Asked Markos ladling potatoes onto his plate.

"Better husband, better." Said Mina. "Peter don't gulp your food so fast you'll get indigestion."

"Sorry Mama," Said Peter looking up guiltily from his plate. "What's his name, has he said yet?" He asked before pushing a forkful of meat into his mouth.

"He hasn't said." Answered Mina, "Put some potatoes on your sisters plate boy."

"Peter has a point." said Markos "How long has he been here, three weeks?"

"Well don't worry over it husband, and it's more like two months, and don't scowl, he'll be fit enough to travel in a week or so."

"Still Mina." said the old man, "He must have a name are you sure he…"

"I've told you more than once, I don't know his name."

"My name is Michael." Peter jumped up from the table sending his plate crashing to the floor, its contents spilling over it. Mina stifled a cry, old Markos got slowly to his feet. Only Lilith sat there lost in her blindness to what was taking place. The three of them stared at the wolf man who stood at the bottom of the stairs. A blanket was wrapped around him, Mina was unable to stop herself from smiling. He looked ridiculous as he moved forward, the slats hanging free and the bandages trailing behind him.

"My name is Michael Cavendish, and I thank you all for my life."

Michael after that first day he introduced himself to the family found it difficult to try and hold a conversation with the old man. Every kind of social intercourse was greeted by a gruff rebuttal by old Markos. It did not take Michael long to realise the old man did not want him there or around his son and daughter. Michael did not find it in him to blame the old man for his attitude, had he been in Markos's place no doubt he would have felt the same. "Tainting the family." Was the expression he had overheard the old man say to his wife, perhaps the old man was right the sooner he moved on the better for all.

The boy Peter liked to talk and from him Michael learnt they were less than a dozen miles from a small village called Mantz. He learnt from Peter that Markos was a carpenter, and proudly pointed out to Michael the old man had built the house and all the furniture in it. Also he was held in high regard by the villagers, where they traded once a month. Michael kept his questioning to general points not probing into the families affairs, for the old man always seemed to be present when he talked to his son. Yet Michael went out of his way to talk to the boy, there was something about young Peter that nagged at him, he didn't know what, but it bothered him. Some half forgotten memory, something said or done, no matter how hard he tried it would not come. Perhaps it was him, how long had it been since he had spent time among humans?

His only ally in the house was the old woman Mina who did not seem to mind his company. She was the buffer between him and Markos, always there, always defending him, she, of them all remembered who and what she was, gypsy. It would be years before Michael found out the boy Peter and sister, Lilith, did not know of the stock they came from. Then it would be too late for all concerned.

The girl Lilith fascinated the wolf man, the way she moved, the ease with which everyday things were done by her with an easy dexterity. The way she communicated her thoughts and needs to the boy, Peter appeared to have no difficulty understanding her strange gruntings. Michael knew from the first time he caught her scent that she had been the one who had found him. On more than one occasion he had shadowed her when she walked in the forest. It seemed that the gods who had deprived her of speech and sight had relented and given her the ability to become one with all the creatures of the forest. He had watched her from a distance as the deer, rabbits, even the birds had come to her . Only once did he spoil it for the girl, he had wanted to get closer to her and his scent had carried on the wind causing the forest creatures to flee. The girl had sat in a frustrated puzzlement as to why the creatures had fled from her. Ever since that day Michael had always made sure he was upwind to her, content to sit and watch.

It was obvious to Michael that they all doted on her, and they loved her , she in return gave her love to them all , but more so to her brother Peter. And her scolding of Peter as he tried to help her would send the old man into fits of helpless laughter. When the old man had returned from the village the whole family would gather around him. As he began to tell them the latest gossip before he read to them from the newspaper, the girl would sit by him. Always she sat on the floor her head resting on the old mans knee, the old mans hand resting lightly on her head. If the gossip was new the paper was weeks old, but that did not matter it was a family affair. Mina would be sat close by, her hands always busy, knitting or cleaning vegetables for the next day's meal, Peter sat at the table carving. The boy had inherited the old mans skills, he could take a piece of wood and carve the most beautiful and intricate toy from it.

Knowing the old man did not want him with the family, Michael would sit in the shadows outside the window and listen to Markos read from the newspaper. He knew he wasn't and never could be part of their family circle, so he sat in the shadows and listened. It was a way to belong, to be a part of something he could never hope to have. Always his eyes rested on the girl, the way her face changed as the old man read to them.

The old mans monotonous voice would drone on and on, Mina would begin to nod, Peter having heard enough would go to his room. Only Lilith would be fully awake listening to Markos, her head on his knee, her arms wrapped around his legs, the gentle touch of the old mans hand on her head , would bring a smile to the girls face. Michael longed to be part of all of this, a member of the family.

"Michael, enough." Said Mina as the wolf man stacked another armful of logs near the door, "Come and sit by me." Mina looked at him, he was wearing only pants and boots. Michael had recovered quickly once he was on his feet, the flesh had filled out and he looked fit and strong. Mina saw a handsome man of around forty, well made but not out of proportion, a body covered in scars. Most of them she knew to be sword marks, as she beckoned him closer the old woman tried to guess his true age and failed. "Sit Michael, you've done enough for the day." Mina was sat on the veranda letting the cool air of the coming night waft over her. She was grateful of the rest that night promised her, the days although short were beginning to seem longer to the old woman.

Michael sat on the fencing that ran the length of the veranda, was this to be one of Mina's serious talks, from her face Michael was left in little doubt it was. "You look fit and strong again Michael." She said. Michael had a sinking feeling in the pit of his stomach, so the time he had dreaded had finally come. Michael felt it was up to him to say the words and save the old woman from doing so.

"And you think," He began, every word he uttered, a knife twisting in his heart, "It is time I moved on." Michael saw a single tear in Mina's eye, it squeezed itself free and rolled down her cheek.

"I have not said that."

"But you think it Mina and your husband would welcome it"

"Markos is an old man, he's frightened for the children, not himself."

"I could never harm any of you." Said Michael, words he would have liked to say stuck in his throat, he wanted to beg them to let him stay, but he knew that he must go. Mina was not telling him anything he didn't know and he should have realised that this conversation would eventually happen. "I'll go when the others are asleep." Michael tried his best to keep the bitterness from his voice, but Mina heard it. The wolf man looked past her and through the window, his gaze resting on Lilith as she sat by the big open fireplace waiting for her father to come and read to her.

"It can never be Michael." said Mina knowing where his eyes rested. "You can never love her." Mina reached out and touched him, Michael tore his gaze away from the girl and looked at the old woman. "Don't try and lie to me Michael." she said. "I have seen the way you look at her, do you think me as blind as Lilith?" Mina put down her knitting, she lay the tangle of wool on her knees. "Another time another place, different circumstances, I believe Lilith could love you, but then,"

"She loves all crippled beast, for am I not that, a beast!" The bitterness which he spoke the words shocked the old woman, Mina took his hand and held it to her, she had never really feared him. Only the once had her strength and beliefs wavered, the night she actually looked into the werewolf's eyes.

"You are what you are and no one not even Lilith can change that." Michael felt her squeeze his hand in hers, Mina bent and touched his hand with her lips. "I could offer you pity, but of what use is that, instead I give you my love."

"Is it dutifully love Mina or is it given freely?" Mina looked at Michael, how did she answer him, this lonely man.

"It is given freely." She said "Oh I admit in the beginning it was duty, but Michael, I have looked into your eyes. And I know that somewhere in that cursed body of yours is a soul. There is goodness inside of you." Michael laughed and startled Mina, Michael laughed again at the startled expression on Mina's face.

"A soul Mina." He said "What I wouldn't give to believe you, look at me Mina feast your eyes on my ugliness, tell me Mina what do you see?" He asked. "I have heard you say that I am a handsome man, a man in the prime of his life." Michael turned her hand and traced the lines of her old age across the back of it. "See this flesh of yours," He said looking deep into Mina's eyes "Once it was smooth like Lilith, now it grows old. Once you were young and eager for life, for love, touch my skin Mina, run your fingers over it, what do you feel? Revulsion? No, no, that was wrong of me to say such words to you. But feel it Mina, touch it, pinch it, it is the flesh of a forty year old man." Again the bitter laugh from Michael, Mina took his hands and placed them each side of her face, Michael felt the wetness of her tears on his skin.

"I am dozen times the age of Markos and more, I was a boy of Peters age when a Stuart King sat on the English throne, but that matters not, and I won't bore you with my life. Within this body of mine flows the infected blood that keeps me a prisoner, here," He said pressing his finger against his heart, "Here inside of me beats a heart that will forever pump the blood that keeps me this way."

"You say I cannot love Lilith, that she can never be mine, you are right but you are also wrong. I see fear in your eyes Mina, but you have no need to worry, I never have and I never will create another like me. I could not bear the thought that I had cursed another to a life like mine."

"You say I cannot love her and I ask you why not? I know it can never be the kind of love a man wants from a woman. I know I shall never know Lilith in the true sense, but someday some man will and I envy that man. But I can love her."

"Soon," Michael continued, "Soon I must leave this place and journey into the outside world, the unknown. I have only heard of this world from the papers Markos reads to Lilith, here you are in a cocoon, for the real world has still not entered this place. Markos reads of things called aeroplanes and electricity, a way in which whole towns and cities can be lit up by the flicking of a switch. The other night he talked of a thing called a telephone and how people can speak to each other over hundreds of miles away. In my time, to speak of such things would get you burnt as a witch or a warlock. Too long have I hidden from this world, hiding my monstrosity in dark places."

Mina held back the words she was going to speak, perhaps it was better to let Michael speak. To let him talk about the things he feared, about the terrible cancer that ate at his heart and his soul. For Michael had to live with the festering knowledge that he was immortal.

In the shadow of the doorway Markos listened to his wife and the man talking. More than once he had thought to interrupt their conversation and take his wife away from this creature. A thing that could talk like a man, act like a man, think like a man. Instead he listened, he listened to the sadness and loneliness in the man's voice. The longing of wanting to belong , to be accepted into human society. The knowing that filtered through his words that he himself knew that he belonged among the dead. The gods that ruled Michael's life took pity on him and the hatred in the old mans heart dissipated. The fallen one took the cold tendrils of hate and pulled them free from the old mans heart. Markos had never really hated Michael for what he was, but he loved his family and had wanted to protect them. He did not want them too burdened with duties the old religion placed on Mina and himself. That thought had sealed his heart and mind against the plight of the moon child. Holding his breath Markos moved closer to his wife and Michael.

"Lilith," Said Michael "Is pure and unspoiled by the touch of man, but like me she carries a curse, perhaps that is why I feel her to be a kindred spirit. But my curse is an obscenity in the eyes of the Christian God and his followers. But Lilith what dark god could have given her a heart full to bursting with love for all things. Then rob her of the sight to see them and the voice to talk to them. Answer me this Mina if you can, are all the gods, Christian and Pagan, dark? Is the fallen angel of your people so biased that he will not lift this curse that I carry?"

"Once, long ago I was told by a woman who loved me that I would have to discover for myself how I would live in this world. She also told me that one day when I was on the point of death, when even I, who despise him, would cry out for the fallen angel to save me. She said I would hear a voice and if I followed that voice I would reach a place to rest." Michael felt the presence of the old man behind him, the touch of Mina's hand on one of his. Markos placed his hand on Michaels shoulder and reached for his wife with the other. Michael felt in that big calloused hand a feeling of wanting to understand and finally offer him help. Markos didn't speak he believed that through his touch Michael understood his action. "When shall I hear this voice Mina?" Asked Michael "I didn't hear it when Lilith found me."

"I'm so sorry Michael, I don't know, we are neither Wych or Guardian, all we can do is help you." Mina struggled to her feet and put her arms around Michael and holding him to her rocked back and forth. Wrapped in the embrace of the two old people, he was held in a silent understanding, that perhaps for a short time they could dispel his loneliness.

From that night Markos began to talk to Michael, from their talking came a form of trust. Not a complete trust for Markos still had reservations as to how Michael would react if he was threatened. But the old man did allow Michael to accompany him into the forest and took a great joy in teaching the moon child how to use his tools. Peter of course took everything in his stride, when he was with Michael he chattered on incessantly about everything and nothing. But for all his trust in Michael the old man still would not allow him to join Lilith as she walked in the forest.

"Michael would you like to come to the village with me?" Markos saw that his offer had caused the moon child to have to think about it. "It is time the villagers saw my cousin from over the mountains, well what do you say?" Markos had spoken of his idea with his wife the night before. "Peter has talked so much about our cousin that I think it's better I show him off, sooner than one of them surprising him in the forest." Mina had mumbled it was about time, turned and went to sleep.

The sights and smell of the market excited him, and he gloried in being part of the human throng. He listened to loud voices haggling over prices, his eyes drank in the multitude of bright colours the women were wearing, men who smelt of tobacco and strong wine. He cocked his head to catch the sound of music, drowned by the raucous laughter of men and women in their cups. Markos saw his eyes open and his head lift slightly as the smell of a certain establishment, connected to the tavern. The scent of sex carried to Michael, above the dozens of different smells he caught this one. Michael closed his mind to it, for he felt a stirring in his loins, he could imagine the sweaty bodies coupled in lust thrusting at each other. He could taste the saltiness of a woman's sex on his tongue, he felt the hairs on his arm stiffen, Michael forced it to the back of his mind. Markos had understood Michaels longings and had offered him money should he wish to go to them. Michael shook his head, "I dare not, for it would not be safe for the woman, I don't believe I would be able to hold back the changing." The two men refrained from discussing the matter further, but the longing for a female remained with Michael for days.

On other occasions he went to the village with either Markos or Peter and sometimes both of them. When the bargaining was done Michael would sit by the edge of the village and wait, avoiding the scents of the brothel. If he was with Markos he did not have long to wait, but Peter would while away hours talking to his friends. To all intents and purposes he was the old mans cousin from over the mountains, he left the villagers alone and they didn't bother him, just nodding when they passed. This way he was able to avoid their probing questions, but always he would look and examine Peter's friends. Should he tell old Markos that he believed Peter was mixing with a bad crowd, for there was the smell of death and deceit about them. When Michael finally made up his mind to speak to the old man, it would be too late, for all of them.

With the passing of the days and his trust in Michael increasing Markos relented and allowed him to join Lilith on her walks. These times would become treasured memories for Michael, for she would take his hand as they walked for hours. The girl was full of the joys of living and Michael took pleasure in her silent company. And at times he would engineer it so that he brushed against her body, just to feel her touching him. Once when he had picked her a bunch of forest flowers Lilith had gently kissed his cheek. Michael had had to fight down the desire to take hold of her and crush her body against his.

Michael even considered changing and going to her as a wolf. It would be easy to feign injury, how would she react, with fear or kindness? Would she pass those hands over his body seeking for his injury? No, not even to feel her hands on him would he change, never again, he would stay human no matter what it took.

He had taken Lilith to her favourite spot in the forest, they were to have had a picnic and Michael at Mina's bidding was to tell the girl he was leaving in the morning. Michael was in a quandary as how to begin when the sound of Mina screaming came from the direction of the house. He jumped to his feet pulling Lilith with him, he scooped her up in his arms and began to run. He sensed the terror in the girl and saw her mouth working noiselessly as she tried to voice her fears. The distance to the house wasn't great and Michael covered it in less than four minutes, the girl weighing nothing in his arms. Leaping the steps Michael shot into the room putting Lilith down as he came to a skidding halt.

Mina stood her fist pressed hard against her mouth, Peter stared stupidly down at his father. Markos lay on his back, near the table , blood jetted from his leg like a red fountain. Michael knelt by the old man and tore at the fabric of the trousers, his hands covered in the old man's blood Michael saw the gaping wound in Markos's thigh. The chisel cut ran from hip to just below the knee, it had split the leg wide open. Michael kneeling in the ever widening pool of blood tried to hold it closed with his hands. Blood pumped up between his fingers and ran thickly from them onto the floor. He had to somehow stem the flow of blood, it was a deeper darker red and old Markos was white with shock and the loss of his life giving fluid. Michael saw death's skull face in the old man's eyes , its white bony features mocking Michael's attempt to save the old man's life. He must stop the flow of blood, the fire, Michael's eyes rested on the burning logs. In his eagerness to reach the fire Michael slipped in the pool of blood feeling it soak into his trousers and shirt. Its tangy sweetness filled his nostrils and Michael fought down his baser instincts. Without hesitation he reached into the fire and gripped the burning log. The flesh on his hands bubbled and swelled, Peter saw the grim determination on Michaels face, the pain in his eyes. He heard his father cry out as Michael pressed the burning log against the open wound, the smell of burning skin, the sizzling of blood. Michael held the log to the wound as long as he was able to bear the pain, when it became too much even for his great resolve he threw it from him. The blood had stopped, the wound was a mass of burnt flesh and congealed blood. Michael felt the pain in his hands and turned them, he saw blisters forming and bursting then filling again. Michael ignored the pain and looked down at Markos, the old man was breathing hard fighting for every mouthful of precious air. Death was stamped clearly in every line of the old man's face. Those few minutes it had taken Michael to reach the house had been too long. The amount of blood Markos had lost in those first few minutes was going to cost the old man his life. He looked towards Mina, she knew , it was written plainly on her face, she knew she had lost him. Michael put his arms under the old man's legs and shoulders and lifted him. Michael heard the sucking sound his feet made as he walked through the pool of blood towards the stairs. He carried Markos up the stairs and into the bedroom and he carefully laid the old man on the bed, the blood soaked trousers soaked the crisp white sheets of the bed. Markos opened his eyes and looked at Michael. "Stupid." His voice harsh and grating struggling to form the words he wanted to say. "Stupid, after all these years, stupid." A deep choking sound came from his throat, a long sad drawing of his final breath, "Mina." The harsh rasping sound filled the room, when it stopped the old man was dead.

Mina's sobs broke the silence of the room, she fell to her knees beside the bed. Her hands sought those of Markos and she held them tight, rocking her body back and forth. Her vision blurred with tears, she wiped them away, Mina saw her husband clearly before hot tears blurred her vision again.

The wolfman reached out to Mina then withdrew his hand, she did not need his touch she had Markos. It would profit him nothing if he tried to speak to her for words were of no use to her now. Michael turned and left the room. All the way down the stairs he could hear Mina's sobbing. In every one of her sobs he heard the love of their years together.

Peter stood where they had left him, the understanding of what had happened finally sinking into his shocked mind. Michael looked at Lilith, her blind eyes rolling madly, that sad awful grunting of her dead voice, wanting an answer. She looked so vulnerable, so alone and lost. Michael walked over to her and folded her in his arms. In a low voice and with all the gentleness he possessed Michael told her of her father's death.

Behind him Peter sobbed, sobbed with the loss of a father and the knowledge that he blamed himself for the death of his father, because he hadn't known what to do. In his arms Lilith's body shook uncontrollably, the awful grunting that came from her torturing his soul. Michael had seen death in its many forms over the years, he himself had killed, but the intimacy of death had never actually touched him before, not like it had this day. He held the girl until the sounds coming from her ceased. Michael looked down, Lilith had taken refuge from her sorrow in sleep.

"Peter." He said softly, "Peter." This time louder and with authority the boy turned towards him. His face was streaked with tears, his eyes red and puffy from weeping. "Take your sister to her room." Peter came towards him, he looked at Michael, at his sister and began to weep again. "Take her boy." Michael raised his voice, startling Peter who almost jumped at the sound of it. "Do as I say boy, take your sister to her room." Without speaking Peter took his sister from Michaels arms. "Peter." The boy looked at him. This time Michael's voice was softer, gentler, "Stay with her, in case she wakes, she will need you." Peter carried his sister out of the room, away from the congealed blood on the floor. Away from the place where their father had died.

Michael looked down at his bloody footsteps leading across the wooden floor to the bottom of the stairs. Without really knowing why he was doing it Michael fetched soap and water and washed away the blood. On hands and knees he scrubbed at the floor until all traces of the old man's blood had been vanished and the floor was clean.

Michael stood before the house and breathed deeply, clenching his hands into fists, forcing his nails to bite deep into his palms. He was fighting the change, stopping the beast inside of him from taking over. He tore at his bloodstained clothes tearing them from his body, he pulled the blood coated boots from his feet, naked he stood there. He cursed the creature that had turned him, he cursed his very existence to an uncaring sky. The death of a man who had befriended him had almost driven him over the edge. Michael lifted his head and howled his anger, was there no hope for him anywhere in this wide world? Was he never going to find peace, was death the only answer?

Without looking back, knowing what he was leaving behind him Michael walked into the forest.

THE VALLEY - Part 6

"What the fuck are we doing in this shit hole Vogel?" Vogel shifted in his chair and looked up from his report at the man who had seated himself across from him, Vogel sniffed and reached for his mug, he sipped at the hot liquid and tried to ignore the man. "Well," Asked the man, "What the fuck?"

"Keller." Sighed Vogel looking up and staring at the man over the rim of the mug. "Why don't you stop whining, day in, day out, whine fucking whine." The little sergeant put down his mug and said "Why don't you go and tell the Major you're not happy. Better still go and tell Mantz."

"And what do I say?" Asked Keller "Excuse me sir I'm sick of this place and I'm sick to fucking death of guarding stinking Jews."

"Tell him you want a transfer to a fighting unit." Vogel grinned at the frightened expression that crossed the man's face. "Tell the Major or Mantz you feel you would be better employed fighting the enemies of the Fatherland." Vogel heard one or two of the other guards stifle their laughs, they like Vogel were getting sick of Keller's constant winging and whining.

"I didn't say that," Blustered Keller "I didn't say,"

"You don't mean you won't fight for the glorious Fatherland Keller." Vogel corrected himself in the chair, he came up from his slouched position at the desk and glared at the hapless Keller. "Why don't you grow up Keller." He said "Do you think any of us like it here, well do you, can't think of anything to say?" Vogel brought the flat of his hand down hard on the desk top. "Answer me." He shouted at the man. Keller jumped to his feet a thin sheen of sweat sprung out along the top of his lip. "Nothing to say Keller, well that makes a change. Listen to me Keller you are a fat ugly ignorant bastard. You are a poor soldier and an even worse dog handler." Vogel was warming to his barracking of the man, not only was he having some fun at Keller's expense he was also directing the men's complaints away from the diminishing food stocks. Vogel let his bright eyes look at every man in his office, the reason they were all here was because he had checked the food supply and found a large quantity of it missing. "I know that you Keller, all of you," The sergeant's beady eyes making each man feel uncomfortable when Vogel looked at them in turn. "Have you been exchanging food with the female prisoners for a fuck." He let them think about it before he continued, "Believe it or not I don't mind you doing that, but if you get caught," He ran his finger across his throat. "Remember what happened to the others. Look lads," Vogel's voice altered to his fatherly one, the one where he convinced them he was right and they were all wrong, and he Vogel knew what was best for them.

"So the job stinks, but we're alright here aren't we? It's comfortable, and best of all it's nowhere near any kind of action. Think on, there's not much chance of stopping a bullet here."

"It still doesn't explain what we are doing here." Damn Keller why did he always have to try and have the last word. Why couldn't they be satisfied to be in a safe place. God knows they had little enough to grumble about, keep the prisoners at work during the daylight hours and pull a night patrol every now and then. Vogel gave them one of his best theatrical sighs and said.

"I don't know why we're here either. The Major doesn't take me into his confidence." He looked directly at Keller. "Now," He said softly, "Before I loose my temper, Keller get out there." Keller moved reluctantly, he hated patrolling the compound at night, even with the dog he hated it. "The rest of you not on duty get out of my office now." Vogel waited until his office had cleared before he allowed himself to smile. Hopefully he had planted the seed of mistrust for their fellow soldier regarding the missing food, he was convinced that Keller would have a rough ride over his visits to the female prisoners, at least it would give them something to think about. Vogel lifted the mug and sipped, he pulled a face at the bitter luke warm coffee. Vogel moved over to the open door of his office, he would stand here and have a cigarette and drink the filthy stuff. Let them think he was checking up on them, rub salt into their already suspicious minds, besides Keller would get the blame for everything. Vogel watched the six man night guard walk past, they had their rifles at the correct angle and they made some attempt to march in unison. The sergeant looked at the dogs, they seemed to be in good health, but one in particular constantly sniffed at the ground and occasionally lifted its head and looked towards the forest. Vogel hoped the wolf hadn't been on the prowl, slinking around the compound.

He pulled at the cigarette and echoed Keller's words, why the fuck were they building the airstrip. There was nothing round here worth bothering about, only mountains, trees and too much fresh air. Vogel and his dogs and the misfits they had given him command of had been stuck in this god forsaken place, without leave, since the end of the winter in thirty seven. He had watched the prisoners work like animals, labouring under terrible conditions to create the airstrip out of the valley floor. He had watched the slaughter of the Poles, the ground turning red with their blood. Vogel lifted his head and looked towards the man made pass, somewhere out there under thousands of tonnes of rock lay the remains of the dead Poles.

The sergeant spit and then tossed the rest of his drink onto the ground, from where he stood he could look directly into Strobel's hut. Strobel and Mantz were having one of their animated conversations, Strobel doing all the talking and arm waving, while young Mantz sat there . He would have given almost anything to have been a fly on Strobel's wall at that moment. Like the rest of the men Vogel was curious as to what they were doing here, the man from the mean streets began to turn over in his devious mind the problem of gaining access to Strobel's office. There must be some kind of a report in the Majors office which gave the reason for building an airstrip here in this particular valley.

Vogel stepped out of his hut, no one would think twice about the sergeant taking a turn around the camp and checking on the officers huts. The old itch returned to his fingers as he cast a professional robber's eye over Strobel's hut, security was a joke he could open the hut with a spoon. An hour, twenty minutes alone, ten even and he would find the Majors hiding place. There had to be detailed orders from some one high up in the party, Strobel just didn't have the clout to be able to do this without party backing. A glimmer of an idea came to him, when he gave his early morning report to Strobel he would give the office more than his usual cursory glance.

Vogel walked back to his hut, closed the door and lay down on the camp bed without undressing. He closed his eyes and tried to recall in detail every thing he remembered about the Majors office. His mind probed every nook and cranny of the sparse office. No pictures on the wall only a plan of the airfield, a desk, two chairs, the iron stove in the corner, a box full of logs. Where would some one like Strobel hide the papers, in his bedroom, no, there was no safe in the office, on his person, Vogel dismissed that idea. He turned on his side, he would sleep on it, as he drifted slowly off to sleep his mind constantly returned to the desk, a lamp, pens, ink, paper, blotting pad, Vogel began to snore softly.

Vogel woke instantly, a grin on his thin face, he knew where the Major would have hidden his orders, under the large leather edged blotting pad.

The sound of Vogel whistling early next morning gave those coming off night guard cause to feel alarmed. The only other time they had heard him whistle was the day the six men who had raped the Jewess were shot. Had one of them overstepped the line, because of Keller was Vogel going to report their indiscretions in visiting the women prisoners. For the rest of the day those that were able, kept out of his way, the others kept a weary eye on the little sergeant.

But Vogel said or did nothing out of the ordinary, he made his morning report to Strobel and examined the office. He wandered around the camp, checking anything that took his fancy, and spent the rest of the morning with his dogs. Vogel was still whistling tunelessly to himself two days later, the men breathed a sigh of relief, concluding that the sergeant had been made privy to some good news that gave him pleasure.

The little man was more than pleased with himself he was ecstatic, he had planned his break in of Strobel's office down to the minutest detail. It was, if he was to believe himself the most audacious plan he had ever conceived. He was therefore somewhat disappointed when he was given free access to the Majors office by Strobel himself. The Major dropped his bomb shell at Vogel's morning report, he and Mantz had to leave the camp on business and since he, here Strobel looked down at the little man, since he Vogel was unfortunately third in command, he would sit at the Major's desk and if the telephone rang he would answer it and if need be write down what was said to him. "All communications from Berlin must be written down sergeant, in a clear concise and legibly hand. They will most probably be just general information, about new prisoners' food supplies and of course new dogs for you. That is of course if Berlin feels we need them." Vogel though about the Major's words, food, yes that would be welcome. Prisoners, well those here now were dying daily. New blood no matter how starved would replace the dead. Dogs, now that was a different matter, the animals he had now were used to the wolfman's scent, a new batch could cause trouble. The little man decided, no matter what Strobel said he would somehow manage to reject a fresh intake of dogs. .

He had waited almost two hours before he eagerly lifted the large blotting pad. Had anyone witnessed the expression on Vogel's face they would have fallen about in helpless laughter. Shock, surprise, disgust, anger and the uncontrollable tears of frustration which rolled down his thin face. Under the pad the desk was bare, there was nothing under the pad or in it, Vogel didn't believe it, it had to be here, there was no other place to hide it. Vogel drummed his fingers on the top of the desk, his brain working overtime, thump, thump, thud. Where, where, where? His eyes closed in deep concentration, he allowed his fingers to continue drumming on the wood, thump, thump, thud.

The little sergeants eyes shot open, he stared down at his hand, very slowly he moved them, thump, thump, thud. His eyes riveted to his moving digits, he sat there, thump, thump, thud, thump, thump, thud. "The crafty bastard." Vogel carefully drew a square on the desk top roughly the size of the pad and with the precision of a surgeon he tapped the wood, listening and grinning each time a finger went thud instead of thump. He looked at the square, he tapped it until he was certain he had found what he was looking for. "Now." He said wetting his lips, "Where's the spring to open it?" Vogel placed his fingers around where he believed the spring to be then stopped. Careful he must be careful, he couldn't afford for anyone to see him, if he got caught he would end up dead. Vogel was beginning to sweat, he had come this far, so a little caution wouldn't hurt. He wondered if he drew the blinds would anyone notice, Vogel snorted his disgust at his idea, of course they'd notice. Curiosity was getting the better of him and his fingers itched to try and open the secret panel, damn it he'd risk it.

He forced himself to concentrate all of the searching into his finger tips, his eyes held the door, if anyone decided to enter he would hear the click of the latch. He held his breath, something moved beneath his fingers, he pressed a little harder. A square a foot by a foot lifted itself up from the top of the desk. Vogel saw the thin sheaf of papers, he licked his lips and forced himself to wait a second or two, he even managed to take a quick look out of the window. The area around the hut was deserted, Vogel rushed back to the desk and pulled the papers free.

He held them in front of him hiding the secret drawer, if anyone looked through the window it would look as if Vogel was completing his report for Strobel.

The hairs on Vogel's neck stiffened, a spider crawled with ice cold legs down his spine. His body trembled with excitement and then fear, his mouth went dry. Eagerly he pushed the papers back, he felt like someone had filled his hands with hot coals. Vogel was sweating profusely, despite his body being enveloped in an icy cold sweat. He clenched and unclenched his hands trying to get his circulation working.

The little man had found himself in some very difficult situations over the years but there had always been a way out. He wished to god that he had never looked at the papers, why did he have to be so fucking curious? The contents of the type written sheets had sent terror coursing through him, Vogel felt the wetness between his legs. "God help me," he murmured "I've pissed myself." His head was aching, his eyes were hot, he didn't know what to do for the moment he was a prisoner. "Mother of god." For the first time in many years the sergeant crossed himself, if the plans detailed in the papers worked the crazy bastards would rule the world.

Vogel made himself a promise, come the fourth of July he had every intention of being miles away from this valley. He knew it meant desertion so he needed to plan everything carefully, because he didn't intend getting caught.

Strobel replaced the hand set of the field telephone. "Everything is ready." His broad smile told Mantz that this little expedition of theirs had borne fruit. "The original date is still the one we work to." He opened his mouth and drew in a lung full of the mountain air, Strobel was a very happy man. He had carried out his orders exactly as Berlin had dictated, the fear that had rode his shoulders for the last few months had been lifted. "We've done it Mantz, completed and ready for test's exactly to the day and date planned and ordered by the Furher himself." Strobel had difficulty in containing himself. "Come Mantz let's go back."

Captain Mantz started up the car while Strobel put the field telephone in the back seat. "Soon Mantz I can tell you everything, things not explained in the papers." Mantz pulled the car around in a tight circle and headed for the gap the engineers had cut in the mountains. "You're a good soldier Mantz." Strobel broke off humming some obscure operatic aria he was particularly fond of. "There's promotion in this Mantz, promotion for both of us." He began to hum again his fingers drumming on the dashboard as if accompanying himself on a piano. "And glory boy." The suddenness of Strobel's shout caused Mantz to swerve, under his breath the captain cursed the man. He gave a quick glance down the ravine, the road cut out of the living rock was only just wide enough for one vehicle at a time to travel on it. Strobel slapping his knee didn't help matters, and it was a hell of a drop to the bottom. Ignoring Strobel he concentrated on his driving, changing down as the car struggled up the steep incline before dropping into the valley. The wide strip of Tarmac and concrete stretched out before him, dissecting the valley. Four years of planning had gone into this project, more planning than Strobel would ever know. He may be a brilliant engineer, but brains immeasurably more talented than his had worked out where the airstrip would be and why it should be there. These minds had worked to a time and a date and they had achieved all they had set out to do, the development of "Iron Fist" and the airstrip had been carefully calculated to come to completion at the same time.

When first assigned to this project Mantz had baulked at it, he didn't want to be buried in this isolated valley guarding Jews and Gypsies and the misfits of the German army.

But an interview with Himmler had changed his mind, especially when Himmler explained why "Iron Fist" was being created. "To strike a blow against our enemies, before they become our enemies. To cut off the head of the snake with one quick blow." Three days later Mantz had joined Strobel's command, his job to watch Strobel, to ensure that the project was carried out no matter what the cost in prisoners lives. And of course to report progress on a regular basis to Berlin. Mantz grinned at Strobel's air of secrecy and his promise to tell him everything and the offer of promotion. Captain Mantz could not refrain from laughing out aloud, Strobel looked at him and joined in the laughter, imagining that his joy had infected the young man.

Taking one hand from the wheel he touched the pistol at his side, he laughed out loud again, here was Strobel's promotion, nickel plated lead. "To glory Major." He said "To the everlasting glory of the Third Reich."

"To glory Captain." Echoed Strobel and again joined in the captain's infectious laughter.

Michael moved slowly back into the main area of the cave, he had just spent the best part of two hours searching the passages. He had been hoping that perhaps there was a way out, he had been disappointed. It would be almost impossible to climb up the rock face and out of the valley, Katji's condition made it impracticable. How, even with the strength the two men possessed, did you carry a heavily pregnant woman up the side of a mountain. Michael had stood before the opening of the cave and looked up at the rock face and the overhang, he could make it and he believed that Tibor could. But the Wych woman, Michael thought long and hard, he would try and climb up to the overhang. If he could get a rope secured up there they could pull Katji up. But first he had searched the cave, when that proved hopeless, he decided to attempt the alternative.

Tibor was fussing around Katji, each time she tried to do anything he was there before her, getting in her way. Finally Katji snapped, she threw the spoon at Tibor, then burst into tears, then laughter as he stood there, soup dripping down his face and into his beard. From her small height she glared up at the six foot six giant, who had the good grace to blush. "Will you cluck round me like a mother hen when the child is crying to be changed or fed?" She asked. Michael thought that discretion was the better part of staying out of an argument between man and wife. He sat in the corner and didn't move until Katji had vent her spleen on the hapless giant. Tibor moved over towards him, looked down, his face said it all, don't say a word.

While they ate Michael explained what he would like to try, "It is a difficult climb Michael." His mouth full of food the wolfman nodded, "But it's worth a try, if we don't go soon,"

"The child will be born in this cave." said Katji, the two men turned to look at her. "My, our" she corrected herself before taking Tibor's hand "Our daughter will be born in our valley."

"A daughter." asked Michael. "You have seen all this?" He asked.

"Yes Michael, I have and I also know that we will escape from the valley."

"Then," said the giant, "That makes everything perfectly alright, we have nothing to be afraid of moon child."

"Oh don't be stupid Tibor, I did not say there would not be danger, I have not seen all that will take place, I only know we will leave this valley," For the rest of that day Tibor said nothing, he ignored Michael and refused to talk to Katji. "The silly man sulks like a spoilt child." But when Katji retired for the night the giant lay beside her his arms wrapped around her.

Michael was awake and ready to attack, his eyes blazed feral, the sound of boots on the path outside the cave. He heard the click of the pistols hammer being drawn back, he turned his head, Tibor was wide awake the gun pointing at the entrance to the cave. Michael looked at him, and placed a finger to his lips the giant nodded, there was something familiar about the smell of the trespasser. "Vogel." he said, his voice low, he eased himself to his knees and then to his feet. "Leave him to me." Once again Tibor nodded agreement with the wolfman.

Vogel breathing heavily, gasping for breath from the long climb from the camp, through the forest then up the narrow path to the cave, stood there.

"Jesus Christ." His frightened voice uttered as Michael's hands grabbed him and pulled him through the opening. Vogel felt himself being lifted and carried, "Michael" His hoarse whisper filled the cave, "It's me Vogel." The wolfman said nothing to him as he dropped him unceremoniously on the cave floor, Vogel grunted at the contact his body made with the hard rock. "What's going" His voice trailed off as the cold steel of the pistols barrel touched his throat. Katji held the torch towards the man on the floor, Vogel twisted his head and looked up at the giant Tibor. In the yellow light of the torch the giant was an awesome sight.

"What the hell are you doing here?" Asked Tibor pressing the gun barrel harder into Vogel's neck "Speak."

"Perhaps if you took the gun away" said Katji. "He would find it easier to speak." Tibor eased the pressure on Vogel's neck and the man breathed deeply. Hard fingers took hold of his chin and turned his face, Vogel looked into the eyes of the wolf and had the insane desire to cross himself.

"Speak little man." Said Michael "And speak the truth." He looked towards Tibor who still pointed the gun at him. "Your life depends on it."

Vogel swallowed hard and began to talk, Tibor never dropping the gun, Michael sat on his haunches, Katji her face turned away from them, listened to Vogel's story. Vogel finished off his story with a petulant, "I've risked my life to get up here." And rubbed his bruised neck, glaring at the giant Tibor.

"How do we know he speaks the truth Michael?" asked Tibor. Vogel felt unable to take his eyes off the gun in his hand. He turned to Michael seeking help from the wolfman, Michael said nothing. "If what you say is true little man," said Tibor, "how is this?" He looked down at Vogel, "Iron Fist" Said Vogel. "This Iron Fist is to be brought here."

"You've seen the airstrip, they must be bringing it in by plane, but it has to be a big one." Vogel tried to move, Tibor shoved the muzzle of the gun hard into him. "Michael." he pleaded with the wolfman.

"Let him up Tibor he speaks the truth." said Katji, she put her hand on the giants and pulled the gun away from Vogel's neck. "Here little man." She said "Drink this." Katji handed Vogel the tin mug.

"Come Vogel." said Michael. "Tell me once again." Tibor didn't put his gun away and his eyes never left the pair of them as Vogel went over his story again. Katji looked at Michael, she could see he was having difficulty in understanding all that the man called Vogel was telling him. Finally Michael got to his feet and walked over to the giant and Katji. "I don't understand it all." He said "But tell me, explain to me what do you understand about this I don't" Katji moved to his side and placed a small hand on his arm, she looked up at Michael and in a low voice she said.

"It has to be stopped, one way or another Michael, it has to be stopped."

"Otherwise the world will never know peace again." Added Tibor, Michael looked from Katji to Tibor to Vogel, he saw fear in all of their eyes. Then he asked the question Tibor and Katji, even Vogel was hoping Michael wouldn't ask it.

"But how do we stop it?" He asked "How?"

At an airfield in the heart of Germany a large bomber painted with the insignia of the R. A. F, taxied to the end of the runway , turned and began to build up its speed. When it had reached maximum speed the lumbering plane lifted up from the runway and its nose reached towards the night sky. Iron Fist was on its way.

LILITH - Part 2

"Hello." said a voice in his ear, Michael did not look up. "Don't I know you?" Michael didn't answer the man's question. He broke a piece of bread from the loaf and dunked it in his soup. From under hooded eyes he looked around the Inn, no one seemed to be taking notice, they were concerned with their own business. He chewed the bread and swallowed, reached for more, "I'm positive I know you." Said the man, "May I join you?" Michael waved his hand at the vacant seat, whether the man knew him or not Michael did not want to bring attention to himself. He looked up from his meal and gave the man a cursory glance, he didn't recognise him, then he had met hundreds of people over the last three years, he couldn't be expected to remember all of them. Michael dipped his spoon in the thick potato soup, since the man offered no apparent threat to him, better to have him sitting with him. The wolfman was aware of the man studying him, perhaps they had met, still Michael could not remember his face.

"Got it." Said the man, Michael looked up, the man had the kind of nondescript face of a thousand other men. "Cousin to old Markos Jurgens." With the spoon between lips and bowl Michael paused, and looked at the man, who for reasons best known to himself was grinning at him. "Never actually spoke to you, but I did see you around the Village with old Markos and that son of his." The man placed his tankard on the table and lent forward. "Michael, that's it, your name's Michael." Michael smiled back at the man, the last thing he had wanted was to be recognised, since it would be stupid of him to deny it, he said. "I'm sorry, I don't remember your name."

"Otto Steiner." The man held out his hand. "The butcher in Mantz's." Michael took the scared hand criss-crossed with many a slip of the butcher's knife. Strange that a man who was a comparative stranger to him should tell him something he had never thought to ask, the family name of Markos. "Didn't see you at his funeral." Steiner's voice broke Michael's train of thoughts.

"No." He said "I was forced to return home." How could he explain to this man or any other the real reason he had left, suddenly Michael wanted news of the family , particularly news about Lilith.

"Bad business." Said Steiner. "Terrible, a good man." He lifted his tankard and drank deeply from it. Michael reached out and put his hand on Steiner's forcing the man to lower his drink.

"How are they?" He asked "Mina and the boy, and how is Lilith?" A look of fear came into Steiner's eyes as if at the mention of the family the subject was suddenly taboo. "You don't know?" He said. Puzzled Michael shook his head and Steiner acquired the furtive look of one who had news about a certain subject that couldn't be discussed in public. "Look," said the man "If you're really interested I'll tell you, but not here, too many ears." The butcher's voice had dropped his words barely a whisper. "Which way do you travel?"

"I hadn't decided," said Michael "But it looks as if I'll be going along with you."

"Right my friend." said Steiner, his voice returned to its normal pitch. "You're welcome to a ride, meet me by the statue in the square, about one." He held out his hand and Michael took it. "Believe me, I'll be glad of the company."

The beast inside of Michael could smell fear on the man, he watched as Steiner left the inn. Nobody appeared to be curious about his going and nobody looked up as Michael paid for his meal and followed him out. The wolfman paused outside the inn, only a craving to spend a few hours in human company had brought him to this town. He had shunned towns and villages for the past three years, only when necessity drove him did he enter one. But Steiner had aroused his curiosity, and he wanted to hear of the girl.

Michael was waiting by the statue when Steiner's wagon appeared around the corner of the houses. The butcher hauled on the reins and the horse came to a reluctant halt, its eyes rolled at the scent of Michael, who quickly jumped up beside the butcher. "Damn horse," Said Steiner. "Time I got myself an automobile." He cracked the reins and the horse after a second taste of the leather finally decided to move on, but not before it had turned its head and looked in panic at Michael. Michael was annoyed with himself he realised he should have stood upwind from the animal, too late to worry now and besides the butcher wasn't happy with his mode of transport anyway.

Steiner hadn't spoken since they left the town, which was now some three to four miles behind them. Michael forced himself to remain silent, he had a thousand questions building up inside of him, but it seemed the butcher needed to build up his courage before he spoke. Michael thought of Lilith, conjuring up a mental picture of the happy times he had walked alone with her. Steiner broke his train of thoughts when he asked a question which totally threw Michael.

"What do you think of the new order in our lives?"

"I don't know what you mean." Said Michael, perplexed at the question Steiner had just blurted out. "I don't understand."

"Where have you been?" asked Steiner disbelief in every word "Buried?"

"News is slow to penetrate where I have been." Michael was beginning to get agitated, he wanted to hear about Lilith, not about how things in Steiner's world had changed. "The family," said Michael, "Tell me about the family."

Again the wolfman smelt fear, he saw it in the man's eyes and the way his body slouched in the seat. Steiner took a deep breath, he had got himself into this, and he realised with a man like Michael he had no way of backing out of it. God, why did he have to go and greet the man, he could have had his drink and ignored him, the man wouldn't have been any the wiser. "Steiner." He said to himself "you always did have a big mouth." The butcher realised he had no option but to tell the man everything, he had to trust Michael to keep his mouth shut when he'd finished his story.

"I hope I'm not making any mistakes with you Michael, but if I am, remember I'm telling you this because you were old Markos's cousin." Steiner turned and looked hard at Michael. "And I can't see a man like you belonging to them." The butcher was beginning to sweat, the smell of fear in every drop of sweat.

"Tell me." said Michael. "I want to know." Michael had grabbed the butcher's wrist and was tightening his hand around it. Steiner heard the grinding of bones and an agonising pain which forced him to cry out. Michael realised what he was doing and let the man's hand go, a numbing pain filled the butcher's arm.

"God man, you nearly broke my wrist."

"I'm sorry Steiner." Said Michael, "But it seems to me that you have a story to tell me, that I am not going to like."

Steiner swallowed hard, his voice shook as he began to tell Michael what had taken place since he had left. And Steiner realised he'd better tell the man the whole truth, the pain in his wrist convinced the butcher that the man sat alongside him was a violent man. He spoke softly of the funeral and the weeks after it, "Then," He said, "Mina died."

"They say it was of a broken heart at the death of old Markos, not me, and not to others who thought the same way as I did. She didn't die because

Markos was dead, she died because of the way her son had turned out. He, you remember the crowd he used to hang around with, well he spent more and more time with them. And when some jumped up little shit came to our village and spoke of the new order about to take our country into a new era, he listened. We always thought he was a quiet boy, and that he would realise that his so called friends were nothing but idle louts. How wrong can you be, the young bastard turned out be the leader of them. And before long they were strutting around the village and the outlying area wearing the uniform of the master race, the Hitler youth corps."

"You wouldn't recognise him from the boy you knew, he turned completely bad, totally evil was the way the old police chief described him. But the old man made a mistake, he called it Peter to his face, one night the old man was so badly beaten he had to be sent away for treatment. The culprits were never found, but we knew who was responsible for it, and god forgive us we were so terrified by this time, we did nothing."

"Do you remember the old clock maker? Well it doesn't matter if you do or you don't. The man was a Jew, a harmless old man who never did any harm to anyone, they kicked him to death in the village square. They broke into his shop and smashed everyone of his clocks, then they burnt the house down." Steiner fought to control the emotions building up in his voice. "They came to my house, the evil bastards came into my house." Steiner's voice was still full of surprise that the event had actually taken place. "They came into my house." His voice trembled with anger at the memory of it. "They came into my house, they ripped the clock the old Jew had sold me down from the wall, they smashed it into a thousand pieces in front of me. They terrified my wife and daughter and told me that this was only a warning, that in future I should be careful not to trade with inferiors."

"I was petrified Michael, scared shitless but I had to ask, why had they done these things, what had the old man done wrong. I could hardly believe the hatred I saw in Peters face and what made it worse was that he actually believed what he was saying. They had murdered an old man, broke into his home and destroyed a life times work and do you know why? Peter said it was because the old man was a Jew." Steiner's voice trailed off and he sat quietly, Michael did not speak he was remembering a tall blonde haired boy. How could this be the boy he had known, the way the butcher was describing him he was a monster, "There's not much more to tell you." Said the butcher. "Peter let it be known that he and his gang of Blackshirts were the law and whatever they said went. And if we did as we were told they left us alone, why we didn't fight back I will never know, we sat there and let it happen, grown men terrified of a bunch of kid's. We covered up the death of the old man and god forgive us all we covered up a worse crime. About six months after Peter took control of the area a caravan came into the village, Gypsies, a man his wife and two young daughters."

Steiner began to cry, tears rolled down his fat cheeks and he was unable to control the sobs that came between each word he spoke. "He murdered them, he shot the old man and his wife in front of us all, because like the Jews they were inferiors who given the chance would taint the blood of the master race. It didn't stop Peter and his friends from raping the two girls before shooting them. There are times I still hear the girls screaming and begging for mercy, but we did nothing," Steiner began to laugh, his voice rose, hysteria was taking over. "Do you know what else this specimen of the new master race did, he killed the horse and the dog belonging to the gypsies, then he forced us to help him burn them."

"The stench was with us for days, the smell of roasting flesh, it is still with us, it will always be with us."

Michael said nothing, in his life he came across thousands like Steiner, who did nothing until it was too late then found out that there was nothing they could do. What had happened in the village had happened more times than the wolfman cared to remember, Peter, well he would deal with him whichever way he thought best. But Lilith, if the new order had decreed that Jews and Gypsies were inferiors, what of the girl, how would she fare under this new order? "What of Lilith?" He asked his voice low and full of concern, Steiner waited a moment until he had full control of himself.

"We do all we can for her, but we have to be careful because of her brother. She still lives in the house old Markos built, she won't leave it. It's heart breaking to see her, its bad enough for anyone normal having to live in these times, but Lilith, the way she is, the loneliness must be intense." Michael listened and thought, he had intended never to set eyes on Lilith again. He had wanted to forget her and the few months he had spent with her, she was a ghost from his past he didn't want resurrected. A feeling deep inside of him told him he shouldn't be going back. That his return was sure to bring further tragedy on the girl, but to see her once more, to look upon her, to hold her to him. Michael repressed the feelings that once more death was riding on his shoulder, he wanted to see the girl.

"I will go all the way with you." He said, Steiner turned to him, his face full of fear and his eyes full of terror.

"What about Peter?" he said "He won't like your coming back, and for Gods sake don't repeat a word of what I've told you, please Michael."

"Told me," Said Michael, "Told me, why Steiner we met by chance on the road. You gave a lift to a man who wished to visit his relative's." Michael tried to put the butcher's fears to rest. "What harm is there in that?" Steiner said nothing, he knew for a fact that if he didn't report Michael the moment he arrived at the village, Peter would find some harm in it.

They arrived on the outskirts of the village, late afternoon of the third day, Steiner had told Michael more of Peter's denigration into the cold obscene creature he now was. Michael still found it hard to believe that Peter had become this nightmarish monster everyone lived in dread of. It seemed his only redeeming feature was his love he still had for Lilith, but as Steiner had told him. Even blind and dumb Lilith had recognised the change in him and refused any and all gifts, even the food he provided for her. "She sensed his evil." Was the butcher's way of describing it. Michael knew that the man wasn't lying, his voice told him that, every word spoken about Peter was tinged with fear.

"So how does she survive?" If Lilith had sensed evil in her own brother, why had she not rejected him. "Stop the wagon." Said Michael, he jumped down, took his bundle from beneath the seat. "I'll walk from here, cut through the forest." He held up his hand to the butcher. "Thank you and your friends for all you've done for Lilith."

"Listen Michael." Now they were so close to the village Steiner had become a bundle of nerves, fear coming out of his body in a way that threatened to overwhelm the wolfman's senses. "I'll have to report I brought you here. I have to go directly to Peter." He let go of Michael's hand and flicked the reins onto the horse's rump, "I'm sorry it has to be this way."

"So am I, but when you see Peter give him my regards, no doubt he'll want to pay me a visit." Steiner was constantly looking around, it was obvious he was eager to be on his way, to be rid of Michael's company.

"Goodbye Steiner and thank you for the lift." Michael watched until the butcher and his wagon were out of sight. He smiled to himself, the butcher had been right to be careful Michael had noticed at least three men in concealed positions watching the road into the village. Michael's return would be reported by more than one person to Peter. He threw the bundle over his shoulder and started down the hill towards the house, he had a little over a dozen miles to go, he would reach Lilith before nightfall.

From the sounds that reached his ears he knew he was being followed, two men at least, the wolfman smiled and stepped off the beaten path. He wondered what would happen should he confront them, he decided against it, now was not the time to cause trouble. He moved silently across the carpet of pine needles, soon the men would be confused, angry that they had lost him, Michael went rigid, he heard the sound of heavy breathing, so they were not so stupid after all, clumsy yes, stupid, no. He waited until the two men had passed him before he changed his direction and moved off, the two men hunting him would be too far away now to hear him running. By the time they finally decided they had lost him he would be only a matter of minutes away from seeing Lilith.

Everything looked the same, the house needed some minor repairs, the smell of cooking carried across the yard. Everything looked the same but Michael knew it wasn't, there was no sound of voices in the house, no Mina sat rocking on the veranda. A feeling of a tremendous loss hung around the clearing where the house stood , it was as if someone had taken all the love the house possessed and ripped it from it. There was an overwhelming sense of loneliness around the house, the kind of loneliness Michael had lived with most of his life.

The feeling that he had made a mistake came back to him, it wasn't too late to turn away, he'd done it before, leave things as they were. Michael turned to go, footsteps sounded on the wooden veranda and he turned to look.

She was still as beautiful as he remembered her, he watched her feel for the edge of the door and move onto the veranda. She stood for a moment her head cocked to one side and he knew she was listening. Michael stood rigid and silent hardly daring to breath, had he not known differently he could have sworn those two milky orbs were staring directly at him. He saw disappointment on her face when the sounds that had brought her from inside the house did not announce the arrival of visitors. Not until Lilith had sadly returned into the house did Michael dare to breathe again. He moved slowly forward, it was too late to go now, had she not come outside perhaps he could have left. But not now, not now he had looked upon her again.

He stepped lightly onto the steps leading up to the house, before his boots had touched the top step Lilith was there. Michael walked over to her and looked down. "Hello Lilith." Was all he said. The girl paused for only a moment before she was wrapped in his arms. Michael held her close, he smelt the freshness of her, he buried his face in her long hair. The joy she felt at his being with her transmitted itself to him. He held her tight, not wanting to let her go, she sobbed her awful grunting cries, her tears soaked into his shirt front. Gently the wolfman held her from him and with a finger he wiped away the tears, he bent forward and placed a kiss on both her closed eyes. "I've come back to you."

How long they stood there, holding each other, Michael could never remember, he only knew he wanted it to go on and on. To feel her pressed against him to touch her, to drink in the sweetness of her scent. Tenderly he took his arms from around her and led her into the house, Lilith seemed reluctant to let go of him even inside the house. Michael sat her down at the table and tried to fetch her some food, but Lilith clung to him, as if by letting him go, the loneliness would return. Even as he filled the plates with food she clung to his shirt. "Eat." he said sitting her down. As he sat down across from her, her hand reached out and closed over his, Michael knew what he was feeling for her. He hoped that all she felt towards him was the pleasure of his company, that she would no longer be alone in the house. Michael watched as she ate the food, he realised how stupid he had been in coming back here, he knew he couldn't stay long, a month, two, maybe three, but eventually he would have to move on again.

Michael looked at her she really was a most beautiful young woman, he reached over and brushed the hair which had fallen across her face, away. Lilith caught his hand and pressed it to her, and a smile brightened her face. With all the tenderness and love he felt for her, he told her how he had heard about Mina. He did not mention anything about Peter, it was possible that if Peter was having the road watched it followed he would keep his eyes on his sister. Although he didn't feel the presence of any others, he had given his word to Steiner to say nothing to anybody what he knew about Peter.

When, finally he did mention her brother's name, her body stiffened and her hand tightened around his. If pretending to ask about Peter's health and well being created this reaction, how would she react if he asked about the rift between the two of them. Michael suddenly realised he was being not only stupid but ridiculous, of course she couldn't speak of Peter, she could only tell him things by her touch and reaction. To say nothing was the best thing to do, wait for Peter, he would pay a visit sooner rather than later.

Michael fetched logs and lit the fire, and when he was satisfied it burnt well he took Lilith and seated her beside it. Sat in the old man's chair, the girl resting her head on his knee, Michael lied to her. How could he tell her for the last three years he had hidden himself away from all human company, that if it had not been on a whim to be among humans for a few hours he would never have known about her, Mina and Peter. So he lied, he told her of the people he had met in towns and villages hundreds of miles away from her home. He fabricated incidents that made her laugh, all the time he rested his hand on her shoulder, not wanting to loose contact with her.

Michael paused in his story telling and looked down at her, Lilith had finally fallen asleep. Trying not to disturb her Michael eased himself out of the chair, bent and lifted the sleeping girl. Lilith did not stir, except to let her head fall on his shoulder, Michael carried her across the room and pushed open the bedroom door with his foot. Carefully he laid her down, and slowly, so as not to wake her, he covered her . He silently moved backwards out of the room, his eyes never leaving her until he reached the door. Michael closed the door and went round the house making sure all the windows were barred and locked, then he locked and bolted the main door.

He stretched out on the bed in the room where Peter had slept, he knew no one could take him by surprise, but he could not get rid of the uneasy feeling that his being here was bound to bring trouble of some kind. Within seconds the wolfman was asleep, but like the beast his senses were still tuned into the sounds of the night and the forest.

He was instantly awake, feral eyes pricked the darkness of the room, teeth moved ready to become fangs if he needed to fight for his life. Lilith stood in the doorway to the room, Michael breathed slowly and allowed the fangs to regress. It had been the sound of her bare feet on the wooden floor which had awakened him. It was the eyes of a man which watched her walk across the room, bend, her hand seeking the edge of the bed. Lilith lifted the blanket which covered him and climbed in beside him, the girl snuggled her body against his and pulled the blanket over them both. Michael lay still, not wanting her to know that he was awake, not until her deep breathing told him she was asleep did he move. He lifted her head and put his arm around her, the warm contact of her body caused the wolf's eyes to flare briefly. Lilith moved and her arm fell across him, her face touched his, Michael fought down the desire to turn to her, press his lips against hers. The longing for her made itself felt in his loins, her female scent filled his every sense, he could smell her, taste her, feel her, hear her soft breathing. Michael lay still, not wanting or daring to move in case he disturbed her rest and slowly the yellow eyes faded. Michael spent the remainder of that night staring into the darkness, holding her close to him, he saw the first faint finger of dawn poke through a crack in the shutters.

It was past midday when Lilith finally awoke, her hand seeking the body of the man she had slept beside through the night. Panic gripped her when she failed to find him, frantically she struggled free of the blanket and off the bed. Had she dreamed it, was Michael only a figment of her lonely imagination. It couldn't be, she had touched him, held him, she had heard his voice. The choking sound of her own voice rebounded in her ears, please god don't let it be, please don't let me be alone again.

The sound of a saw being dragged across wood brought her to a stop. She stood in the centre of the room her heart pounding wildly. Lilith felt her body go slack as the tension inside of her subsided. She did not move until her heart had slowed to a regular beat and her nerves had stopped jangling. The sound of the saw was like the sweetest music she had ever heard, Michael was still here. She had not dreamed it, and suddenly she felt happy, for the first time in months she felt happy. It's only a little happiness her mind told her, but if Michael stayed it would grow and grow. She had to believe it would be so, she wanted and needed it to be so.

With accustomed practice and ease she moved towards the stove, a fire already burnt in it, Michael had been busy. With the deftness that all blind people learn to live with, Lilith opened cupboards and found the food she wanted.

Michael paused in his work at the sound of pans banging on the stove, so the girl was finally up and about. He had left her side just after dawn, needing to feel the morning's freshness on him, to think about the situation he had placed himself in. He half turned to go to her, but changed his mind, the girl was probably happy doing what she was doing. Let her make him a meal, to take her mind off, of what had happened to her. He could still smell her scent on him, and he realised that it was not danger he had brought to Lilith. Not the kind of danger he had anticipated, but a kind of danger more deadly than any foe he would ever meet. It hit him with a suddenness he wouldn't have thought possible, his return had given her a reason to be alive. "God forgive me." he should not have returned, he had felt it , known it, now it was too late . From the moment he had set foot on the steps to go into the house, he had known, now he knew he could never leave her again. He rested the saw against the log he had been sawing and tried to think of other things, the repairs to the house. Old

Markos had built it well, it had withstood the elements for the last fifty years. The only real damage Michael could see was the broken railings around the veranda.

What had he done to her, stupid was not the word he would use for his recent actions, thoughtless, selfish. What did he do now, like many a confident beast before him, he had willingly walked into a honeyed trap. Think about other things, his brain screamed at him, forget the girl for a moment, Peter think about Peter.

Michael cleared his mind and looked towards the road, he had spotted the two men easily, one lay on the edge of the forest. The other on the slight incline, hugging the ground trying to imitate the rocks he was hiding behind. Michael guessed that these were the same two men who had tried to follow him yesterday. He knew that Peter would be coming soon, if all that Steiner had told him was true , he couldn't imagine the boy leaving it too long before he made an appearance.

The banging of an iron skittle on a metal pan told him his meal was ready. His eyes still on the two men he walked over to the bucket and plunged his hands into it. It had gone tepid with the heat of the sun, but he didn't care, he splashed it over his chest and arms, then he trust his head into it. Michael took a mouthful of the water, swilled it around his mouth and spat it out, using his shirt he rubbed his head and hair, feeling drops of the water run down his back. Michael stood there letting the sun dry the excess water from his body. Lilith banged the pan incessantly, Michael smiled even a woman without a voice could show her disapproval of a meal going cold.

The two men hadn't moved, Michael smiled yet again, let them stay there they were causing him no bother, unless they decided to move closer. Then he saw them as a threat not only to himself but to Lilith, then he would do something about them. But until that time let them stay where they were he intended to enjoy the meal Lilith had cooked for him.

Michael ate his meal in silence, the situation he found himself in upper most in his thoughts. Looking at Lilith he knew he would never ever leave her, but he couldn't take her away from this place, she would never survive in his world. The one thought that went round and round his brain disgusted him, he could not, would not attempt to turn Lilith. Michael was learning something new, to be wanted , needed just for himself. It was an experience he wasn't totally confident of handling. Then suddenly it came to him, of course he could take her away from here, Markos and Mina had been born gypsies. Any tribe would welcome her, Michael's hopes were dashed at the sound of boots on the wooden steps and he recognised the wearer. "Come in Peter," He said without lifting or turning his head to look. At the mention of her brother's name Lilith grabbed his hand, he felt her nails digging into his flesh. It was unbelievable that she was actually terrified of him, he could smell her fear of him, it clung to her like a cloak. Michael bent his head towards her, "Don't worry." He said and he was rewarded by a weak smile. He turned towards the man just inside the door, a handsome, blonde haired, blue eyed young man, tall, powerfully built, the perfect picture of the new master race.

Michael examined the man stood before him, the highly polished riding boots, the jodhpurs style breeches, the black jacket with its silver buttons. Tightened at the waist by the wide leather belt which carried his pistol, it was hard to believe that this was the boy he had once known. Michael realised he was looking at a man who held absolute power, and knew how to use it. "It's good to see you again." Said Michael.

Peter did not walk into the room, he sauntered in, his cold blue eyes taking every detail of the man sat at the table, Peter sat on the edge of the table looking down on Michael and his sister. He rested one booted foot on a chair, and appeared to be inspecting it, he flicked away an imaginary speck of dirt with his riding crop.

"I." He began his voice as cold and as dead as his eyes, "We, my sister and myself, didn't expect to ever see you again." There was no warmth in his voice as he continued to speak. "Why did you come back?" It was a direct question from a man expecting a direct answer, not asking for an explanation demanding one.

"I heard about Mina, I met this man." Michael paused, pretending to think, "The butcher, Steiner, that's it, Steiner, he told me what had happened, and I thought perhaps I could help."

"Why?" Asked Peter, the question like the rest of their conversation, short, demanding an answer.

"Because I owe you all my life." If Michael expected some kind of reaction to this from Peter he was disappointed, there was no emotion of any kind on his face. Peter drummed his fingers on the table, ignored Michael and bent to kiss Lilith on the cheek, the girl shuddered at his touch.

"Dear sister," He said, slowly as if measuring every step, he crossed over to the door. With a theatrical gesture he stopped and turned. For a second Michael thought he saw the faintest glimmer of affection in his eyes towards his sister. Then it was gone, the eyes were cold and the voice devoid of feeling, "Come with me please Michael." Without waiting for an answer Peter left the room, Michael knew he had little option but to go after him. Lilith tugged at his arm, Michael looked at her, she was shaking her head, Michael bent and brushed her lips with his. "I won't let him hurt you." How could Peter have fallen so low that someone so full of love for every living thing could be so afraid of him as Lilith was. Peter held no fear for Michael for if the need arose he knew he was capable of tearing Peter and his men apart.

Peter was stood beside a large black stallion, its harness sparkled in the sunlight, its coat a glossy black from the attention of an experienced groom. The black began to shy away as Michael approached, Peter tugged savagely at its bridle. The horse stopped tugging at the reins, but it stood there trembling with fear at the scent of the beast.

"As you can see Michael, my sister is not happy with my presence." He smiled and tapped his crop against the horse's neck. "Still," He said, "That is one of the reasons I don't often visit her. Still it is none of your business." Peter turned and put his foot in the stirrup and pulled himself into the saddle "While you visit with my sister, my men won't molest you." He pulled at the reins beginning to turn the horse. "Be warned Michael, don't overstay your welcome."

Michael grabbed the horse's bridle and stopped it from turning, anger flared in Peters eyes and he lifted the riding crop to strike Michael. The warning he saw in Michael's eyes stopped him, for the first time in his young life he was looking down at a man who wasn't afraid of him. "I have lived too long to be terrified of a boy." Peter glared at him, his face getting redder by the moment. "When I think the time is right, or Lilith does not need me anymore, then I will go and not before."

"I could snap my fingers and have you killed, I have given you a warning, don't stay around too long."

"And Lilith?" Asked Michael "What becomes of her?"

"She is my sister and while I live no one, no one will hurt her."

"Not like you have Peter." The boy was suffused with anger, his eyes burnt with an anger Michael had rarely seen in a human, his lips a tight slash as he ripped the reins free of Michaels grip.

"One day I do believe I will have to kill you." His free hand moved to the pistol by his side, Michael heard his words and knew that Peter was not making idle threats he was simply stating a fact.

"That would be a terrible day for all of us." Said Michael, "Especially you." Was this the sense of foreboding he had carried with him, was he to kill Peter and so cause Lilith more hurt than he could ever hope to repair. He saw death in the young mans eyes and he hoped Peter could see death staring back at him. Peter turned the horse and raked it with his heels forcing it into a gallop. Michael saw the crop rise and fall across the horse's rump, Steiner had been right, whoever or whatever had seduced Peter he was now totally evil.

Michael watched until Peter disappeared around the bend in the road, he then searched for the two men, they had also vanished. From now on he would have to be careful, he would never leave Lilith on her own unless it was absolutely necessary. The sound of her strange mewing made Michael forget everything else as he ran back to the house.

Had he not been preoccupied with thoughts of Lilith, he would have caught on the soft summer breeze a well remembered and hated scent. Had he caught the scent he would have been prepared for what was to happen, his mistake, for he would always remember it as his mistake. It was to end in an orgy of blood and death for the villagers and the woman he loved.

Lilith came again that night and shared his bed, like an innocent child she slept soundly in his arms. After that second night they moved upstairs and shared the large double bed, not once in all that time did Michael have to fight the change. The days and weeks that followed were spent walking hand in hand in the forest, or Michael did the few repairs the house needed. Lilith changed, Michael hoped it was because of him and the fact that Peter had kept his distance. Lilith was, Michael believed, happy, as happy as it was possible for him to make her.

So the summer passed without incident, and the first leaves began to turn brown and Michael smelt snow on the winds. The heady scents of summer vanished under a blanket of white and the warm winds turned a bitter cold. Sat by the fire, Lilith sat beside him her head on his knee Michael realised that time was passing by too quickly. His resolve to stay only a month or so had been stretched to over six. This realisation had come when the snows began to melt, and the forest began to sing with the sound of new life announcing the arrival of spring. Throughout these winter months he and Lilith lay in each others arms, though he longed to take her to him. Lilith showed no inclination for any sexual contact to take place and Michael had to convince himself this had to be right. They neither saw nor heard anything of Peter and had he not known that the village was barely twelve miles he could believe that he and Lilith were the only two people on earth.

It did not seem like being in solitude to them, there was no loneliness in their private world. They had each other, Michael loved her with every fibre of his body and he hoped that she returned his love, he never spoke of it for he felt it unkind to profess his love when she was unable to. The fact they had not consummated this love did not bother him for he knew it would come in time. He had waited and prayed for a time like this when he was to be loved and wanted just because he was a man.

It came when Michael least expected it to happen, they were sat by the fire, the first day of spring gently fading into darkness. It came with a lingering kiss from Lilith, it came with a depth of tenderness and all consuming love that he could only surrender to. It came slowly, there was no urgency to their lovemaking just a gentle but sensual exploration of each others bodies. From their first kiss to the overpowering climax Michael burnt it deep into his memory. The feel of her naked flesh against his, the heady smell of their sexual juices, the touch of her hands on his body, these things would never leave him.

That they had made love did not change anything between them except to bind them together with an iron band of love. The daylight hours became longer their nights together shorter, the words he spoke to her took on a new meaning. Their touching accidental or on purpose became precious moments to cherish. At night they lay wrapped in each others arms, during the daylight hours Michael hardly left her side. By the time he took stock of his life more than a year had passed.

The passage of time meant little to Michael and Lilith, they cared little for the happenings of the outside world. The colossal changes that had and were taking place throughout Europe. They had each other and Michael believed that at last he had found the peace and contentment he craved. The only blight on his horizon was that his love would grow old before his eyes, while he remained forever young trapped in the immortal curse of the werewolf.

He drove these thoughts from his mind, there was time left to him yet, before he had to take the only solution possible. For the time being he would be content with the gift the fallen one had seen fit to give him.

On the first day of summer seated on the veranda Lilith by actions and gesture told him she was pregnant, she was expecting his child. At his failure to respond to the good news Lilith's face crumpled and tears filled her sightless eyes.

Michael did not know how to respond to such astounding news the words he wanted to say to her would not come. He pulled her to him and sat her on his knee and rocked her back and forth gently. Was it possible, had the fallen one taken pity on him and decided to end his curse. Could such a thing truly happen, Anna had said it was impossible for the werewolf to propagate. But he had given his seed to this woman he loved, she was carrying his child, god in heaven let it be untainted. Please don't take this from me, to what god should he pray, Michael lifted his face up to the sky. If there is someone up there who can show me pity, I beg you please to allow this thing to happen to me. Michael held her close, the thought that he could have all he ever wanted, please don't let me loose it. He rocked back and forth holding her tightly never wanting to let her go.

Michael woke the next morning to the sound of a different noise, one he had never heard before. From the widow he saw his first car, he had been shown pictures of these vehicles, as he had seen pictures of aeroplanes but because of what he was he had spent too many years in hiding to be able to satisfied his curiosity over them.

He watched the car come down the small incline and move easily along the road until it reached the yard, at any other time no doubt Michael would have examined the car with great interest. The black sleekness of the car didn't interest him, it was the man seated in the back, Peter. As he looked upon the man, the brother of the woman he loved a sadness touched his heart. To whatever god Peter had succumbed to in the first place, it now owned him totally. The face was different, Peter's boyish looks had gone, only the cold handsome face remained the same, but even that was devoid of any trace of humanity.

The car stopped and the driver jumped out, Peter waited until the door had been opened for him before he stepped down. Once he had walked and strutted with the knowledge of power, now he moved with the spectre of death on his shoulders. Peter stood before the house, he appeared to be examining it, perhaps, Michael hoped, that somewhere inside the creature he had become he was trying to remember his past.

Michael and Lilith were seated at the table long before Peter decided to enter the house. She clung to the man beside her, the months of happiness wiped away in one visit by a brother she had once loved. Michael ached to go outside and ask him what he wanted, but he would not leave Lilith, she would not let him. The sound of footsteps on the veranda, the click of the latch and Peter walked into the house and Michael invited evil to sit at the table with them.

He looked at Michael and then at his sister, his lips curled in a sneer when he saw that Lilith was pregnant. "So little sister," He said, blowing smoke from his cigarette in their direction, "You appear to have grown up, become a woman." Peter removed his cap and placed it on the table, pulled out a chair and sat down before he continued, "I can only assume you are the father of the child she carries." Peter smiled as Michael's features tightened in anger. "Well, you would have to be, wouldn't you?" Michael did not answer him, his answer was curled in a tight fist beneath the table, he pressed the nails hard into his flesh and the claws retracted. For whatever reason he had decided to visit, Michael knew it would not be to their benefit. "Well Michael I had hoped you would be gone, it seems I was wrong, but" He said dismissing Michael's presence with a casual nod "It's Lilith I've come to see. I intend to take her with me to Berlin when I go there in three days time. There are doctors there that can help her." Lilith gave a croaking cry and shook her head vigorously. Peter blew a thin stream of smoke from the corner of his mouth, and tapped the table, Michael was aware that Peter was fast losing his temper. "Oh for gods sake Lilith, listen to me, I know your not stupid, I know you understand me, you will accompany me to Berlin," Lilith continued to shake her head, making those soft mewing cries of hers. "You will come." Said Peter "And let go of the man's arm, must you cling to him like a leech."

"Enough Peter." Peter turned to Michael, and gave him a quizzical look. "It's obvious she does not want to go with you."

"Let me say this so that even you can understand it, there are doctors in Berlin who think it's possible to give her back her voice. You," He said looking at Michael with the same contempt with which he regarded a slug, "You have planted your filth in my sister's belly, but I have told you and I have told Lilith, when I go to Berlin she goes with me." Peter stood up as far as he was concerned the interview was over, he had said what was to take place and that was an end to it.

He walked over to Lilith and put both hands on her shoulders, Lilith held her breath at his touch. "Lilith." He said, his voice soft, "You are my sister and I love you, and if what I am can give you," He never finished the sentence, for

Lilith had placed her hand over one of his, just for a moment the old Peter had broken through, Michael saw the look in Peters eyes , then the mask slipped back into place and he snatched his hand away. "Three days." He said. "Be ready to leave."

Michael stood up, and placed himself in front of Peter, "And if I say I won't let her go." Peter looked at him, he had expected this, well it was time this man was put in his place.

"You won't let her go." He said. "Michael must I continually repeat myself to you. Are there things you don't or won't understand?"

"Oh I understand Peter, but I asked you a question, what if I say no, Lilith stays here?"

"You fool." Peter laughed "You, don't be ridiculous how could you hope to stop me." There was no threat or challenge in Peter's words, he simply spoke them secure in the total belief that he held the power of life and death over them. "Don't even think about trying."

"Peter look at me." Michael did not move, their eyes met and Peter blinked, had Michael's eyes changed. He shook his head, for one second of time he believed he had looked deep into the eyes of the beast. Peter's mouth went dry, he tasted the bile of last nights wine, for one more second he tasted fear. Michael lent forward and his words were low and full of menace. "If you try and take her away from me, from this house, I will kill you." The words sank into Peters brain, cold and matter of fact, as if Michael was simply stating an everyday thing. "Be warned."

Peter swallowed and moved around Michael, he picked up his cap and fought to regain his composure, once beyond the eyes of the man he turned, nothing had changed, Michael was still Michael and the room was the same. He would have to take care of how much wine he consumed, it befuddled the brain, made you see things that were not possible. Secure now that he was away from Michael, Peter reverted to his normal self, he was no longer afraid of the man, but he still curled his hand around the pistol. "Three days." He said "I'll be back in three days." Michael sensed evil leave as Peter left and the house smelt clean again.

Lilith came to him and wrapped her arms around him, her whole body shaking with fear, Michael lifted her chin and kissed her. "Don't worry." He said holding her to him. "I won't let him take you away from here. Or from me." He whispered under his breath. Michael had to get her away from here, but where, would the villagers help him, he doubted it, Peter had too much power over them.

Three days was a long time, he could take Lilith and vanish long before Peter returned. But where, where could they go, he needed time to think, time to plan. It would be easy enough to take Lilith with him now, but in a few months time, the child would be due. He needed to be on his own, but he dare not leave her, tonight, when she slept, he would walk the forest, perhaps the answer would come to him then. Michael lifted his head and looked at the disappearing car, perhaps he should have told the arrogant young bastard that he was born of the same race as those he persecuted. That would have knocked the smirk from his vile face, but what would have happened had he spoken of Peter's blood? The man Peter now was would have committed any crime to hide it from his masters. Too late, too late for Peter to change, too late, damn there must be a way to get Lilith out of his reach, there just had to be. He had found too much to let it slip away from him, now!

From the fringes of the forest a pair of violet eyes watched the departure of the men in the car. They watched the house looking, checking every movement. The man in the house was dangerous, she had been told so. Be careful of him he killed without a seconds thought if he believed his life was in danger. But it wasn't his life they wanted , not yet anyway, the woman would die first and then he would feel the pain and suffering her mate had lived with for centuries. The black she wolf Petra settled herself on the carpet of pine needles and watched and waited, tonight she would sneak up to the house. Her violet eyes narrowed in hate at the sight of the man who slowly returned to the house, he had crippled her mate, he would die for it.

Michael was thinking like a man, his animal sense not in tune with the sight and sounds and smells of the forest. But even had he been in tune with nature he would not have caught the smell of the black she wolf she had hidden herself upwind. While the man paced back and forth across the veranda the she wolf watched, as she had watched the house for months. Petra was pleased with herself, only once in those long hours of watching had she made one little mistake, but then he had not detected her. She had been so close to the man and his mate that had he reached out he could have touched her. She had watched as they made love in the forest, the way he explored her naked body with the hands of a man. She could have killed him there and then but she dare not, his life belonged to her mate. It had sickened her to see them coupling, had the grey wolf forgotten how it felt to mate like a wolf. And the mate he had chosen for himself, a travesty, blind, voiceless, she could not run with the pack. How could she call to her mate, how could she voice her joy to the skies, Petra decided that she herself would claim the life of the grey wolf's mate.

Her eyes glittered with the thought of the woman's blood on her tongue, the grey wolf had made a bad mistake, he should have sensed her, he didn't, now his life was forfeit. He should have moved on, it never paid to stay too long in any one place. They had hunted him over the years, always missing him, but now, now it was too late for him to run, soon it would be the hour when the killing began.

Michael was unable to sleep, he tossed and turned on the bed, he sensed that something was wrong, and it had nothing to do with Peter. By his side Lilith had finally fallen into an exhausted sleep, nothing he could do or say would put her fears to rest. His brain could not stop working, over and over he thought of ways of taking Lilith away from her. There had to be a way, there just had to be. Michael closed his eyes, he would have to rest, now more than ever Lilith needed him.

The eyes of the grey wolf flared, the sound of footsteps on the veranda, the furtive movements of somebody trying hard not to be heard. Michael was up and off the bed and looking through the window in the time he took to think about it. He stared down into the darkness, his wolfs eyes seeking and searching every shadowy corner, carefully he opened the window. Felt the cool night air on his naked body, he sniffed, like a bullet from a gun it came to him, the scent of a werewolf. Michael could not stop the growl which started deep in his stomach and forced its way though his clenched teeth.

Below the window deep in the farthest corner of the veranda Petra heard the challenge of the grey wolf, questioning the right of any other wolf daring to trespass on his private domain. She knew there was no way she could win a battle with him so she had no choice but to run. Leaning on the windowsill Michael saw the figure run from the shadows and off the veranda, the shape and form of a woman.

It was the werewolf that landed beneath the window, Michael would have preferred changing completely, but he knew that when he caught her, if she was in wolf form, they would fight to the death. He didn't want that, he needed her alive and able to talk, where was she from, why had he never detected her presence before. The she wolf disappeared into the forest, the man-wolf tracked her easily, her scent left on everything she touched. He knew he was not far behind her, he could hear her crashing through the undergrowth, when the noise stopped the werewolf stopped and listened and sniffed the air.

Slowly he advanced towards the sound of her laboured breathing, then he saw her. The black she wolf was in a half altered state, the grey wolf looked at her with its yellow eyes searching her face, digging into the recess's of its memory.

She meant nothing to him he had no recollection of her, growling, claws extended towards her the werewolf moved in. The black she wolf stood her ground, inviting the grey wolf to attack if he dare, she snarled her defiance at him. The wolfman jumped and saw the trouble it was in too late. The hand he had thought was resting on the tree was holding back a thin sapling, it hit the wolfman in mid jump. The werewolf cried out in pain, the sapling striking him hard and fast in the chest, catapulting him backwards. The werewolf rolled over and over, a tree stopping his progress, sky and earth spun round in one continuous whirl, Michael on his hands and knee's spit out his own blood, the pain in his chest a reminder that the black she wolf had bested him. Michael was forced to stay on his hands and knees until the whiplash pain of the sapling had faded. He still found it difficult to breath, even to walk correctly, her tracks were plain, her scent strong, there was no pretence, she did not intend hiding herself from him. So vicious had been the blow that it took Michael the best part of an hour before he felt able to follow the tracks of the she wolf. She was no novice at this game, in less than two hundred yards Michael had lost her track and her scent, damn it she was playing with him. He could imagine her laying hidden close by and laughing at his futile attempts to find her.

The problem of Peter became irrelevant, the fact that another werewolf had found him became his immediate problem, he was not on his own he had Lilith to consider. On his own he could wait his time and sooner or later he would have the black she wolf by the throat. But he didn't have time on his side, whoever she was the she wolf had decided for him, he must run and take Lilith with him. Michael got himself downwind and sniffed the night air, nothing, whatever scent she had left had been deliberate. As he walked slowly back to the house he needed no animal instincts to tell him that his finding had been no accident. Was it never to end, would they hunt him for the rest of his days until he destroyed all of them, or more possibly they took his life.

The scent of the she wolf was strong on the veranda and Michael found what he was looking for. He had guessed right, this was no accidental finding, the she wolf had defecated in the corner, letting him know she had been there. He spent the rest of the night seated on the veranda, he didn't expect her to return, but the moods of a female werewolf were unpredictable. So confident had he been that he would run her down he had grown careless, and because he had failed to catch her he now needed to be cautious around Lilith. She had the ability to second guess his every mood so their travelling arrangements would have to seem as normal as possible.

What should have been a long pleasant day, lazing in the summer sunshine or simply sitting on the veranda enjoying each others company, was to both of them a day that frazzled the nerves, each jumping at everyday sounds and noises. Michael was aware that Lilith sensed trouble, from the way she moved around the house never venturing far from the main room. She who loved to have the sun on her face, to feel the wind blowing her hair anyway it pleased, refused to step outside. Michael fretted the day away, his eyes constantly returning to the edge of the forest, seeking the she wolf's hiding place. When finally the summer light faded and night brought its few short hours of darkness Michael took Lilith upstairs and lay by her until she slept. Carefully he crept out of the bedroom and went downstairs to wait for the she wolf to show. He did not ask himself how or why, he knew that she would come again tonight he just knew.

He sensed her long before she howled across the clearing to him, Michael eased himself out of the chair and walked over to the door. The she wolf stood at the edge of the forest, her naked body highlighted by the moon. Even from this distance Michael saw the perfect proportioned body of a young female, probably not more than twenty. But Michael knew this meant nothing, she could be one hundred, even two, it only mattered when she had been turned. The she wolf beckoned him, using her body to make him come to her. Michael stood there not moving, allowing the change to take him over gradually. The she wolf put her hands between her thighs, opened the lips of her sex and made a thrusting movement towards him. The man inside the body of the werewolf realised what she was doing, well if she intended leading him into a trap, she would be the first to die. The werewolf started to move, then stopped and went back inside the house, it went slowly up the stairs and then paused at the bedroom door.

Michael bent over the sleeping Lilith and brushed her forehead with his lips, he took her face between his hands and kissed each eyelid. "I love you Lilith." She moved in her sleep but his restraining hands held her face towards him. He had the strangest urge to wake her to tell her how much she meant to him. Words tumbled around and around his brain, words that meant everything to her, words that he somehow realised would be too late. His eyes riveted on her sleeping form Michael backed out of the room, forever stamping the picture of her in his memory, "Until death beloved." he whispered.

Petra waited, why had he gone back into the house, was it all going to go wrong. The plans to entice Michael away from the house had been thought out over a period of time. Where was he, Petra lifted her head to howl a warning to the other members of the pack, when a grey wolf crashed into the bushes a little distance from her. Petra her heart beating rapidly turned to run, he had tricked her, he had learnt a lesson from last night. Strong fingers caught her dragging her back, Petra struck out and was rewarded with the feeling of her claws tearing flesh. The hand released her, and the she wolf bolted, there was no time for tricks now, she had to run to save her life. Petra realised there was no time to change into a wolf, she must stay as she was and do her best to escape him. She had seen the grey ones face only briefly, but it told her there was no mercy for her if he caught her. Petra ran like she had never run before, now she was beginning to understand what it felt like to be hunted. She risked looking over her shoulder and saw that the grey one was only yards behind her , why hadn't he caught up with her , there was no way she could out run him. The miles disappeared beneath her feet, still the grey werewolf stayed just far enough behind her to give her a glimmer of hope that she might escape. Then she understood what he was doing, she herself had done the same thing when hunting, he was wearing her down, he would strike when she was unable to run any further.

Her breathing became ragged, the heart that pumped the blood around her body was ready to rebel. The she wolf fell, unable to stop herself she rolled over and over down the slight incline of the river bank. Petra lay on her back in the river gasping for breath, she knew she was finished, she could run no more. Panic in her eyes she looked up, the grey one stood at the top of the bank staring down at her. A terror gripped her as the grey werewolf prepared to jump down to her, the grey wolf paused and listened.

On the clear night air the sounds of gunfire and the screams of the dying came to him, the she wolf heard them also and began to laugh. , "Vengeance grey one," she snarled at him "Vengeance." The grey werewolf began to understand what she had done. Twice now she had decoyed him away from the house and, "Lilith." The one word was torn from his throat in a scream. He hit her before she had time to laugh again, his weight bearing hers under the water. Hard fingers curled into her hair and dragged her to the surface, a clawed hand exploded at the side of her head and she fell face down in the water. When she surfaced a second time the grey one had gone, fighting for her breath Petra clawed her way to the river bank, digging her fingers into the soft soil she hung on.

When the change came he welcomed it instead of fighting it, inside twenty paces he had changed from half-wolf to complete wolf and it was the big grey wolf that raced thought the forest. It ran in a straight line knowing it had very little time to reach its mate, its eyes blazed with a killing fever. All the time it ran eating up the miles, the sound of guns being fired and the screams of humans carried to it. The grey wolf swerved, something was coming towards it, a body crashed through the bushes and small trees. Whoever it was, was not used to being in the forest, the grey wolf willed itself to change.

Michael looked into the terrified face of the butcher Steiner. The man was babbling incoherently. Michael grabbed him and the man began to scream, Michael shook him until his teeth rattled together, his eyes rolled until only the whites showed. Steiner uttered one word before he collapsed against Michael. "Wolves." Michael heard the growl and dropped Steiner, both man and wolf instantly recognised each for what they were. Without warning the wolf leapt at Michael, Michael waited until the last possible moment before he moved. He grabbed the wolf by its throat and ripped open its belly, before the wolf had chance to scream out in pain, Michael lifted it over his head and broke its spine.

Hot blood and intestines poured over him, he threw it from him.

In the distance the boom of a shotgun, the howl of a wounded animal, Michael grabbed Steiner by the shoulders. "Soldiers." he said, "Fetch the soldiers." He pushed Steiner from him and the frightened man looked wildly about him before he began his shambling run. Michael waited until the man had vanished into the darkness, in the village his kind were killing for killings sake. He doubted that even the soldiers would arrive in time to save any of them, he couldn't waste his time in trying, he had to get to Lilith.

He ran with the cries of the dying ringing in his ears, forcing himself to ignore it. Half-man, half -wolf he skirted the village, his senses alerted to any danger that threatened him. He smelt them all around him, the stink of their bodies overriding all other scents. These were not his kind, they were the degenerates who cursed with immortality preyed on their human counterparts as food. The scent of blood was everywhere, the blood of the werewolf he had destroyed clung to him like a second skin. A werewolf dragging a screaming woman bumped into him, it growled at him, the grey werewolf didn't answer its challenge. The woman's begging sobs for mercy died as the werewolf tore her throat out, the sound of the werewolf eating was the last thing he heard before he came to the clearing before the house.

He stared at the house, the lights were on, the door closed, he sniffed the air, bent to the ground, they had been here. Human instinct told him to rush into the house to see if Lilith was safe. Animal instincts demanded caution, the werewolf was reasoning with its human brain, it knew that something was wrong. Yellow eyes examined every part of the house, the light, when he left, Lilith was asleep upstairs, even if she had wakened up and come downstairs, she would not have lit the lamp, she had no need for it. He moved forward cautiously, stopping every other step, sniffing the air, they were still here. The werewolf moved ever closer to the house, nose, ears, all his senses alert for any sign of his enemies. He didn't approach the house from straight on, he moved at an angle and climbed over the railings to the veranda.

He caught the sound of movement from inside the house, the werewolf melted into the shadows. He heard their movements but not the sound of their voices, he was certain that they would not be waiting for him as wolves. They would be like him retaining the human side of their nature, the killing part. The werewolf put its eye to the window and looked through the lace curtains Lilith was so proud of, but had never seen. From his advantage point he could see most of the room, they stood, one either side of the door, one by the table. One of them knelt by Lilith, who was sat in her fathers chair. He could not see her face. The werewolf kneeling by his mate turned and the grey werewolf lost all control of himself, "Julius." They heard his cry inside the house, Julius jumped to his feet catching the seated woman. Lilith fell forward onto the floor, a red gaping hole where her throat had been. The human part of the grey werewolf lost control to the beast.

The door splintered, ripped free of its hinges it flew inwards, a large splinter of wood pinning one of the werewolves to the wooden wall. The two others made to rush the in coming figure, when they saw the blood drenched grey werewolf they paused, it cost one its life. The grey werewolf opened its mouth and grabbed the nearer of the two, fangs tore into its unprotected throat. Blood and flesh hanging from its mouth it threw itself at the second one, they hit the floor hard. The grey werewolf came to its feet first, took hold of the smaller werewolf and lifted it over its head and threw it with as much force as it could against the wall. The wooden wall cracked under the impact and the small werewolf its legs and one arm broken was unable to lift itself.

A third werewolf threw itself at the grey one, who caught it, spitting and snarling trying to free itself it clawed at the grey wolf. The grey werewolf heaved it from him, the wolf hit the table, howled in pain and rolled. It came to its feet fast, ready to fight, a clawed hand ripped away most of its face, a second blow took out its throat. Holding the werewolf by its hair the grey one struck again, its clawed hand taking the wolf's head from its body.

Claws raked the grey wolfs back, a fourth member of the pack had joined the battle. The grey werewolf staggered forward, the one who had struck him clinging to his back. The grey wolf dropped forward and at the same time reached behind him, his clawed fingers found soft flesh and sunk in. The attacking werewolf found itself being dragged over the grey wolfs head, slowly it was being lifted. Higher and higher it went, kicking and squirming trying to free itself from the grey wolfs grip. It screamed in agony, holding it above its head the grey werewolf was slowly and deliberately breaking its back. It gave one long agonising scream as its spine snapped, blood gushed from its mouth. With a gesture full of contemptuous savagery the grey werewolf let the broken wolf drop. It lay there unable to move, its feeble kicking stopped when the grey wolf tore out its throat.

"Now Julius, you die."

"I warned you Michael." Spittle covered the muzzle of the dark wolf, "When you killed the Countess, I warned you."

"And I told you not to come looking for me." Slowly the grey wolf advanced on Julius, it saw how the dark one dragged its leg, it would not be able to move as quickly as he could. "You came seeking death Julius and you have found it." The grey werewolf leapt at Julius, its mouth open, fangs seeking to reach its throat, to rip and tear.

The body of the black she wolf hit the grey wolf in midair, its hurtling body knocking the grey wolf from its target. They hit the wall together the fangs of the black she wolf tearing flesh from its shoulder. The grey wolf knocked her away, she rolled out of his reach and came to her feet beside Julius. The grey werewolf felt no pain from his wound, it had only one thought in its head, to kill Julius. The grey wolf crouched waiting for their next attack.

"Here Michael." Julius stood before the shattered door holding a lamp in each hand. "Here." he screamed and threw the first lamp. The grey wolf followed its passage through the air, watched it as it hit the floor and exploded in flames, "Here." Julius shouted. "And again, burn you bastard, burn." A second and third lamp burst on the floor, hot oil scolded the grey wolf's hide, flames licked around it. The burning oil seeped into the wooden floor, flames leapt and danced over it, hungrily they ate at the staircase, the grey wolf snarled his defiance at an unbeatable enemy.

A wall of flames between them Julius laughed and screamed, thick choking smoke filled the grey wolfs lungs and he gagged against the taste of it.

Michael the werewolf bunched himself to leap through the flames to reach his enemy. Michael the man saw the flames licking at Lilith's dress. He saw the thin fabric burst into flame, he beat uselessly at them. He saw her dead flesh blister and bubble under the eager tongues of fire.

Michael the man sank to his knees accepting defeat, he tore the blazing fabric from the dead body. He held Lilith's body next to his, he kissed the dead eyes and dead lips . Here with the woman he loved he would die, the flames would consume their bodies, holding his world in his arms he would find the peace he had longed for.

The insane howling of Julius came to him over the roar of the flames, Michael tried to ignore it. Let Julius win, what did it matter, he had nothing left to live for. He held Lilith to him watching the fire move ever closer, he felt the intense heat of the flames on his exposed flesh. "Until death." He whispered in her dead ear.

A voice soft and low entered his mind, a soft incessant voice that wouldn't leave him alone. With the voice came a vision of eyes older than time itself staring at him. "I will not let you die yet." Michael tried to shut his mind to the voice, "Anna." He shouted. "Anna help me." From beyond the grave he heard her calling to him, the beautiful red haired she wolf, "Live Michael live." He saw again her body in the pool of his secret place, she smiled that bewitching smile of hers and beckoned him. "You must live Michael, your time has not yet come."

Michael opened his eyes and looked about him, he saw the flames, tasted the smoke, he had been dying , why had they brought him back. Then he knew why, he could stay here in the flames, he would not die, it would burn the flesh from him, leave him a crippled travesty, but it would not give him the peace he wanted. He lifted Lilith and placed her in her fathers chair, he touched her lips once more. "Until death."

Michael the man leapt into the wall of flame, it was the grey wolf that landed on the ground outside the house. The grey wolf rolled over and over in the dirt trying to ease its singed skin. It lifted itself and trotted away from the burning house. At the edge of the forest it lay down, placed its head on its front paws and watched Lilith's pyre.

"Sir , sir." Peter turned, the corporal held out a blood soaked shirt. "This was found over there." Peter took the shirt from the man and without a second glance at it, he dropped it onto the ground.

"Yes." He said "It belonged to the man." He had no idea if it had been Michael's or not, it didn't make any difference now. He looked at the smoking pile of charred wood that had once been his home, the fire had left nothing. His men had scoured the ruin once it was possible to do so, they had found charred remains of what could have been a man and a woman. Obviously they were the bones of his sister Lilith and the man Michael. He had no idea who the other set of bones belonged to. Perhaps some of the villagers had managed to make it here. He tapped his leg with the ever present riding crop. "Get your men corporal, there's nothing more we can do here."

The shambling wreck that had staggered into his camp he recognised as Steiner, but the only thing they were able to get out of him was "Wolves". His troop had pulled into the village early that morning, the sight that met their eyes was unbelievable. Blood seemed to be everywhere, splashed on the walls of the houses inside and out. Even the small statue of the shepherdess in the village square appeared to have been daubed in blood. The bodies of the villagers, when they finally found them had been dragged into the church, all of them showed signs of being partially eaten. Peter realised that should a thing like this get out, questions concerning his governing of the small town and its surrounding countryside could hurt his advancement. His cold mind saw no other alternative but to do something about it. "Burn the village." He said, his sergeant looked at him, had he heard the commander right. "Burn the village?" He asked, Peter turned and looked at the man in surprise, surely he had given his orders clear enough. "Burn it all, every house, everything, including the bodies. Then forget it corporal, you and the men, forget it." Peter smiled at the man. "A thing like this would be better left here in ashes. After all who would believe animals could do something like this?" That the men would obey his orders was beyond question, they like him wanted to belong to the inner circle of a new order.

Not until he was satisfied that the village was burning correctly and that no trace of it would remain to embarrass them at a later date did he call for his driver. Common sense told him that if a pack of wolves had attacked the village in large numbers then there was little hope Lilith and Michael had somehow survived. As the car carried him toward the house a thick pall of black smoke and the stench of burning flesh followed him. He looked once more at the charred timbers and then down at the blood soaked shirt, his last tenuous strand with humanity was broken.

The smoke from the burning village had thinned out, tendrils of black smoke were being driven about by a playful wind. Peter knew he would never come back here, there was nothing at all left of his former life. "Drive." He said, the driver turned to him. "Sir, Berlin?" Peter took out a cigarette and lit it, "There's no need to go now." He pointed with his riding crop at the remains of the house. "This has saved me putting Lilith into one of the special camps, and of course now I don't have to shoot Michael, drive." Peter settled back and pulled deep on the cigarette, he blew the smoke at the back of the drivers head. All he had now was a future, he was burning his past, there was power and glory to be had under the leadership of the little man with the toothbrush moustache.

From the edge of the forest the grey wolf stared at him, he had no time now to kill this man, one day he would, but for the moment others demanded his attention.

The grey wolf had spent the last two days hunting the trail of the pack, he had lost it when a torrential downpour wiped it out. The storm had been so violent that the grey wolf had, had to seek cover from it. The river had swollen until its banks were unable to hold the water back, it burst its banks and flooded the field on both sides. Trees were torn free from the spot they had occupied for hundreds of years, the swollen river carried them with it, roots and branches tearing the soil free from its banks. The water turned a dirty grey, ripping and tearing, changing the landscape forever. The grey wolf paced angrily back and forth along the banks, knowing that the flood was too dangerous to cross. The twisting and turning jumble of trees, tangled up with young bushes could cause it serious injury. It stared at the swollen waters, its yellow eyes blazed, somewhere under the flooded fields the trail of the pack was being destroyed forever.

The grey wolf sat on its haunches, the human part of its brain told it, change, swim across as a man. Intelligence told it, this was too dangerous, as wolf or man the floating jetsam could cripple it. The grey wolf was on a killing quest, it would wait, the waters would subside sooner or later, it was the nature of things. Somewhere beyond the flooded fields the trail of the pack would still be there, and he would find it. The grey wolfs blood sang in its veins, it could taste revenge , no matter how far they ran he would find them. It fretted at the amount of time it was losing, but the death of the black wolf would be sweeter for the waiting. The grey wolf reluctantly left the banks of the raging river and returned to its hiding place.

Under the pale yellow of the moon the grey wolf ran arrow straight, the moon touched the trees and grass which sparkled a shimmering white under the first frost of winter. The wolf's breath was a visible tremulous stream of white caused by the beating of its heart. Powerful muscles drove it on, they bunched then relaxed as it cleared the obstacles in its path. Sure-footed it leapt up and over the rocks, its claws scrabbled on the frosty surface, the grey wolf heaved itself up and over.

Its prey was near, for weeks he had hunted the surrounding area, three days ago it had finally found the packs trail. Resting for only short periods it had single-mindedly followed their scent. When it was forced to stop and rest frightened animals bolted from its presence. Startled frightened creatures, hearts beating, wild eyed hugging whatever cover they could. Grateful to be alive when the grey wolf moved on.

The stench of their passing had permanently stained the ground over which they travelled. He could almost taste the stench of Julius, visions of the Countesses black dog filled its mind and heart with a cold, murderous vengeance.

They grey wolf pulled itself onto the top of the rocks, its chest heaved with the effort, its breath clouding its vision. Below it stretched the frost covered plains, its quarry running across it. If it was possible for a wolf to smile then what passed for a smile crossed the grey wolf's face. No sound came from the grey wolf, he would not warn his prey, he was hunting to kill.

The grey wolf shook its head as the first fat flake of snow fell on its nose.

Yellow eyes watched the falling flakes as they drifted lazily down. He sat and watched as they settled onto the rock, fat, swirling, spinning flakes slowly but surely covering the frost covered rocks and the plains. He had come too far to loose the pack now, he could not allow the snow storm to let the murderers run free. Gingerly it moved down the snow covered rocks, each step carefully taken, until it reached the bottom. Once on the flat it burst into a run, like a bullet from a gun it zeroed in on its target.

It was less than half a mile behind them, now was the time to slow down, but not to loose contact with the pack. The wind , gaining in strength with every minute that passed , blew their scent to him. The snow was by this time falling thick and fast, the grey wolf could not see his prey, but the wind carried it to him and led him on.

The grey wolf was less than dozen yards behind them when the pack turned into the trees. Here, though the snow had partially covered the ground, the trees held the snow storm at bay. As the grey wolf followed them it became obvious that the pack knew exactly where it was going. They fell into single file moving up and into the narrow ravine, twisting and turning around the tight bends following the well worn path.

When they disappeared into the opening of the cave the grey wolf stopped and lay down. Now was not the time to show itself, he had come to kill, not as a wolf for he could not kill Julius that way. He must face Julius half and half and if Julius wished to defend himself he must also be in the shape and form of the werewolf. The grey wolf lay down and waited for the change to come, it would take only a few minutes, the pain would be brief after all these years, but never the less it would be an agonising pain which enveloped his body. The grey wolf closed its eyes and waited.

Julius had chosen well, the cave could be easily defended, the path twisted and turned and had he not been what he was, he would most probably have never found it. A smell came to him, it was the sweet sickly smell of rotting human flesh. Michael got down on his stomach and crawled into the opening, his shoulder touched the roof, the tunnel to the main cave was going to be tight. As he moved further in he felt the rocks pressing down on him, for a moment he felt panic grip him, he was held tight by the tunnel. Michael was stuck fast, his eyes clouded over and he felt the teeth move in his mouth. He could not change now, he held his breath and fought down the panic of the trapped beast, Michael pushed with every ounce of his strength, he moved six inches. He should have entered the cave as a wolf, it had to be the way Julius and the pack had crawled down the tunnel. But he knew that to have entered his enemies' lair as a wolf his chance of winning was slight. He lay still, took another deep breath, let it out and reached forward again, fingers dug deep into the soft soil of the tunnel he pulled. Another few inches, reach, pull, reach, pull, inch by painful inch he pulled himself along the floor of the tunnel. Michael felt his shoulder break free of the confining tunnel, they were raw and bleeding, he allowed the change to begin, hands equipped with hard nails he dug in and pulled his body completely free.

From where he stood the cave sloped down to a sandy area, it was fifty to sixty feet in circumference and at least twenty feet high at its lowest point. From the rock face a spring carried fresh water down to a pool, at the far end of the cave he could see half a dozen dark recesses. Michael guessed these would be the sleeping areas of the pack. He had guessed right, one of the pack, the violet eyed she wolf crawled out of one of the holes and scrambled down to the pool. She bent her head and began lapping up the clear water. The pack had all it needed here, it was warm and dry and it had fresh water.

Michael looked back at the she wolf she had finished drinking and had crawled over to a pile of bones in the corner of the cave. She picked through the pile until she found one that took her fancy, he heard her teeth grind against it. In the strange fluorescent light of the cave Michael stared at the she wolf that had decoyed him away from Lilith. No doubt she had been beautiful before she had been changed. Michael pushed these thoughts out of his mind, it did no good to imagine what she could have looked like. Now, with her hair matted and filthy, hanging in rat tails about her face, her full woman's body streaked with her own filth, she was more beast than human, as she sat sucking the marrow from the human bone in her hands.

Unaware that he was there allowing the change to take him over she shifted her hands through the pile of bones. Michael lifted his head and howled, the she wolf jumped and turned, crouching ready to defend herself. The challenging cry of the werewolf reverberated around the cave, the black she wolf snarled, the grey one had somehow found them. She licked her lips, her tongue touching the protruding fangs. The grey werewolf moved down towards her, his eyes never leaving her. She heard the sound of the other members of the pack crawl from their holes. She heard them issue growls of warning, the grey werewolf totally ignored them. The grey werewolf towered over her, she had been the one who had stopped him from killing Julius during the battle in the house. The pack snapped and growled at him but he knew they would stand back, he had issued his challenge of a fight to the death to their leader Julius. But this one she would need to be watched, he knew she would aid Julius if possible.

"Julius." His voice was low, no need to shout, Julius would be aware of his presence in the cave, "Julius it is that time." The grey werewolf moved backwards away from the pack, his back against the cool wall of the cave. His eyes flashed constantly back to the she wolf, who still assumed a posture of defence. If in fact she was Julius's bitch then for once in his life he had chosen well. "Julius do you still fear me, are you still the dog that clung to the Countess's skirts?" Julius gave him an answering growl as he crawled out of his hole, standing up once his body was clear of the hole. Slowly he moved around the pack until he was stood before Michael, the grey werewolf again noticed that he dragged his right leg.

"Still a dog." Snarled the grey werewolf. "Still hiding behind a woman." Julius curled back his lips and showed his fangs to Michael, the scars on his face and body put there by the Countess, a vivid white against his dark skin. "I once warned you never to come looking for me Julius."

"And I told you that one day I would kill you." Spittle drooled from his fangs with the words he spoke, his eyes burnt with an insane hatred of Michael. Froth gathered at the side of his mouth and dripped down onto his chest, Julius was mad. Michael risked a quick glance toward the pack, all but the she wolf had retreated to allow them space to fight, the she wolf glared at him. "You killed her." screamed Julius, the anger and hatred he felt towards Michael causing the change to come over him, thick black hairs springing out all over his body. "You killed her." The sound that was torn from his throat, a cross between anger and a sob. "You destroyed her."

"She deserved to die." From the corner of his eye he caught the she wolf moving closer to him, the grey werewolf looked at the pack. It sickened him to think that he was tainted by the same cursed blood as these cannibals. "We are all better off dead, you, me." The she wolf launched herself at him, Michael moved to one side and caught her by the throat. The she wolf was jerked back in mid-air, the grey werewolf dug his fingers into the soft flesh of her throat, feeling her blood run down onto his hand. The she wolf howled, struggling in Michael's grip, her feet held clear of the floor, he squeezed tighter, the she wolfs eyes rolled in her head, her breath a rasping choke, as he slowly strangled her. "You took the life of my woman Julius." He said "I repay in kind." With a contemptuous gesture he threw the woman at Julius. Julius jumped out of the way, the she wolf hit the wall, rolled and lay still. "Now I am going to kill you."

Julius stared at Michael, it was the same confident voice of the man who had killed the Countess and crippled him so badly. It had taken him years to recover. He had defied the flames to seek him out, he looked down at the she wolf he had created, she had not moved, had this man once again ruined all of his plans. He had warned the Countess that this one was different, to leave him alone or kill him before he had been turned. She had not listened to him before it was too late, Julius 's eyes found the thing he sought, the mark of the pentacle .

Julius snapped and hurled himself at the Grey werewolf. Michael hit him hard, Julius's head jerked back and Michael's clawed fist struck him again. Pain exploded in Julius's brain, he went down and rolled, crouched and attacked again. The hatred they felt for each other was in every blow they inflicted on each other. The pain and anguish they had caused each other relived in every bite of fang and tearing of claw on flesh. Over and over they rolled striking the cave walls in their frantic struggle to attain the killing stroke. They were no longer human men they were a pair of snarling beast's.

Michael felt himself being lifted and then thrown, he crashed against the cave wall. His vision blurred, he only just managed to avoid Julius's charge, he rolled and struck out, his clawed fingers ripped into the crippled leg of the dark werewolf. Julius screamed and blood spurted from the leg in a thick stream onto the cave floor. They stood panting, claws outstretched, gulping in lungs full of air, Michael felt the pain of his battered body. The hurt in his chest where Julius had raked him with his claws. Blood dripped into his right eye, a flap of skin hanging down partially blinded him.

Julius hobbled, blood pumped from the wound in his leg, with every movement he made the grey werewolf had ripped him open to the bone. Nothing remotely human remained in Julius, he had gone completely insane, a shambling, gibbering beast with only one thought in its head, to kill its tormentor. They both knew that the end for one of them was near. Michael made to attack, Julius moved with him, Michael feigned yet another attack. Julius struck out, the grey werewolf twisted and came in low and fast at a different angle. He hit Julius with a force that carried them both to the ground, he felt his fangs sink into Julius's neck and he tasted blood on his tongue. The grey werewolf screamed as Julius ripped him from under the armpit to the top of his thigh, and feeble as Julius's push was, he fell back. The grey wolfs left side burnt with an intense pain, a blinding agony that threatened to engulf him.

Julius tried to stand, his legs gave way, his hand clutched his throat trying to stem the flow of blood. Michael rolled over and over until he came up against the smooth wall of the cave. Struggling to retain his senses he saw through pain filled eyes Julius crawling towards him. The grey werewolf called on its last reserve of strength and forced itself to its feet, blotting out the pain he waited for Julius to reach him. He couldn't die yet, not while Julius lived, his chest heaved as he pulled air into his tortured lungs.

Julius was on his knees, both hands pressed against the gaping wound the fangs had made, red frothy blood bubbled between his fingers. The dark werewolf tried to speak, his words lost in a gush of blood which burst from its mouth.

One hand holding him away from the cave wall Michael waited, Julius was slowly forcing himself to stand. Michael readied himself for one final attack, Julius, one bloody claw held before him came at Michael. The grey werewolf knew that Julius was already dead, but his insane mind driving him on to one last attack against his enemy, but he wanted him to come closer. He wanted Julius dead at his feet, that is what he had come for to finally kill Julius. The grey werewolf struck hard and fast, his clawed fingers ripped into Julius, gouging out flesh, entrails and bone from the rib cage. Every last remaining ounce of Michael's strength went into the blow, such was the power of the strike to Julius's nervous system that he went rigid with shock. Then with an action of the utmost barbaric cruelty the grey werewolf thrust its fingers into the gaping wound, ignoring the jagged bone that tore at its flesh. It closed its seeking fingers around the still beating heart of the dark werewolf and tore it free.

The grey werewolf held the beating lump of flesh before Julius's eyes, if he was aware of it Julius was unable to acknowledge it. His body began to jerk and tremble, his arms and legs shaking in a grotesque dance of death. A fountain of blood erupted from Julius's mouth and his brain received its final message, Julius fell dead at Michael's feet. The dead body of Julius at his feet, the bleeding lump of flesh he still held, the cave, the pack, all swam before his eyes as he fought to remain conscious. He failed and as the dark whirlpool opened up before him Michael fell into it.

A soft crooning filled his mind, he did not fight it, he allowed its soothing music to bring him slowly to his senses. Michael looked up at the roof of the cave, it was minutes before he realised where he was and what had taken place. The first movement he made sent pain raging through his body, clenching his teeth against it he forced himself to sit up. His back against the wall he waited, his vision blurred and the blackness threatened to swamp over him yet again. Even sat as he was, not moving, the pain coursed through his body, not a sharp pain, but a constant flame that burnt him to his very bones. If ever he needed the curse of the werewolf it was now, he needed it to help resist the agony that held him.

Senses reeling he forced himself to his knees, all the time the incessant crooning went on and on. No longer a soothing balm to tortured pain filled body and mind, it grated on his nerve ends. His brain demanded that he get to his feet, his body refused the command, Julius had hurt him badly. He knew that the wound was not a mortal one, but it was causing him great difficulty in functioning properly. Michael reached round and his probing fingers touched the open wound, his body reacted violently. The whirlpool opened up again , so inviting, so comfortable , all he had to do was let go, let go and find rest for his battered body, allow himself to fall in and find a deep , healing, restful sleep. Michael was being drawn ever deeper into the whirlpool, not fighting it, gently going with it. He rocked slightly his fingers touched the wound, with that one single touch the blackness of the whirlpool exploded into a red agony of all consuming pain. He heard himself cry and then somehow he was on his feet, his head throbbing and spinning he fell against the cave wall. Hands pressed against his eyes he stood there unable to move until the crazy kaleidoscope of pack, body and cave stopped spinning. When he moved, he moved with extreme caution, every tiny movement a calculated risk to avoid the blackness returning. Michael let his body rest against the coolness of the rock and slowly he managed to focus his eyes on his surroundings.

The sight that met his eyes brought back memories of the Keep and a beautiful, evil woman, and Julius holding her severed head against his face, crooning to it. The she wolf was holding Julius's body against her, his head resting on her breasts, the crooning was coming from her, it hissed through her clenched teeth. The rest of the pack cowered against the far side of the cave, uttering threatening growls, but even now when he was too weak to defend himself. They were still too afraid of the grey werewolf to attack him.

Michael knew he needed help, he also knew he would not get it from the hands of the pack or the violet eyed she wolf. He looked at the disgusting travesty of what they had become, Julius had taken them down this path from which they could never return. How would they fare now that he had killed their leader, Michael was finding that revenge left a bitter taste in his mouth, but he had followed Julius to kill him, he could not undo what he had done. Again he had broken the law and took the life of one of his own kind, he had marked himself for death at the hands of any werewolf that cared to challenge him. He had taken the life of one of the fallen angel's children for the love of a woman, a human woman.

No matter how depraved they had become, he, not they was the outcast, they still had their own kind to cling to. What did he have compared to them, nothing, he had rejected the pack and tried to live like a human and he had failed. A memory stirred inside his mind and the words of the red haired she wolf Anna came to him. "The werewolf always destroys the thing he loves the most." They belonged, he had nowhere to belong, he could try and live among the humans, but what if his secret was discovered. He would be driven away, he was the unspeakable in their midst, the evil among them. His own kind lived in fear of him because of the mark he carried on his shoulder. The fallen angels kiss, the pentacle, made him different from them, it allowed him to cling onto one of humanities finer feelings. Hope, hope that one day he would find peace and deliverance from the curse of the werewolf.

He must get away, away from this cave, away from his past, his present and his future, he never had been and never would be a member of any pack. His life lay somewhere beyond this place, he would try and find a life that offered some semblance of freedom. It took every ounce of his self control and will power to force himself to walk to the opening of the tunnel. Every step he took sent an agonising pain to the very core of his being. The she wolf gave out a prolonged howl, and Michael was forced to turn, she had given her challenge, he had to listen to it.

The pack had gathered around her and the body she held to her, Michael believed that he could taste the hate she directed at him. "One day." She screamed at him. "One day I will find you, and on that day I promise you death, grey one."

"Is it never to end?" He asked looking at her unforgiving face, each word he spoke sending pain through him, "Must we murder each other until the end of time?" He held his hand towards her, a pleading gesture whose seeds fell on stony ground.

The she wolf pushed away the filthy rat tails of hair from around her face, let him look upon her, let him see that she meant every word she uttered. "Even unto eternity." She began to croon again, rocking back and forth, Julius's dead head nodded in agreement with her.

Michael fell to his knees, he was in too much pain to risk changing in such a confined space, but he had no option but to go on. Michael would never remember how, without the aid of the curse, he managed to drag himself down the tunnel and into the ravine. He stood in utter darkness, the moon hidden by the confining walls of the ravine and the snow storm that raged over head, unable to shed its light on him. A bitter cold wind blew down the ravine and playfully sought out his wound, Michael tried to fend it off but couldn't.

Why hadn't she killed him when he lay unconscious on the floor of the cave. Was she like her dead mate so consumed with hate for him that she needed to look into his eyes at the moment of the kill. Michael knew she would never give up the hunt for him no matter how long it took, he also knew that she would convince the pack to hunt him down. He had to get away from here, now, he needed a place to hide , to rest and allow his wounds to mend, regain his dissipating strength. And if and when she came be ready and waiting for her.

Michael began to walk down the ravine, he allowed the eyes of the wolf to show him the way. The journey down the ravine seemed never ending, he knew if he was to escape the pack he needed to travel faster. He came out of the ravine and walked into a blinding snow storm, never before in his life had Michael been so happy to be in the middle of a storm. Snow fell upon snow, fat swirling flakes driven and tossed by the wind, flakes which fell into the imprint of his foot, quickly filling and hiding his passing. He felt only the cold now on his naked flesh, the icy winds had sealed his wound, blood and snow congealing.

He paused for breath, hanging onto the trunk of a tree, the wind picked that moment to give itself a rest, before it gathered its strength to throw itself once more against man and nature. He heard the baying of the pack they had come sooner than he expected, he pushed himself erect, now was the time to begin running.

"This way moon child, come to me." The words struck him like a blow stopping him in mid stride. "This way." Michael cocked his head and listened. "Come to me moon child." Michael turned, sure of the direction from which the voice came, he began to run, the voice of the Wych woman pulling him on.

THE VALLEY - Part 7

"I loved her." Michael's voice trailed off, Tibor said nothing. Instead he looked towards the sleeping Katji. He could feel what Michael was feeling, if it came to it he would kill to protect or revenge Katji and the child she was carrying. Tibor had never given it much thought, before Michael had released them there had been no need to, but how could he go on living if he lost Katji? And as if to give him his answer Katji moaned in her sleep, her hand reaching out and searching for his. "I loved her." He hung his head, thick grey hair fell forward and covered his face. Something hot and wet ran down his cheek, followed by another and another. Michael realised he was crying, crying for his lost love and his lost life, he forced himself to smile and to remember. There was hope for him yet if he was capable of showing human emotions other than anger. Michael allowed the emotions to take him over, tears filled his eyes and he let himself remember happier times.

Tibor got to his feet and quietly moved away from him, now he needed to be alone. Michael had discovered that he was still able to shed tears, to bury the animal part of him and mourn his lost love. Katji moaned again, Tibor moved quickly to her side, her time must be near. He sat beside the sleeping Katji and took her tiny hand in his. "Sleep." he said "Sleep." Carefully he moved until he lay beside her. Pulling the blanket up to her chin gently tucking it around her, he lay back and closed his eyes. When he did sleep he was finely tuned into every sound or movement Katji made.

Long after the giant had fallen asleep Michael had sat, quietly he allowed his brain to recall memories, these would never leave him. He turned and looked at Tibor his arms protectively around Katji, then his thoughts turned to Vogel. If half of what the little man had told him was the truth, then the horror they were bringing to this valley was far too big for the three of them to stop. He realised that the step he was about to take would forever change his life and those who were with him.

There was only one choice, a choice he was prepared to accept, no matter what it brought to him. They must leave the valley, forever.

Michael crossed the floor of the cave and touched Tibor's shoulder, the giant came awake the ever present pistol in his hand, "What is it, do you smell trouble?" He asked. Michael shook his head and placed a finger over his lips and beckoned the giant to follow him.

"Listen to me Tibor and please let me speak before you say anything." Tibor shrugged his shoulders as if to say carry on you have me at a disadvantage. "I know," said Michael "that when the soldiers came you and Katji stayed because of me. Don't shake your head you know I speak the truth." Michael pointed down at the airstrip at the shadowy figures of the prisoners working under the lights. "I have been blind, stupid and selfish, I realised this when I told you how I lost Lilith, Katji must be taken from the valley. Once before I delayed such a move, I prayed to gods I didn't believe in. I lost everything I lived for, I do not intend that this should happen to you and Katji."

"I look down there and I see those little men with their guns holding the power of life and death in their hands. And I know I am safe, they cannot kill me with their bullets, but they can kill you and they can kill Katji. We must leave the valley, now."

"Impossible." said Tibor "I have Katji to think of, there's no way she can walk out of here." Michael had foreseen that this would be one of Tibor's objections and he said, "We carry her, we have the strength between us."

"Do you understand what this will mean to you moon child?" Michael turned away from looking down on the valley and looked at Tibor. It had been more than a year since anyone had called him that. "You have never lived in the world beyond these mountains, the real world Michael, not villages and towns but cities and,"

"Once." Said Michael interrupting the giant "Once long ago a woman told me that I was different to every other werewolf created, very few of us carry this mark." He pulled off his shirt to expose the mark of the pentacle. "It has taken me centuries to understand her words, but being here with you and Katji. Loving Lilith, I think I understand. I can if I wish, want to so badly, live among mankind without discovery."

"I don't understand why you were marked with that star Michael, I don't even want to understand why men and women were born to help. But you are right in the things you say, yes if you want it badly enough you can learn to live among them. And yes Michael you are right I only stayed in the valley because I knew Katji would not leave you, it is simple, I love her and we were born to protect you."

"I released you both from that vow, now answer me, do we leave?" The two men looked at each other, then without a word they reached out and clasped hands. "We go?" Asked Michael.

"We go." Said Tibor.

"Then lead and I will follow you." Said Michael, a puzzled looked crossed the giant's face. "What?" Asked Michael.

"I don't know which way we have to go, the only way out is closed to us by that." He said pointing down into the valley, "The pass is the only way out. We need the one they call the rat."

"Vogel?"

"Yes Vogel, he must know the land beyond the mountains, for we cannot go back the way you came, we can only go forward, do you think he would help us?" Michael nodded his head and when he spoke he said the word confidently in the belief that the little German would go with them. "Yes."

"Then you must seek him out we have very little time, I will speak to Katji." Michael saw the giant shake the sleeping Katji, he saw the bemused look on her face of a woman roused from a deep sleep. It would be better if he left them alone, stepping out of the cave he stripped and concealed his clothes beneath a bush. He moved quickly from the rocks to the forest heading for the prison compound.

Strobel tapped the map with the blunt end of his pencil, if all went well in twenty four days London would feel the power of 'Iron Fist'. He reversed the pencil and drew a circle around the city and with a grim satisfaction wrote 'end' inside the circle. "The end to a war." He said and sat back and literally beamed at Mantz. "That has not yet begun."

"My God." Mantz thought to himself , the man actually believes that he is wholly responsible for it all. Mantz opened his cigarette case and took out a cigarette, meticulously he tapped it against the case, turning it so that both ends received the same number of taps. Mantz carefully examined it then decided not to light it, he lifted himself out of the chair and walked over to the window. The ridiculous effervescence of the man was making him sick. Strobel was a complete idiot, did he honestly believe that the construction of the airstrip was the beginning, middle and end of 'Iron fist'. He looked at Strobel who was bent over the map his pencil constantly going around and around the circle he had drawn.

The man was sweating profusely, his tongue flicked in and out licking those fat slobbering lips of his. God, the man was disgusting, he would take great pleasure in putting a bullet through the man's brain when the time came. "Before the war has even started." Mantz put the cigarette between his lips, hostilities had already begun, Hitler had marched his troops into Poland, Germany was at war with Britain and France.

The airstrip was clearly visible under powerful arc lamps, from its inception 'Iron Fist' had been created to deliver one telling and final blow to the enemy Hitler feared the most and admired the most , the British. The inner circle had decided that since Britain would not fight alongside of them, they by necessity had to be the first to be vanquished. The enormity of the plan was so immense that the Furher himself had refused to believe in it. The nameless little man who had nurtured the idea of `Iron Fist' finally convinced the Furher and the inner circle that it could and would succeed.

He himself had been a simple Corp. commander at the time the team was being assembled, but his single minded devotion to Hitler and the cause brought him to the attention of Himmler. It also brought him promotion and though he wasn't privy to the plans of the inner circle, he was clever enough to realise that here was his ticket to eventually joining the hierarchy of the Third Reich.

The weapon that was to become known as `Iron Fist' was not easy to bring to a satisfactory conclusion, what had been promised in a month took nearly a year. The price paid by those working on it, all converts to Hitler's thousand year Reich, was horrendous. Some died in screaming agony, the flesh rotting on their bones with a nameless disease. Others died by the bullet, when they realised the horror of what they would perpetrate on the British people, they refused to carry on working. Their refusal meant death and they were duly rewarded for their lapse of faith, the work on 'Iron Fist' went on.

The aeroplane that would deliver the ultimate weapon on the unsuspecting people, proved to be a problem. Mantz remembered the words of the scientist in charge of the project, "It's all very well saying that we need a British bomber, how do we get one?" The man had looked around the table when he received no answer he went on "Providence will not provide one and I hardly think the British will lend us one."

The little man in the rimless glasses had said nothing, all through the meeting he had occupied himself by doodling on his papers. Smiling the snake like smile of his he lifted his head and said, looking pointedly at the head of the Luftwaffe. "I'm sure, no certain our good friend Herman, can get us one, or," He added. "If not, arrange to have one built." There the meeting had ended and after it Mantz had received his promotion and his orders.

Mantz dropped the cigarette and ground it out beneath his boot, in less than fourteen hours the plane which would carry 'Iron Fist' would land on the airstrip. At the same time a wagon would leave the factory where the weapon had been built, carrying the firing mechanism. Strobel would not have his twenty four days, or his test flights, when the two parts of 'Iron Fist' came together, the plane would fly. Even allowing for a large margin of error in the timetable, in twenty four hours or less `Iron Fist' would burst into life on the city of London.

Mantz giggled at the thought that came to him. "Was Chamberlain really a Jew, or was it Churchill?" He doubted that either of them were Jews, still in less than a day it wouldn't really matter.

The shrill ringing of the telephone caused him to stop thinking and listen. Strobel didn't speak, just nodded his head in agreement with whoever was speaking on the other end. Strobel replaced the phone and turned to Mantz. "Phase two has begun." Strobel turned and left the room, Mantz knew he would be going for the brandy, well one drink with him, then he would have to turn the rest of his orders into action. Strobel held out a glass, "To the glory of a thousand years Reich." Mantz allowed his glass to clink against Strobel's.

"To the Furher, victory and the Fatherland."

So intent on eavesdropping on the conversation between Strobel and Mantz, Vogel's heart missed a beat as a hand closed over his mouth. He found he was not able to move in the grip of the wolfman, Michael carried the little man into the forest before he took his hand from Vogel's mouth.

"God almighty are you trying to kill me?" Vogel spluttered, rubbing his mouth, tasting his own blood, he spit out the bitter taste. "What the hell's wrong with you?"

"I needed to talk to you." Said Michael, watching Vogel touch his mouth with a finger, winching in pain when he did touch it. He glared angrily at Michael, he would have liked to say something, but it was obvious that the wolfman demanded his attention. "Well." He said.

"We are leaving the valley and I want you to come with me."

"Are you crazy?" Asked Vogel "You want me to desert, they'd hunt me down." Michael looked hard at him, surely he hadn't made a mistake with Vogel, did the little man want to stay in the valley.

"What about 'Iron Fist'?" said Vogel "You said, you would do anything to stop it." Vogel wanted an answer from Michael, he had risked his life sneaking out of the camp and going up to the cave. "You said,"

"We are only three, if there was a way, do you think Tibor would ever want to leave this valley, this is, was his and Katji's home."

"The woman can't move anyway," said Vogel, "She's too close."

"We carry her."

"Use your brains Michael, have you learnt nothing?" Vogel was growing angrier by the moment, "How the fuck do we get out, fly?" Vogel shook his head, he had to talk to them all together, there was nothing he would like more than to be miles away from this valley. "I have to speak to the man and woman, I must." He grabbed Michaels arm, urgency in his voice. "I must talk to you, them." Michael wanted to say no, there was no time left to talk, but if Vogel felt so strongly that he had to talk, so be it.

"It must be now?" Asked Michael. "At a time like this?" Vogel nodded and when Michael turned he followed after him.

They sat and listened to him as he spoke, Tibor his arm around Katji, Michael his arms wrapped around drawn up legs. Vogel told of the feelings which had taken hold of him when he found the papers. How he had spent nights hiding outside Strobel's hut listening to their conversations. Katji lifted her hand and placed it on Tibor's mouth when he thought to ask a question. The little man continued, he told how he had spent long hours mulling over the things he had heard. It was only when he finally managed to piece it together he realised the enormity of it.

The horror and death it would bring sickened him. Vogel knew he would never be cast in a heroic mould, but he would rather die than be associated with 'Iron Fist'.

"Michael says to run, perhaps he's right, run and keep on running, but where? There is a disease creeping over Europe, a disease that will embroil us all in war. Do you honestly believe that they would be satisfied with one bomb? There would be another to bring Russia to heel, then another to show the Americans the power of the third Reich. He" Said Vogel pointing at the giant "He said that if this bomb was dropped the world would never know peace."

"There is no need to go on," said Katji "I understand what you are trying to say." She turned to Tibor. "Help me up." Tibor put his hand under her shoulders and lifted her to her feet. "Michael," she said, the wolfman turned his face to look up at her. "You once said that you would like to meet the fallen angel face to face. If you allow this thing to happen, your creator will rule this world."

"Why should I care about a destroyed world, perhaps if it is destroyed I will find peace."

"You stupid, stupid, selfish man." Katji's voice was filled with an anger she could not suppress. "Do you think that Tibor and I have spent years of our lives hidden away in this valley, locked away from the real world," Katji was at a loss as how to continue, she was struggling to find the words. She pointed her rigid finger at Michael. "No more self pitying platitudes from you. I am the Wych woman, the guardian of your kind. You owe me more than your life, you owe me your soul." Tibor was taken aback at the venom in Katji's words, he recoiled in surprise when she tore her hand from his and walked over to look down at Michael. "Forget what you are, forget the old religion, forget the fallen angel, trust in something more powerful. Trust in fate and whichever god rules it, it keeps us in this valley." Katji did not move she remained standing over Michael waiting for him to answer her, when he didn't Tibor could see she was beginning to get even more agitated. Tibor wanted to rush over and hug her, but he also needed to defuse the tension.

"It seems we are to try and put a spoke in 'Iron Fists' wheel."

"And that bastard Mantz," said Vogel "Do you know how he got his name, Mantz isn't his real name, I found these papers," Vogel reached inside his tunic and pulled out a thin brown file. "I stole this from Strobel's office thought it might help me, but all it is, is about that bastard" Vogel opened the file and quickly scanned it. "Here," he said "Captain Peter Mantz, changed his name when he got promoted. Called himself after the village he burnt down, though he thinks no one knows about that, his real name's Jurgens, Peter Jurgens son of a carpenter named Markos."

Michael was on his feet and rushing at Vogel before anyone realised what he was doing. He lifted the little man by the throat and smashed him against the wall, "What did you say?" he snarled. Katji cringed at the sight of Michael's face undergoing the change. More beast than man he snarled at the struggling Vogel, "Repeat what you said." The choking Vogel was unable, Michael's hands were too tight around his throat.

"By the gods," the giant threw himself at Michael. "Mantz is Lilith's brother." He thrust his great arms between the struggling Vogel and the wolfman. The muscles in Tibor's arms stretched and bulged as he tried to squeeze Michael. Michael shrugged his shoulders, gave a small grunt at the pressure Tibor was exerting on him. Tibor tightened the bear hug in which he held Michael, the wolfman gave an almost effortless shrug and broke Tibor's hold. Michael turned, his face contorted with rage, Tibor braced himself for Michael's attack. Michael poised himself on the balls of his feet and leapt towards the giant.

He changed directions in mid air, while his body was still clear of the cave floor. The pregnant Katji stood between him and Tibor, the sight of her brought some sanity back to him. He landed feet apart and glared at them, Katji, ashen faced but defiant. Tibor ready and waiting to test his strength against that of the werewolf. Vogel in a crumpled heap coughing and spluttering, fighting to get his breath. The three watched the regression from wolf to man, fangs retracted, the muzzle of the wolf became human. The eyes flickered between wolf and man before turning grey.

"Once again the nature of the beast rules you Michael." Katji refused to move from the front of him, forcing him to look at her. "Do you, who has recently professed love for the man's sister, hate him so much." The question hung in the air, filling the cave with its implications to them all. Katji had thought that Michael was safe, she had felt the emotions he had been feeling when he attacked Vogel. For the last few months Michael had walked a fine line allowing his human side free rein, now at the mention of one name he had regressed, he had become the beast that was forever inside him.

Michael struggled to come to terms with himself, his mind a whirling jumble of thoughts. He had attacked his friend Vogel, he could have quiet easily killed him. And Tibor, he had even wanted to attack him, at the mention of Peter's name he had wanted to rip and tear. The words of Anna rang in his brain. "The werewolf always destroys the love of those who love him." Frantically he searched the faces of Vogel, Katji and Tibor, was death stamped on their faces, would he be the bringer of death to them.

"I do not ask you to ask our forgiveness Michael, for that is not in the nature of the beast." Katji turned her back on him and walked away, her bitter words burnt into him, she had called him a beast. He cast hurt eyes in her direction, the tiny woman, swollen with child, had defied him and brought about the change. Katji was still the Wych woman, she above all others was still able to exercise control over him. Michael burnt with shame, he looked at the little German, at red marks of his fingers on Vogel's throat. Katji had her back to him refusing to make the first move, the giant glared at him still ready to try and defend his woman. The wolfman moved over to Vogel and reached out towards him. Vogel's eyes widened in fear. "I ask your forgiveness." Vogel eased himself up into a sitting position and looked at Michael. "Vogel I am truly sorry, you gave me friendship and I repaid it with violence." The wolfman was searching Vogel's face looking for a sign that the friendship still existed between them. "Will you still follow me?" Vogel smiled at the wolfman, he had given his loyalty to this cursed man, and where Michael went he would follow.

"It would make me a lot happier though Michael, if you didn't do these kind of things often, especially to me." Michael reached out and gripped Vogel's hand and gently pulled him to his feet. Michael looked at Tibor who was still undecided as to the wolfman's next action, Katji laid a hand on the giants arm and looked up at him.

"I need to speak to Vogel." Said Michael "There are things I must ask him." Katji said nothing but pulled at the giant to follow her, reluctantly Tibor did as she wished. "Vogel, how did you get this?" he asked holding the thin brown file, Vogel took the file from Michael and put it down beside him.

"I stole it." he said "Like the papers referring to 'Iron Fist' I found them in Strobel's desk, there's one on every man in the unit." Vogel smiled "Mine makes good reading, I didn't recognise myself." Vogel eased himself he was still sore from the experience at Michaels hands. "I guess Strobel thought he'd have some kind of hold over us all with these."

"But when he finds them gone?"

"He'll shit himself thinking that Mantz has them."

"Is that the truth, is he really Peter Jurgens?" Vogel saw the look in Michaels eyes, damn it, which way would Michael jump. If he went after Mantz they were as good as dead. "I promised I would kill him." Michael's words were said with no more emotion than any man commenting on the state of the weather. "Why did I not sense him, why? How many times have I been down to the camp, I never picked up his scent." Michael looked at Vogel. "I always found yours." Michael was asking questions about one specific thing that he had missed and it was clear to Vogel that it disturbed the wolfman that he not picked up on a hated enemy's scent. The werewolf's eyes suddenly went feral, yellow eyes glared as he spit out. "I promised to kill him !"

"If any man deserved to die it's Mantz, but think on Michael. The smell of dogs, the stink from the camp, petrol , diesel, and when you came to me you where only smelling for me, not him" Said Vogel "If you try and get him now you know about him," Vogel left the rest unsaid, he did not think he had to explain why to the wolfman.

"I risk all of your lives." Michael shook his head, he knew no matter what he was feeling that this was not the time to indulge himself in his personal vengeance. Peter would have to wait to die.

"Good god almighty." Shouted the little man, Vogel pushed past Michael and ran across the cave to where Katji lay, he had watched her suddenly stop and keel over. Tibor stood stupidly looking down at her, the little man shoved at him. "Get out of the way, Christ she's having the baby." Vogel bent over Katji who opened her eyes and looked at him, "Easy," He said "I help you." Katji smiled again and reached out and took Vogel's hand in hers, she didn't speak, she didn't have to. From the look in her eyes to the touch of her hand on his Vogel knew he had her complete trust.

The giant moved around them like a mother hen protecting its children, aware that they were in danger, but not knowing what to do about it. Vogel barked his orders and the giant jumped, if Vogel wanted hot water he would get it. "Michael."

Tibor turned and looked when the little man called out Michael's name. Vogel got to his feet and directed Michael gaze towards Katji, she was laid, eyes closed, pain visible on her face. "Look." He said "I think this is going to be a difficult birth, damn it," Vogel paced back and forth as if thinking hard. "I have to trust you Michael." The wolfman stared at him quizzically. "To help Katji I need certain things, I don't have them here, I need certain items from a white box marked with a red cross, will you get them for me?" Vogel actually knew the answer before he'd asked the question. "It means you going down into the camp, and Michael," Vogel took hold of Michael's arm and held it tightly. "No matter what, you must return here."

"I must not be seen, and I must not try and find Peter."

"That's exactly what I mean, for if you are seen, it could mean Katji's death."

"Then I will not be seen." Tibor sat dejected and feeling useless as Vogel described the items he required, Michael said nothing just nodded from time to time. Then Vogel said in a voice loud enough for Tibor to hear.

"Just get the box and bring it back." Tibor watched the wolfman leave and he prayed that Michael would remember all that Katji had done for him. As if to quieten his fears Vogel touched the giant on the shoulder and said.

"He will come back, trust him."

"Do I have any other choice?" Asked Tibor.

"No." said Vogel "No you don't, but I'll give you something to think about, do we really want Michael in the cave when the child is born." Tibor was puzzled over the little mans words, what difference did it make if Michael was in the cave or not when Katji gave birth. "I am sorry little man, but I do not understand." Vogel shook his head, smiled down at Katji who gave a little sigh at the befuddled thinking of her husband. "Tell him." She whispered.

Vogel pushed his hands in the pot of hot water and began soaping them, he hoped he'd made the right decision in sending Michael down among his enemies. It was a risk, a calculated risk but Vogel believed it was the right one considering Michael's previous show of anger. "When a child is born." He said "There's a lot of blood." Tibor's eyes widened in alarm when the truth of what Vogel was saying hit him.

"But he wouldn't hurt Katji or the child would he?" Why was he looking to Vogel for any kind of confirmation concerning Michael. He knew all that any human should want to know about the werewolf, or did he? Listening to Michael tell his story he realised that perhaps the Wych and the guardian didn't know everything. He knew the power and the strength of the werewolf for he had felt it, he could still feel the way Michael had shrugged his shoulders and sent him flying. Had Katji not pulled on her reserves of power he knew for certain he could not have stopped Michael from killing Vogel. They, he and Katji were there to help Michael's kind, but who was there to help them if the wolf turned. The answer was quiet simple, none was there to help them, like Michael they too carried a curse , the burden placed upon the Wych and the guardian by the leader of the old religion was as much a curse as the one Michael carried. He allowed these thoughts to twist and turn in his brain, the word curse shrieked at him. Cursed, all of them, he, Katji. Michael, even the little German who had given his loyalty to the werewolf, all of them were cursed in different ways. Katji's cry brought him out of his revelry. "It is time." said Vogel, Katji her face contorted by pain tried to smile.

Michael moved from shadow to shadow, moving past the sentries like a ghost, a grim smile on his lips. He could have easily killed them all, not even when the dog by his side whined did the sentry move, the fact that the dog stood trembling, he attributed to the cold night air. Michael was aware that the dogs knew he was prowling the camp. It could be that he still retained some of Vogel's scent about him. They smelt him, the scent of the wolf was causing their trembling and fear. It had been so easy to enter Vogel's office and take the box with the red cross from where it hung. It had taken him less than fifteen minutes, if he turned now he could be back at the cave within a matter of minutes. But he had to look upon the man who had threatened to have him shot and his beloved sister incarcerated in one of the special camps. He moved to the edge of the hut, the area he had to cross was brightly lit, he knew before he even set off at a run he was endangering the lives of three other people. He blotted out that thought, one overriding factor burnt in the wolfman's brain, to look at Peter.

Had the sentry turned he just might have caught a glimpse of a man running, but he didn't turn, and Michael was safely across and in darkness once more. He slowly sidled up to the window of Peters hut, Vogel had not asked why he wanted to know where Peter slept and Michael had not enlightened him. The light from the window threw a shaft of light, dispelling the darkness. Michael eased himself ever closer, until he could look in at the man. At the sight of the man sat in a chair Michael felt his heart begin to pound and his fingers clench and change. Michael did not fight it, he allowed it to take him over, the yellow eyes of wolf glared at the man he had promised to kill.

Peter, unaware that his enemy was outside his window and he was the thickness of the huts wall from death, yawned. His mouth tasted foul, too much of Strobel's brandy and far too many cigarettes, sleep was the medicine he needed. If he was lucky he'd get about four hours before the lorry arrived in the valley. He threw his jacket over the back of the chair this time they had to get it right. The original date had come and gone, Hitler had no intentions of waiting, war or no war Iron Fist would fly. Now, they were at war, but that seemed to be going well at least. The German war machine was pushing the British back, the last reports he had had from Berlin told him that within hours the whole of the British army would most likely be trapped on the beaches at Dunkirk. If that happened and 'Iron Fist' did fly on time, then the war would reach a victorious conclusion for the Third Reich. Peter looked at his watch, round about now a team of Storm Troopers should be heading for the valley, they'd been dispatched three days earlier to give them time to gain access to the valley from the high cliffs at the far end. He lay on the hard bunk, for gods sake let's hope it came together this time, too much time had been wasted already. It had been Strobel's fault in July, constant bickering and whining about the plane not being able to do this and he needed another dummy run. The snow had caught them out and the men in Berlin had not been pleased, but Strobel had survived by the fact that the firing mechanism had failed to work.

To hell with it Peter tried to get comfortable, forget Strobel, forget everything and try and get some sleep.

Michael pressed himself against the side of the hut, the boy was still handsome, but now the stink of corruption hung about him. Murder was in Michaels heart, it held him in its vice like grip, tightening around his heart until he thought it would burst. This was Lilith's brother, the man he had promised he would kill, he was near , so close, the wolfman could smell him, it still bothered the wolfman he had not picked up Peters scent over the many months he had visited the camp.

"You made a promise Michael." Katji's voice bore into his throbbing brain, drilling its persistent message again and again. "You made a promise Michael." Michael's clawed fingers tore into the wood, splinters drove themselves into his palm, he felt the warm trickle of blood. Peter had to die, he deserved to die, Michael pressed his face hard against the wall of the hut. It would be so easy, the walls were thin he could tear them apart in seconds, he lifted his hand, the hard claws glittering in the light from the window. Michael drew back his hand and measured the distance, an almost impermeable cry filled his mind, a small cry, the cry of a new born child. Peter would live, the werewolf would not kill him tonight. Michael turned away from the hut the sound of the child pulling him back to the cave.

Peter shot bolt upright on the camp bed his body covered with sweat. "God." He murmured, the nightmare had been so real. A man with the yellow eyes of a wolf had come to kill him, he reached under the pillow and his fingers touched the cold metal of his pistol. Sleep was a long time in coming to Peter but when it did it was populated by men with yellow eyes.

The sentry cocked his head to one side, the drone of aeroplane engines overhead, it appeared to be coming from beyond the mountains. In the still of the night they sounded like a million angry hornets trapped inside a glass jar. The sentry dismissed it, he had lost count of the number of times planes had roared over the valley in the last five days, heading, god knows where. He stamped his feet and cursed the whining dog, hell it gave you the shivers just listening to the bloody thing. Once again that night he missed the running man so distracted by his own discomfort that he took no notice of the dark shadow which fell across the cringing dog. He'd give Vogel a piece of his mind in the morning, that's if the little shit showed up, nobody had seen him since last nights guard roster, and nobody had bothered looking for him. The sentry hunched his shoulders deeper into his great coat. "Hope the little bastard's laying dead somewhere." Vogel's threat over the female prisoners still rankled. "Serve the little fucker right if he'd fallen into a water logged ditch and broke both his legs in the process." The sentry smiled to himself and pictured the sergeant laying in a ditch, trying to scream for help and the filthy water running into his mouth and choking him. Keller grinned again and even looked kindly on the dog, Vogel's hopeful demise gave him something to focus his tired mind on.

Michael suddenly stopped and looked down at the case in his hand, he tested the weight of it. His lips pulled back in a smile. "Clever little man," Vogel had tricked him, he hadn't needed anything from the case, but why send him down to the camp. Michael felt a cold finger trace its way all down his spine, he couldn't be trusted, not even by those sworn to protect him. The birth of the child, the scent of blood, they didn't want him there, in a bloody rage he wasn't to be trusted.

The sound of the new born babe came to him, it came not to his human side but to the beast within him, surely they understood he could not, would not hurt them, but he had tried to hurt Vogel. But the child, how could they believe he would hurt the child? There was one course of action open to him, he could leave, he had done it before, run away. Vogel would lead them to safety, he would make sure they survived.

How long he had been stood there he wasn't sure, the beast inside him told him to go. The human side of him telling him not to, Michael bent and picked up the box, not this time, no more running away. Both man and wolf wanted to look at the child of Katji and Tibor.

"Good God." Vogel jumped up at the sight of the big grey wolf, the box gripped firmly in its teeth, entering the cave. It padded slowly over to the little man and dropped the box at his feet. "The bastard things laughing at me." said Vogel. Looking in alarm at the giant, "It's laughing at me." The wolf looked at Vogel and growled, Vogel pressed back against the wall. The wolf turned and walked over to where Katji lay, Tibor held the pistol, pointing it towards the wolf.

Katji smiled wearily at the wolf, the wolf stared back, "It's alright he just wants to see our daughter." The wolf pricked up its ear and scratched the floor with its paw. Katji pulled the cloth from around the child, the wolf moved closer and stared down. Tibor, sweat running down his face tightened his grip on the pistol, the wolf lifted its head and looked directly into his eyes. For a moment they locked eyes man and beast, then the wolf looked away and into the Wych woman's eyes. Katji exposed more of her child, the wolf lowered its head until its cold nose touched the baby, the child whimpered and squirmed at the touch of it. The wolf's tongue ran gently over the babies exposed arm then its tongue touched the baby girl's eyes.

Tibor relaxed his hold on the pistol, so tight had he held it that pain flooded into his fingers. Vogel let his breath out in one long sigh. The wolf backed away its yellow eyes never leaving the child's face, for a moment it paused at the exit to the cave, then it was gone.

"Sweet Jesus." Said Vogel letting himself slide down the wall and slump onto the cave floor. Tibor's big hand reached out and he gently touched his daughter with one thick finger. "Why?" He said looking down at his wife, "Why did he come like that?"

"To prove to us all that we will never have to be afraid of him again." She looked towards Vogel. "I believe he knows you tricked him."

"I'm bloody certain of it." Said Vogel "God, he scared me, coming like that, it was worse than his attack." Panic suddenly gripped the little man, "He's not gone has he?"

The Wych woman shook her head and snuggled closer to her husband, who had put a protective arm around both of them. "No, he has not gone," Katji carefully pulled the blanket around her child. "He'll never leave us now." She pressed her head against the giant's arm and hugged the child closer to her. "He has given his life to the child." Vogel looked at the giant who stared back at him. They had both seen what Michael had done, so they had to believe it happened. Vogel made a mental note to quiz Michael over his actions, when the time was right, he drew up his knees and rested his head on them quietly thinking.

There was no going back for him now, he had burnt all his bridges behind him, he was a deserter. The more Vogel thought about it the more he was convinced he had made the right choice. From that moment in the forest when he had witnessed the transformation of wolf into man, he had been Michael's man. His last thought before he finally fell asleep was "I always will be."

Michael lay in the deep shadows watching the compound, he watched the guards moving around the circuit, taking their time. Their complacency surprised him, they were soldiers and should never take anything for granted. Even the dogs looked and moved with a lethargic disdain for their surroundings. Perhaps that was why it had always been so easy for him to enter the camp without discovery. The sound of the prisoners carried to him on the breeze, some of them moaning in their sleep. Others crying, begging their god to release them from the pain they were suffering. The hum of the generators keeping the landing strip alive with light. He also heard the sounds of the forest around him, he lay still, watched and listened.

His decision to go to Katji's child in the guise of the wolf, was the only gift apart from his total love, he had to offer. Michael also realised that he had bound himself forever to the small, wrinkled human, who at that moment lay sleeping in her mothers arms.

Major Eric von Marsten touched the arm of the driver. "Pull over." The driver slowed the lorry down and gently braked , von Marsten had opened the door and jumped out before it had stopped. "The lights," he hissed, the driver turned them off. The major waited until all the lorries had stopped and his men had climbed out before he motioned them over. "We walk from here, and we go quietly, sergeant." The big man moved quickly to his major's side, "You take the lead, take Cruger and Sholzt and be careful."

"I thought there was no one around here sir."

"There's not suppose to be, but we are not here to be seen by anyone, Rilla," The young storm-trooper saluted and started to click his heels. "For gods sake man." snarled the major. Rilla had the good grace to blush, grateful that his men could not see him in the dark, "Get your climbers ready, when the sergeant returns we go." The major flipped off the watches leather cover and look down at the luminous dial. "We're behind, get moving sergeant, the rest of you stand easy, and no cigarettes." Von Marsten moved until he was able to rest his arms on the tail gate of the lorry, he pulled out the map and carefully shone his torch on it. "To be perfectly truthful Rilla," He said, "This is about as much use as a glass eye." Von Marsten folded the map and flung it into the back of the lorry. "We're going in blind, your men better be up to it." He opened his watch and looked at it again, the sergeant had only been gone ten minutes, and why in gods name he was worrying he didn't know. They had lost far too much time getting here, the operation was supposed to go like clock work. Still he thought to himself if it all went pear shaped he could always lay the blame at the door of that cocky young bastard Mantz. His information concerning the back road to the valley was total and geographically wrong, where he said there were roads they turned out to be paths. Damn it, why had he been given this job, not because he was the best man for it, even if he thought he was. This was a simple mop up job, it would have been better left to the Gestapo, he and his commando's could have been having a go at the British "They're back sir." The major sighed and waited for his sergeant to come to him. "Let's get in there and get it over."

"It shouldn't be a problem getting down sir, once we shin down the cliff face we're right into forest." Well, mused von Marsten, at least Mantz got that part of it right.

"Right sergeant all the information to the captain."

The coughing drone of the bomber caused Michael to look up, the plane was a large bat winged shadow flying across the night sky. The plane banked and turned, the pilot making his landing approach. It floated down, its engines roared as the pilot throttled back, rubber squealed on Tarmac and the bomber was down. It taxied down the runway and slowly the lumbering plane began to turn. Propellers revved and the plane started its laborious journey back to the end where it had landed.

Michael watched as a car shot from between the huts and raced towards the bomber. The headlights of the car flashed on and off as it neared the plane. The engine of the plane whined and spluttered as they slowed down before completely shutting off. A door opened in the planes fuselage and a ladder dropped, Michael counted the men who climbed down it, five. In a group they moved away from the plane towards the rapidly approaching car. Strobel leapt out of the still moving car and reached out to take the pilots hand in greeting. There was no sign of Peter.

The noise of the plane landing brought Peter out of his sleep, he heard Strobel shouting at the driver of the car to get a move on. He had to get off the bunk, he should have been there with Strobel to meet the plane. He swung his legs over the edge of the bunk, his head ached, it pounded sharp fingers of pain into his brain at the least movement. He had slept badly, and the nightmare had returned to haunt him. This time there was no man with the yellow eyes of the wolf, it was a woman. A tall beautiful woman who floated towards him, a woman with milky orbs instead of eyes. Lilith had floated on air her arm outstretched, one finger pointing accusingly at him. He had watched her open her mouth and he waited for that terrible croaking sob. "Why Peter?" Terror gripped the sleeping man, he wanted to wake up but couldn't, he cried out to her in his tortured sleep. "Why Peter?" she asked him, the two words had come from a throat that had never spoken before. Peter Mantz had felt himself falling, falling down a long dark tunnel, he had screamed soundlessly. Hands tried to grip the smooth wall of the tunnel, he actually felt his nails scrape against the wall. He knew he was lost and that should he hit the bottom of the tunnel he would never awake.

The roar of the engines and Strobel's voice had dragged him back from the edge. He inhaled the rank smell of his own sweat, he was trembling with the fear of a man remembering his nightmare. Along with the pounding in his head a pain was constantly pecking at his eyes. Peter sat there, begging the pain in his eyes to go away . When it did subside a little he forced himself to stand and walk over to the sink. A shaking hand turned the single tap and the cold water gushed out, Peter stuck his head under it. The freezing cold water sent shock waves through him, intensifying the pain in his head. Cupping his hands he threw the cold water over his face, chest, it ran in icy rivulets down his chest and dripped onto the floor forming a small puddle. Again and again he threw water over him, soaking what few clothes he had on. Not until he believed some semblance of humanity had returned to him did he stop. Peter Mantz could never remember having a nightmare before, he hoped to god he never had another.

Freshly dressed he looked at himself in the mirror, he tightened the belt and shifted the cap to a more rakish angle. Satisfied with how he looked he walked over to the door, it mattered little to him now that Strobel had greeted the aircrew, in a few hours Strobel, the guards, the prisoners, the camp, all would be a distasteful memory. He pulled open the door and stepped out of the hut, Mantz sniffed the cool mountain air, he looked at the thin grey light that announced the coming of a new day. He smiled, it would be a perfect day if everything went according to plan.

Von Marsten watched as the last of his men landed safely, they left the ropes where they were in the event that something went wrong. Leading his men down the narrow path, he stopped suddenly and brought up the machine gun at the figure which stood before him. Vogel had chosen the most inopportune moment in his life to leave the cave to relive himself. The butt of the machine gun hit him under the jaw sending him backwards into the cave, before Tibor had no time to react before he was looking down the muzzles of half a dozen guns. Von Marsten moved into the cave and looked around, he knelt and examined Katji and her child before he said, "Tie these two up, I'll talk to them later, Rilla, you and two others stay here, and make sure they stay quiet. Damn", What was going on, didn't Mantz check on anything? He motioned the rest of his men to follow him, he was beginning to get a very bad feeling about this operation.

Michael stiffened, the sound was barely audible, the sound of cloth rubbing against a branch. The silent swish as the branch returned to its normal place, but he heard it. He also heard the sound of boots treading carefully on the ground beneath the trees, unable to avoid the pine needles. Michael merged into the background and listened, mentally he counted the different sounds, at least twenty men moving, trying not to make a sound. Before they had reached the spot where he had been standing, Michael was concealed in the lower branches of the tree. From between the branches he stared down at Von Marsten and his men creeping forward through the undergrowth.

So intent were they on reaching their objective that none of them even bothered to look up. The line of armed men made hardly any noise, these were hunters, men who knew what they wanted and what they were after. Each man wore a black boiler suit, each carried a machine gun, across their chest a wide leather belt which held spare ammunition and half a dozen hand grenades. They never spoke, using their hands to indicate what they wanted. The scent of killers drifted up to the wolfman. At the edge of the forest they stopped, their leader made a chopping motion with his hand, this was as far as they were going. The men lay down and hugged the ground, Michael knew that from the camp they would be almost invisible. He would have liked to stay where he was and wait to see what was going to happen. But he knew that wasn't an option, cautiously he slid down the tree trunk, he backed away from the armed men, his eyes never leaving them until he knew he was safe. Then he turned and began to move quickly but carefully towards the cave. Using all the cover available to him he moved with the self preservation of a trapped beast. These killers had come from somewhere, and it was obvious that they had entered the valley somewhere near the cave. His one thought now to reach Katji and the others, but with caution, just because he hadn't seen more of them it didn't mean they were not here.

The deep imprint of boots coming down the path from the cave stopped him, he lifted his head and sniffed the air. There were more of them in the cave, his friends were in trouble, it never entered his head that they could be dead. Katji would have found a way of reaching him, why hadn't she. If they had touched her in any way at all, the invaders in the valley were dead men. He cleared his mind of all thoughts of their present danger and allowed the change to take him over.

The wolfman did not panic, he did not even consider charging up the path, yellow eyes sought out a way he could climb up to the cave. He bunched his muscles and jumped, reaching as far up as he could. Hard nails on feet and hand found tiny cracks in the rock and the werewolf hung on. Yellow eyes sought out more hand holds and he began to pull himself up, hard nails found invisible cracks and the werewolf moved ever closer to the cave. Michael went up the rock face at an angle, so that if there was a guard he would be able to come down on him from above. The sound of boot nails on the path, a man yawning, there was a guard.

Michael looked down. The guard moved to the edge of the path and opened the front of his boiler suit, he died holding his manhood in his hand. Michael tore the man's head from his body, the mans bursting penis spraying the path with urine. The werewolf grabbed the headless body and held it from falling, the headless torso sprayed blood all around it. The wolfman standing on the path lifted the headless body above his head and walked into the cave.

Tibor was bound tight, Vogel lay beaten and bleeding, they had taken pleasure in beating the little man, a deserter from the army. Rilla was still stood over him, he nudged the little man with his foot and prayed he hadn't killed him, Von Marsten would show him no mercy if he had. Perhaps they shouldn't have gone too far, he turned and looked at the giant who glared murder at him, at the woman who had gone into a trance the moment he had touched her. He had never intended to rape her, she wouldn't be worth it, she had just given birth, besides the Major had promised them some time with the female prisoners when it was all over.

Not until the werewolf growled did Rilla realise they were not alone with the prisoners. He turned, his gun levelled, the sight that met his eyes sent him rigid with terror. They were trained killers who had tortured and maimed the weak, the innocent in the name of the third Reich, they had never faced a werewolf.

If the sight of their headless companion in the arms of the werewolf was not enough, Michael picked that time to change into half-man, half-wolf. Rilla could not move, he felt his bowels move and then the smell of his own defecation. He didn't have much time to think about his plight, the werewolf took a handful of flesh from his throat. The second man tried to make a run for it, Rilla's death galvanising him into action, he got about three feet before the werewolf bore him down. His scream choked off as fangs sank deep into his throat. The mans jerky movements stopped, the werewolf opened its jaws, it tasted hot blood seeping down its throat. The werewolf shuddered, coarse hairs began to cover its body, its spine began to bend trying to assume the shape of a wolf. One hand changed into a wolf's paw, the werewolf growled, the taste of hot brassy blood infecting it.

Michael fought the change, he didn't want it, he needed to stay human, the shock of its human side fighting the change sent pain coursing through his body. The pain swelled until it filled every part of his body, he felt as if it was tearing him apart. Michael sank the fangs into his own flesh, feeling the pain it brought, he tasted his own blood, he dug his nails into his palms , he felt the exquisite agony of self inflicted pain. The fire he needed to make the change regress.

Slowly his spine began to straighten, it creaked and cracked as muscle and sinew returned to its proper place. Before his blurred vision thick grey hairs retreated back into his flesh. On hands and knees Michael gulped down great lungs full of air, he gasped at the burning sensation it caused. Again and again he drew air into his tortured lungs, gagging against the taste of human flesh and blood which had tainted his mouth. He had fought the change and won but the price was high, he was experiencing an agony he had not thought the human body capable of. Sweat poured from every pore of his naked body, so intense that it ran from his body and formed a pool on the cave floor. Through red rimmed eyes he looked at his friends, Tibor was struggling against his bonds, the veins in his neck visible. Vogel still lay in the corner, not moving. Michael stared hard, his heart lightened at the slight movement of Vogel's stomach rising and falling. Katji sat rocking the child a far away look in her eyes, humming a strange song to the sleeping child.

Michael scuttled across the cave floor to Tibor, blood stained fingers tore at the knots in the rope. Once he had untied the giant, still on hands and knees he crawled over to Vogel. The wolfman tenderly lifted the little mans head, there was an ugly cut on Vogel's head. His face was covered in blood, his lip split, a bruise forming under his eye. Vogel's chin was badly bruised and cut from the major's gun. Michael lay him back down and hurried to get some water, using part of Vogel's shirt he wiped away the blood, Vogel groaned as the cloth reopened the cut on his lip. The little man opened one eye and looked at Michael, his mouth twisted into what could have been a smile. "Bastards." He groaned again at the pain, talking caused him.

"Easy little man," Said Michael, pressing the wet cloth against Vogel's lip, "Rest easy." Michael bunched Vogel's coat and pushed it under his head, "I thought I had lost you" He said.

"I would not have liked that." Vogel grinned up at him, his hand squeezed Michael's. Michael smiled again and gently touched the little mans face.

"Friend," he said and turned away lest Vogel should see the tears in his eyes. The question on Michael's lips died when he looked towards Tibor, he was cradling Katji to him, tears streamed down the giants face. He was muttering to her in the sing song language of the old religion, Katji was staring straight ahead her eyes locked on something that only she could see. Michael laid his hand on Tibor's shoulder, the giant looked up at him. "What is it?" Asked Michael, "What's wrong with her?"

"I don't know." Tibor's words were slurred by sobs that racked his giant frame.

"Did they touch her, did the soldiers touch her?"

"No, yes, he just put his hand on her and she went into this trance, it just happened, Vogel, he told me not to fight." the giants words were full of regret, had he fought perhaps this would not have happened. "She held our child to her refusing to let her go" Tibor sniffed, his mouth trembled , he was trying not to break down completely. Michael stared deep into Katji's eyes she did not blink, not even when he passed his hand across her face, her eyes remained wide open and fixed on some invisible object. Tibor said nothing, he was once more engrossed in talking to her in their strange tongue.

"Go on Michael," The wolfman turned, Vogel had managed to crawl over to them. "Go, get rid of the bodies." Vogel groaned as he bent over Katji. "Go on, I'll do what I can."

"Easy." Von Marsten put his hand over the sergeant's gun barrel, he had watched the young man in the uniform of a captain in the Gestapo walk out of the compound. The man had spent some time near one of the vehicles, looked at his watch and slowly sauntered towards their position. To all intents and purposes it looked like Mantz was taking a leisurely stroll before breakfast. He walked steadily towards where they were concealed by the undergrowth, six feet from them he stopped, pulled out his cigarette case and carefully selected one. Von Marsten counted the number of times that Mantz tapped the cigarette on the case. Peter Mantz had given the required signal to the commando's that he was their contact. The sergeant lowered the muzzle of the gun and clicked the safety back on. The captain settled himself down on the ground before lighting the cigarette, "My name is Peter Mantz." He said "I hope you can hear me if not please say so." When he didn't receive an answer Mantz carried on talking. "Sometime within the next few hours a vehicle will drive into the valley. This vehicle will contain a very important and valuable object." Peter paused and removed his cap, he pushed his fingers through his hair.

Peter opened his case and took out another cigarette. "Your orders Major, and I have to tell you that these come from the Furher himself is to ensure that every prisoner, man, woman and child, including the guards stay in the valley, that means"

"I know what that means Mantz, it means we murder them." von Marsten felt his stomach contract, and the bile rise in his throat, murder wasn't his game, he was a soldier. How could this arrogant young bastard sit there and carry on a conversation that called for the death of hundreds and still remain calm. If this was the breed of man who wanted to rule Germany perhaps it might be better if they were defeated by the British and French. But from information received it seemed that the British were taking a beating, Von Marsten realised he had little choice but to do as he was ordered, he had a wife and family in Berlin.

"A strange choice of words major, I should have used, expedite, terminate, but not murder, they are after all enemies of the Reich." Von Marsten did not answer, so Peter continued, "Do you see the three huts close to the edge of the airstrip? good, the last one on your right. Once everything is ready for you I will stand at the door of that hut, and" He held out his lighter for the major to see "One, two, three" He said flicking it on and off. "That is your signal to attack, if for any reason I light it a fourth time do not come in, the operation will have been cancelled."

"What about the guards? They're not going to just stand there."

"Shoot them, it will save time later on." Peter got to his feet and brushed himself down. "Oh, one other thing Major, no, no, I mean two other things, under no circumstances do you or any of your men go in the hut or near the plane." Without waiting for an answer Peter started to walk back down the incline to the camp. The major lifted his gun and trained it on Peter's back, one quick pull of the trigger and the evil young fucker would be dead.

"It's not worth it sir." Von Marsten turned to his sergeant, of course the man was right, but he would have derived great satisfaction from doing it.

"I fear sergeant," he said "That within a few years we will be fighting for our very lives on German soil. Men like him will make the whole world our enemy."

Michael followed the footprints from the cave, he saw the ropes hanging down, he pulled at it, someone had fastened it securely, so this was the way they intended to return. Grabbing hold of a rope he began to haul himself up towards the edge of the cliff, reaching his hand over the edge he pulled himself over. Kneeling he examined the ground, the crushed grass trampled by the soldiers boots, and he carefully followed the path they had made to reach here. Cautiously Michael moved, back tracking their footprints in the soft soil and across the blanket of needles and fallen leaves. There was something about the bushes that wasn't right, the way the branches lay, Michael eased his way to them. He smiled, they had broken down branches and tried to hide the transport Tibor and Vogel had told him were called wagons or lorries. He had never in his life been so close to one of these things and for a minute or two he was lost in the wonder of it. He ran his hands over the big rubber wheels, stroked the cold hard metal of its body, here he knew was their way out of the valley.

The soldiers must be confident in their own abilities to leave these things unguarded but that made it much better for them. He would return to the cave and speak to Vogel, the little man would know what to do.

"My God Michael do you realise what this means, yes, I can see you do." Vogel's voice was full of excitement. Michael's discovery of the three vehicles was wonderful, they only needed one of them. Drain the fuel from the other two, and in less than twenty four hours they could be a hundred miles away from the valley, free. "We can't risk it before dark though, and from what you've been telling me of the men down there, they won't attack until dark." Vogel groaned as he got to his feet and began walking back and forth, muttering to himself. Apart from a cut lip, one eye which had closed and turned a multitude of colours Vogel appeared to be alright. Michael smiled to himself, the little man was loving every minute of it, he was in charge, he knew what to do, but despite his excitement Vogel looked at the Wych woman with each passage he made.

Katji had not moved, she sat holding her daughter, eyes fixed forward. The giant had remained at her side refusing to let her go. "What about those two?" Asked Vogel "The woman we can carry, I think," He said rubbing his arms "but him?"

"Tibor will listen to me. I am sure of that."

"Then I'll make a start on getting things together."

"Vogel." Said Michael, the little man stopped what he was doing and turned to Michael. "We will find a way, you and I." Vogel thought before he answered, then he grinned, which caused him to winch. A final nail had been driven that was to cement their lives together for as long as they both lived.

"Yes Michael." He said "We will."

"She comes out of her trance just long enough to feed the child." Tibor explained in a voice fraught with concern for his wife and child. The giant's features were drawn and haggard. The strain was beginning to tell even on his mighty resolve, his love for Katji was slowly breaking him. "I've tried to recall her, I've used every prayer of the old religion I can think of, nothing works." He looked at Michael, for the first time in his life Tibor was asking another person for help and that person could not help him, Michael did not know what to do.

Michael knelt before him, reached out and touched Katji's face, she was cold. He looked at the child who lay sleeping in her arms, something or someone must be watching over the child, barely three days old, fed at irregular intervals, still it flourished.

Michael explained to the giant what was going to happen, Tibor who never stopped uttering to Katji in their strange language, just nodded his head in agreement. Michael left them alone and wandered over to Vogel, the two men collected what Vogel thought they would need, in silence, all they had to do now was wait for dusk. Michael walked over to the cave mouth and carefully slipped outside trying not to show a light.

Below him the valley was a blaze of light, the arc lamps illuminating the prison compound, the huts, the plane. In all the time he had spent here in the valley he had never once explored it, now he never would. And Peter, what of Peter, would he ever be so close as this again to the man. Michael lifted his head and looked up at the darkening sky and prayed to the fallen angel to one day put Peters life in his hands. He considered looking at Tibor and Katji's valley with the eyes of a wolf, to look upon a place that had given him hope and friends, but there was no need to, unless the fates or the whim of the fallen angel called him back here, he believed he would never set eyes on the valley again. The wolfman turned and made his way back inside, it was time to leave.

Vogel stood on the path beneath the rope and watched Michael disappear up it, it had taken them a little over ten minutes to reach this spot. Tibor had refused to let either of them help him, he had insisted on carrying Katji and the child. Vogel felt Michael tug on the rope he was over the top, "Tibor." He whispered, the giant turned, "Tie Katji to the rope." He whispered again and had a ridiculous thought, why in hell was he whispering there was no one else about. "The rope man, tie her." Vogel shook his head and tied Katji to the rope, making sure the child was safe he gave it a tug. Katji and the child were hauled up. When Michael tugged again he wrapped the rope around the giant and gave the signal. Michael heaved at the rope, his muscles creaked at the effort of pulling up the dead weight of Tibor. It would have been easier to change, by the time he had pulled Tibor over the top he was sweating.

Vogel's grinning and bruised face appeared at the edge, his hand reached out and Michael grabbed it and hauled him over. Vogel, without a word to the others took his knife and cut the ropes. "They won't follow us this way. Come on." Once Katji was loaded in the back of the wagon, Vogel got the two men to push the wagon backwards first. He spun the wheel and then got them to push him forward. No point in starting the lorry until he was certain they wouldn't be heard.

At the touch of his sergeants hand Von Marsten came awake, it was dark already, how long had he been asleep. He felt the sergeant put something into his hand, chocolate, he smiled and bit into it. What he'd have liked was a cigarette, but that was one luxury he couldn't afford. "No signal yet sir." The sergeant gave an unneeded explanation, Von Marsten wondered what his sergeant would have done if the signal had come while he had been sleeping. He gave instructions to the sergeant and chewed on the chocolate bar, and started to get that feeling again, that something was going to go wrong. He lifted the night glasses and trained them on the hut, until Mantz signalled they could only wait.

Peter Mantz checked his watch yet again, where the hell was the lorry, it should have been here before dark. The whole operation should have been over by now, the timing had been crucial, Von Marsten's men should have attacked the camp at dusk. He reached for his greatcoat, looked at the aircrew, he had taken them to his hut. "Better," he had said to Strobel "That they do not hear any communications from Berlin. They know they are on a very secret mission, but it is better they don't know what could happen to them when they release the bomb." Strobel had agreed with him and now the aircrew were lounging about his quarters. "Stay inside the hut." he ordered "I must do my nightly checks around the camp, everything has to look normal." He looked at the airmen they appeared not to be listening to him, he lifted his foot and knocked the feet of one airman off his desk, the man jumped to his feet his face red with anger. Peter stared him down. "Is it understood, you don't leave the hut." The airman bit his lip and nodded, Peter looked at the others, they all nodded in agreement. "Good it's nice that we can all agree, gentlemen." He said and opened the door, "Cocky bastard." He heard one of them mutter as he shut the door behind him.

Peter settled his cap on his head and made for Vogel's hut, strange that the little man should vanish. He didn't think Vogel had it in him to desert and leave behind his precious dogs. Still it didn't matter, at this late stage in the game, the little mans name would just be added to the list of those who had fallen for the glory of the Third Reich.

Where the hell was that fucking wagon? What if something had happened to it? A tyre burst, it could have hit something, he needed to know. The firing mechanism to explode 'Iron Fist' was being carried in it, he'd take a car and go and look. Drive up the pass, find it, find the others as well. The more he thought about it the better the idea appealed to him. Two minutes later Peter, behind the wheel of a car drove out of the compound and headed towards the pass.

Von Marsten looked hard at the driver of the car, he wasn't able to see the man's face, he had his collar turned up. Whoever it was, was driving at breakneck speed towards the pass. He lifted the flap on the watch and looked at the time, it was all going wrong.

The airman yawned they'd been cooped up for god knows how long, what with the smell of food, the stink of sweat, he needed some fresh air. He desperately wanted another cigarette but he didn't want to smoke it in here, the air inside the hut was already stale from too many cigarettes. "Sir." he said shaking the man's shoulder, the pilot opened one eye and looked up at him. "Uh." "Is it alright for me to smoke near the door?" The pilot thought about it and said "O.K, but don't go outside, just stay inside." He sat up wishing the whole damn thing was over and done with. He and the crew had trained for months on the mock up of a British bomber. But it was nothing like the real thing and he should know, the reason he was heading this mission was because he had flown British bombers while training in England. The plane was a brilliant piece of work, it looked like the real thing pure imitation right down to the last nut and bolt. But the bloody thing handled like a pregnant pigeon. "No further than the door, eh." The young crewman nodded and opened the door to Peter's hut.

He pulled the packet of cigarettes from his tunic pocket, turn his head against the draught through the door, the match went out. He looked appealingly at the pilot, who shook his head, sighed and threw him his lighter. The man lit the cigarette and pulled at it. Allowing the smoke to dribble down his nose slowly. He looked at the lighter and flicked it on and off, one, two, three.

Von Marsten lowered the glasses. "Let's go." he shouted and jumped to his feet glad at last to be doing something, even if it meant killing innocent's.

The guard looked up and his mouth dropped open, a line of armed men were moving down on the camp. The big Alsatian at his side began to growl, straining at the lead, panic gripped the guard as he began fumbling with the rifle over his shoulder. The animal sensing the man's panic pulled hard at the lead, the dog ripped it from the man's grip and shot arrow straight at the oncoming men. The guard, the rifle finally in his trembling hands fired, it was the first shot he had ever fired at another soldier, it was his last. The other guards alerted by his shot rushed out of their hut just in time to see their comrade go down under a rake of machine gun fire. "We're being attacked."

The charging Alsatian was torn apart by the bullets, it was thrown backwards to drop and slowly fall into two halves at the feet of one of Von Marsten's men. A volley of fire from the compound guards, three of the advancing commandos went down. The cry of a thousand nickel coated bees of death as von Marsten's men opened up a concentrated field of fire. An enterprising guard opened the dog pound and twenty snarling dogs hurled themselves at Von Marsten and his men. A man went down screaming as the dog sank its fangs into his shoulder, the sergeant shot the dog in the head. Before he had time to help the man up another dog had its mouth around the wounded mans throat. The sergeant gritted his teeth as teeth ripped flesh from his leg, a soldier staggering blindly around, blood pouring from his face hit the sergeant, they both went down. Half a dozen blood crazed dogs tore into the two men. Von Marsten threw himself down, the dog hurtled over him, he rolled and fired. The dog hit the ground and lay still. A body hit the ground next to him, rough hands grabbed him and hauled him up. One of his men his face covered in his own blood, a bullet had nicked his nose. "What's happened major?" He cried "What the fuck's gone wrong?"

"I don't know, how many of us are down?"

"At least ten sir, and god knows how many to those fucking dogs."

"If it moves soldier, shoot it." Von Marsten ran for cover behind one of the huts a fusillade of bullets rattled into the wooden side of the hut. The major peered around the corner, some of the guards had decided to make a stand. "You, corporal, throw them a fucking present and fast." A half dozen hand grenades floated across the space between the two huts. Orange fire blossomed, soil, wood and bits of human flesh flew up into the air mingled together. A second batch of grenades hit the ground and exploded before the sound of the first explosions had subsided. The hut was blown apart, great chunks of wood sailed through the air, four of the aircrew died instantly, the one man who had wanted a cigarette was impaled by a seven foot splinter of wood.

The pistol in Strobel's fist belched three times, the man flew backwards out of the door. Strobel minus his jacket raced through the door, the hut exploded behind him, the blast picked him up and sent him skidding along the ground. He felt the skin being burnt from his chest and knees, he came to a sickening halt, hitting one of the posts to the prisoners compound. Strobel, shaking his head, used the post to get to his feet, what was going on? Why were they being attacked, it was unbelievable that they should be attacked , who were they? He shot the man running towards him and snatched the machine gun from his hand. Strobel stuck the pistol into his belt and looked around him.

Death and destruction was all around him, the huts lay in ruins, bodies lay in their grotesque ending, limbs shattered by the explosions. Flesh riddled by bullets, Strobel's mind unable to comprehend what he was seeing went crazy. Another larger explosion threw him back to the ground, the prison huts were being systematically destroyed. He heard the screams of the prisoners unable to escape the carnage, he saw them mowed down by gunfire as they tried to run. A figure dressed in black came towards him, the smoke had blackened his face, only the white of his eyes and teeth were visible. Strobel believed he was looking on the face of death, he screamed once at the sight, then pulled the trigger. The man twisted and turned under the impact of the bullets. Strobel still held his finger on the trigger long after the magazine had emptied itself.

He began to giggle, then laugh, a high hysterical laugh, he had conquered death, eyes wild, he twisted and turned looking for a way to escape. The car, the car was less than thirty feet away, flinging the empty gun away he raced towards it.

Strobel snatched at the car door, cried in pain as the hard metal cracked against his knee, then he was behind the wheel and with a calmness that only comes to madmen he sat there and lovingly ran his hands over the dashboard. Still giggling he turned the key, the engine roared into life, a great shout of joy was ripped from Strobel's lips and he rammed his foot against the accelerator. The sleek black car shot forward, mowing down the two men charging towards it, it drove over one of them. Strobel heard the screams and the sound of bones crunching under the cars body, the sounds of fighting had been driven from his mind. The car lurched, jumped and broke free of the body, what remained of one of Von Marsten's commando's was left behind. The madman had only one thought in his mind to reach the plane and defend 'Iron Fist'.

Von Marsten lined up the speeding car and fired, the windscreen shattered under the impact of bullets, Strobel swerved the car, the car shuddered as more bullets riddled the body. Strobel was half stood, his hands gripped tightly on the wheel, his eyes riveted on the plane. "Stop him." Von Marsten shouted, working quickly he slammed another magazine into his gun, beside him two men opened up.

Strobel shot upright lifted from the car by the bullets, a neat row of death traced its way from the base of his back to his head. The bullets exited Strobel's face tearing it away, blood, bone and brains splattered what remained of the windscreen. "The tyre's, hit the tyres." Von Marsten's shout came too late, the car slammed into the body of the plane. Strobel, car, and plane were enveloped in a ball of gasoline. Flames eagerly caressed the fuselage, licking hungrily at the thin fabric that formed the body. Strobel's fire blacked body stood upright, pointing an accusing finger at Von Marsten, then a second explosion obliterated him. A finger of fire shot into the air fuelled by the aviation fluid, a rain of fire descended on the valley.

Von Marsten stood there unable to tear his eyes away from the flaming wreck, he ignored the droplets of fire which burnt his face and hair. A ball of fire 'whooshed' from what remained of the plane before it collapsed onto the Tarmac.

"Jesus fucking Christ."

In the remnants of Strobel's hut, a wire which had miraculously survived all the destruction around it carried its message to the telephone. No one heard the incessant ringing, which went on for nearly six minutes, when it finally stopped the man in Berlin looked up at Himmler. "No answer sir, there must be a fault somewhere on the line." Himmler nodded and turned to go back into his office, they would try again in the morning. He could just imagine Strobel's face when he received the message that `Iron Fist' was not going to fly after all. Hitler had decided that since the British and French were already beaten they would save the bomb to use on the Russians when their time came.

"How many?" Asked Von Marsten, the corporal took a deep breath before speaking, the major turned on him "Well, how many?"

"There's only the four of us left alive sir." the corporal tried to deliver his message as coldly as he could, but he couldn't disguise the tremor in his voice. "No wounded."

"Destroy everything, burn the fucking lot, prisoners, our men, the others, leave nothing, not a single trace, do you understand me?"

"Yes sir." Von Marsten watched the man walk away, he was going to have one hell of a job explaining this away. They waited until the bodies , soaked in petrol were burning, hopefully by the time the fire died down there would be nothing left, he wrinkled his nose at the smell of burning flesh. A thick black column of smoke rose into the air and settled over the valley.

"Let's get the fuck out of this god forsaken place."

THE WAY HOME

Vogel pulled the wheel sharply to the left narrowly missing the tree that loomed up out of the darkness. "Sweet mother of God." He was going to have to use the headlights, he had hoped to be clear of anyone in the valley seeing the moving vehicle. Vogel pulled the switch and the twin beams illuminated the area around the wagon. He had wanted to follow the path the wagons had used to get up to the cliffs above the valley, but he had lost it a way back. The little man thumped the wheel and peered at the way ahead, they were not making good time. In the green instrument lights Vogel more than resembled the rodent they had christened him. He did look and act like a rat. His eyes constantly switching back and forth from the bright swathe of the headlights. He gripped the wheel and twisted, another tree missed, god, how long could he carry on like this, sooner or later he was bound to hit something.

From behind them came the rattle of gunfire and minutes later an explosion that sent a tremor through the ground that he felt through the body of the wagon. Vogel slammed on the brakes, pulled hard at the handbrake and shoved open the door. He stared at the column of fire that reached high into the night sky. He sensed Michael near him, neither of them spoke both realising that the column of flame was not only destroying the valley but burning away part of their lives.

Peter Mantz heard the explosion and turned the car into a skidding turn, he almost lost control as the car hit the solid rock of the pass. He heard, rather than saw the right hand side of the car being ripped away, he howled in pain as a piece of razor sharp metal pierced his arm. The pain spurred him on, he jammed his foot down hard and the car tore itself free of the rocks. He felt the blood running down his arm and filling the leather glove, the wheel becoming slippery under his right hand. He ignored it, his mind totally occupied with one thought, something had gone drastically wrong. When he reached the head of the pass and saw the flames he slowed the car down, letting it roll forward until the whole of the valley opened up before his eyes.

He stared in horror at the remnants of a shattered dream, mesmerized he got out of the car and walked towards it. Peter was in a daze, eyes and brain refusing to believe what he saw, everywhere was destruction. His eyes fixed on the ruin of the plane, he smelt the foul smell of burning fuel, and tasted the bitterness of total defeat. He saw men moving towards him, but he did not move, not even when Von Marsten took his arm could he tear his eyes away from the burning wreck of the bomber. The major passed his hand across Peter eyes, they remained fixed on the valley, Von Marsten smiled, so the mighty were realising how hard it was when they fell. "Get him in the car." The corporal took hold of Peter and dragged him over to the car and literally threw him onto the back seat. Peter forgotten for the moment he checked the car over, apart from a missing right wing the car was still mobile. Von Marsten sat behind the wheel, the others jumped in, the major slowly reversed the car and turned it away from the valley. He did not know where he was exactly, what he did know was that he'd left the map in one of the wagons, but if recent information was to be believed , somewhere to the east on a beach the German Army had trapped the invading British. He would head that way, if he was lucky perhaps a British 'Tommy' would get even luckier and save the army the pleasure of a firing squad.

Vogel's head dropped forward, he was falling asleep at the wheel, the wagon swerved, Vogel fought to keep it on the road. Michael opened his eyes and turned to the little man, he could see fatigue written in every line of Vogel's face. The little man needed to rest, he was the only one among them who knew the way to safety. "Stop and rest." Vogel jumped at the sound of Michael's voice loud in the wagons confined cab, he eased his foot off the accelerator and allowed the vehicle to roll to a stop. Vogel pushed in the stop and the engine died, he let his head fall on the wheel and before Michael had left the cab he was fast asleep.

Michael pulled back the canvas flap and climbed into the back of the lorry, Katji to his surprise was sat feeding the baby. She looked up and smiled at him, never even considering to hide her exposed breast from his eyes. Tibor lay sleeping, his back against the wooden side of the lorry. "Let him sleep Michael." She said.

"Are you alright now Katji?" He asked, he moved closer to look into her eyes.

"For a time." She said and looked down at the child, gently she wiped away the dribble of milk from her chin. "When I feel the time is right I will tell you of my dream." She handed the sleeping child to Michael, who looked terrified at the prospect of holding so frail a bundle. Katji carefully pulled her dress together and sat back. She found it amusing to see Michael the man cursed as a werewolf gently rocking the sleeping baby. His life, his curse, the whole world was lost to him as he gazed lovingly down at Katji's daughter. Katji did not want to break the spell Michael was under but she knew she had to be told what had taken place from the moment the men walked into the cave. Michael would tell her and she knew he would hide nothing from her, and, she sighed , when the time came she would hide nothing from Michael.

Katji reached up and felt inside her dress, she touched the gold medallion at her throat, many times over their years together Tibor had asked how she came by it. It was the only time she had ever lied to him, how could she tell him, that only in death could she be parted from it. "Michael," the wolfman turned to her at the sound of his name. "How is the little man?" She asked.

"He sleeps."

"When he wakes I would like to talk to him." Michael nodded and continued to rock the baby, he had heard her and when Vogel woke he would tell him, "I will sleep now," she said "I leave my daughter in your care."

Michael could not believe he could be so happy, all the years he had lived and no one, not even his beloved Lilith had taken so fierce a hold of his heart. Was this how it felt to hold your own child, he had been denied that by Julius and for that he had killed. And he knew that should anything threaten this child he would kill again, this innocent would be the reason he would have blood on his hands.

Vogel yawned and looked at the map he had found in the back of the wagon, he knew he was on the right road. But getting to the coast wasn't going to be easy, if what he heard listening to Strobel and Mantz was true, between them and the coast would be German soldiers. If he drove all night and tried to hide by day he guessed it would take them at least three, maybe four days to reach the coast. "What the?" He rubbed his eyes, surely he was seeing things, Michael with the baby in his arms, he started to grin then saw Michael's face.

"Katji wishes to speak to you." Michael watched Vogel go round the end of the lorry then lean back and grin at him, making a rocking motion with his arms. When Vogel returned some forty minutes later his manner was quiet, a worried look in his eyes. "Well?" Asked Michael. The little man ignored him and climbed up into the driving seat. "What did Katji want?"

"Nothing." Said Vogel, "It was just, oh nothing." He turned the key in the ignition and put his foot on the accelerator, "Come it's time to go." Vogel sat there gripping the wheel until Michael returned and climbed in beside him. He pushed the lorry into gear and the vehicle lurched off. Michael listened as the little man slammed the gears in, swearing under his breath all the time. He would say nothing, let Vogel work whatever it was bothering him out of his system.

"I know this road sir." Von Marsten turned to the man beside him, "It leads over the border and into Belgium." The major started to talk to the man and asked questions concerning the countryside around Dunkirk. If it all went well, somewhere along the way they might be able to change cars. If not, at least they would be able to get fuel from the army, if they found it.

"What about the captain?" He asked.

"Like a Swiss clock sir." He twisted his finger in his ear, "Cuckoo."

"Very funny corporal, very funny." Never the less Von Marsten had to smile, it felt good to know that his men were in good spirits even if he wasn't. Once they reached an army unit he would turn Mantz over to them, they could do what they wanted with him. The soldier had said it would take at least three days to reach the coast road to Dunkirk.

The she wolf followed the smell of the grey wolf, her eyes found his marks on the ground and at the entrance to the cave. Petra, knowing there was no one inside walked in, it would soon be dark and she needed somewhere to spend the night. Petra moved around the cave, memorising each scent that had been left here, two other men and Michael, a woman, and a child, newly born. The she wolf smiled to herself she would take great pleasure in tearing the child to pieces before Michaels eyes. She threw the lump of human flesh into a corner of the cave, she had found the carnage in the valley. The sight of half burnt bodies of human and animal welded together by the flames did not bother her, she only saw a source of food if she had to stay around the valley looking for the grey wolf. Petra curled up on the floor of the cave and drifted off into an uneasy sleep, she had to find Michael.

The she wolf touched the rock, the grey wolf had climbed up this way, Petra bent and picked up the ropes. They were no good to her if she wanted to find Michael she had to follow his scent up the cliff face. Petra willed the change to come over her, she rammed hard nails into the cracks and began to climb.

Vogel had been driving almost non stop for the last two days, what sleep he managed to get during the daylight hours was not enough. No matter what, come daylight he was going to tell them, no more travelling for at least a day, he needed rest. Too late he saw the car coming from the other side of the road, he tried to turn the lorry, but failed. Metal screamed on metal as car and wagon collided. The car tipped over on its wheels, Vogel fought the wheel trying to keep the lorry on the firm road. The lorry's wheels churned great lumps of earth from the roadside, grass sods struck the windscreen, snapping the wipers away.

Von Marsten shouted and swung the car away from the lorry, he saw the large wheels inches from his side of the car, heard a crack as the door handle was torn away. Dazzled by the headlights of the lorry, his own lights pointing upwards Von Marsten twisted the wheel hoping and praying that they would break free. The lorry's rear wheel mounted the running board of the car, dragging it closer to it, at the last moment the wheel ran off the running board and the car swerved into the hedges.

Peter picked that moment to look up and his eyes gazed directly into those of Michael. Peter flicked his eyes towards the other man. It would be a few hours before he realised who the two men were, the car hit the hedge and the roadside bank, it lifted the car up and threw it through the hedge and into the soft soil of a field.

Vogel pulled the lorry back onto the road, rammed his foot down hard and shifted the gears up one, relieved that they responded. He had no intentions of stopping, it had only been a brief glimpse but he had seen both uniform and guns. He hoped that they had been knocked out or better still killed, his heart missed a beat, then the lorry started to pick up speed. He had no time to decide which road to take, he just left his foot where it was and drove as if the devil was on his tail.

Von Marsten wiped the blood from his face, spit out a loose tooth, damn that had been a little bit too close for comfort. They had been lucky no one had been hurt a few nasty bruises but nothing broken. There was nothing they could do until daylight, but from the feel of it the car was out of commission. In the back of the car Mantz began mumbling to himself, Von Marsten had forgotten about him, hell to be saddled with an idiot at a time like this. The major took out his cigarettes and put one in his mouth, he drew the smoke deep, held it there savouring it, god it felt good. He settled himself on the driver's seat and lay back, when he'd finished the cigarette he would get some sleep.

Peter Mantz screamed, Von Marsten shot out of the car, the gun in his hand cocked and ready to use. "Fucking daft bastard." He heard the corporal shouting at Mantz. Mantz was on his feet, eyes staring wildly, his mouth moving but nothing coming out. The major saw the froth around his lips and the thick white spittle running down onto his chin. The hairs on the back of his neck bristled and he went cold, the man had gone insane. He lifted the gun and aimed it at Mantz , better to shoot him now than risk harm to any of his men from him.

Peter Mantz turned to the major and said "I know the men in the lorry." His voice was low and cold, much as Von Marsten remembered it. "One of them is a deserter named Vogel, the other," Von Marsten watched his expression change. "I should have killed him years ago." Mantz sat down and looked around him, he was back in control of his faculties, the sight of the two men had brought him back. "I believe they are responsible for the failure of 'Iron Fist'."

Von Marsten laughed at him, they were responsible for what had happened, well at least the man had a sense of humour. "You find me funny major?"

"Not funny Mantz," He said "Sad, you're all sad, sad little men wanting to be gods."

"You swore an oath to Hitler."

"I also swore one to my country, that's why I fight."

"You will take me after those two men, now." demanded Mantz, the major laughed out loud, Peter Mantz shot him. Von Marsten looked down at the blood soaking his tunic front, surprise written all over his face. Slowly he fell onto his knees and looked up at Mantz. "You stupid bastard." Von Marsten keeled over and fell face down in the soft soil. Peter Mantz got out of the car, put his pistol behind the major's ear and pulled the trigger. He turned to the two men before the sound of the shot had faded, the pistol pointing at them.

"Are you with me or not?" He motioned with the gun at the body of Von Marsten, "Well?" He asked.

The corporal looked down at the major's body, its head a mess of blood and brains mixed with hair. He turned and looked at Mantz, saw the madness in his eyes and decided that he wanted to live.

"We'll go with you Captain, how I don't know, the cars fucked." Mantz looked at the other man and smiled, oh yes they'd follow him they were too terrified to do any other.

"We walk until we find something." Said Mantz, he slipped the pistol back into its holster. "I want those two men."

"I'm sorry" Said Vogel, he looked around him at his three companions, they like him were tired, but Vogel himself was near the point of exhaustion. Tibor went over to Katji she was sleeping, he carefully pulled the blanket from the babies face. He still had great difficulty in actually believing this tiny bundle was his. Michael was sat, his back against the stone wall, his head resting on his knees. They had found the abandoned farmhouse just before dawn, Vogel had turned the lorry into the yard and waited until they had all got down, before he drove it into the barn. The roof of the farmhouse had been practically shaved off during the fighting which had taken place a week before. But the downstairs rooms offered them protection against the weather.

Vogel, more than any of them, had been surprised how easily they had been able to drive across a country embroiled in war. They had not run into any troops and when Vogel had pulled up and pointed to the signpost which read Dunkirk, the promise of freedom beckoned to them. Leaving Katji and Tibor in the farmhouse Michael and Vogel searched the surrounding area, scavenging, they found potatoes and turnips in plenty. And when they'd returned to the farmhouse the smell of cooking had caused them to stop, Katji had found eggs in the barn and a chicken that had foolishly returned to his coop. Vogel had spent some time outside staring towards the coast, there had been no sign of troop movement, but the sound of fighting could be heard clearly.

"I'm sorry," He said again letting his voice trail off, neither Michael or Tibor said anything, Vogel let his head hang , he was suddenly feeling defeated. Michael reached out with his foot and nudged the little man.

"It's not your fault." He said "You haven't failed us."

"I thought," Said Vogel "I banked on the British being here, I didn't expect them to be shoved back so easily." He looked helpless, it had been his idea to head this way, once they had reached British lines, he hoped and prayed they would get a boat to England. "I believed we would get away from here."

"There must be a way." Interrupted Michael "We have come too far to give in now." He shoved himself to his feet. "Come with me." He said and Vogel obediently followed him outside, Vogel was glad to leave the room, anything was better than listening to Katji and Tibor conversing in their obscene guttural tongue.

Following the dull thump of the bombs, the horizon became a riot of colour. The drone of planes, the spiteful coughing of their guns. "Some bastard is catching it." He said, Vogel kicked a small stone. "Out of the frying pan and into the fire." He lent on the remains of the stone wall and watched the sky change colour as each shell pounded the British defences. He turned to say something to Michael and his stomach churned with terror.

Michael was on his knees, his arms wrapped around his body, rocking himself. He lifted his head and looked towards Vogel, Vogel looked into the yellow eyes of the wolf. Michaels face began to swell, mouth stretching to accommodate the fangs that were pushing their way through. Thick grey hairs sprouted along his jawline and up his face. Michael's fingers began to lengthen, nails grew into sharp claws, Vogel heard the bones in Michaels body crack and snap, he could almost believe he heard the sound of sinews stretching. Michael uttered a long agonising cry, his spine began to arch. Michael scuttled about on hands and knees, the clothes ripping and dropping away as the wolf tried to escape out of its human prison.

The howl of the werewolf shattered the night, Vogel clasped his hands over his ears, again the wolf howled drowning the sound of battle. Vogel was rooted to the spot, terror held him, he had watched the wolf become a man. But to watch the transformation of man into werewolf. No matter what his brain told him, his body refused to listen, and the little man stared in terrified horror at the thing Michael was becoming.

The sound of a woman's scream tore into his numbed brain, Vogel refused to open his eyes, he dare not look at Michael. . "Vogel." He heard the rasping sound of his name. "Vogel" Again came the deep guttural cry. His mind still full of terror, he opened one eye, he stepped back and came to a stop against the wall, his breath came out in a wheeze. "Sweet mother of God." More wolf than man Michael reached out to him. "Help me." The hand that begged for help was more claw than human. Sweat drenched the little man, it ran into his eyes stinging them, he tasted the saltiness of it on his tongue and lips. Vogel wanted to laugh out loud, he felt ridiculous, he had wet himself with fear, and his nose was running. He felt the urine running down his leg and into his boot and the little man wanted to cry at his own discomfort.

The werewolf fell forward and lay still, then its body began to jerk and twitch, at the sound of his name Vogel looked down. He saw a wolf's face and a wolf's yellow eyes but he heard Michael's voice. "Vogel, help me." And the little man realised that a battle was being fought inside Michael's body.

The clawed hand reached out to him again, this time Vogel took it, his fingers closed around the werewolf's. The horny claws began to retract, the grey hair vanished into the flesh of the man's hand, Vogel pressed his fingers tight against Michael's. Michael's eyes rolled until only the whites were showing. Lips stretched tight across teeth, gums flecked with blood. "Katji, take me to Katji." It took all of Vogel's strength to help the wolfman to his feet. He staggered under Michael's weight but somehow he managed to get him back inside the farmhouse. Michael pushed himself free of Vogel and lurched towards the standing figure of Katji holding her child. "Why?" He asked her. "Why now?" He fell full length before her.

Katji handed the child to Tibor and came to Michael, she knelt beside him and lifted his head until it rested on her breast. The lines on Michael's face smoothed away and the last fine grey hairs disappeared from his body. Michael's mouth opened and the fangs regressed with a strange sucking sound, Katji gently wiped away the blood from Michael's lips.

"Michael." Her voice was low. Vogel mesmerised by what had happened strained his ears to try and hear her words. "Michael." Her voice barely a whisper, Michael opened his eyes, only the whites showing. "Listen to me Michael, listen, there is only the short ticking of life's clock left to me." Katji heard her husband gasp and say "No." Katji turned and smiled at him, "hush" she said to him, Katji motioned to Vogel to join them, she reached up and took the little man's hand and pulled him down. "Listen to me, all of you, but," she said , still holding Michael to her "You Vogel you must listen most of all."

"Michael I have been visited by the fallen angel, that was the reason for my strange trance, in my dreams he spoke to me. You are his chosen one Michael," She let her finger touch the star shaped scar, she withdrew her finger quickly, the sound of sizzling flesh filled the room. Katji stared at the blister forming on her finger tip. She placed it back on the pentacle, the blister burst and the fluid ran onto the star shaped scar. "He spoke to me of a time when another woman told you that she believed you were special, she hinted that perhaps she knew more than she was telling, she knew a little but not all. Even I do not know all, and soon I will not be here to help you, but another will take my place."

"You are to live and escape from this place and return to the land of your birth. One day, many years from now you will meet the fallen angel face to face. You are to take my child with you, you and Vogel, for Tibor" Katji felt her husband's hand touch her shoulder, she reached up and covered it with hers. "Tibor and I, we must remain here, it is the fallen angels wish and his word is our law. We will not fight it, for we knew that one day this would come to us, all we can do is accept the fallen angels will."

Vogel bit his lip, he wanted to shout at her, fight it, she was welcoming death, not only for herself but for the silent giant. "Don't just sit there fight it." He felt his eyes prickle, he felt embarrassed that he should feel the need to cry.

"Friend Kurt," Vogel looked at her through tear filled eyes, she had never used his name before, Katji's hand touched his face and she held it there for a moment. "My little rat, oh don't brindle so, I call you that in affection, for you will defend my child to the death if necessary." Vogel took Katji's hand and with a gesture of supreme gentleness placed his lips to it. "Will you be the good uncle to my child?" Vogel could not answer, he simply nodded his head in agreement, Katji leaned forward and whispered in his ear, Michael saw Vogel shake his head. "No." He mouthed, Katji smiled and said "Yes."

"I have little left to say to you Michael, but to warn you, remember where you buried your sword, for one day you will need it again. Those that seek to destroy you are near, the woman with black hair, the fallen angel will not allow you to meet her yet. For like her he too fears you Michael, for you have the power to lift the curse of the werewolf from all those tainted by it. Don't ask me how you will do this, for I do not know." Katji sighed and tightened her grip on Tibor's hand, the giant said nothing. When she moved Michael to get to her feet Tibor pulled her up, she held out her arms and he placed their child in them.

"The man who should have called you brother, he is close to us, soon he will be in this room and he brings death with him. It is the fallen angels command that you face that battle alone. You must make the decision as to if he lives or dies by your hand." Michael looked down at her, then at Tibor, who stood glowering ready to defend her, and Vogel who didn't know what to do or say. Katji stiffened and said "He is here."

"Well, well," Said Peter Mantz "What an unpleasant surprise I must be for you Michael." He stood in the doorway of the farmhouse his pistol pointing at Michael, by his side more guns aimed at them, the two men who had followed Peter. Peter smiling strode forward into the room, hooked his foot around the only chair and pulled it to him. He tested the table before he put his weight on it, then lent forward and brushed the dirt from his sleeve. "I thought you were dead Michael, burnt in the house with my sister, how did you manage to escape?" He held up his hand, he needed no answer, he was talking . He pulled his cigarette case from his tunic pocket and took out a cigarette, lighting it before continuing. "Please don't move yet Michael or I'll shoot you. I saw you and this thing," he said pointing at Vogel with the pistol, then he tapped the side of his head. "It took me hours to remember who you were, kneel Michael. That's better, I hate looking up at anyone." Peter studied Michael as one studies a moth before pinning it to a board. "Still not interested in why I couldn't remember you, no, well I'll tell you." Michael kneeling on the farmhouse floor listened to him as he told them about the destruction of the plane and the death of hundreds of people. And Michael realised that with each word Peter spoke he was convincing himself that they were to blame for the disaster in the valley. "So you see Michael I need a scapegoat, and I don't think you'll have to guess too hard who it's going to be."

Michael opened his mouth and managed to get out one word. "Peter" Before Peter struck him a savage blow across the face with the pistol. Michael felt the skin split and blood seep down his cheek. "Don't speak." Peter spat the words out. "Don't speak." He lent back on the chair and selected another cigarette, Vogel looked at him and saw the light of madness in his eyes. Peter totally misunderstood the look, he looked down at the cigarette case and then at Vogel. "Would you care for one sergeant?" He asked offering Vogel the case, Vogel reached out, Peter laughed and snapped it shut. "Oh sergeant," he said "Not too close, too soon for you to die." He threw the case at Vogel, "Enjoy it sergeant, it's a condemned mans final smoke." He turned his attention back to Michael, failing to notice the look that passed between Vogel and the giant. Tibor nodded and turned and took the child from Katji's arms and placed her in the open kitchen cupboard. Katji smiled at him, the corporal followed his movements with the muzzle of his gun. He breathed easier when the giant lent back on the wall and folded his arms across his chest.

For the first time Peter appeared to notice Katji, he stared at her long and hard, her calmness bothered him, Katji turned her face and looked at him, two white orbs fixed themselves on Peters face. Peter went white and his temper broke. "Enough." His voice loud and teetering on the edge of hysteria. "It's time for you to die Michael."

He was half out of the chair when Vogel flung the cigarette case, it hit Peter in the mouth, the gun went off as he toppled backwards striking his head on the wall. Michael went from kneeling to attack , his hand shot out and the soldiers scream was cut off as he twisted the mans head . Tibor grabbed the corporal's gun, the man's finger tightened on the trigger and the giant grunted. The corporal opened his mouth to scream as Tibor's fingers tightened in an iron band around his throat. He felt himself being lifted clear of the floor while Tibor's fingers dug deeper and deeper into the soft flesh of his throat. The corporal died with his finger on the trigger of his gun, the bullets tore a neat row of holes in the giant's chest. They exited from Tibor's back in a shower of blood and bone, Tibor crumpled in a heap on top of the corporal.

Peter grunted and tried to move, Vogel pushed the pistol hard into his mouth. "Move you bastard and you're dead." Peter gagged against the metal, feeling it rip the inside of his mouth, he tried to spit out the blood , the pistol barrel stopped him. Vogel turned to look at the others, Tibor lay still on the floor, Michael was holding Katji to him, blood pumped from between her fingers from the hole in her chest. Vogel struck Peter hard at the side of the head, Peter slumped to the floor unconscious, using shoe laces from the dead soldiers he tied Peters hands and feet. He tried to turn the giant over, it was no good he wasn't strong enough. "He's dead," said Vogel, surprised that such a thing could happen to the giant. "He's dead." Katji lay in Michael's arms, he held her to him his hand pressed against the flow of blood.

"You can't stop it Michael," She said "Look to my child." Vogel jumped to his feet and took the child out of the cupboard, Katji saw him smile. "Take me outside Michael, please I don't want to die in here." Michael picked her up and carried her outside into the darkness of the night. "By the wall." She said, her breath was coming fast and she seemed to be fighting to get her words out. "Vogel stay with me while he fetches Tibor to me." Vogel held the child so that Katji could see her daughter. "Now Kurt." She pulled open the neck of her dress. "Take it now." Vogel lifted the medallion from around her neck and slipped it over his head. "Now you are his protector, you have witnessed him changing and around your neck you hold the power to stop him or bring him back." She turned her head as Michael carried the giant to her. "Here." She said, touching her breast. "Put his head here. "She was white and drawn, the stamp of death trying to take away her beauty. "Remember us Michael."

"I owe you my life."

"I tried to save your soul." Michael touched her face and let his finger trace her beauty as he sealed it forever in his mind. "Look after my child." Blood sped from her mouth and onto her chin, Michael wiped it away, but still it came. She tightened her arms around the dead giant, turned her face and pressed her lips against his. "Goodbye." Katji closed her eyes, for the second time that night Vogel cried unashamedly holding the child close to him.

Michael howled his anguish to the sky, once again he brought death to those who loved him. He remembered Anna and the vengeance he had wrought on the pack. He remembered the woman he had loved and who had loved him in return, yet again he had sought vengeance on the pack. It had gained him nothing, still they came after him, would he have no rest until he destroyed all of them, or he himself was destroyed doing it. Inside the walls of the farmhouse the brother of the woman he had loved, like the Countess, like Julius, Peter had come looking for him wanting him dead. There was rage inside Michael that tore at his soul, a rage against humanity, a rage against heaven and the dark god it had thrown to earth.

Murder begat murder and vengeance gave birth to more vengeance, could he really kill Peter. Anna had asked if they were a colossal joke, no they were no joke, only the most obscene mind could have contrived to create creatures like himself, the werewolf. Michael would look into Peters eyes and decide if he should die or not.

"Help me to bury them."

"Michael for gods sake, we don't have that much time."

"Katji promised I would return home." He said "And you would come with me." He looked at Vogel and down at the child. "There will be enough time." Michael fell to his knees and the claws of the werewolf began to tear up the soft ground, Vogel watched the man. Naked and covered in sweat and dirt Michael tore deeper and deeper, how he was managing to hold off the complete change Vogel could only imagine. Only when he lowered Tibor into the hole did Michael look to the little man for help. Vogel put the child down and lifted Katji's body into Michael's arms, gently the wolfman lay her on Tibor's chest. He took the giants arm and placed it around her, and Katji's arm he placed around the giant's neck. They were like lovers entwined in sleep as Michael covered them first with the stone from the wall and finally the dirt. "Sleep in peace."

"Give me the gun and leave me." He held his hand out to Vogel. "Take the child and go."

"Michael don't do it, come with me now."

"Friend Vogel, I will follow shortly." He still held out his hand for the pistol, reluctantly Vogel handed it over. "I will find you and the child." Vogel didn't want to leave him, but he knew that this was the test that he must face alone.

"I'll head that way," said Vogel "Away from the fighting, there has to be another village somewhere along the coast." He started to walk, constantly turning hoping that Michael would change his mind and follow him. He reached up and touched the medallion, should he try and use it. "Leave him." Said a voice in his head, "I told you he must face this alone." Shaking his head against the low insistent voice Vogel climbed over the stone wall and into the field.

Michael took the boot laces from around Peter's feet and pulled him upright, Peter glared at him, "I heard you that day Peter, I was hiding in the forest when you came to the house. I heard you say that Lilith's death saved you from putting her into special care. Vogel has told me about the camps you called special care, you would have let her die in torment." Peter said nothing, if the man was going to kill him, why didn't he get on with it? "She would have known a fear that no human should be subjected to." Michael reached out and took the bindings from Peter's wrist. "I am going to show you fear Peter, a fear not even you could inflict on others." Peter's eyes opened wide as Michael held out the gun to him. "Take it."

Peter snatched it from him and curled his hand around it, a finger on the trigger.

"If you believe I won't shoot you Michael, you're a fool." Confidence had seeped back into him, he was armed and Michael wasn't.

Michael spread his arms wide. "Go ahead Peter, shoot." Peter pulled the trigger, the shot knocked Michael backwards. He struggled to his knees, Peter fired again, Michael was twisted sideways under the impact of the bullet. Michael was on his feet, still smiling at him, anger and fear gripped Peter and he pulled the trigger until it clicked empty. Michael was thrown backwards, he struck the wall, fell to the floor, but still he got back on his feet. Peter counted every hole on Michael's body, neat round holes that seeped with blood.

"No." He said as Michael came towards him. "No." This time he screamed it. "You have to be dead." Michael took hold of him and pulled him close.

"Why?" He said "Why must I be dead? I told you long ago you could never kill me." He let Peter go, Peter flung himself at Michael, Michael caught his wrist in his hands, Peter screamed in agony as Michael exerted pressure, pressing flesh into bone. "Watch Peter." Peter Mantz went totally mad as Michael's face underwent the transformation from man into werewolf. The young man held in the vice like grip of the werewolf slobbered and cried, his words incomprehensible. He stared at the yellow eyes that bore into his brain, the fangs that came ever closer to his throat. Then he was tossed across the room, he hit the far wall, bones snapped and Peter screamed now in pain. He was being lifted again, face first he struck the wall, his nose breaking, blood poured down his face and into his open mouth. He was hauled upright and a hard fist struck him, his lips split open, he tried to cry out for Michael to stop. He was experiencing the terror and the pain he had delighted on inflicting on others. Peter tried to crawl away from the punishment the werewolf was inflicting on him.

Michael reached down and pulled him up, he lifted the slobbering Peter until he could look into his eyes. There was nothing, no recognition, he had broken the boy mentally and physically, he would not kill. Peter would live if his life after this could be called living. In one last blind moment of anger, the wolfman flexed his muscles and threw Peter at the window. Peter hit it head first, a thin sliver of glass in the otherwise empty frame penetrated his left eye. It stopped a hairs breath from his brain, his left cheek was sliced to the bone by the jagged wood of the frame. Peter struck the wall, he did not cry out, not even when his bones snapped and tore through the flesh.

Michael looked down on the boy, Peter did not move he lay in a broken heap at the wolfman's feet. Michael turned his face and looked towards where Vogel had gone, the yellow eyes saw the little man walking across the open fields.

For two days Peter lay there not able to move, his mind knowing only pain and the terror of dying alone. He did not see the dark shadow that flitted from cover to cover, a creature hunting for a prey. The woman's hair was matted and filthy like her body, she crawled slowly toward him, a beast instinct knowing the man was not yet dead. The black haired she wolf sniffed the air, the scent of the grey wolf was all over this man. Hands with dirt encrusted nails turned the man over, the grey wolf had extracted a terrible vengeance on this man. Petra lowered her head and listened, the man's heart beat steadily, he was young and if she decided to help him he would live. Petra turned her head, she smelt the flesh of the dead soldiers, hunger gnawed at her, she had forgone the pleasure of hunting food to catch up with Michael. They would provide her with the nourishment she needed, if after she had eaten the man still lived, she had the knowledge to turn him. Petra had known from the moment she set out to find and destroy Michael she would need allies. Her baser instincts told her that if the grey wolf could deliberately inflict such punishment on this man, then he was the one to help her. Once she had turned him he would have such a hatred of the grey werewolf, a hatred nurtured into a killer who would not turn or be stopped no matter how great the odds.

"I'll find you grey one, you and the Wych's whelp." Petra threw back her head to howl, her mouth snapped shut, no it would be foolish to warn him she was so close. There was all the time in the world to seek him out, no matter where he went she would find him. Petra crawled over to the corpse and touched it, fresh meat would have been better, but she had no time for that, fangs tore into the dead flesh and Petra chewed the meat before she swallowed. Hunger finally satisfied, her thoughts returned to the injured man, bones would mend, there was nothing she could do about the man's eye or the wound on his face. If she saved him, he would learn to live with them.

The she wolf bent over Peter, who chose that moment to open his eye, he saw the fanged mouth moving down on him and begged that he be allowed to die. Sharp teeth sank into his throat and he heard the obscene sucking of the woman's mouth. His brain whirled , he heard the loud thumping of his heart, he tried to cry out, he found himself falling in a bright red mist. He was experiencing a pain far more terrible than the pain Michael had given him, he felt his body jerking and threshing and the woman's mouth sucking his life blood from him.

Peter was on the point of death when Petra stopped, she could hear the feeble beating of his heart, her own heart was thumping loudly in her ears. She forced open the man's mouth and bent down and covered it with hers, blood gushed from her into Peter. She held him until he had swallowed every drop of his and her combined bloods. Now she must wait, Petra took hold of Peter's legs and dragged him into the farmhouse, he would feel no pain, yet, when she had finished turning him then he would feel pain. She pushed the flap of flesh back onto his cheek, carefully she withdrew the splinter of glass, then she sat and examined him. Once he had been a handsome man, a powerful man, he would be powerful again, he would make a good mate. She would nurture him, her enemies would be his. The man moaned and Petra moved his head to look into his eye. Peter saw her, and he saw the fanged mouth coming down on him again.

Vogel was beginning to fret, they were still not far enough away from the theatre of war to suite him. He could hear the boom of the big guns, the thud and detonation of shells as they landed, occasionally the sound of machine gunfire, the softer bang of hand grenades, and the crack of rifle fire. The British forces still refused to surrender to the German war machine. It felt ridiculous to Vogel that they should be stood listening to sounds of battle, when all around him the life of the countryside carried on. Birds chattered to each other in the hedgerow, small rodents moved beneath it, a stalk of grass trembled with their passing. A bird of prey swooped, whatever it was after it missed, it flew away its talons empty.

On the horizon the last rays of the sun glinted on the sea, at any other time Vogel might have been content enough to sit and watch the day reluctantly give way to night. Vogel sighed and turned, they had to find somewhere to rest, and food, they needed food. He could hear the sound of the sea rolling onto the seashore, waves breaking on the sand. God, they were so close.

His stomach rumbled, telling him it required feeding, Vogel rubbed it, how long was it since he last ate? It rumbled again, he swallowed the juices that filled his mouth, he suddenly realised that he still carried the child. If he needed food this badly, how was the baby managing without food? He moved the blanket from the child's face, it was still sleeping, it had slept through the fight in the farmhouse. Vogel didn't like what he was thinking but his brain refused to stop the thoughts that came to him. The child was a liability, on his own he could vanish into the ranks of grey clad soldiers, even with Michael he might make it. "Shut up." He said aloud when his stomach rumbled yet again. "God, what I'd give for a cigarette." He was wishing he'd picked up Mantz cigarette case. "Oh shit." What was the use of wishing, wishes didn't solve their immediate problem.

Michael was walking ahead, his mind was thinking of things other than food. He had had Peter exactly where he had wanted him, and let him live. True he had broken the man, it would be months, if ever, before Peter would be of any use to anyone. He had made his choice as Katji said he must, why then did the thought keep on returning to him, that he had made a mistake, he should have killed Peter.

They found a place among the sand dunes, it would shelter them from the sea breeze and also hide them from the road that ran about a hundred yards away. Vogel had said nothing for the last hour, simply huddled up with the child, Michael watched him, it was obvious that he was bothered by something.

"Your thoughts are troubled little man?" The suddenness of Michael's voice caused him to jump, the words struck like a drum in the silence of the dunes rebounded from their sandy walls. Vogel looked up, he couldn't see Michael but he knew the wolfman could see him and was studying his face. "Is that fear I smell on you Vogel?" He asked "Fear for us, or the child you hold so close?" Vogel coughed and sought for the words he needed, he coughed again, what was the point of saying it, he had given his word to Katji. As if he knew what Vogel was thinking Michael said "I know it would be better if we could find somewhere to leave the child in safety, but,"

"And it's a big but Michael, we have to get away from here." Michael said nothing let the little man get it out of his system. "We're too close to the fighting for safety, any time now there will be thousands of German soldiers on their way to finish off the British. We need food, well I do and the baby does, and I need a change of clothes. If I'm caught in these I'm a dead man." The eyes of the wolf saw the little man move, "God damn slap fucking bang in the middle of Hitler's war machine."

"Vogel I know the trouble we are in and I don't blame you. Without you we would not have got this far." Vogel felt the werewolf's hand on his shoulder, he had not seen him move over to him. "Friend," said Michael "One day I will tell you my story, when we have the luxury of time, as for the child, do not worry over her she is the child of a Wych, she will survive." Michael reached out and took the child from Vogel, the little man needed something to focus his mind on. "We are on the coast." said Michael "surely we, you can find us a boat somewhere."

"I suppose so." said Vogel "I can try, but I'll bet the entire coast is crawling with the German Army." Michael did not expect the little man to answer him straight away, he had poised Vogel a task that would not be easy to fulfil. For years Michael had relied on others, Katji, Tibor, Anna, even Lilith, now in a time when the world was about to be embroiled in war that would involve the whole world, he needed Vogel. This was the little mans time, his world, Michael realised that if they were to get to England it would be Vogel's guile and not his supernatural strength that got them through.

Vogel got to his feet, "I'll have a look around." He said "I won't be long. I hope." Michael smiled to himself, Vogel was nearly back to his old self, the wolfman knew that he had a better chance of finding the things they needed, like food, and checking the area out, but he let Vogel go. The little man was worrying too much over the child, but how did Michael convey to him that the child was in no danger. Perhaps when Vogel returned he would talk to him about things, he would wait and see. Michael listened to the fading sounds of Vogel scuffling along the sand, the cool sea breeze hurling itself at the sandy hillocks, shifting the millions of grains of sand to a new position. A battle that had been fought for countless centuries forever changing the shape of the coastline.

There was a deadly silence to the south of him, the guns had stopped firing, only occasionally was that silence broken by the spiteful cough of a snipers rifle. Michael understood how the men on the beach must be feeling, cold, terrified but determined to fight to the bitter end. He had been in that position more than once on the battlefield, but unlike the men trapped at Dunkirk, he had always had an escape route. With the sea at their backs they had nowhere to go.

Brilliant lights cutting through the darkness drove all thoughts of the men on the beaches from his mind. He pressed his body tight against the soft sand and looked towards the light. A convoy of wagons, engines breaking the stillness of the night, labouring even on the straight road, weighed down with men. The wolfman never took his eyes from the single file which moved towards the encircled army. Suddenly from out of nowhere a single plane swooped down from the darkness the leading lorry lifted high in the air as its petrol tank exploded under the impact of bullets. The lorry came down on its tail end, cartwheeled into the following wagon, the screams of men dying, crushed and burning. Again the plane made a pass at the convoy, this time concentrating on the last vehicle, Michael heard the explosion of tyres, the crack of petrol igniting. Then the plane was gone, it had struck back, the cost to the Germans would not be that high, but the lonely airman had delayed the inevitable for a few more hours.

Not until a faint line of grey announced that this was a new day did Michael realise the little man had not yet returned. He had watched the soldiers fight the fire, drag dead comrades to the side of the road and shove the broken vehicles into the ditches before continuing on. So intent had he been in watching, for danger of any kind to them, that all thoughts of Vogel had been put to one side, but now he had time to think about the little man, Vogel should have returned hours ago. Michael scurried down the valley between the sand dunes, he could see where Vogel had walked towards the tide line, the little mans footprints had been washed away by last nights tide. Michael stared at the way Vogel had gone, he could see nothing but miles of deserted beach, broken by the mounds of the sand hills. Somewhere out there the little man could be lying injured or worse, Vogel could have been captured. Only the child stopped Michael from risking all and going after the little man, he would wait, he had no other choice. If the little man had not returned by nightfall then he would go after him.

As the day wore on, the minutes becoming long drawn out hours, the wolfman was becoming more and more frustrated and irritable with the situation he found himself in. He was slowly becoming a caged beast, unable to escape, his anger was at boiling point. Constantly he crawled to the end of the sand dunes and looked for Vogel, returned and checked the child. Michael lifted the blanket from the child's face, it looked to be sleeping but the beast in Michael knew differently, the child needed nourishment. It was not an immediate problem, but sometime within the next few hours he would find the child food, no matter what the cost.

Vogel opened one eye, the pain in his head was intolerable, slowly so as not to increase the pounding in his head he opened his other eye. He looked around the small room, light was streaming in through a crack in the curtains, he settled his head back on the pillows. He smelt the freshness of the sheets that covered him, he was warm and comfortable. The smell of food , it smelt like bacon, he heard the sound of voices, no doubt Katji would be scolding the interfering giant and. "Sweet fucking Jesus," Vogel shot from under the sheets , Michael and the baby, where the fucking hell was he. Head throbbing, Vogel expecting it to explode at any second he tried to put his thoughts together.

He remembered the house, a woman stood by a table, talking to someone he couldn't see. The feel of cold metal against his neck, the door opening and being pushed into the room. The woman looking at him, a big man grabbing him by the shirt front. A voice calling him a kraut, the slam of something hard at the side of his head. The cry of the woman "No," and then a blackness. The little man realised he was totally naked, who the hell had undressed him, he reached up, a bandage had been fastened around his head.

A Tommy, the bastard what hit him had been a British Tommy, what the hell had he walked into. He had to get out of here, back to Michael, the wolfman would be close to coming after him. "Good morning." Vogel jumped at the sound of the woman's voice, he turned and looked at her. She must have been about forty, pleasant looking, and, good god he was naked. Vogel made a grab at the sheet and struggled to wrap it around him. The woman grinned and had to force herself from laughing out loud at the antics of the little man. "I've brought you some food." Holding out the tray towards him, Vogel reached for it, and dropped the sheet. The sight of bacon and eggs caused his stomach to give out a loud noise, Vogel had the good grace to look embarrassed. "Eat little man, and I will tell you what happened to you last night," The woman sat on the bed next to him, "you are very lucky the British corporal wanted to shoot you." Vogel swallowed the mouthful of food and said nothing, there was still time for the Tommy to carry out his threat. The woman reached over and lifted the medallion round his neck. "This" she said "Saved you, how did you get it little man?"

"It was given to me, and the name is Vogel, Kurt Vogel, and I have to get back to my friend and the child." Vogel was trying to decide if he could make a run for it, he doubted it, but he had to do something.

"Is your friend cursed?" She asked, Vogel turned to her, how did she know, "Well" she said "Is he, and are you his protector?"

"Who are you?" Asked Vogel, he looked hard into her eyes, was she like Katji, no, that would be too good to be true. "You're not a Wych." He said, the woman smiled and clapped her hands, the bedroom door opened and the two British soldiers walked in.

"I told you he was safe." she pointed at the men, "they managed to escape from the fighting, and,"

"Look." said Vogel "You know I'm no threat to you, but I have to get back to Michael." Vogel looked pleadingly from the woman to the two men. He held up the medallion to the woman. "You know what this is don't you?" The woman nodded her head. "Then you know why I must get back to him?" she nodded again, smiled and got off the bed.

"A child you said, a Wych child." She watched the little man's face, yes she had been right about him, he hadn't found the medallion, it had been handed onto him. She turned to the two men, who looked at him while she spoke, both shaking their heads, the word "Kraut". The woman lifted her voice and said, loud enough for Vogel to hear. "You want my help?" They both nodded their heads "Then we help the little man and his friend." Vogel felt relief at her words but why did she insist on calling him little man. "When it is dark we will go for your friend."

"I think," said Vogel, alarm bells ringing where Michael was concerned "I'd better go alone."

The woman looked at him for a long time then said, despite the objections of the two soldiers "yes." She said "Perhaps you're right."

Petra lifted Peters head and using her finger forced open his eye, the pupil was dilated, the surrounding eye, red. She bent her head and listened to the beating of his heart, it beat with a regular healthy beat. Petra smiled, the man would live, soon he would begin to feel the pain of the changing. She had to get him away from here, hide him until he became like her. So close to the grey wolf and she had to let him go free, Petra snarled and raked her fingers down the kitchen wall. She could not do it, she could not allow the grey wolf to escape without knowing where he went. She returned to the man, she could hide him in the woods, it would mean going back a few miles. But once Peter was safely hidden she never doubted that she would not be able to pick up his scent. Peter made no sound when the she wolf threw him over her shoulder and headed back the way she had travelled following Michael.

Michael carefully wrapped the baby in her blanket, making a loop at the top, a wolf could hold it easily in its mouth without harming the child. Michael sat back, the day had wore on and on, the beast inside getting more and more agitated. He held himself ready and lifted his face to the dark night sky, it was time to allow the change to take him over. He felt the pain begin, first in his fingers as they began to lengthen and the nails becoming hard and sharp, bursting free of his flesh. His mouth ached with the pain of fangs forcing their way through his gums. He tasted his own blood, he swallowed relishing its bitter and brassy taste. Michael's spine curved and twisted, he fell forward on all fours, thick grey hair spring free of his pliable flesh.

The werewolf lifted its head to howl, free once more of its human prison, yellow feral eyes looked upon the little man.

Vogel cradled the wolfman, holding the hot sweaty body, "I'm sorry Michael, god, I'm sorry." Michael lay shaking , every part of his body racked with the pain of regression, grey eyes filled with a burning pain trying to focus on Vogel. Vogel had found him just in time, and he was still surprised that Katji had passed it on to him. He had stood before the werewolf and the power of the

Wych had flowed from him to the werewolf, and slowly the wolf turned back into a man. Vogel held Michael in his arms for a long time, was this how it was going to be every time, would it always work? Vogel prayed that for Michael and his sake it never failed. Vogel spoke of his little adventure from last night, about the two British soldiers and the woman, "The woman knows about you Michael, she knows about this." He lifted the medallion so that the wolfman could see it. "She knows what you are." He felt the man stiffen in his arms. "Easy." He said "She can be trusted." Vogel breathed easier when the body he was holding relaxed.

When Michael was ready to move Vogel handed him the bundle he had brought from the house. "Clothes." While Michael was dressing he went over to the baby, he looked and inspected the way Michael had fastened it. "You were coming after me?"

"Yes." Said Michael, he didn't say more, but the little man picking up the child grinned to himself.

"Come on Michael." He said "Let's go."

When they entered the house the two soldiers jumped to their feet, both holding pistols, the woman smiled. "Come in Michael." Michael moved towards her he wanted to look into her eyes. Vogel was right about her, she knew but she was not a Wych woman. "Sit down, I've food ready for you and the child, here," she said to Vogel "Give her to me." It wasn't until he had sat down and was eating the food she had placed in front of him he suddenly realised he had never told her the child was a girl.

"The names Andrew Calthorpe," said the taller of the two men holding out his hand, Michael dropped the spoon and looked up, staring hard at the man. Calthorpe backed off, he had suddenly seen something in the man's eyes that caused his flesh to creep.

Then Michael smiled and said "I once knew a man called Calthorpe a long time ago, Amos Calthorpe." Michael gazed questioningly at the soldier.

"My great grandfather was called Amos, but" He said "I doubt if you mean him, you're not old enough."

Michael looked towards the woman who shook her head and said "I suppose it's a common name in your area, come eat up, we have to be ready to move in less than two hours." Michael turned back to the food, he would have to be more careful in the future, but he knew that this young soldier was a descendent of the man who had helped him. The woman waited until the two men had left the room to collect what few belongs they had managed to save. She walked over to Michael, still sat at the table, watching Vogel with the child.

"Well little one what do we call you, my mothers name was Elsa, but," He said, ticking the child's chin, "She wasn't very nice, you wouldn't have liked her." Vogel looked up and caught the others staring at him. "What?" He said "What?" He turned his back and continued talking to the child. Michael felt the woman's hand on his shoulder, he looked up as she pulled the shirt back and looked down at the five pointed scar on his shoulder.

She sat down beside him and said, "When you leave here, I will be coming with you, don't ask questions now Michael Cavendish, there will be plenty of time for that later. My name is Elisabetta, I was sent to you by the fallen angel." Vogel who said nothing had been listening attentively to their conversation, his ears pricked up when the woman told Michael he would never have a need for money. Once they reached England a place would be found for them, away from prying eyes. "Well," said Vogel to himself "That solves one problem." Where they were going to go and how they would live had occupied Vogel's thoughts for days. It seemed that the fallen angel was still watching over Michael.

"Are there others like me in England?"

"Michael, we have no time for questions, later."

"Answer me." Michael took hold of her arm and held it tight, he watched as the woman went white with pain, Vogel jumped to his feet and put his hand on Michael's arm. "I need an answer." said Michael, letting go of her. "Tell me."

"Yes I believe so, but they are young, and they are rogue's."

"Then I won't know peace."

"They will not seek you out Michael, believe me."

"I believe many things Elisabetta, for I have lived too long, but," He said, "you are not here to protect me are you?" The woman did not answer him "No, you are here to watch over the child." Michael smiled at her, and she smiled back, for a moment they locked eyes, and an understanding passed between them. But Michael spoke the words so that all present understood. "If the fallen angel, touches one hair of Katji's daughters head, I promise you this. I will find him and when I stand before him, one of us will die." The woman reached out and took Michael's arm, she then let her hand move down it until her fingers entwined in his.

"When the time is right, I will explain it all to you, now there is no time if you wish to go home." She let go of his hand and stood up, Vogel holding the child stared at the two of them. He was wondering what Michael was going to do next, the woman turned. "This I say to you Michael Cavendish, the Wych child has nothing to fear from me."

"For gods sake Michael." The wolfman turned and looked at Vogel, then at the woman, "Michael." Vogel held out the child to him, Michael shook his head.

"Let Elisabetta carry her." Michael gently took the baby from Vogel and held her out to the woman. "I can give you no greater trust." said Michael "For you hold my soul in your arms."

"Thank you." She moved the baby to the crook of her arm, "But we must go, now."

"You may call me Albert." said the man who was waiting for them at the prearranged place. "All is ready." He looked at Elisabetta who was carrying the child, a woman and a baby, he had not been told of them, but it didn't matter the boat was big enough. "I am sorry there is no transport, and we move quickly." He handed out a parcel of food. "In case you are hungry, but you must eat as you go, we dare not stop, my contact reports German troops in the area." In the dim light of his torch he caught a question forming on Vogel's lips. "Questions have to wait my friend." Without another word the Belgian turned and started to walk away leaving them no choice but to follow him.

For the best part of an hour they marched parallel with the coast, always in the water leaving no footprints for anyone to find. Albert walked with the confidence of a man who had done this before, who knew where he was going and what he expected to find at the end of the walk. Even before Albert slowed down, Michael had caught the scent of others, men living on a knife edge, risking their lives. He saw Albert flick the torch on and off and receive an answering signal, the Belgian waited until the party had crowded around him. "I have to ask you to trust me for I must go to these men alone." Michael allowed the eyes of the wolf to study the man, they had come too far to fall in any kind of a trap. There was no deceit in the man's eyes, he was telling them the truth. "Those men are guarding our means of escape, and if they are not sure of anything they just may shoot first." Albert started to move away from them, and then suddenly turned, "if things go wrong, and god forbid they do," He shrugged his shoulders

"I'm sorry to say you will be on your own." Of the group Michael was the only one who had noticed Albert's actions, it was obvious he was worried, and like them he would no doubt feel a lot safer once they were at sea. Michael watched Albert reach the men and saw the exchange of hugs between them.

He bent and whispered in Vogel's ear. "He's coming back." A torch flashed and from among the dunes a dozen men lifted themselves upright, all of them armed. It was good that they should take no chances. Michael smiled to himself, it was a pointless exercise spitting in the face of death.

"Quickly." said Albert "There's no time to waste, it seems a German patrol is taking an unhealthy interest in this beach." They made the short journey to the boat at a run, the men guarding eagerly helping them on board. They began shoving the boat out before they had all managed to sit down, Vogel cursed as he fell headlong. The men gave the boat one last push and the turning tide grabbed it and carried it away from their hands. The boat was being pulled forward by the sea, the men on the beach watched until the boat was carried almost out of sight by the outgoing tide, then they ran from the beach.

A multitude of scuffed footprints was the only witness to them ever having been on the beach, when the tide turned in the morning even that mute witness would be washed away. Albert turned to Calthorpe and told him to hold the tiller and keep the boat on its present course. The Belgian knelt and lifted a cover, reached in and pulled, a small diesel engine rattled into life. Albert laughed and took the tiller from Calthorpe. "Now." He said "We go to England."

Unbeknown to the occupants of this one small boat, whose prow pointed the way to freedom. Hundreds of little boats were braving the Channel and the German war machine to pick up the ravaged forces of the British army from the beaches of Dunkirk. This moment in history would allow Michael and his friends to land unnoticed among thousand of battle weary men.

On the beach a half naked, a dirt encrusted woman threw back her head and howled her frustration and anger at the tiny speck floating on the sea.

Michael turned and looked back, the eyes of the grey wolf saw the she wolf standing on the beach. The trail of vengeance was still following him, she would never give up and Michael knew that one day he would have to kill her, for if he did not, Vogel, Elisabetta, the child, his life would never be safe, not while she still lived.

When even the eyes of the wolf could not see her, Michael turned back and stared ahead. In a few hours he would set eyes on England and for the first time in over three hundred years he would stand on his native soil.

Michael was going home.

The End